WHO CATHARTED?

Blair Styra

For permission, serialization, condensation, adaptions, or for our catalog of other publications, write to Ozark Mountain Publishing, Inc., P.O. Box 754, Huntsville, AR 72740, ATTN: Permissions Department.

Library of Congress Cataloging-in-Publication Data

Styra, Blair – 1960 -
Who Catharted by Blair Styra

Being a Spiritual Being doesn't mean you stop being a Human Being.

1. Spiritual   2. Soul   3. Meditation 4. Metaphysical
I. Styra, Blair, 1960 - II. Metaphysical   III. Spiritual   IV. Title

Library of Congress Catalog Card Number:2019944977
ISBN: 9781940265759

Cover Art and Layout: Victoria Cooper Art
Book set in: Gabriola, Californian FB
Book Design: Tab Pillar
Published by:

OZARK
MOUNTAIN
PUBLISHING

PO Box 754, Huntsville, AR 72740
800-935-0045 or 479-738-2348; fax 479-738-2448
WWW.OZARKMT.COM

Printed in the United States of America

To my friend Dolores Cannon,
a great soul whose life touched the world and made it sing

Contents

Introduction

Life speaks to us all the time; it's full of funny, sad, perplexing, and downright astounding stories all day, every day. We are not only participating in these stories, but creating them every nanosecond of our Mind, Body, Spirit existence. All too often we let life simply swallow us up and our experiences seem to disappear in a myriad of systems and structures, rules, routines, feelings, actions, and thoughts. It's so important that we all stop and listen to what we are saying to ourselves through the way we are living our lives and what the world is saying back to us!

Over the last twenty-seven years as the channel for Tabaash living my life has sharpened me up, enabling me to be a greater observer and participant in my life. I know for sure that I have literally created all my life, all its realities. In my first book, *Don't Change the Channel*, I said, "Being a spiritual being doesn't mean you stop being a human being."

I have been on my "soul road" since my mid-twenties, and now in my late fifties life is still a perplexing expedition offering up more to create, more ways of growing, and more ways of growing up! Despite my soul understanding I find that I can still be a complete ass about some things, make mistakes, fall over, be afraid, and all the other human nature things that we are all involved in. That's the journey, though, and it's not that those things are good or bad, but they *are* the journey and obviously at some point in the expedition of life we get to the place where we can see how to make better arrangements. And so while we are doing this let's remember that we are all so brilliant and yet we can all still be so silly at times with the way we feel and think and participate in life. It's important that we are serious in our intentions but at times not take ourselves so seriously and to laugh at some of our endeavors and no doubt along the way offer up a good laugh for others.

Blair Styra
Wellington, New Zealand
2017

Chapter One
Quivering New Vibrations!

Twenty-seven years, who would have ever thought? That's how long I have been a channel for spirit. When I first started publicly on this path I really had no idea what I was doing or why I was doing what I was doing. I never had a sense of where is this going to go. Perhaps I was being rather naive but then do we not all have the energy of naivete when we begin a new venture in life? There are times when one just feels that this is the thing to do and so you take that first step and have a look at what view is offered up once you do that. One thing that I have come to understand is that

As you change through your experiences you have to ensure that you change your life to fit with what you have become.

I see more and more now that everything we do is simply an opportunity to expand on the ideas of what we can make possible for ourselves. In those early days of channeling in the 1990s there wasn't the abundance of self-development material that there is today; the door had been opened but people were still learning how to walk through it. I walked through a door and initiated the biggest experience of my whole life. Anyone who is a light worker will understand that what they have agreed to be is not just the way that they will serve human nature but it is essentially the way that they will serve themselves.

It's an agreement to face your self in ways that people who have not aligned to source consciously will never experience. When one does know that you are source, you understand that what you are involved in is all your making and you can't help but change the dynamics of how you see and create your life. For a start, there is no one else you can blame for the errors you make in life. You find yourself constantly facing other selves that you are made up of. You call them in through the thoughts and actions you have in life. And one finds at times that you still have that conflict of interest going on between the God part of you and the human part of you. This is not so much a fight with the selves, but more an honest meeting of two opposing energy forces that strive for some continuity, therefore enabling better cooperation between the two.

You become more conscious of the realities that you are creating and the way you participate in them. One finds that you are observing self more, rather like following yourself around watching what you are doing; if you take your eyes off the road, so to speak, then you can easily set up a collision with an experience that was created by you to remind you of the importance of watching the road! It's a daily training and at times it is not an easy thing to do, but as you establish this "following yourself around" then you notice what you are doing and as a result make the relevant changes. Many years ago a client commented to Tabaash that they thought all this spiritual stuff was supposed to make them feel better and improve their lives as they were finding that facing themselves was quite an ordeal at times. Fair comment, too, as the moment you step into the realms of self-development you seem to expose all the issues that are important for you to consider. I suppose that's the whole idea, isn't it?

You lay yourself raw before your self, exposing the issues that you committed to in this lifetime. If you persevere without being too severe then invariably you will expose more of the productive aspects of self. This is where things even out and one feels "better" because you have created an order that fits in with what you know to be authentic to your higher nature. And to quote a famous New Zealand businessman, "It's the putting right that counts."

*Through our whole lives we are always finding
new ways of putting things right.*

Putting things right does not mean that one is always finding remedies for the wrongs but repositioning life differently so that you get the best out of it. I imagine it like a room full of wonderful objects but they are not quite in the place that you feel they should be. You wander around first getting a sense of everything, observing carefully, and by doing so getting ideas about how you relate to what you see. Then new feelings emerge about how you really want the room to look, and you begin to move things around in such a manner where it gives you the complete picture that supports your new vision. Having done so, you have completed your alignment to your satisfaction.

Anyone who engages on the road of self-development has done so because there has been an urge to evolve. There becomes the need to disengage oneself from the old patterns that have now become counterproductive, establishing unsettledness in one's life. Often people misinterpret these feelings as "what's wrong," whereas, simply put, you have completed the tasks that were essential and now it is time to move on to the next ones. I feel it's so crucial to our evolution to identify the time when that occurs, so that we are able to make the appropriate alterations to our lives and ourselves. This is when we have to "listen to the whispers of life," to quote Tabaash. Life really is whispering to us all the time like a subtle nonphysical voice in the background, always there to remind, support, and suggest. If we don't listen to these whispers, then the volume is turned up, and the voice translates itself into strong feelings or events in a way to try to get our attention. We will keep getting these "reminders," and the more that we ignore them, the louder this nonphysical voice becomes. It's unfortunate for us that when we totally ignore this that we can turn our lives into places of fear, disease, anxiety, and regrets, to name a few outcomes.

*The whispers of life are our connection with source energy that is
always prompting us to take the best course possible.*

There is never going to be a moment in anyone's life when
these whispers stop.

They are an inherent part of our soul makeup and we have
them even when we no longer have our bodies and once again
are nonphysical. The more that we engage in a relationship
with our self as soul, the more we can train our bodies to be
aware of receiving these messages more consciously. When
you spend twenty-seven years involved in spirit as I have, you
get to a point where you understand that once the connection
is made it's actually what you *DO* with the energy that makes
the difference in your life.

You have to first decide what changes you need to make
and then formulate a plan that engages the Mind, Body, and
Spirit.

*Having a plan is essential to how the Mind, Body, Spirit
engage with themselves.*

Having a good relationship with your *GOD NATURE* is a
requirement to the success of your plan. That, after all, is the
part of you that knows everything and feeds you all the answers
you need through your feelings. The better the relationship with
those feelings, the better you are able to translate those feelings
into positive events in your life. As I wrote that, the thought
occurred to me that all my life I have had a good relationship
with the God part of me but have battled the human part of
me. I can really feel the God part of me simply being me. So
therefore I must have created that degree of separation that
did not allow the God me to flow unconditionally, hence the
battles! And don't we all do that without even realizing that we
are? When we separate ourselves we actually end up drawing
a battle line, and the moment that occurs all our many selves

start preparing for the battles that will ensue. Our minds and bodies don the necessary armor that is needed, therefore disabling us and making our progress in life arduous and encumbered. The more we do this, the more that we take on this armor as a second skin, and its attachment to us becomes like a disease to our bodies and minds.

It's best to be able in life, not disabled.

So much of this is done quite unconsciously of course and before we know it we seem rather entangled in our own energy web rather than flowing freely with it. Too often have we tripped up simply because we were not paying enough attention to what as Gods we were trying to tell the human nature. I've tried hard to stay conscious of what's what, but those old energies keep reigniting themselves, not of their own volition of course, since nothing can ignite anything but our own thoughts and actions. Tabaash has explained that we all carry ENERGY SHADOWS. These energy shadows portray themselves as life without features. They may have featured at some point in our lives as actions, attitudes, feelings, thoughts, etc., but they have served their purpose and therefore there is no need for them to be a part of our lives. They will hang around, though, and need to be removed! Removing them is not an onerous task. According to spirit if we speak directly in our thoughts to them or out loud if you choose to gather all the shadow energies together and then tell them that you have created a shadow room where you will presently position them. You herd them into the room and quite simply close the door. They have no power to open the door because only we can do that by allowing them to once again become a feature in our lives. This exercise is recommended weekly, though one could do it more often if you feel it's required.

Such an exercise seems vital to our well-being more than ever these days. I'm totally dizzy by all the energy changes that seem to be happening presently. The regularity of the changes seems to be the constant these days, therefore the need to "purge" is imperative to maintain a good balance. The natural shift of consciousness that is occurring is manifesting a great blend of diverse energy that everything is susceptible to. I'm not meaning just as human beings but literally *EVERYTHING* that is of this planet, on this planet, and beyond this planet.

A great shaking off of the old energies has occurred and the consequences of this are the need to adapt with the new pulse of life. It's as if everything went into some vibration cardiac arrest and needed to be revived. Once it was, a new way of existing had to be carefully constructed, and that's what I believe we are all doing now, constructing new ways of living. You can have it thrust upon you in very ungracious ways, or you can be very gracious about it as you allow self to adjust to new rhythms. There is only one rhythm, that being the God rhythm.

We don't need to confuse ourselves by creating an assortment of rhythms that align to all the aspects of self. Just go direct to what everything is made of, the source energy of God itself. Go direct to that and you pass GO, collecting life along the way. In my own journey I created such pressure on myself by believing that I needed to separate life into factions and endeavored to find out how I was to filter in the God energy. Whereas all I needed to do was remember that all those factions were God anyway and already carried the vibration. So ... if I simply practiced being God doing those things or thinking on that level then I can bypass all the confused efforts of trying to be God and "get on with the act of actually being God." Ah the pressure of walking your talk! As a light worker you really do feel the responsibility of doing the best you can. You're rather a conscious representative for God, and you want to feel that you are coming up with the goods. After all, when people come to see you it's important that you reveal yourself as someone who is actually living all this stuff and that it actually works, otherwise it's like going to a dermatologist who has really bad skin. This makes you more conscious of self and at times self-conscious of self.

All of that is a good thing but, hey, no pressure! It's not that I'm constantly looking for faults but I am more aware that I actually have them and how they can affect my life and of course the lives of others if overplayed. We've got to be easy on ourselves, otherwise we're going to generate so much heaviness of Mind, Body, Spirit that it can render us afraid.

You are Gods and you will still make mistakes. You're going to wake up some mornings and feel like shit. You're going to walk through some days being the ultimate misery guts and you're also going to wonder and ponder, and be up and down and go sideways. You will still wonder if you are doing the right thing or presenting yourself in the right way. You will wonder what the hell the right thing is, and you will doubt and want to withdraw and wish that you had done something else like becoming an architect or a cheese maker. You will feel that you want to get away from it all and move away where you can just grow your vegetables and count how many eggs the hens have laid that day. That's just a part of the road, but of course it is not the whole road. There is no price to pay as we were all born with a life credit card that credits us with as much as we want and there is no bill at the end.

Making a choice to be born again into a body is like stepping out onto the high diving board except this diving board is higher than any you have dived off in human terms. What it must be like from up there looking down, knowing that you are about to make the dive into all of that going on down there. It's amazing that any of us ever take that step and off we go! So, why do we do it? We do it because we are actually accomplished divers as we have perfected our diving technique over the lives we have had. Imagine all the different pools of consciousness that we have dived into throughout history! I'm suddenly getting a picture of times when we must have resisted, and there we are as souls right on the edge gazing down at Earth and everything that's happening. One can imagine the conversation you would have with the souls who are in spirit encouraging you and guiding you to take that leap.

"Oh, come on, you want me to go down THERE?"

"It will be fine, just jump and you will be guided, it will be fine."

"That's all good for you to say that, you're staying up here all being light and uncomplicated, and from where I'm standing at present believe me that looks a far better prospect."

"You know you want to do this. It's something you have done so many times before."

"Why do you have to talk to me in that misty voice and exude light from your being?"

"It says in your script that's how we are supposed to speak, in misty mystical voices and exude copious beams of radiant light. We are, after all, your reality, therefore we are simply playing the role you have created for us."

At that point that's probably when we make the jump.

And so down, down, down we fall once again into human nature and all that it entails. For some of us it will be SPLAT; for others, it will be like a gentle feather floating gracefully down into the existence of human consciousness. For others, it may be "WHAT THE F***!!! Once we are there, we've got to pull all ourselves together and get on with the job of creating the best life with what we come with.

And not only do we do that every life that we engage in, but we also dive off that high-dive board every morning before we wake up, plunging back into the body, back into Earth life (or whatever planet you happen to be involved with at the time).

Our souls are expert swimmers always going for gold.

Being expert swimmers doesn't mean that we are always going to win the race or swim our best time, though. We might start off strong and determined, but then one can unexpectedly feel the weight of some human issue and we slow down or we feel like we are sinking. And it's at that time when, if truth be told, we have to remember all the training we have put ourselves through and swim to live in a manner where we know we have accomplished the best for the situation. We should never resign ourselves to just crawling through life thinking that's the best we can do because of the circumstances. We may be weighed down by what's happened or happening in our lives and that's when we have to swim stronger because it's that action that will inevitably make the difference. For every time that we make a step that we thought ourselves incapable of taking we have made an impact on the way that we move forward. I have found through my own personal experiences that when one does take that step it often shakes up a lot of counterproductive thoughts, past actions, and feelings. I believe that's part of the process of perfecting oneself. By shaking up those energies it gives you the prospect of confronting them, thus enabling you to organize those energies so as to not disable you. I do think, though, that we create a natural disablement so we can bear witness to these energies. We simply can't ignore anything and when we do and don't make the changes that are needed then the issues just get worse. Your personality choice and life deals will determine the way that you cope with things. I admire those who are able to just toss stuff aside and not let it get the better of them! I have come with a personality that overthinks things and therefore I mull over stuff far too much and create issues that were never there in the first place. I can't stop being that way as it's never about stopping but more about being industrious with harmony and having better ordered thoughts. Thinkers can't stop thinking and feelers can't stop feeling. You have to think and feel in a manner that's going to allow both energies to blend.

It's hard to think positive thoughts when you don't feel positive, and it's hard to feel positive when your thoughts have scrambled themselves up.

And so what are we all supposed to do when we get into that sort of tangle? That's when we have to go to God. That's throwing it all up to the part of us that is not getting beleaguered by the intricacy of the human nature. After twenty-five years of consciously connecting with the God force I totally get this and endeavor to make this concept a daily element in my life. We do still feel pain, though; oh, how we still feel pain at times! Perhaps some people have an unrealistic approach to what self-development will bring to them? In my observations, some people seem to think that by giving it up to God or the "universe" that means they don't have to take the responsibility for their life and expect the "forces" that be will sort it all out. That just makes us puppets without any free will and that's NOT what we were created to be. When we go to God we are expanding our idea of ourselves, and we take our thoughts and feelings to a place where we can put them into a better order. Here we can disassemble the tangle and see an order of energy that provides information, feelings, thoughts that will make possible more industrious ways of living our lives hence creating better outcomes.

We will never stop creating and telling our story. We are all constantly bringing in new plots and new characters. Every time we do this we engage in a relationship with new vibrations that offer up new ways of creating and living our story. Even though we are creating our realities we have to remember that we ourselves are the creation of other people's realities. We only exist for them because they have put us there, and they exist for us because we have done the same. It's a bit like "What comes first, the chicken or the egg?" To keep it uncomplicated for yourself you have to remember that as God you are the very center of consciousness and you are organizing what's going on around you. If you get too involved in other people's realities then you are getting tangled up in an energy that will distract you. Hah! This is where I confuse myself because my brain starts thinking that other people's stuff is still your reality and so you are really dealing with yourself all the time. That's it then, you are actually all the time dealing with yourself, loving yourself, being angry with yourself, being in conflict with yourself, and you have created everything around you to show you that. When you are involved with someone you have created that involvement, so that you could be drawn in to opportunities that allow you to know yourself. It's a chance to either improve that who you are or change that who you are. The same could be said for any event you participate in or any country you find yourself in.

At the end of the day it's your world and you are the very epicenter of it. We are all directing the creation of everything from our own unique vantage point.

As we find the appropriate rhythm that exudes harmony then this energy influences our personal creation. It's interesting to note that as we engage in this way of living, life starts following us around in more definite ways. As we recognize what we are feeling and seeing from that we are able to direct the course of our thoughts and actions more specifically.

The other day I had some free time and it being an exceptionally beautiful sunny spring day I decided to take a book, grab a coffee, and go and sit on the beach and read. I had been thinking a lot about the excess baggage that as individuals and as a collective we all carry around with us. I started to consider as an individual what I might still be carrying with me, what "trash" was necessary for me to rid myself of. As I was driving to the beach I found that I was coincidentally "following" a local council rubbish truck. It obviously was going in the same direction I was, as I ended up "following the rubbish" the whole way to the beach. Then as I was driving home the very SAME truck was coincidentally following me but the rubbish had been emptied! How often do we keep following the rubbish in our lives, and how often do we allow it to keep following us? The signals are all there for us to read if we allow ourselves to notice them. When the recognition is there that's when we put a new plan of action together to ensure that we are free of all the trash. That's why it's so important to keep writing the stories of our lives, creating the new plots, positioning ourselves in such a manner where the story flows and all the characters involved in our story are complementing our endeavors to create a happy life, that has no ending but a continuum of creation and harmonious participation.

So it seems obvious that life is following us around and that's exactly what it's supposed to do. The trick is that we recognize that it is and realize that we allow it to follow us around. And that brings up this point, which is, *"We have to start following life around so that when it follows us we are happy about that!"*

The more we follow it, the more we see what we are creating; the more we do that, the more we are able to distinguish what works more to our advantage and consequently we can make the relevant changes if it's not working in our favor. Easier said than done, eh? Hah, I have been following myself around for years and I still keep losing myself! There are aspects of myself that are very elusive and others that are downright in my face, while other aspects are so obvious that I hardly notice them, or perhaps don't want to notice them. And this is why we keep creating new stories in our lives so that we can present to ourselves chances of changing the story and of course learning what we need to. Once we do that more constantly I find that things seem to fall into a better rhythm. I have learned that being God is a lifetime commitment, and that as we evolve we have to keep changing the rules to fit in with our new vibration. No mean feat when one considers that the constant now seems to be consistent change. It's exhausting at the best of times to keep up with what we are all being bombarded with. I try earnestly to practice following myself around through the day remembering that I am God as often as I can, affirm how I want the day to pan out, make sure I'm asking the right questions of myself. It's a routine, yes, but one that will bring good benefits. It's the sticking to it that counts! When I get pressured or unhappy or just categorically pissed off with my lot I still ask, *"What the bleep am I doing this for?"* and of course the moment I ask that is the moment my authentic self throws at me all the reasons why. You can argue with your authentic self, but it has a propensity to know what's best and can make you feel ashamed for not listening, which is ridiculous considering you are only listening (or not) to your own self!

I shall continue writing new stories in my life, and I shall persevere with following myself around so that I don't get the better of myself. And what better way to turn the tables for the better!

Chapter Two

"Excellent Footwork, Mr. Bond"

I never wanted to go to the show in the first place. I had just returned to Wellington having spent a week in Christchurch working, and I was really looking forward to a nice relaxing evening, settling in and seeing my wife, Kay. Within minutes of greeting Kay and lugging my suitcase in, she announced that she had some tickets to go to a show hypnotherapist of some renown, a fundraiser that was to be held in the hall of a local high school, and she thought it would be fun to go. The authentic part of me said no straight away, but then Kay said that we would catch up with friends for dinner first at their place and then go on to the show from there. She seemed really keen on going and so I allowed myself to be persuaded. Not wanting to be funny here, but it was literally *a dark and stormy night!* As I dodged the bullet-size raindrops to get the car out of the garage I could feel my whole being resisting to going out and muttered and grumbled to myself as I backed the car out of the garage. The rain beat a hard drum on the roof of the car, and I'm sure it was going HAHAHAHAHAHAHAH!

Kay didn't seem perturbed that she would have to go from house to car in the waterfall, but then she had a husband carrying a giant umbrella over her ensuring she stayed DRY!

As we drove through town the traffic was atrocious; not only was it wet and cold but it was also rush-hour traffic and we were caught up in a slow crawl out of the city. This was the first sign that I should have heeded. Heading out of the city I decided to take a route to our destination that was easier and less traffic, but when I went to take the turnoff the road was blocked and there was a detour, which was the second sign I should have heeded! By the time we got to our friends' place I was beginning to take on the distinctive characteristics of a grumpy middle-aged man who was somewhere he really did not want to be and had no qualms about expressing that! We were half an hour late getting to our friends' place and so dinner was not the nice relaxed prelude to the show but more a frenzy of gulping down the food and making our way to the event.

We arrived at the venue and I dropped Kay off at the entrance and proceeded to set out on a "find a car park expedition." The dark and stormy night still prevailed and eventually I found a park far away from the entrance, enabling the torrent to send rivulets of water in places upon my person where no man nor woman should expect to find them. I made a mad rain dance to the entrance and gave myself a good shake and made a few adjustments. All the others had found a seat by then so I squelched into the hall and sat down next to Kay. I sat there gathering myself from the puddle that was forming at my feet and tried to send out messages of love and harmony to quiet my deluged self but felt I was failing miserably. The hall was full of echoes and it was cold and smelt damp. I wished more than anything that I was at home in the quiet and warm enjoying a hot cup of something rather than being where I was. Why had I allowed myself to be talked into this or rather why had I created this reality in the first place? What could I possibly be learning from this situation?

The hall was full of the usual chatter of anticipation that preceded a show and as I looked around I recognized a few people that I knew. It was rather uncomfortable sitting on the hard, wooden bench, but it was a school hall and hell, a fundraiser and all that. Relax, Blair, create the reality that you are going to enjoy yourself and be part of the energy. Yeah, right.

We can all look back at our lives and see that we had certain experiences that needed not to have happened should we have simply listened to the little whispers of life earlier on.

For some time I had been getting little nudges from all angles that I needed to slow down a bit and re-prioritize. There was always so much to do, though, and in the back of my mind I did hear the messages but ignored the warnings. And so like so many of us I had to force myself to change by creating an event.

The hypnotherapist came on stage and the audience quieted down and he gave his introduction speech. I had heard about him over the years but had never been drawn to attending any of his shows as it just wasn't my sort of thing. People clucking like chickens and pretending they were strippers, all very amusing, I'm sure. He started the show with a bit of audience participation where we all had to put our hands in the air and grip them tightly together. We all did this for a few seconds and when he told us to let go there were gales of laughter as several people, including myself, could not un-grip their hands. It's not like they felt glued or anything like that and I knew that if I really tried I could do it but it was if I felt compelled to stay in that position. Looking back now I wish that I had made a more concerted effort to do so as it would have saved me an awful lot of hassle over the ensuing months! As it was, my hands stayed gripped together and so my fate was sealed. Others who were in the same predicament were then asked to come on stage.

I dutifully made my way up to the stage where there was a row of chairs facing the audience. All of us on stage were asked to sit down and that's when the show really started. Based on some past-life regression that I have done in the past I knew that I hypnotized easily and that night was no exception as the hypnotherapist went behind each of us sitting in the chairs and put us under. It's an interesting feeling, you're not really "out"; you are aware of yourself and everything going on around you, noises, smells, feelings, etc. It's as if you have stepped away from a part of you and another has stepped forward. All that I totally understand, knowing that we are made up of source energy and always have access to our many "selves."

All the things that I expected from such a show happened. We all had to be washing machines at one point, spinning and agitating. Then we had to swim across the Cook Strait, a body of water that separates the North and South Islands of New Zealand. The woman sitting next to me was made to have a sudden desire to stroke my hair and be in love with it. Now I absolutely hate it when someone touches my hair or head and yet the hypnotized me took it all in its stride and encouraged it!

Things went on in this fashion for a while and then as we were coming to the end of the first half of the show the hypnotherapist told us to go back to our seats but before we did he said that when we heard a piece of music, which he then played, we would all be filled with the compulsion to come back on the stage. The piece of music was that familiar tune from the James Bond films. He told us that when we heard this music we would all remember that we were spies and as we made our way back onstage we had to take out all the KGB agents in the hall. This of course made total sense to our altered states of mind and so we all made our way back into the audience and to our friends. Kay and my friends greeted me with laughter at the antics that had been displayed onstage. I chatted away and felt quite normal as we waited for the second half of the show to unfold. After about twenty minutes the hall was suddenly filled with the strains of the James Bond theme music and I found myself on high alert. I stood up and then dived for cover under a chair, and felt that there was a weapon in my hand. I literally ran around the hall like something demented knowing that I was being pursued by the KGB and in danger for my life. The hall had erupted with laughter as my fellow spies from the stage acted out similar antics and we all made our danger-filled way back to the stage.

The thought came into my head that I had to make a dive and roll onto the stage and so I ran toward the stage egged on by the audience. I noticed that the others had gone up the short flight of stairs, but my mind was saying that they were sabotaged and the safest way was the way I was going. I tell you, the compulsion to do this was so strong even though there was a part of me that was wondering what the hell was I doing running around like this making a complete ass of myself, there really seemed to be no other way. As I leapt onto the stage I did a roll and as I went to stand the rubber sole of my shoe stuck to the floor and my foot twisted and I heard a distinctive crack. I was able to stand and I made my way backstage. I could feel a little pain and thought I must have twisted my ankle. Once I got backstage I sat down and felt a huge wave of nausea overtake me. I tried hard to fight the feeling and thought I was going to faint, but then the feeling passed as quickly as it had hit me. The hypnotherapist came over and asked if I was all right and I replied that I was okay but just needed to sit for a moment.

He and the other spies went back onstage and carried on with the show. After about five minutes I stood up, felt okay, and went back onstage to great applause. The show carried on and as it got to the end he came up to each of us and gave us a task to carry out. For me it was that I had to stand up and dance the Lambada with him. He had a rose between his teeth and so together we gyrated and swayed in the floor, and the whole time I felt fine and had no pain at all in my ankle. The show finished and the hypnotherapist presented us each with a DVD of one of his previous shows. I made my way back to my friends, and as the audience dispersed I was greeted with congratulations and more laughter. My poor body wasn't laughing, though, as I suddenly felt sharp pains in my leg and ankle as the effect of the hypnotherapy started to wear off.

It was still pouring with rain and my journey back to get the car was a slow and painful hobble. As we drove home the pain really started to kick in and I was breathing heavily fast. I felt like I was giving birth as the waves of pain increased and decreased. It occurred to me that I had obviously done some sort of damage and that I had better get this checked out and fast. I dropped Kay at home and called a taxi to take me up to the hospital.

As I hopped feebly up to A&E (Accident and Emergency) I felt like a complete idiot as I explained what had happened. The pain was worse up the left side of my shin and I thought that was an odd place to feel the pain considering I felt I only had a bad sprain. I sat down and a nurse came over and gave me triage. As she felt my leg and ankle she also seemed to think that it was a bad sprain, and she gave me some aspirin, sat me in a wheelchair, and gave me some forms to fill in. When it came to the part that said, "How did you sustain your injury?" I thought, *this is going to be good!* So, I truthfully wrote, "Injury was sustained when taking out KGB agents while under the influence of hypnosis."

And so I waited, and waited, and waited. I sat in pain watching other people come and go. An hour went by, then two, and the pain was getting worse to the point where I was on the verge of tears. This is not good, I thought, and I was getting pissed off and feeling very UN God like! I wheeled myself over to the receptionist and explained that the pain was quite excruciating and that I had noticed that people who had come in AGES after I had arrived were being attended to. She blanked me out with a cold stare and announced that it wasn't first come, first served. Then she turned her back on me and carried on a conversation she had been having with a colleague. Suitably chastised I wheeled myself into the corner of the waiting room and waited some more. I had arrived at A&E at 10 p.m., and at 1 a.m. my name was finally called and I was seen to. The doctor looked at my notes I had filled out in regard to my injury and with a complete straight face read out what I had written. He did an examination of my leg and ankle and then into X-ray and back to a room where I sat quietly awaiting the verdict. When the doctor came in and informed me that I had broken my ankle, damaged the ligaments, and fractured my tibia on my left leg I stared at him for a second and then burst into laughter. He was a bit taken aback by my reaction and no doubt put it down to some sort of post-traumatic reaction. He then proceeded to put a temporary cast on the offending area. He also informed me that I would need an operation to insert a pin in my ankle such was the damage. They did not know when they could do this so I had a few nights in hospital ahead of me.

A nurse came in and wheeled a canister of nitrous oxide at my side, slipped a mask over my face, and told me to breath in deeply as the intern was going to push my ankle into place while he plastered me. As he pushed and pulled I felt no pain at all; in fact, I was feeling rather euphoric and at one stage I recall having inhaled deeply of the nitrous exclaiming rather loudly.

"OH, THIS IS THE WAY THE WORLD IS AND SHOULD ALWAYS BE!!"

The doctor and nurse looked at me and grinned; I'm sure they had heard it all before and no doubt more. Having been temporarily plastered I was wheeled up to a room where a male nurse came in and presented me with the latest fashion in hospital gowns to change in to. He looked at the tight black jeans I was wearing, the left leg of which was rolled up above my damaged leg.

"Well," he exclaimed with some degree of masochistic pleasure. "There's no way you're going to get those off. I'll just go and get some scissors to cut them off."

Having announced this with some relish and a satisfying look upon his face, he turned and walked out of the room in search of the offensive scissors. I lay there considering this and thought there is NO WAY he is going to cut up my favorite American Eagle black jeans that I had purchased in Santa Monica, and so with great presence of mind and dammed determination I managed to scriggle my way carefully out of the jeans. This was helped enormously by the fact that the fabric was slightly stretchy. As the nurse came back in the room brandishing the scissors like some sort of execution weapon, I was laying up in bed brandishing my jeans like some trophy I had won. The look on his face was sheer disappointment. He must have been majorly pissed off as he never came back, and in his place was a pleasant female nurse who laughed when she read my notes about how I had sustained my injury.

I was wheeled into a ward that had two beds in it. It was then three in the morning, and at this point I was exhausted. The curtains were drawn between my bed and the other occupant so I had no idea who was there. I was in the bed closest to the door, and I soon fell into an exhausted and restless sleep. All through the rest of those early hours the nurses would wake me up and take my blood pressure, denying me of any real form of sleep. I felt silly and foolish and really pissed off with myself for having created the situation, and yet I could see the funny side of the whole debacle. About 8 a.m. a doctor popped his head around the corner and said, "Good morning, Mr. Bond." I smiled at him wryly and thought, "great, now everyone is a comedian." No doubt the joke was discussed at my expense in the staff room. He explained that they were not sure when they would operate and so I had to be nil by mouth until it was decided. That proved no problem for me as the food was so atrocious that what they had offered up to me was instantly rejected. In the end I spent three days there not eating a thing. It was like a self-imposed fasting retreat.

I had no sense of time or even if it was day or night as the curtains around the adjoining cubicle that was near the window were pulled over the whole time I was there. I drifted in and out of sleep not even having a sense of myself. I looked down at my leg elevated before me and felt no attachment to it at all. I could feel the presence of spirit around me and thought they were probably shaking their heads and saying, "Told you so!" Why did I have to create this situation? I thought to myself, and then followed that thought with wondering how

I could make the most of this self-created sabbatical from my normal routines.

I needed a shave and a shower and badly wanted to pee. For anyone who has had to pee in bed under the covers into the appropriate vessel, it's a lesson in focus and abject concentration. I assumed the blank concentrated expression usually performed in urinals and waited for my body to do what should come naturally. At last the fast-flowing stream of urinary consciousness presented itself, and I wondered if the bottle was big enough to hold what was emitting from me. God, it seemed to go on and on and on, and I felt a slight panic that I was going to give a good physical rendition of "Overflowing Waters." My fears were unwarranted and after a few shakes I finished the job in hand, so to speak. Now, what to do with the blooming bottle? I'm no prude but I wasn't in the mood to display my liquid offering so blatantly to the entire hospital world to see and open up to possible comments on a healthy bladder. I rummaged around and found a small hand towel in a drawer and so wrapped the vessel with it, no doubt making it more conspicuous. I hoped like hell I didn't have to take a crap.

There I lay feeling drained and not very much like my God self in any way at all. My Libran self so used to order and structure was in dire need of some rebalancing and I was also wondering how I was going to let my mate Remi, whose wedding was in two weeks, know that I as his best man was going to bring a cast and crutches as extra guests.

As the morning progressed copious amounts of nursing activity prevailed and the night shift bid farewell to the day shift that instantly took my blood pressure again even though it had been taken minutes before. I'm sure they were all on some sort of blood pressure quota system. Perhaps they thought I would get excited at the prospect of the new shift. Next door the curtains were still drawn, but there was a flurry of nursing activity that came and went through those curtains over the next hour. After a while my roommate struck up a conversation through the curtains. His name was Laurie and he was in his nineties. He had flown fighter planes in England during World War Two. We became friends and yet I never set eyes on him the whole time I was there. We would talk for a while and then there would be a comfortable silence as he or I drifted off to sleep or into some altered state of consciousness. Then one of us would pick up the conversation where we had left off or make some comment about something that we had been thinking of. We joked about trying to pee into a bottle while lying down. He was old school and a total gentleman, and I felt it was a privilege to spend the time I did with him.

It's incredible what sort of people we attract in the most unusual of circumstances.

Of course, this was my reality and in the world of my reality it was natural that Laurie was to be a part of that. And, of course, this was his reality and I was only his creation. Each was participating in each other so that we could understand our self. So why did I need to only hear him and not see him? Was that my authentic nature reminding me of the importance of listening and not getting distracted by always seeing what was in front of me?

It's interesting developing a friendship over such a short period of time when you have no visual reference of that person. One has a sense of the person therefore engaging you with your own sensory abilities. I could feel my soul connecting with his soul. We were energy-to-energy and voice-to-voice and it made me realize how much we all rely on what we see. We place demands on ourselves and others through the expectations we have when we see life and others through our eyes. What judgments are we making, what conclusions do we come to simply because we see someone?

It reminded me of a client who had been coming to see Tabaash for some years.

He was of the nature who was constantly being distracted by what was going on around him and was often not paying attention to what he should be doing or listening to as he was always waiting to "see" what was happening. He was not a very present person and all that he was seeing was a great distraction to him. One day when he came to have a session with Tabaash, Tabaash presented him with a mask to cover his eyes and announced that he wanted to have some of the session with the man's eyes blindfolded. He explained that it was an opportunity to listen with his soul instead of seeing with his eyes. Always up for a challenge, the guy readily agreed and for the first twenty minutes he was comfortable. Then Tabaash went silent and walked around the room very quietly so the guy didn't know where Tabaash was. Tabaash would then speak again and then be silent. Having no visual reference point what manifested in the guy was fear, and of course the feeling that he wasn't in control of what he could not see. Then Tabaash, always the comic, decided to play a joke on the guy. He again went silent and then very quietly went and sat next to the guy who still had no idea of where Tabaash was. Then Tabaash leaned over and whispered BOO! The guy almost went through the ceiling and then he just laughed and laughed.

"You see," said Tabaash, "that's what life does if you don't stay present and focused on what you feel."

And we do get so distracted by what we are seeing that we at times forget to feel what is before us. Feeling I believe gives us a new vision and a vision that allows us to see beyond our human nature. A good thing perhaps to engage in is when you are "seeing" then ask what you feel about what you are seeing.

So spending those times in the hospital *NOT* seeing Laurie gave me more of an authentic version of him as I was allowing *my soul* to see him not my *human nature*.

As the days progressed and the news of my spy escapade started to become common knowledge among my friends, I started to get visitors. First was my best mate David, who did the appropriate things and laughed at me and told me I was an idiot and then took my picture as I lay there unshowered, unshaved, and uncomfortable. You can always rely on your mates to put things into perspective!

Then I got a text from a mate who said, "Hey, come and visit me as I'm in hospital with a broken knee." He was on the floor above me and since neither of us was physically mobile at the time we kept each other informed by text the whole time we were there. Then another mate appeared that day on crutches (obviously not a good week for my mates), his bottom exposed to the masses as his hospital gown flapped away, open to the breezes. He had fallen off a ladder or a chair or something and had ripped the quadricep muscle off his thighbone, ouch! We commiserated with each other for a while and then joked about what past lives we must have had to create our situations, and then he hobbled carefully back to his ward. People came and went through the day, and I became more restless as the day passed and no operation seemed imminent. I had been nil by mouth for three days and by this stage I was in a rather altered state due to the imposed fasting. Having no sense of the day or time of the day I drifted in and out of sleep only to be awakened by yet another nurse brandishing the blood pressure equipment. I tried to meditate and make good use of having to stay reclined but it was no use. I think my meditative self took one look at the situation and booked a holiday somewhere else.

Finally on the morning of the third day a miracle happened; a surgeon actually appeared at the foot of my bed. I thought I was seeing a vision at first. He informed me of the procedure and with a colored marker he had in his hand he made a map on my leg and ankle showing me what he was going to do. And so that afternoon the porter arrived to take me down to theater. I bid farewell to Laurie and was wheeled away. There was a nurse who walked beside my bed as I was wheeled down to surgery. She carried a clipboard in her hand that had all my vitals written down, and she kept looking at the board and then at me. Then she proceeded to ask me questions and the conversation went like this:

"Now what is your name, please?"

"Blair Styra."

I began to think this is not a very good start.

"Can you tell me what you are having done?"

God, I thought, what is this place, don't you know?

"What leg, please?"

Considering the amount of artwork the surgeon had made on my ankle and leg I would think it was pretty obvious which body part was afflicted, and the fact that my left leg was suspended seemed to me to be enough evidence for anyone. Perhaps she had spent far too much time taking people's blood pressure? I was not feeling very confident, and it got no better once we got into surgery.

"Hello," an anesthetist or nurse or someone said to me; they all looked the same in their gowns and caps. It could have been the cleaner for all I knew.

"Can you tell me what your name is and what you are having done today?"

Is this what you get for free medical care? I thought as I gazed up at the man in my pre-op haze. I wanted to yell, "Just give me the drugs and please don't chop off my leg!!"

Eventually I was sent to anesthetic heaven and later woke up in recovery with a new leg plaster and a titanium pin holding my ankle together. I was wheeled back into the ward and Laurie greeted me with a hearty voice, commenting that I was at least still alive and that he hoped that they had managed to get the right leg. I mumbled some reply through my post-op cloud and then drifted off to sleep. Later on in the day the surgeon arrived and announced that he had done an excellent job and that I would be fit and ready for my next mission in no time at all. A nurse arrived and though she was a grown woman she had a very annoying little girl voice that you would expect from a five-year-old. She had brought some crutches and proceeded to demonstrate to me in her girlish tones how to use them. I hauled myself out of the bed and did a few crutch circuits while she smiled endearingly at my efforts simpering and commenting on my success in her little girl voice. There was a slight patronizing tone in her voice and it was all I could do to not ask her when she was going to playtime. The surgeon came by early in the evening announcing that I was able to go home the next day. He then swished out of the room, no doubt thinking another job well done and went off into the sanitized hospital sunset.

As the new day dawned so did the dawning of my new situation. Adapting and walking with the assistance of crutches was easy to get used to but suddenly I realized I couldn't go at a billion miles an hour that is my normal speed. I was fast discovering and appreciating my body in new ways. The hour of my departure arrived and before I hobbled out into the world again I stood by the curtain and said my farewells to Laurie. Many nurses were attending to him and I had a feeling that he would not be alive much longer. He thanked me for being his roommate and said that he could not have wished for a better person. And then his strong but aged hand appeared from a gap in the curtain and I grasped its parched but powerful grip. We held onto each other's hand for a moment in silent farewell and then the hand withdrew. I turned and moved my way out of the ward, out of the hospital, and at last back into the sunshine.

I hold strong onto the image of Laurie's hand reaching through the curtains that surrounded his bed. That hand said everything about his life, and who he was.

Even though I never met the rest of him that hand was attached to a man who had experienced a lot in the world and he was wise and strong and loving. Having not seen him I could feel that.

Chapter Three
"These Boots Were Meant for Walking"

I've got this thing for boots; always have had as far as I can remember. While a child growing up in the sixties I loved the boots the men wore with their bell-bottomed trousers; you could not get any more Austin Powers than the boots of those times and I *LONGED* for a pair. I finally did get some when we left Canada to live in New Zealand, and I felt so cool in my tan-colored ankle-length boots with my red-and-white-striped flared seersucker trouser. I was the man!

My late teens were in the late seventies and *Saturday Night Fever* introduced me to a whole new boot extravaganza! The first time I saw John Travolta slip on his black leather high-heeled boots and strut his stuff down the streets of New York City to the strains of "Stayin Alive," it was boot nirvana for me. I saved my money till at last I was kitted out with a pair of soft black pointed boots with five-inch heels. Looking back now it's hard to imagine I actually functioned normally in those things let alone boogie down at the discos! As the years progressed, as did my income, the family became larger by the pair till eventually I had my own "boot" shelf or shelves to house the ever-expanding foot encasements!

Perhaps I had been majorly deprived of footwear in some of my past lives, or perhaps boots had been my major footwear in some of those lives. Needless to say, I always felt comfortable and kitted out when I donned a pair. I recall one incident while I was walking through town on the way home from the gym. I was slowly meandering, window shopping as I made my way home and as I passed one of my preferred shoe shops I saw these astonishing pair of highly polished brown leather pointed-toe boots that screamed at me to instantly relieve them of the boring shelf existence that they were currently living. I walked into the shop and gazed up at them. I'm sure they smiled at me and projected boot thought transference to take them home and live a happily shod life ever after. My feelings and my brain started at this point to have a major conflict of interest.

Brain was saying:

"The last thing you need is another pair of boots, turn around this instant and walk out of the shop!"

My feelings had other intentions though.

"You really need these, they would be SO useful, and go with heaps and heaps of the things you have. They look so cool and so comfortable, and LOOK THEY ARE ON SALE! You can't really pass up on such a deal. They really are Blair boots."

Brain replied:

"Kay would not be very amused if you came home with yet another pair of boots that you don't really need. She would think that you were over indulgent and wasting your money that could go to some of the house renovations."

On that day the brain won the bout, but all was not lost as a few days later when Kay and I were having a wander through town, I by mere coincidence steered us by the shoe store and to my utter surprise Kay insisted that we go in and have a look. I feigned disinterest and grudgingly was persuaded to have a look. The boots were still there beaming up at me as if to say:

"We knew you would come back. We knew you would not forget us, as you can see we're still here waiting for you."

I am certain that they waved to me and batted their lashes at me grinning enticingly. As Kay wandered around the shop, I sat down on a leather couch pretending that this was the last place that I wanted to be. I watched Kay carefully out of the corner of my eye as she veered toward the shelf where the offending boots were positioned, and waited. I didn't have to wait long.

"Oh look!" she exclaimed.

I glanced her way oblivious of course to what she was looking at.

"Have you seen these boots? Aren't they nice?"

I stood up and wandered nonchalantly into already chartered boot territory and stood by her.

"Oh yes," I replied, knowing the game was already won, "they're quite nice."

"You should try them on, Blair," said Kay. "And look, they are on sale and that's a really good price."

"Well," I replied casually, "I don't really need another pair of boots but maybe I will just to see how they look."

The sales assistant went into the back while I feigned complete indifference to the situation. I tried them on and of course they were a perfect fit and they looked everything I knew they would look, SHOEPENDOUS!

Kay walked around me and made appreciative murmuring noises and started to tell me that they were really nice and that I really should buy them.

"Yes, they look great. Now come on, buy them and let's go and have a coffee."

I looked up at her and then down at the shoes, did a little twist of the ankle here, then there to get the best angle.

Oh well, twist my arm.

Another day, another shop, this time in an outlet mall. I was by this stage moving from any previous lives where I had gone barefoot and was channeling Imelda Marcus and her shoe closet such was the growing collection of footwear.

There was the most awesome of shoe shops in this mall and I accelerated our pace in case there were offending people who had the idea of depriving me of podiatry indulgence. The shop was small and it did not take long before I spotted them. They were suave in their black suede; they were sophisticated and stylish in their low-heeled Italian design. They were desperate to be worn by me and so of course I bought them. As I was driving home I could feel their joy as they were deported out of the shop where they had spent many a lonely hour with only inferior shoe species to keep them company. Nothing else spoke their language but me. I got them home and took them out of the bag, marveling at how I could have been so remiss that I had not discovered them before. I was desperate to wear them right away and so slipped them on and felt their instant embrace of welcoming. From every angle they sang of glory but it was Sunday night and we had no plans to go out and so I reluctantly slipped them off and placed them in the care of the rest of the family. We had dinner and after that I settled down with a good book but my mind kept wandering to the pair of black gold that was residing in my wardrobe awaiting their public debut.

And then by some sort of divine shoe providence, no doubt orchestrated by the shoe gods and goddesses, Kay announced that we had run out of milk and that I would have to pop down to the supermarket and get some. Did I resist? Did I say that I would wait till the morning? Don't be so ridiculous, I was out of that seat and into the wardrobe where I bedecked myself in some tight black denims, shirt, and black leather jacket and, of course, the boots. The effect was most satisfactory and I left the house in anticipation of the cataclysmic effect the boots would have on all who beheld them, such were their magnificence. As I walked out of the house Kay commented that I was rather overdressed considering that I was only going out to get milk. Such statements can only be treated with the complete contempt they deserved and in ignorance of what she said I left the house.

It was a cool night and with a slight wind blowing so I was glad of the leather jacket and of course the boots transformed my feet into small heating devices. Even though it was only a bottle of milk I needed I was compelled to walk down every aisle of the supermarket to make sure that the boots were getting good exposure. Being later in the night the supermarket was fairly quiet but the few people that I passed in the aisles smiled at me in a way that suggested to my mind that they were really impressed with the boots. Aisle after aisle I traipsed gazing at things that I would never buy like capers and pickled cabbage. I stood and stared at a can of baby food till my back ached so desperate was my need to show off the boots. After a while I realized I had spent far too long in the supermarket to warrant a bottle of milk and so reluctantly went to the checkout. People were still smiling at me but I did start to notice that there was something odd about the way they were looking at me. I began to feel self-conscious; something didn't quite seem to fit.

At the checkout the operator looked at me, stared, and smiled. She seemed to be trying to conceal a little laugh and so feeling rather puzzled I handed her my money and walked out, looking back I noticed she was staring at me and saying something to another co-worker and then they burst into girlish giggles. I checked my fly to make sure that everything was intact and felt my face to make sure there wasn't anything stuck to me but all seemed fine and so I made the passage home pleased with the boots inaugural outing.

The walk home was a short one and a cool stiff breeze had got up since I had been in the supermarket. I turned the collar up of my jacket and as I did a gust of wind blew up and blew my hair around my face. As I lifted my hand up to brush my hair away my hand caught in something in the side of my hair and my hand closed around a strange round object. I thought the wind had blown a leaf in my hair but when I opened my hand I stared for a moment and then burst out laughing. While I had been reading at home before going to get the milk I had shoved my bookmark behind my ear while reading. In my haste to get those boots on I had forgotten that it was there. And so thinking that I was so shit hot in my boots and black denims, I had traversed the aisles of the supermarket with this BIG plastic poppy behind my ear. No wonder people were giving me odd smiles and looks. And no wonder the checkout operator was suppressing her girlish giggles. I laughed all the way home and looked up to the heavens and said,

"Oh, very funny, obviously I needed a lesson in humility. Well, I got it!"

As you become more involved in "your authentic self" I have realized that being God points out to you in subtle ways if not more obvious ways, certain idiosyncrasies of one's personality that are important to pay attention to. Doing this allows you to look at things that need to change or simply have an awareness of characteristics that may not be very endearing! Each day I comprehend and appreciate what we are dealing with here when we start paying more attention to ourselves. Our awareness of the bigger picture of life permits us a view of ourselves that assists us in the fine-tuning that we are all involved in. None of our habits or idiosyncrasies are wrong but at times we have to make alterations to those habits and actions that make us project a vibration that entangles us in our own egos. All of us in some way through our lives can't but help throw out the energy of "Look at me!" Not that this is a wrong thing but it may attract life to us in ways that may challenge other people! And this makes me think about the finer aspects of being God on Earth. It is about moving away from acting out life through our egos and acting out life through our souls. I could have just walked down to the shops in my old trainers and jeans and got the milk and come straight home. The ego in me, though, insisted that I did it another way and though this wasn't wrong it was putting me in a situation where I had to humiliate myself in some way to get my attention so changes could be made. I'm working on that!!!

Chapter Four
The Space Invader

I like the fact that my line of work takes me to all sorts of interesting places in the world, and wherever I am I love to participate in the day-to-day life of the people whose hood I am visiting and be a part of the local rituals.

I was working in Surfers Paradise on the Gold Coast of Australia. With its long golden beaches with squeaky sand and its lack of the "back of beyond," I reveled in its complete dedication to tourism and consumerism. It's a party place and it knows it! When away my work schedule offers up little opportunity for decent daytime indulgence and so often I would get up early wherever I was and peruse for an hour or two before the work of the day. While in Surfers I would get up at 5:30 every morning and walk for an hour, watching the sun make its appearance and herald in the new day. Actually I had little choice to get up as at that time of the morning without fail a car alarm would go off or the noise from council rubbish trucks would float up and invade my slumber.

It's an awesome time of the day to be awake. There is just the tip of the night energy still there teasing you and the morning energy excels in making its presence felt. You can't help but feel that you are on the brink of something wonderful. There was always warmth in the air despite the fact that the sun was still to show its face and an all-pervading air of peace and stillness was most agreeable. As I walked along the promenade adjacent to the beach I would always have what I call my "morning conference." This is when I would inform my body and mind selves about the day. Basically it was "I" the soul having a chinwag with my other selves setting up everything for the day and inviting in the appropriate energy that I wanted for the day.

"Hey, life, it's me, God, speaking, you know the one in complete charge of how this day will pan out? We've a whole new day in front of us and so here is the structure of the day."

Then I would outlay the plan to my selves, tell them what I wanted of them and that they would have to report to me often through the day with the best results. Hopefully I would be listening as the results came in! Having done this, then I would focus my mind on how far I was to walk that morning, keeping in mind that if I were to walk too far the return journey would be more of a rapid run rather than a pleasant morning stroll along the seaside. By 6 a.m. the place was packed full of early morning joggers, walkers, dogs, and other contemplators who were no doubt having their own morning conferences with their authentic selves!

With some others, there seemed more of an urgency to get this part of the day over and done with, and they didn't seem to have a sense of anything "higher" than the sun moving up in the sky.

It was a serious business this morning walk, a ritual needed to be practiced by the eager indulging masses. Women of a more mature age seemed to use this as a chance to catch up on the latest gossip and traveled in dangerous packs of pastel velour, their voices overriding the sound of the surf hammering the beach. They must have had a season pass to the same hairdresser who seemed to be of the opinion that an Eton crop in shades of gray or blonde looked good on women of advanced years. They all looked like aged versions of a Stepford wife with their perfect tans and perfectly manicured nails. They were bedecked in the ubiquitous gold chains and bracelets, and the diamonds on their fingers blinded and dazzled you as the early morning sun caught them.

There were the serious jogging babes with their pert breasts thrust out followed closely behind by their scantily clad rounded bottoms. The babes were plugged into their IPods, no doubt listening to words of highly motivating wisdom that would establish a balance and harmony equal to their perfect breasts and bottoms. The faces of these women all carried the same concentrated look of indifference to what was going on around them and it reminded me of people at the gym on the running machines, plugged into their own sound but seeing nothing. And then came the serious jogging dudes, whom I noted like the female joggers of advanced years were often seen traveling in packs. Perhaps this was to protect themselves from the pertness of the serious jogging babes. These pack dudes for some reason found it essential to talk at the top of their voices about serious stuff that when spoken and heard didn't sound serious at all. They usually talked at the same time and it became a sort of a consistent drone moving up the path. Looking onto the beach I noticed several black masses, and on closer inspection saw that they were Japanese tourists in suits, standing in the sand and watching the view. Many of them had their trousers rolled up to their knees and they had discarded shoes and socks. Cameras ever ready, they looked a comical sight as they welcomed in the day with their formality and politeness. With that and the blend of early morning surfers and serious swimmers in their budgie smugglers, it was almost farcical.

I love watching people's routines, love watching them simply being themselves and getting on with living life in the way they know how, that being totally unique to them. I love the fact that I am by their creation, a part of their reality as well. It's also entertaining when you have found that you have inadvertently upset someone's routine, as I found out.

Having walked for half an hour I decided to stop for a moment before turning back and rested on a little patch of lawn that overlooked the beach. I watched the surfers and the tractor mowing up the sand for the day and gazed out into the sea as it sparkled in the rising sun. I could not suppress a laugh as I saw that some of the Japanese besuited businessmen had been besieged by several large waves hitting the shore, catching them unawares and drenching them. They flailed around on the beach trying to keep their footing. Gesticulating and loudly exclaiming no doubt Japanese expletives, they still managed to maintain a high semblance of dignity despite their baptism.

After a while I became aware of someone else standing nearby and noticed a man in his early sixties who was looking very agitated. He kept throwing me glances that were a mixture of sheer frustration and immense annoyance. He seemed to be lining up to want to say something, as his face was a concerto of suppressed expressions. By inductive reasoning it came to me that I was probably standing in "his spot." No doubt every morning for the past zillion years he had stood at the very spot I now occupied and now this foreign interloper who evidently had no regard for what was proper and decent had come and invaded his home turf. I was in his hood and he did not take to it at all.

It was my intention to at some point put him out of his misery and move on but before I did I felt it my cosmic duty to make him endure my unwanted presence just a little bit more.

I looked at him and gave him the biggest and most endearing smile that I could muster.

"Nice day," I said, making it look as if I were going to be there for the rest of the day.

He glared at me in unconcealed disdain and said nothing. He shuffled a bit clearly needing with ever-increasing moment to find ways of reclaiming his territory. He stared at me with bulging eyes and I could feel the increasing desperation oozing out of him.

"Yep, it's going to be a really nice one, I reckon," I continued, plunging the knife in just a little bit deeper.

Shuffle; shuffle agitated movements and more glares.

He stared out into the open sea, no doubt wishing he could cast me out into the depths and planning strategies that would remove me from his own piece of hallowed turf so he could once again reign supreme. There was a little tick in his cheek that was moving rapidly and his face was becoming the color of a nice ripe pomegranate. Not wanting to bring on a cardiac arrest I decided to put him out of his misery and abdicate my position.

"Well, I had better be on my way," I said, still standing my ground. I bent down to tie up my shoelace that did in fact not need attention at all. He shuffled a bit closer as if in fear of some other miscreant taking my position. I stood up as if to move on but instead did a few hamstring stretches and twisted side to side smiling at him the whole time as if we were the very best of friends. At last I moved away and at once he reclaimed his prize land with furtive glances of the surrounding area particularly paying heed to a busload of tourists that had just pulled up. He stood his ground, making it clear that no one was going to hoist his or her personages onto his space. So I left him and as I walked away he stared at me to make sure that I was leaving for good. I waved my hand to him but really felt that I should have saluted.

Chapter Five

Requiem for a Gym Brother

The day after I got out of hospital I was determined to get on with my normal routines as soon as possible. Having to adjust to the crutches was no mean feat as I discovered. Trying to get a glass out of the cupboard suddenly became an exercise in determination and expert choreography. I was no Mikhail Barishnakoff in my maneuvers, believe me, as I clumped around the kitchen perfecting my balancing act. I had been in the hospital for three days but you would have thought I had been away for three months as my body was agitated and tired for having been prone all that time. I started to inform my body more about what had happened and now what I wanted the result to be. All through the day I was affirming that I was healing well and that the healing process would be half of what the surgeon had said. I became a one-sock one-shoe guy and had to give the skinny jeans a sabbatical.

Having to learn how to use your body in a totally different way became my new sort of training. I soon perfected quite a speed on the old crutches and started back to work within days, easily scaling the staircase up the side of the house to my work premises. I did wonder how Tabaash was going to cope with the cast on my leg but he did so admirably, resting my leg up on some cushions and making jokes about my adventure, at my expense of course. I hoped that having his energy in my body through the day would assist in the healing process and I must admit at the end of the channeling day, I felt the full force of source power flowing through me. I made sure I spent a few minutes at the end of the workday relaying that energy to my wounded ankle and leg, not wanting to waste what I was feeling.

I was desperate to get back to the gym and felt that exercise would help in my recovery. The gym was only a ten-minute walk from our place and it was a fairly straight run so I thought I could easily manage to hobble my way there. So I kitted myself out with all that was needed and with backpack attached I proceeded on my adventure.

Bloody hell! After five minutes I felt like I had done the iron man! I had to stop several times before I even got to the end of our road. A forty-second journey to the end took me all of five minutes. I forgot that out road had a slight incline to it and going slightly downhill was an act of hard-going concentration. My shoulders ached and so did my back. I could feel my body tensing up such was my concentrated focus. And as I passed some workmen at the tile shop at the end of the road I was greeted with derisive comments such as "hop-along" and other such expressions that fitted my situation. It was all said in good humor so I stopped and chatted awhile, taking the opportunity to rest and catch my breath. I looked ahead of me and saw the road stretched before me now looking like some conquest of the crusades. Being a stubborn and determined soul I manfully proceeded to fulfill my mission.

As I crutched my way up Courtney Place people gave me curious glances, and I could see that they were wondering what had happened to me. Some tall blonde woman exuding "I'm expensive" gave me a cold dismissive look as if to say, "get out of my way, I'm much more important than you and you're in my way." It was obvious by her demeanor that she didn't have many lights switched on, and so, I lifted up one of the crutches that was concealing an AK 47 and gunned her down. Well, actually I didn't really, but man some people!

Every crutch step up the road was a feat of endurance and I could feel the sweat pouring down my back and soaking my t-shirt. Maybe this wasn't such a good idea after all, I began to think, but one must soldier on and not give in to defeat. I called in all my walking guides to assist me but I think they must have gone shopping or something as I felt very much like "You're on your own, my lad." After half an hour I finally reached the building where the gym was and went up to the lift that would take me to the first floor where the changing rooms were. Of course, there was a sign that said "Out of order," and so I resigned myself to ascend the two flights of stairs that hovered before me. Climbing carefully I met up with one of the trainers I knew and he burst into laughter and said, "Oh dear."

In fact, I noticed this with most of the people I knew well, they would always laugh and then give me that "What have you been doing" look, whereas a complete stranger would give me the appropriate look of sympathy.

Going up the staircase was a sort of step, clunk, step, clunk process but I got there in the end, got changed, and had my workout. It was good to get back into exercise and I could feel my body's gratitude.

Divesting myself of the now-offensive gym gear I headed for the showers. I wrapped up my leg sufficiently in enough plastic bags from the supermarket so that if they ever ran out they would have to know where to come to. Off I went rustling in the breeze and into the shower cubicle. Have you ever had to have a shower standing on one leg? Have you ever had to become a contortionist in a space just wide enough to turn around in, carefully? Well, don't, unless you want to audition for Cirque du Soleil. I stood under the water with my left leg thrust out and up behind me. I had no idea before just how much water really traveled and trickled everywhere. I turned around in the effort to wash my hair and tilted my head back with my leg now thrust out in front of me as if I were kicking the winning goal in the rugby world cup final. My other leg and back and hips and everything else that was unimpaired were definitely having a conference about what I was doing and they were not very happy about it. Still, I managed to denude myself of any odious aromas I may have incurred during my workout and did it all without getting the cast wet. Thank God for New

World supermarket plastic bags.

Out of the shower, back into the changing room, more laughter and comments from people, and back on the road to hobble home. What a waste of a shower, as by the time I got home I was drenched in sweat and feeling exhausted and pissed off to the max. I collapsed into the nearest chair and in the process did myself some damage by getting tangled up in the crutches.

As the weeks melded into each other I perfected my journey to the gym; i.e., I got in the car and drove!

It was a Sunday morning, a beautiful cornflower blue-sky day. The early morning sun already had delicious warmth to it, the sort of day that spoke to you of the happiness of life and the joy of living. I was to drive up north to Hawke's Bay to work for the week. I was looking forward to staying on the farm where I usually went; it was a little haven among the rolling green hills of the bay area. I was up early Sunday to get that last workout in before I went away as gyms were far and few in the area so it was usually a gym-free week. The lift up to the first floor was at last working again so I didn't have to negotiate the stairs anymore. As I was getting changed I struck up a conversation with a guy that was usually there the same time I was on a Sunday morning. I had seen him for years but never knew his name. That's the way it is at the gym. It's usually mate or pal or dude or bro. You only ever meet those guys at the gym and so your shared world for that hour or whatever is regulated to bench presses, leg presses, and the like. Not to mention shared grunts and gasps and the sneaky farts that were emitted during strenuous pushing. It was all part of the gym ritual, though, and so this nameless gym bro and I chatted about our gym routines and how the week was and just the usual "stuff." He went off to do his workout and I slowly made my way by stairs to the second-floor weight room. Obviously the gym budget had not stretched to putting lifts through all the floors! I think there was a lift at some other part of the building but even on crutches it was quicker to go by the stairs!

I got into my workout and saw the guy I had been talking to doing some leg extensions. I passed by him and I smiled at him, which he returned, and then with a wave went up to the third floor to do some stretching. A quarter of an hour later I was coming down the stairs and I noticed that the doors to the second floor were closed and locked. The small windows in the door were covered and as one of the staff went by he looked really rattled and I asked him what was up.

"A guy's just died on this floor doing leg extensions," he replied.

He told me that the guy had just stood up and dropped dead. One of the other members had administered CPR but to no avail. The man who had died was the gym bro that I had been talking to in the changing room. I stood stock-still and the bottom of my stomach seemed to drop out of me. I was dumbfounded. I felt blank and shocked at what I had just heard. The energy in the gym became very weird. An odd quiet descended upon the place as the news filtered through to others who were at the gym. Sunday morning was always quiet and there were a small group of us gym stalwarts who were always there on Sunday at the same time. We all knew each other but we didn't. No one said a thing but our faces spoke volumes. I went back to the changing room and sat down and looked at the locker of the guy who had just passed. All his things were still in there. I could hear his mobile receiving texts. His life was there but he wasn't. There were people who were trying to contact him but they didn't know they would never do that again. His body was still laying up there on the second floor; his life had finished but it still seemed to be in action.

I showered, got dressed, and made my way back to the car. As I looked at the few cars that were in the car park I wondered which one was his. I sat in the car for a while and noticed the arrival of the ambulance and police. I thought about the gym bro and wondered if his soul was still hovering around the second floor watching all that was going on. As I drove back home I could not get out of my head what had just happened. What plans had he made for the day? Was there washing in the machine, had he made his bed? It was bizarre, my mind; it just went round and round with all these trivial and trite thoughts. I thought of all the processes that his dying had set off. I thought of the building and the room where his body lay and of all life simply going on, people getting on with their Sunday morning and not being aware of what had just happened. I thought about when he woke up that morning not realizing the countdown for his physical demise had just begun. When he closed the door to his house or flat, that would be the last time; he would never return. Driving to the gym for that last time, that last workout, last conversation, that last sip of water out of his drink bottle. Had all his guides surrounded him the whole time knowing he was about to return to spirit? Was there a part of his soul that already knew what was about to transpire and was that part of him already stepping in? Now the family would have to be informed; did he have a wife, children? The people at his place of work would no doubt be shocked at his sudden demise.

I then recalled some years ago that a woman in her early twenties had booked a personal session with Tabaash. On the day of her session she was rather late so I rang her contact number that turned out to be her work number. The receptionist answered and when I asked if my client was free to talk there was an audible gasp and a silence. She then asked who I was and I explained the situation. She put me on hold and then another person came on the line that was the manager.

"I'm very sorry to have to tell you this but she died in the weekend."

Apparently, she was going to have a bath and the water heater in the bathroom was one of those old gas calophont things that heated the water when you lit it. It had leaked and the woman had been gassed and had died. In a strange turn of events, the woman who had died happened to be the stepdaughter of someone I was well acquainted with, whose own daughter incidentally passed away at a young age a few years later. Bloody Hell!

When I got home from the gym I was feeling awful and the moment I got through the front door I promptly burst into tears. I felt rather silly actually, but the tears kept flowing as I thought about this poor man in the prime of his life and in a moment it had all ended. I felt empty and sad but at the same time ridiculous that I was reacting this way considering that I didn't even know his name. It pushed some button in me that initiated some sort of purge to my system. Then I thought that I was part of his energy web and he had positioned others and me around him that day. By that positioning, were we there as energy to somehow assist him on his way? Were we part of the formula of the day that he chose to die?

I thought about how we are all source energy and that we are inherently each other. And so would the physical demise of someone have an impact on us as individuals? The closer we were to that person certainly would have a greater impact on our lives. The further we are from that individual emotionally, the less the impact would be, but nevertheless from a collective point of view it would impact our lives in some way, most of the time we would never know that of course. I think of the events that have happened in history and more recent events that have had an impact on all of us. World-changing events like 9/11, the advent of ISIS, the world recession, all had an effect on the way we think and the way we feel about the direction this world is going. The collective thought that transpires from these events can't help but direct certain thoughts and feelings that will influence the outcome of our own personal lives and the direction that humanity itself is taking. As a collective energy, we are one mass of pulsing living energy that is in a continuous state of expanding and perfecting. So the death of one particular individual will have an effect on everything.

In view of this, it means that we are in this ever-changing mind, body, spirit environment that is an ever-changing vibration, and not only are we participating in it, but we are also creating it by the way we respond. What lays before us are varied choices that influence the outcomes of our personal and collective existence. When a person physically dies that does not mean that they are no longer effective in regard to this theory. They are simply creating and participating from a different exemplar and from an all-prevailing point of source. They would see the bigger picture, feel the bigger picture, and understand in more specific ways that they are consciously influencing what is happening. While we are in our physical incarnations, the majority of us are not aware of this and so don't feel and see the influence that our lives are having on everything and everyone. Also we are not consciously taking advantage of the source of life that is available to us.

It's rather mind blowing actually. Think of all the people who daily are passing into spirit and how that actually changes the world. When we become aware of change by something we hear on the radio or watch on the television or read in the newspaper we are receiving information that alters our whole being and therefore alters the whole world. Even if we are not "paying attention" consciously we are being influenced by the ebb and flow of altering vibrations as we simply get on with living. And so, if we do pay attention then perhaps we can "catch" that vibration in such a manner that encourages us to direct the vibration in more specific ways, consequently enlightening the world. It's so easy just to be a nameless face in the crowd or at the gym. We are all so involved in our routines and structures that we forget how to find ways of engaging with each other and the world on a more personal level. Here we all are sharing this planet and yet without realizing it we are mostly avoiding each other though I'm sure this is not the intention. I think of all the people who live in my street and apart from the closest neighbors I have no interaction with anyone. And even with the close neighbors it's usually just a polite hello. I was made aware of what I shall call the "close but safe distance" in October 2014.

I had been out in the front of our property water-blasting the paths. I had finished and was cleaning up when my wife, who suffers from Alzheimer's, came out and stood by me watching what I was doing. I had my back to her and turned suddenly as I heard a strange guttural noise. My wife had gone rigid and before I could catch her she fell back and smacked her head on the concrete step, splitting open her head. It later transpired that she had suffered a cardiac arrest. There was blood everywhere and I ran to ring the paramedics and was talking to Kay at the top of my voice. Ambulances arrived and attended to Kay. I sat there in shock and noticed that a couple of the neighbors had walked by and peered over the fence as if there was a mildly interesting event happening and then walked on.

Our neighbor next door had watched all of this from the upstairs window of their flat and later commented to me that everything seemed to be in hand and they didn't want to disrupt things. Luckily for me a good mate was passing and when he saw what was happening he ran to me and put his arms around me in comfort and support.

It seems it's too easy to ignore and too easy to be ignored. What are we all doing to each other?

The death of the gym bro had an interesting effect on those of us who had been at the gym on that Sunday morning. We made an effort to find out each other's names rather than just be a dude who was at the gym the same time every Sunday morning. We talked to each other and found out about each other. We helped each other out with our workouts rather than just let each other have space and do our own thing. We shared a coffee or a juice after the workout rather than rushing off. It's funny, though, how no one ever talked about what had happened on that day and about the guy who died. I saw in his death notice that he was only forty-two. I often wonder what effect his death had on the other people who had been there that day.

Making an effort of course does not mean that we have to be best friends with each other. I make the effort more now when I go to the supermarket to look at the name tag of the checkout person who is serving me and I always greet them by their name and thank them by their name. I find out who's living next door and have a chat now and then. I put myself in their picture and place them in mine so we are real faces and not just another blank. One afternoon when I was walking to the deli to get some lunch an elderly lady was coming up the footpath.

She looked up at me with the usual blank expression most people would have as they pass a stranger. I smiled at her and said hello and asked how her day was. She looked rather taken aback and slightly suspicious. Then she peered at me and asked if she knew me. I said no, I just thought I would say hello. She then smiled at me and said:

"Well, that's very nice, thank you," then carried on her way.

Making an effort always has its simple rewards.

Chapter Six
Come Fly with Me

Traveling will test the patience of even the most enlightened of authentic beings as I discovered on a trip to the US in June 2014.

It was a warm humid morning in Springdale, Arkansas. I had checked out of the hotel where I had been staying for a week attending Dolores Cannon's Transformation Conference. The birds were tweeting and the trees were doing I suppose what trees do, being trees. I was heading to Sedona in Arizona where I was to spend a week with friends and was waiting for the shuttle to come and pick me up and take me to the local airport. While I waited, I mentally emptied myself of the energy of the week, an exercise that spirit had taught me to do, saying that it is important to make the energy gear change from one event to another and as often as we could. That makes so much sense particularly in important events of one's life. You don't want to carry the old energy with you into the new experience with its new energy.

What I usually do is inform my body and mind what we are about to do and what I wanted as the desired result. Generally this works quite well but I think that morning my mind and body must have been having a late checkout based on the events that were to follow. The shuttle arrived and a very nice woman drove me to the airport. I was the only one in the shuttle and we chatted about stuff strangers usually do when thrown together in a moving vehicle for a twenty-minute ride. I was deposited at the airport, shook the hand of my female chauffer, and with great anticipation of a smooth and uncomplicated flight I went into the terminal. Checking in was no problem and for once I did not have to take an item out of my bag because I was over the required weight. Upstairs I went and through security where I had to take off my shoes but was allowed to keep the rest of my clothes on, but as usual I was sent through the full body scan.

Now I really have to make a point about this because since 2009 when I started to travel to the US regularly, without fail I have been subjected to the full body scan. I have often wondered if there was a room in the basement of some government department where scanned images of my personage between 2009 and 2014 have been deposited among others who have been subjected to the same process! Imagine, though, if it were a full body aura scanner; they could see if your soul was any danger to national security.

And so having survived the rigors of security and given some sympathetic murmuring sounds of commiseration to a young woman who had her hairspray and expensive hand lotion confiscated because it was over the level of ounces allowed, I felt the call of nature and went to the nearest appropriate receptacle for it to receive my liquid offering. I glanced up at the departures board to see if my flight was on time and seeing that it was went to complete the task in hand, so to speak!

Apart from the normal relief of relieving oneself, I also experienced the relief of any traveler who is traveling offshore must experience having conquered the machinations of a foreign airport and its systems. I stepped back out into the departure area and once again glanced up at the departure board. My eyes scanned for my flight and in the time it took me to have a pee saw that my flight was now ten minutes late. This was slightly annoying, as I had to fly to Dallas-Fort Worth first and get a connecting flight to Phoenix. It was a bit tight but if they kept to the original schedule it was doable. I made some adjustments to my authentic self so that I would not overindulge in being pissed off and I made my way to the assigned gate.

The flight was scheduled to board at 1 p.m., and so when I arrived at the gate to see that it had been changed to 1:30 p.m. the adjustments that I had made to my authentic self earlier did a bit of a dive into being a human being really pissed off.

As hard as I tried I could not find any "soul" reason for having created this delay as my reality. If it was there, then it was certainly practicing strategic avoidance maneuvers. The repercussions of this delay in departing had a huge ripple effect. I joined the long queue at the desk and observed that the female traveler in front of me had finished her business but then decided that despite the line of people behind her that it was an excellent idea to empty the contents of her handbag in the pursuit of a brush or a lipstick or whatever. I could feel the wave of energy emitting from the people behind me screaming silently in annoyance. She certainly felt it as she quickly turned around and then got all flustered and dropped her boarding pass and then quickly shoved the contents of her life back into her handbag. I picked up her boarding pass and handed it to her with an encouraging smile from my authentic self.

My human self on the other hand was going by a different script and really wanted to say:

"Hey, don't worry that you have held us all up while you were rummaging around in that mess in your bag, we don't mind standing here patiently while you get your life sorted!"

I'm sure that most of the people in the line behind me wanted to throw her out onto the runway.

When I got to the counter I informed the woman that there was no way I was able to get my connecting flight due to the delay and that she would have to find me another. My original flight had me leaving Dallas at 2:35 p.m. and she said that the only space free was leaving at 6 p.m. That meant a four-hour wait in Dallas and yet an even longer wait for friends who were meeting me at Phoenix and an even longer wait for the friends in Sedona whom I was staying with. My arrival would be hours later as we still had a two-hour drive from

Phoenix to Sedona. My friends who were to pick me up had flown from Carolina and we had synchronized our flights so that we would all arrive at Phoenix at the same time.

The woman at the counter did give me some excellent news to my baggage, though, as apparently it could still board the original flight and could have hours of fun going round and round the luggage carousel while it waited for me to catch up. Needless to say, without consulting the views of my luggage I opted that we travel together. This of course meant that the woman at the desk had to contact luggage dispatch to re-tag my bag and hopefully ensure that it wasn't going to end up in Albuquerque or some other far-reaching place. All that done, I hope that my bag didn't feel too deprived if the now impossibility of any baggage assignations as I'm sure that as I was checking in it was flirting with a Louis Vuitton.

I do pity and admire those champions at the gates. They must have to put up with an awful lot of crap from the public when flights get delayed. It's funny, though, isn't it, that you can go from being full of rage and self-righteous indignation because the airline has fucked up for whatever reason, to feeling extremely sorry for the unfortunate individual who has to bear the brunt of it. You just all want to join hands and start singing "Kumbaya."

Airports are a cesspool of human consciousness at its worse. You can feel the air ridden with anxiety and suspense as people from all walks of life are thrown together in one big boiling human energy soup. There's nothing as satisfying as observing and feeling this people energy when you yourself are a part of this recipe for human consumption. It's a feast of everything you can possibly experience in human emotions and actions. From the corporate women and men in their immaculate suits and even more immaculate pods, pads, and all the ITHINGS one can imagine, to the hassled mothers with their hassling children, it's a great feast of human behavior that can be endearing as much as it can be annoying, disgusting, and heartbreaking.

Call me sentimental but I can't help but shed a tear or two when I see people greeting each other at airports. I find it so moving and it fills me with joy and happiness seeing people greeting each other with such raw emotions. It speaks volumes to me. And for some reason I always think of the theme music to *Born Free* as an excellent backing music for such meetings.

Having changed my ticket and resolved myself to the inevitable wait at Dallas-Fort Worth, I then had to contact my friends to inform them of the change of plan, and having done so settled down to read my book. Reading though in the crowded environment of the departure lounge seemed more like a distraction and so I put the book away and instead observed what was going on around me.

An older couple was sitting across from me and the woman kept looking in her handbag to make sure that the tickets were all there. The husband just sat there staring into space; actually I'm not even sure he was alive as he showed no signs of any form of animation the whole time we were sitting across from each other and by the looks his wife kept giving him she was happy he wasn't.

A young woman was sitting on the floor to my right constantly playing with her hair and texting. More than likely she was texting her friends that she was sitting on the floor and playing with her hair since these days it seems essential for young people to keep each other informed about the slightest movement about anything that in essence has no meaning at all. One can imagine the conversation would go something like this:

Txt: Like, I'm sitting here on the floor
Reply: Like, really the floor?
Txt: Like, yeah
Reply: Wow, the floor
Txt: And like, I have hair and I'm playing with it.

And so this meaningful and highly informative conversation of sorts would no doubt be forwarded to all her friends.

Txt: Like, Melissa is sitting in the floor and like, she has hair, and like she is playing with it and like we are all completely brain dead and it's like well you know like.

No doubt it filled in the hours while she waited.

Personally I am no fan of social media though I do accept that it has its uses. The hours of life that are lost through staying connected though must be staggering. I also think that at times it is used as a dangerous platform by nasty people who vent their own inadequacies by anonymously posting remarks about others and never have to be accountable for their actions. It allows bullies and the faceless with no real power to have a platform and the unfortunate circumstances of this is that it can be exceedingly destructive.

After about a zillion years of waiting we were called to board the flight and so off to Dallas at last we flew. I found myself sitting next to a very amiable and chatty woman from Idaho. We chatted about soul stuff as invariably I find that whenever I am ensconced in a small environment where there is no possibility of escape, the person next to me will generally be one of "those people" you know, like me of the like persuasion shining with quivering vibrational portals. The man next to her in the window seat looked as if he had been brought up in the Bible belt and exuded the energy of strict religious upbringing. The energy that was coming from him as he couldn't help but hear Idaho girl's conversation with me was of a distinct uncomfortable nature. There he was, trapped, and we were no doubt in his mind assailing him with the forces of evil and the work of Satan himself. He probably thought we were in league with Beelzebub. He was distinctively sweating and I'm sure he was muttering a prayer quietly to himself in the desperate hope that his soul would still be intact once we hit the tarmac.

Once we did land we did the decent thing and let him out first, his poor tortured soul leaving the dust of spiritual contamination in his wake. I like to think that my soul companion and myself had subconsciously surrounded him with source energy helping him on his way to salvation!

Idaho girl waved farewell. I was initiated into the art of "gate dancing." For those of you who have yet to be initiated into this fine art form, some explanation is needed. You arrive at the gate number that was printed on your boarding pass only to find that the gate had been changed. In an airport the size of Dallas-Fort Worth this meant that you would get onto the Sky Bus, a monorail system that surrounds the airport and links you to the gates. I found this fascinating and tremendously efficient. Okay, I had four hours to kill, and for whatever reasons my authentic self thought all of this must be great fun and since time is an illusion anyway let's just keep on having this fun going round and round and round as the gates keep changing. After about an hour of gate dancing I found myself in places that I'm not sure even the airport staff knew existed. In fact, there were no doubt departments that have existed for years and no one knows really who is there and what the people are doing. There were lots of people pushing carts and things around and if I had gone up and asked what their jobs were they would have no doubt replied:

"To push carts and things around."

I did eventually find a gate that hopefully a plane would leave from and as I looked up at the screen I imagined that it would announce something like this:

"YES, THIS IS THE ONE! CONGRATULATIONS! WE HOPE YOU HAVE ENJOYED YOUR JOURNEY AROUND THE AIRPORT AND ITS FACILITES. WE ARE REALLY SORRY FOR SENDING YOU ROUND AND ROUND THE AIRPORT SEVERAL TIMES BUT WASN'T IT FASCINATING! YOU HAVE HAD A GOOD LOOK AROUND AND ARE THOUROUGHLY

EXHAUSTED AND NO DOUBT PISSED OFF BUT WHAT A BETTER WAY TO SPEND THE TIME THAT YOU HAVE HAD WITH US. WE WOULD LOVE TO SERVE YOU A COMPLIMENTARY LUNCH BUT DUE TO THE FACT THAT WE ARE FUNDING PEOPLE WHO PUSH CARTS AND THINGS AROUND ALL DAY WE ARE UNABLE TO DO SO. HAVE A NICE DAY!!"

I was hungry, though, and so once again I meandered through the airport this time in search of something delectable that would satisfy my burgeoning hunger. Isn't it awful that when you are hungry and you feel a sort of innate desperation to fill your body up that you invariably end up eating something that you wish you hadn't? As I stood in front of all the possibilities I asked my authentic self what it thought I should eat. All I got was a blank so I thought it must have been on a diet or still be trying to find the right gate. In the end the choices came down to:

"TRY OUR HOTDOG IN A PRETZEL" (Oh Yum) to a rather greasy and overcooked Chinese buffet, which really was the lesser of the two evils. So with chopsticks in hand and a bottle of water to swirl the grease around into a congealed mass that encouraged my stomach to protest I found a place to sit facing the window and chewed manfully through rubber dumplings and plastic chicken kebabs. The water was probably the only natural thing on my tray and I was trying hard to convince my body that what I was eating was actually for my higher good. My higher good had other plans as it was doing its best to resist what I was putting into my stomach.

There was an adult family group at the table in front of me and one of the guys had stood up and walked away. I looked down under his chair and noticed that his wallet had slipped out of his pocket and onto the floor. The guy had gone so I brought the wallet to the attention of the others at the table. They made a variety of replies.

"Oh my God, his wallet?"

"On the floor?"

"It's his wallet?"

"You found his wallet?"

"On the floor?"

At this stage the man had reappeared and in a highly agitated manner announced:

"My wallet, it's gone!"

Hi agitation turned to huge relief as his friends explained that I had seen his wallet drop out of his pocket and that I had brought this to their attention. He came up to me and shook my hand and thanked me and then thanked me again.

I thought that maybe in the grand scheme of things this is why my flight had been delayed. My soul must have been scanning for situations where I could serve and so positioned me to sit where I would see that he had dropped his wallet. Who knows what events would have unfolded if I had not been there. Well, why not?

Having had my moment as the good Samaritan I looked at my watch and saw that there were still a couple of hours before the miracle of a plane actually taking off would happen. I wandered around for a while and then decided that I might as well take my mind, body, and spirit to the departure gate and find a pew to rest. A few travelers had already claimed their seats but there was still plenty to choose from so I positioned myself where I could look out a window but covertly observe my fellow travelers. A tall man with dyed blond hair and fluorescent pink trainers sat nearby. He must have been all of sixty and wasn't wearing it well. The very tight minuscule denim shorts he had on didn't add anything to his desire to portray the impression that he was young and gay and free. Like most people around me he was plugged into his IPOD shutting out the world. Have you noticed that regardless of whatever music they might be listening to the majority of people plugged into their IPODS all have the same deadpan expression on their faces? There is no indication that they are even listening to music at all. No bopping to the beat, or showing any sign that they are in point of fact enjoying what they are hearing. I suppose one has to take into consideration that it would look rather grotesque to the observer if people were actually being animated while they listened to their IPODS. It would be like a communal outbreak of Tourette's (no offense intended, of course) without the words.

Now this reminds me of when I was nineteen and staying with a cousin of mine in Canada. I have this habit of singing songs in my head and one day while reclining on the sofa reading I was singing some current song in my head and unintentionally bopping away to the music that no one could hear. After a while I looked up to see my cousin standing at a safe distance watching this obviously deranged Kiwi import gyrating around on the sofa. There really was nothing I could say to him.

There was a family group at the departure lounge who seemed intent on shoving as much packaged food into their fat faces to possibly see how much fatter they could get. I was totally engrossed in their personal grossness such was their unconscious personal need to keep feeding their faces. They were also plugged into their IPODS as well as texting and basically doing everything else but actually pay attention to each other. Apple could create an app especially for people like them and call it IGROSS. I sat and observed and wondered if they ever thought of themselves as souls rather than feeding machines intent on shutting out everybody as well as the world; it seemed highly unlikely. The look in their eyes was of a dull detachment. To me they seemed like their machines, plugged into to charge until they ran out of juice, only to be refueled at the next point.

Occasionally an announcement would be made concerning I assume something to do with flying as such was the clamor of music blasting through intercoms and sounds coming from televisions suspended from the ceiling that you could not discern what was being said. I wondered how many people had missed their boarding call or gate changes because their own personal aural services were being assaulted from all directions. At the gate across from where I was sitting was a desk attendant announcing the departure of a flight. He sounded like Howdy Doody being a commentator on the radio but at least you could actually hear what he was saying. I gazed around me in bored indifference and then decided to commit the ultimate sin when one is struck by intense tedium; I started taking selfies. I couldn't help myself; some sort of pictorial indulgence of the extreme kind possessed me and in all of those I took I have the same expression. A sardonic smile matched by glazed and weary eyes. My authentic self must have found an earlier flight and was enjoying the in-flight service, as there was nothing soul-like about the pictures I took. Just a fed-up human being who wasn't very happy about the way the day had unfolded and wearing a resigned countenance that there was more of the journey yet ahead.

I was abruptly shaken out of my selfie excess by the not very dulcet tones of a woman complaining loudly to someone she was talking to on her mobile. Actually the whole of the terminal if not the state of Texas could hear her such were the amplifications of her tirade. She had, from what I could piece together as I carefully eavesdropped, taken acute exception to the way she had been treated by security and for the next hour she regaled what seemed like all the contacts on her mobile and anyone else who wanted to listen about her mistreatment.

Man, was she mad, her face was a study of emotional animation that would challenge any constipated person intent on making a movement.

Her face was all red and she was profusely perspiring. I looked around her and you could feel the negative energy oozing out of her being. No wonder people were giving her a wide berth and also the fact that she had an aura around her that was saying, "Don't mess with me!" During this verbal diatribe of everyone's aural senses my flight to Phoenix was finally called and everyone dutifully, or in my case thankfully, made our way to the gate. The "Don't mess with me woman" was still purging incessantly while we were all in line. She never seemed to draw a breath and as she handed her boarding pass to the attendant she simply carried on her invective all the way down the bridge to the plane. I was in front and was comfortably seated when I could hear her coming down the aisle. I was in mortal fear that she was allocated a seat next to me and I sent out all messages, pleas, promises, etc., in the hope that this would not happen. Thankfully she positioned herself two rows up from myself and I really did feel sorry for the man who looked up as this walking, talking mass of energy clamored over him to get to the window seat while she still prattled away on the phone. She was not of the physical constitution that would be called lean, more the opposite, and as she squeezed her ample form over the man, mounds and mountains of scantily clad flash assaulted most of his upper body. At this stage of the proceedings the cabin crew were demonstrating the emergency procedures and the recorded voice had just announced:

"In case of a drop in cabin pressure an oxygen mask will appear from above."

In this man's case, it was more likely a rise of pressure and oxygen was unquestionably called for!

As we taxied she was still on the phone and only hung up when the wheels were lifting off the ground. I wondered how long she would be able to contain herself since she was unable to continue her outburst to all and sundry but she soon found comfort in the contents of the food trolley as it passed by. I ordered nuts and a soda and spent the rest of the flight watching her as she twitched and sighed and then to my downright surprise struck up a conversation with the man she had fleshly impaled and for the rest of the flight talked about baseball with him. Of course all good things come to an end and we finally landed in Phoenix and departed the plane. The flesh impaler having been liberated from her mobile Coventry soon took up her cause again and as she disappeared onto the horizon I could hear her all the way.

Now to the luggage carousel where I hoped to be reunited with my bag and prayed that it hadn't run off with the Louis Vuitton it had met in Arkansas. The computerized sign said that I was standing at the right place and so I waited and waited and watched as my fellow travelers collected their bags and went back to the real art of living. And still I waited but to no avail. Then I looked up at the sign and it said that the collection point had changed and so I had to walk to the next carousel where once again I waited and waited. By this stage my authentic self had caught up with me and drew my attention back to the original carousel where with relief I saw my bag going round and round waiting in eager anticipation for me to collect it, which of course I did.

The energy of hours of delay and waiting, the aimless wandering around airport terminals, the gate dancing, the luggage carousel, all seemed to converge in one point of me being majorly pissed off. Fuming I went up to the "desk" where a man stood. The sign above him said it was a place where you could make any complaints and so, I did. Not that I believed that it was going to alter the state of affairs in national airports around the US but one still needs to vent one's frustrations. And anyway, the sign said I could.

With a mixture of great relief, frustration, and excitement I wheeled the bag out onto the arrivals/pickup area where I saw my friends waiting. Since the sun had already set by this stage we could not drive into the sunset but instead investigated several streets numerous times while we endeavored to find the way out of the terminal area, back into the world, and on the way to Sedona. I have composed a little ditty to the strains of "America" to sing along should you so feel inclined.

From shuttle to the terminal
my bags were checked in well
Security was a certainty
x-raying my human shell
Oh airports of America
How challenging you are
From all of the hours of waiting
You made my journey hell.

It's frustrating when you're contemplating
Amongst the gathering crowds
The hours you are wasting
You want to shout out loud

Oh airports of America
How challenging you are
From all of the hours of waiting
You made my journey hell

I need a shave and stink to hell
My clothes aren't wrinkle free
My body it's exhausted
And I badly need to pee

Oh airports of America
This is the final call
A plane will fly
And I will cry
At last I'm airport free!

Chapter Seven
"Blanket Man"

The "Blanket Man" is dead. For those unfamiliar with him the Blanket Man aka Ben Hana was a homeless man who for some years lived on the streets of Wellington and had rather became an institution. His Wellington hood was in Courtney Place where you would see him often intoxicated, smoking, asleep, or sitting on the curb in his loincloth attached to his IPod and grinning away at passersby. At times he would break out into a maniacal laugh at something that he found amusing around him or whatever was going on in his head. He was often unwashed and if you were standing downwind from him you were bound to get a whiff of his sordid aroma. Ben Hana was a gentleman, though, and as I could feel a very spiritual man. If you actually made eye contact with him you could see and feel his spirit. Of course, the world is full of people like Ben Hana who for whatever reasons choose to step away from the conventional way of living. Perhaps it's because of mental illness or they are unemployed. Conceivably it could be their choices are fueled by drug and alcohol addictions. Whatever the reasons, it's a reminder to us all about the diverse ways as souls we make choices about how we are going to evolve through the way we live our lives. Every time I walked by Ben Hana I wondered about his life. He had been born and raised like us all, a soul making the choices of his upbringing stimulating in him the deals that he had made for this lifetime. He would have gone to school and had mates and maybe he played rugby. He would have had aspirations and visions of his possible futures. No doubt he created relationships and perhaps had been married and had kids. Speculating on all of this makes me rather in awe of people like Ben who create in their lives a point where they step off the center line so to speak and take a path so diverse from the path most of us would take. You have to admire the courage of that soul who takes themselves to such an extreme junction point.

I'm sure Ben was an offense to those who chose to see him in that light. You could not get any more blatant than the Blanket Man, and it was this blatant attitude that seemed so odious to some people. Perhaps his unconcealed exposure of his whole being was really the point to his existence? By flaunting himself before the world he was also challenging the world and all its "wrap it up and position it somewhere" attitude. It's far too easy to "not see" what's before us because we feel the connection with something that perhaps we find too uncomfortable to face. Personally I believe it triggers some deep-seated memory that reminds us all of our connection with source and that we are facing all who we are and what we have created. And so people like Ben Hana may bring out in us some deep-rooted memory that we are concealing and needs to be looked at.

Tabaash has taught that the way we respond to other people tells us about ourselves. So fundamentally Ben Hana and those like him are figuratively an aspect of us. We may choose to see this or not, but whatever our choice is we are having ourselves daily flaunted before us, offering up a response.

The vagrants of the world bring out in all of us an essential need to look at ourselves. It's not that we have to take responsibility for who they are and what they are doing but more a need to take more responsibility for who we are all as a whole and the part we have to play in creating the need to have the vagrants of the world at our doorstep. Now this may be a bone of contention for some who no doubt would point-blankly refuse that they have anything to do with the choices that people make in their lives. The more I understand what being a part of collective consciousness means, the more I grasp the subtlety of what being a creator means to the outcomes of life. In this case it does mean that we have everything to do with everything and basically "everything" is an opportunity to fine-tune our own ideas about how we want life to be. So in effect that means that all of us need to decide if we need vagrants in the world, conflict, economic difficulties, social inadequacies to mention a few. We are inflicting upon ourselves constant reminders of how we as a whole are not riding the river of life's energy mutually. So that means that some are going with the current of life and others against it, the result being that there will be collisions along the way. These "collisions" present themselves as socioeconomic imbalances among the populace, leading to indifference, apathy, and at times conflict. Life is pointing its finger at us all the time and saying what are you going to do about yourself so you can have a positive influence on the collective energy of life?

Recently there was a television program aired called the *Kindness Diary*. It was about this Englishman who was going to go around the world on the kindness of others. While I was watching this program the thing that stood out for me was that those who had very little were the ones that often gave the most. At the end of each segment the Englishman would show kindness back by assisting someone who had shown a great act of kindness that really touched his whole being. He approached one man and asked if he could have a bed for the night. The man replied that he was actually homeless but he was very welcome to share what he had and could sleep in the doorway where he usually did. At the end of the show the homeless guy was told that they would organize him to have a home and also that they would fund him to take the hospitality course he had been intending to do. I don't think there was one program where I didn't shed a tear as people's stories of life unfolded. We are all living here on this planet together and yet we are all so separate in our survival. *The Kindness Diary* showed huge degrees of kindness that people can show but also it showed up the indifference, fear, and suspicious nature that human nature seems to have cultivated. Is it really that difficult every day to practice some act of kindness to someone or even to the Earth itself?

And so back to Ben Hanna and a great act of kindness that was shown after his death. A wealthy businessman funded his funeral and made sure that by doing so Ben was given the recognition with respect that he deserved. The façade of the ANZ bank became a memorial board for messages from of all walks of life who wanted to pay tribute to Ben. The Maori flag was flown, and people gathered at the place where he always sat.

It was not Kensington Palace and Diana Princess of Wales but hell, this man got one hell of a send-off considering the way that he lived his life. This makes me thank God I love New Zealand and our people and what we represent. I've seen it time and time again, where the people of this country step up to the mark when there is someone in need. And this makes me believe that we really do care about the blanket people when it comes to the crunch. At his end he wasn't a vagrant and wasn't treated as such. He was a person like us all who made choices, and in those choices he reminded us all of the many faces of life and the varied roads that can be traveled. It doesn't matter that somewhere along the road of the Blanket Man's life that he got all tangled up in some sort of human knot that for whatever reasons he could not or would not unravel. That was simply his journey and through that journey he was evolving and so because of it so were we. All of us at some point in our own lives get into a tangle that challenges the way that we are living and by doing so we set up a platform where we can view all the possible experiences that will of course lead to some outcome. The moment we "commit" to a particular path we align ourselves with many potential outcomes and with those come the "right" people that will be a part of that journey. We attract the emotions and ideas that are part of that experience, we express the "right" way of participating in that adventure. I see more and more that we are gatherers of the unlimited lifelines that are floating around us all the time. As we become more alert to the bigger picture we teach ourselves to recognize which of those lifelines are suitable to a productive outcome. If we get into a "manic panic," to quote Tabaash, then we blindly grab at any lifeline that is there in the hope that this will offer up the best conclusion and by doing so end up weaving an energy that brings about a confusion and at times an inability to cope with the situation we are dealing with. We can of course untangle ourselves but one needs to approach it with patience and calm. I elude to as an example the venetian blinds that we have in our dining room at home. Our dining room is an octagon made of very large and tall Gothic windows that many years ago came out of an old convent that had been demolished. The blinds are floor to ceiling and there is a string to pull them up that is forever getting tangled up. If it's too much of a tangle they won't go down to the floor. It's a bugger and it's constantly challenging me! I can get myself into an impatient frenzy trying to untangle the string and therefore making it far worse. When I calm down and approach it with ease and harmony the bloody things always untangle easily. I can almost see their "told you so" energy as they slide down easily. And when I'm not easy they fight all the way!

I now think of lifetimes I must have had where I was like the Blanket Man, all tangled up in the lifelines that I would have gathered. I wonder what I did with those lifelines and what had happened to me to make me want to experience such a life? I know that I still carry the energy of that experience with me and it is because of that knowledge I responded in the way I did with Ben Hana. I must have been at peace with that part of me as I found that it was very easy to be at peace with him.

And so, Ben Hana, you've gone home and we will miss you. God's no doubt wrapped you up in the finest of blankets and washed you so that you are clean and fragrant. God has taken away the tangles from your knotted hair and said to you:

"Ben, you have done well, your life taught a great deal to so many and you will always be remembered and people will talk about you and write about you for a long time."

So, Ben, you have a good long rest now and when the façade of the ANZ is repainted and the tributes to you are gone the essence of your spirit will linger for a long time. Whatever your problems were, you had an abundance of courage to truly walk your talk in the way that you did. And I think that had you lived your life in a country that wasn't so generous to people like yourself you probably would have ended up like some John Doe, unwanted, unrecognized, and undesirable, your body put in some pauper's grave, just another statistic.

Well done, Ben, for becoming someone.

Chapter Eight
Mangatarata

I truly believe that God directs certain people to us in our lives and conversely God directs me to certain people. These situations are presented to us at a certain point in our lives because we need those connections. There are varied explanations for this of course but whatever they are it is an opportunity to serve as much as be served. How often have we "coincidentally" connected with someone or some people only to find that we have been offered the prospect of expanding our lives? These situations if recognized for what they are offer up a chance to learn, resolve, and enlighten our lives.

For me such people were Judy and Donald MacDonald, who run Mangatarata Station, a sheep and cattle farm in Waipukarau Hawke's Bay. I first became acquainted with their daughter Kate through my work and was soon to meet Judy and Donald. Some months after my meeting with them I received a letter from Judy extending an invitation to come and work and stay at Mangatarata. Judy was to organize a week's work for me and I was to stay on the farm. It's about a four-hour drive to Hawke's Bay and it's a part of New Zealand that is fertile not just in farming, horticulture, and agriculture but in love and kindness and a special spiritual energy that pervades the landscape. I drove over the Rimutaka Ranges and they are like a gateway to a wholly diverse world, leaving behind the city of Wellington and its harbor, replacing it with an ocean of green fields and undulating carpets of emerald hills. It's a great thing about New Zealand, within moments you can find yourself by the sea or in the midst of the country and from that moment you capture a new experience breathing in a potent energy. The four-hour drive takes you through small-town rural New Zealand and whenever I drive up there I can feel my city self unwinding and moving into a more sedate gear. There's something very content about being in rural New Zealand that speaks to me of calming down and moving away from the weight of twenty-first-century living and the constant pressure that so pervades this time. It's like for a moment one can transcend time and just be in an energy that isn't so severe on our being. As I passed through all the little towns, Featherston, Greytown (where interestingly enough, Arbor Day was first inaugurated), Carterton, Masterton, Woodville, Eketahuna, and more, each town offered up energy unique to that place and an inimitable look at rural New Zealand. The ubiquitous sheep dot the hills and you vy for road space with cattle and dairy trucks. I would always stop at Woodville and rummage around the big junk shop that was on the left as you made a right turn. Years ago there was some good stuff at quality prices but these days it really can be totally defined as a junk shop. Across the road was a real Kiwi bakery where I would indulge in a good old New Zealand cream doughnut, freshly made with that little dab of jam on the top! It couldn't get any better I tell you! Feeling content I would get back on the road hoping it wasn't going to rain and that I wasn't behind a sheep or cattle truck or worse a campervan driven by some over anxious tourist who's never driven on our side of the road!

The journey to Mangatarata Station took about four hours and since this was my first sojourn on these roads everything that unfolded before me was uncharted territory. Not knowing what was in front of me made me feel exhilarated and also full of trepidation in a positive way. And there is life's journey, don't you think? Filled with the exhilaration of what's before you but also with the trepidation of a new adventure, new ways of creating and experiencing yet another reality. As I drove nearer to my destination I became conscious that this was my reality and nobody else's. All those sheep on the hills were only there because I wanted them to be there. The very road in front of me presented itself so I could drive; I was in a constant state of making life happen around me to suit my purpose. I remembered that I wanted this experience, I wanted to make all the new connections with the people I would see that week. I wanted to have this new adventure so that I could expand my reality and therefore create different arenas in life. All this was so I could practice living out the qualities that I possessed and perhaps resolve issues that I needed to. My life was the exploration of all my thoughts, words, and deeds consolidated into experience.

Mangatarata Station was about a ten-minute drive from the small rural town of Waipukarau. I drove through the main street observing the locals going about their business. I didn't pay much attention as my eyes were on the directions to my destination; there was plenty of time through the week to have a wander around. New places are filled with new energy and the expectation of experience, new people, different horizons, and all good fodder for the soul! There was a sort of sleepy busyness to the place that I liked. Life was happening but there was no frenetic pace and there seemed to me to be an order to the energy that felt rewarding.

The directions I had said turn right and follow the road that climbed and twisted and seemed to go on ceaselessly. Sounds an awful lot like life sometimes! The hills on the left banked steeply down and as I drove the sheep stared impassively chewing away on Hawke's Bay nutritious grass. Gradually the winding road opened up to a narrow stretch carved through carpets of lush green, and farmhouses were dotted here and there. Dogs barked, birds sang, and the sky was an expanse of cloudless blue. All this touched the rural part of my soul inviting in memories of previous lives I have had in the country. Feeling happy and peaceful but with a natural sense of nervousness that comes with uncharted territory I came to the end of the road. The road carried onto the right leading up to a large white painted red-roofed shearing shed nestled into the land looking like it was a natural part of the terrain. To my right was the drive that would take me up to the house, presently hidden by a canopy of trees. Bumping over the cattle stop I drove carefully up the gravel drive, which on turning to the right took me up to the house and I saw Jude standing on the wide front veranda waving to me. It was a big beautiful rambling farmhouse. All on one level the house had high studs and spacious hallways where rooms flowed off their big double-hung windows and it was full of the energy of all its past history mingled together to create a serene stillness, open to your soul but still guarding its secrets. I loved it and felt at home instantly.

Jude served us morning tea on the wide front veranda and I felt it was a bit of a "getting to know you time" before we settled into the week. As we sat and chatted I looked around at the land surrounding the house, feeling the very obvious energy of spirit in the land and in and around the house. I thought it must be odd and brave for Jude and her husband to invite me to stay for the week having really just met me, but then when we are aligned to source the laws of attraction play out. We finished our cuppa and then Jude showed me around the house and told me to choose a room to stay in. We walked down a long wide hallway and I was drawn to a room at the end on the right. Jude gave me a curious glance as I told her which room I would like.

"That's interesting," she said. "That was Hamish's room."

A little explanation is needed here. Hamish was Jude and Donald's son. He died in a plane crash in his early twenties. As I walked into the room it was full of Hamish through his life. Bits and bobs, books and sports equipment, and I noticed a pilot's helmet sitting securely on the shelf along the wall. Jude left me to unpack and get settled and I hoisted my case onto the bed and started to unpack. As I was doing so a movement in the corner of my eye caught my attention and I turned around to see Hamish's pilot helmet tip onto the floor. I stood quietly for a moment feeling the presence of Hamish in the room. Bending down I picked up the helmet and sat on the bed holding it.

"Hey, Hamish," I said. "Thanks for letting me use your room, hope that's okay with you. Also thanks for directing me here to this beautiful place you grew up in with your parents and sister."

I could feel deep peace in the room and sat for a moment just enjoying the connection. I felt like Hamish was saying it's okay that I was in his room and that he was glad that I was there. I finished my unpacking and joined Jude in the big farm kitchen. Of course, I told her about the helmet and she looked at me with a quiet smile. That week was the beginning of many a week that I was to spend in Mangatarata, and Hamish would make his presence felt in all sorts of ways. In a deep sleep one night I was awakened to the sounds of heavy footsteps coming up the hall and then the bedroom door suddenly flew open. Other times I was just aware of his energy in the room. Once when I was sitting in the veranda after a day's work looking out onto the land I saw the MacDonalds' little Scotty dog Mac running up and down the drive looking up as if someone was running beside him. Jude later told me that Hamish used to run up and down the drive and Mac would chase him. It reminded me that we are living in all the worlds that make up life. Of course, when you are sensitive to those other worlds it opens up a whole lot of new energy possibilities. We are so defined by ideas that create unnecessary restrictions in our soul capabilities, consequently denying *ourselves* of a relationship with a life that takes us beyond our mortal perceptions. We have all these "other worlds" that we can relate to and by doing so it gives us a wider perspective of what we are and what we can do. I think back now about my time at Mangatarata over the years and see it as a sojourn into worlds that redefined my connection with spirit and my relationship with myself. Also it enhanced my connection with nature and the energy of the Earth that I would often feel as I went on walks at the end of my workday.

One particular warm summer's day, I decided to walk along one of the roads on the farm. It was a straight stretch of dirt road embraced by paddocks and hills on either side. In the left paddock was a herd of young bulls grazing and as I walked they followed me with cautious curiosity. When I stopped they would stop and eye me suspiciously, no doubt wondering what my next move would be. Some of the braver or perhaps more curious would venture to the fence line wanting to get a closer look at this interloper in their territory. I had walked about ten minutes and had quite a bovine following by this stage. I decided to try something so I walked right up to the fence line and stood still. The bulls gathered before me and stood stock still gazing up at me jostling for space. I felt I had to say something profound to them.

"You realize of course that we are all God," I said.

They pushed further toward the fence line wanting to get closer to me. I stepped as close as possible to the fence, some of the bulls panicked a bit and cantered away, others stood their ground and looked at me as if to say, "Yes, go on, we are listening."

I told them that I understood that the soul was not a human soul and that as souls we are all able to incarnate into any form of life. I said that I acknowledged that as souls, they choose to incarnate as bulls and that this was the experience that they wanted to have. I said that we were all life and that there was no division between anything. We were just one mass of collective energy expressing ourselves through our chosen life forms. I had their rapt attention; they had even stopped eating and snorting and doing all the things that bulls would normally do! At one point in my conversation one of the bulls let out a loud bellow and all the other bulls at the same time turned and looked at that bull in what I could only describe as a "SHUT UP, CAN'T YOU SEE WE ARE LISTENING HERE" look. The bull that was making all the noise suddenly shut up and bowed its head as if to say "sorry." I lay down on the dry bleached grass and closed my eyes. Several of the bulls came up and gave me a good sniff and investigated further this strange human. I could feel the warm breath and the smell of freshly eaten grass, and I could feel the open curiosity emanating from them and the energy of trust and acceptance. I slowly stood up and they backed away just a little, and I carried on with my walk. They continued to follow me for some distance until they eventually had enough of me and went back to feeding and being bullish.

As the years have gone by I identify with the idea more than ever that there really is no degree of separation to anything. To quote Hermes, an ancient Coptic philosopher:

> *"If you want to understand life you have to conceive of the idea that you are everything."*

That makes so much sense to me as I progress on my personal spiritual path. By allowing the idea that we are everything, we invite a much fuller experience of what we are involved in and that opens us up to an awareness of what life can offer us if we are open to relieving ourselves of our need for identity. Rather than looking to what to be, is it not more what are we? And if we are everything then what are we denying by being separate from being the whole experience? Next time you take a walk through the woods or by the beach consider that you are actually the very trees and the path you walk. The sounds and smells, the touch of things, all of these are you. The whole world is offering us up the exclusive prospect of knowing ourselves through the complete experience of being everything. Now, that's got to be exciting?

Over the years I spent at Mangatarata there were plenty of those walks where I allowed myself to be the very atmosphere that embraced me. The summers can be hot, stinking hot in fact. The grass gets bleached and the ground becomes hard and cracked. I pitied the poor sheep in their woolen coats not being able to cast them off and get some relief from the heat. On one very warm day I went for another walk, this time up into the hills that surrounded the right side of the property. I climbed high to take in the complete view of the surrounding country, marveling at the silence and the expanse of the world below me and above me. The heat that day was searing and it seemed to be like a pall of warm energy placed over everything creating motionlessness that I was a part of. As I stood on the top of the hill I recalled a book I had just finished by Neville Shute. It was called *On the Beach.* It was set in Australia and the general gist of it was that there had been a nuclear war in the Northern Hemisphere. Human nature had at last achieved its annihilation and a great wave of radioactive energy was slowly surrounding the Earth in a fatal embrace. Standing on that hill in the heat I imagined myself to be the last person on Earth waiting for the radioactive cloud to claim me. It wasn't hard to imagine being the only being on Earth as I stood there surrounded by silence, hearing and seeing no other sign of life apart from the nature around me. I would just sit down and let the invisible energy that would bring about my death claim me. I would leave my body and there it would lie until the elements ground it back into the Earth. Another life complete, my soul replete with yet more experience. The Earth perhaps after thousands of years would once again be purged of the toxicity that had been unleashed by certain factions of human nature in its need to get one over another. Then a new cycle would emerge and the process of life would establish yet another opportunity for a new wave of souls to create or annihilate.

As I lay there pretending to be dead, life seemed to call me back but it was also getting awfully hot there on the ground. I felt like I was in a slow cooker, the sun just beginning the job. I stood up and stretched and seeing that there wasn't a person in sight proceeded to take off all my clothes and continue my walk through the hills completely naked. For sake of comfort I kept my trainers on and feeling the relief of abandonment started running along the hills, to the startled amazement of several sheep who stopped in mid munch to behold the sight of a naked man running through the hills. I whooped and yelled and then took a great leap onto what I thought was solid ground and found myself thigh high in putrid muddy water.

I stood there stupefied for a moment and then burst out laughing. I pulled my legs out of the mire and beheld my now mud-ridden legs, that now looked like I was wearing gray stockings to mid-thigh. I could have auditioned for the nude version of *Chorus Line*. The stench of the mud was repellent to even the most seasoned of major sinus sufferers and I knew I had to wipe it off as much as I could before the sun baked it onto me like a cast. I walked on a little until I found a small pool of water that was sufficiently clean and with my man pants in hand endeavored to clean myself up as best I could. My pants were definitely for the bin after I finished so I rolled them up into a tight ball and put them into the mucky mess that I had recently ascended from. As I gave them a little shove with my foot I considered that in the future this decomposing pool of vegetarian effluent was bound to dry up consequently exposing my cast-off Calvin Klein's.

And so years later some farmhand or visitor on a quiet stroll through the hills would come across them and would no doubt be perplexed as to how someone had come to discard their knickers in the middle of nowhere. Such events are the fertilizer for vivid imaginations!

This was nothing though in comparison to what happened when Donald took me up in a small plane to have a look at the farm from the air.

I had just had lunch, cauliflower soup and a chunky Kit Kat. Donald came into the kitchen and said he was going to do some aerial surveillance of the farm and would I like to come with him. It appealed to me, as I had never been in a small plane before so jumped at the chance. We drove the short distance to the airfield and soon I found myself closer to God and over the farm. We twisted and turned and I soon started to institute some of my very own gastric aerials. Now I have never been airsick in my life, in fact I have never suffered from any form of motion sickness, but as Donald tilted the plane at extreme angles, plunged up and then down again to the extreme, I could feel that I was about to become more intimately acquainted with my semi-digested lunch. I tried very hard to "go with the plane" but it was to no avail. Donald turned and looked at me with a look of concern on his face.

"You all right?" he asked.

"Yes, fine," I replied and then turned away from him and proceeded to empty the contents of my stomach onto the inside panel of the plane.

In a way only a Kiwi could, Donald looked at me and in a very matter-of-fact tone of voice said,

"Well, I reckon we better head back."

I felt much better having upchucked and said so but thought yes it would be a good idea to go back.

We landed and the extent of my digestive excretions became obvious. The whole front of my jeans was covered, as was the paneling on the left passenger side. And to ensure that I had done the job thoroughly it had managed to ooze its way down the inside of the panel. This we discovered as we cleaned up, as we had to unscrew the panel and wipe the inside down. I had the decency at the time to cover my mouth so that blocked the propulsion of my heave, otherwise it no doubt would have splattered far and wide. Having attended to the plane I now turned my attention to myself. I surveyed the mess I was in as I stood in the men's room at the airstrip, and I concluded that it was not advisable to get into the car in such a state so I discarded my jeans, cleaned myself up, and made my way back to the car in my t-shirt and boxers. Donald laughed as he saw me and continued to laugh as we drove back to the farm. I gave him a wry smile and said:

"I wouldn't laugh too much, you're the one who's driving in the car with a man who has no pants on."

We got back to the farm and Jude came out to meet us. When she saw me she gave me a concerned look and I laughed and told her what had happened. She gave Don the "wife" look and said "Donald" in such a way that anyone who is married can interpret as "You are slightly in the doghouse!"

During the years that I went up to Mangatarata I embraced the energy of the place and its surrounding countryside and in my own way made it part of me. Jude and Donald and their daughter Kate became to me my "Hawke's Bay" family. I felt the warmth and privilege of being a small part of them. It reminds me that through our whole life we are always looking for others to complement our life and as we pull these people toward us we embrace another opportunity to evolve our sense of being in all ways. When it's easy as I found it with the MacDonalds, it's a validation of the fact that souls are for eternity putting out the call to each other. When they meet, the circumstances can be many and varied. We must never forget that we are always on the search for those that complement ourselves, choosing to live in a world where there are other GODS having a human experience.

As the energy of life changes we must change with it. Being involved with an energy that complements your own seems vital to our survival more than ever now. With such conflict pervading our life be it personal or collective we must embrace the opportunities of goodwill that can be found in the connection with people we love. To recognize a kindred spirit is one thing, to develop that connection aligns us with the power of source and transports us further in our development as a human race. I can't help but think we are all making decisions about ourselves, being more aware that the life that we are living is us presenting to ourselves the need to advance our position in what we believe, and how we live what we believe. As like attracts like there is a merging of energy that permits an automatic expansion of life force. The consequences of this expansion is that we are exposed to possibilities that alter the path of our life and the path of our history as a people on Earth. I urge you to align with the people that are your kindred spirits. Recognize in each other the power to create and to support that power through these powerful connections. And never cease to express your love.

Chapter Nine
Bert

I want to immortalize my friend Bert in writing about him. Such was his impact on others and myself in his life, that he deserves a chapter in this book. For most of us, once our life is complete we simply become a blend of everything eventually forgotten as we are replaced with the new wave of souls coming to Earth. We become a picture in a frame, eventually removed from the shelf and placed in a drawer. I have pictures of ancestors in frames that are now in drawers. On occasions I come across them while searching for something. They stare up at me through their sepia world, these people who had no idea of my existence, no concept of the world that I live in. These pictures that speak long ago of picnics, weddings and christenings, that first day at school, that first Holy Communion. Their world is not the world that we live in now and yet it is because of them that we exist.

Bert lived a long life; he was ninety-nine when he passed in December 2015. I met Bert because he was the father of my great friend Martyn Rix. I met Bert because he was a soul that I knew and we needed to connect in life once again. At ninety-nine Bert to me was a bundle of walking history, you couldn't help be that when you reach such an age. He carried the vibrations of a world we will never see again, of morals and values that have been discarded. He was a representative of a generation that was influenced by a time before this insanity we live in now became the constant. He breathed through history; I think how many breaths does a person take in ninety-nine years, how many steps do you walk, through the changing landscape of such a long life? Recently Martyn showed me a picture of Bert and his wife, Peggy, and some function. Bert looking dapper in his dark suit and tie, a pencil mustache lining his upper lip, Peggy in her evening dress, elegant and feminine, a nice young couple enjoying a night out. In his early nineties Bert was Peggy's primary caregiver as she succumbed to Alzheimer's. He did everything for her until the pressure became too much for him. Peggy went into care and passed some months later. Bert breathed a lot of love into Peggy and it would have made her journey easier. You stand by the ones you love like that, it's what you do. My wife has Alzheimer's and like Bert with Peggy I was Kay's primary caregiver. I did it for five years until late September 2016 when Kay went into care. I thought a lot about Bert caring for Peggy while I was caring for Kay. I gathered such strength from the knowledge that a man in his nineties could do that, it kept me going at times. I knew what Bert had gone through and in that common experience we spoke the same language. It would have taken its toll on Bert but he seemed to just hunker down and get on with the job. You can't help but admire a man who at that time of his life was faced with such an enormous challenge and loss. I feel for what he must have experienced during that time and am in awe of his strength.

I've a picture of Bert taken on a cruise ship where Kay and myself had joined Bert and Martyn and Martyn's wife, Marion, and her brother and sister-in-law who were visiting from Holland. There was a formal evening and Bert was resplendent in his suit but did not have a tie. I lent him one, a pink silk tie, which he wore with aplomb. I told him I wanted to take his picture and positioned him against the wood paneling of the wall. He didn't know what to do with his hands and so I told him to be like Prince Charles and hold onto your ring. He burst into laughter and that's when I took the picture. His face is full of light and you can see he is caught up in the fun of the evening, being around people that loved him.

Watching Bert with his son Martyn and daughter-in-law Marion was a complete lesson in unconditional love. M&M,

as I like to refer to them, devoted to Bert their attention and love in a way that helped Bert maintain his sense of dignity and independence. They were always there for him but were conscious of Bert's need to be his own man. I see people deal with their elders like they are something they have to put up with. And when they do indulge them it's as if indulging a naughty child that knows no better. It's degrading, it's condescending, and it pisses me off enormously. It seems these days too easy to cast aside previous generations as superfluous, as something that has to be accommodated until they pass rather than enjoy and benefit from. That seems to be human nature these days, though, doesn't it? It's been said many times that we live in a throwaway society, and it seems all too easy to throw away people when they have seemingly passed their sell-by date. That's not just indicative of the way we treat our elders, though. One sees this in business practices, marriages, friendships, and material possessions. We seem to always want to keep replacing what we have even though we've never fully appreciated what we have got and I'm no exception. Since Kay moved into the care home I've been going through the house and doing a major purge of goods. I'm shaking my head in constant amazement that I even purchased some of the stuff I'm getting rid of.

After Bert's wife, Peggy, passed, Bert went to live with other family in their house. He had to accommodate himself to their way of living and being. I think he emptied himself a little of being Bert. It was too hard to stand up and continue to be himself such was the unspoken pressure. Must be awful to feel that you are in the way and that there is no way out. He never felt that with M&M, though. They kissed and hugged him; they indulged him, made him feel that he was a part of everything and that he was truly wanted. They embraced him as part of their lives, not placing him apart from them. When Bert lay dying Marion sent me a picture of Bert asleep and he was holding onto Martyn's hand. You can see in Bert's face the process of him letting go of life, but to do so he's holding strong onto his son's hand because his son is giving him the love and the energy of life to let go. Son, I gave you life and now the circle is complete as you give me life.

I cry every time I look at that picture, it is one of the most moving and powerful depictions of love I have ever seen.

When I was looking after Kay while she was still at home, I made sure that every day, through the day as often as I could, I would hug her and let her know how much she was loved. When she got to the place where she could not make an intelligible sentence she would touch my shoulder or my hand and lean toward me with a look in her eyes that spoke the love. It awed me, this simplicity of such a simple gesture that said everything.

Bert was full of love that emanated from him like a lighthouse shining the way. And he received great love from the people who in their authenticity were able to shower him with this great force of life that I know supported him. When you met him his joy at seeing you was obvious and the love he exuded reached out like tendrils of energy wrapping around you gently. Like a lot of older people who have a lot of love internally, Bert would reach out a hand and touch your shoulder or your hand. His hugs were full of warmth and they spoke of the need to be held.

When I was caring for Kay I was conscious of the need for her to be held and told she was loved. At times she would cling to me like a child that needed protection or reassurance and I could feel her soul absorbing the love that she was so needing at that very vulnerable time of her life. When I go up to see her now in the care home often other residents who are in the dementia ward will come up to me and take my hand and hold on. Some will reach out and touch my face and you can feel in them the need to be close to someone. I'm sure for many the hugs have stopped and there is no longer anyone to hold their hand. We never stop reaching out for love. I look at the photos of Bert that Marion sent to me in his final days and can see and feel in him the way that he was loved by the people around him as he peacefully moved to his passing. I can see that he was better off because of this and that his way to spirit was paved by the sacred love that he reached out for from those who cared.

It's not hard to love or be loved. Or is it? There seems to be such resistance around love. Loving to me is a form of respecting that we are all source energy. Love is a way of recognizing our deepest foundations. When we love we are remembering that we are all created by the same source and our love for each other is a way of advancing source energy as well as encouraging the ability we all have to be creators of a better life reality. I also believe that feeling love is like a code, giving us access to so much more life. Without that code, how can we possibly move from the places of conflict that so permeate our world and some of its people? As has been proved when we receive love, give love our biochemistry alters allowing positive hormones to flow through us consequently promoting well-being. As our way of being changes through our life's experiences so too does our way of loving, and our way of needing love. As we mature and particularly as we become elderly, love becomes a form of security and reassurance. It becomes an anchor to hold onto enabling one to stand steady in life and to navigate oneself through the journey of aging. And love is a light that shines onto the path of transition, showing the varied paths of life that we are allowed to be available. Through love we make the transition from life in bodies to life in spirit, the greatest love of all.

When I first started meditating I would lie on the floor and concentrate on words like *God* and *Source*. One day as I focused on the word *God*, the word *Love* also popped into my thoughts. It became a mantra and I could literally feel the rhythm of the energy pulse through me like waves. The intensity of the energy built as the thought became more pronounced as a vibration through me. Then this great wonderful feeling of such absolute love washed over me and took me out into source. I have never felt such love and such absoluteness. I transcended time and when I came back my arms were reaching above me and tears of great joy and love were coursing down my face. It was the word *love* that when added to *God* took me on the journey out there.

Some months before Kay went into care I had reached a dreadful place within. I was so exhausted and full of the stress and anxiety of looking after Kay. The years of care giving were taking their toll and too many people were beginning to ask if I was okay, as I didn't look so well. I was going through the motions, the routines, I was surviving, not living, and it felt like I was standing completely alone even though I knew that spirit was with me. I knew it, but I couldn't feel it anymore and something in me was being destroyed. One evening after a particular arduous time of getting Kay to bed I just sat down in the dark in a sort of stupor. My mind was a blank and I stared into the dark of the room. The word *angel* appeared in my thoughts and then the word *music*. My phone was with me so I Googled "Angel Music" and scrolled through the choices that were available.

Having made my selection I plugged in my earphones and listened as the choral sounds of heavenly voices filled my head. Almost instantaneously I began to experience a journey, some would say a vision but I wasn't seeing it. I was literally having the experience. I was walking down a very wide causeway that was glowing with a soft gold light. Towering on either side of me were majestic clouds tinged with gold and pastel colors, and the most exquisite voices emanated from those clouds. They weren't so much as singing words but singing sounds. Sounds that spoke of the great love that God has for us. Sounds that told me how we were all connected with love and that we were all so loved and cared for and were never ever alone. I could feel my body being relieved of all the anxiety I had been feeling. And then I stood before this swirling galaxy of gold light and felt myself falling into it face first. As I fell into this swirl of light I became one small point of light and then a great hand that was God's descended from above and carefully took me into the palm of its hand and the moment that occurred I was lost in a wave of bliss and love and happiness, and once again I knew I was connected.

It was a very profound experience and afterward I felt very connected to source and exceedingly healed of all I had been going through over the last months. I sat there slowly coming back to the reality of the living room and the sound of Kay's gentle breathing coming from the bedroom. I went and stood by Kay and watched as she slept and wished with all the love that I had and all the source connection available to me that I could place my hands on her and heal her. I knew, though, that was not her journey and so I just kneeled down and held her hand and loved her, accepting the choices that her soul had made.

Bert was hugely independent. And very capable of looking after himself as we found out on a trip to Sydney when we somehow misplaced Bert. Sydney was our final port of call after our cruise around Australia and New Zealand. We had a couple of nights there before we all flew back to our home destinations and so we spent those days touring around Sydney. One day we hopped into one of those buses that you can get on and off at your leisure. We had been out to Bondi Beach, had a taste of the water, some lunch, and headed back into the city. The bus was a double-decker and Bert found the stairs that led up top too much so he stayed downstairs while the rest of us went up. Eventually we descended and started to make our way back to the hotel. As we headed back Marion said to Martyn:

"Where's Bert?"

"I thought he was with you," replied Martyn.

We all stopped and looked at one another, wondering what to do.

As it transpired, Bert not knowing that we had all got off the bus was still on board and he was having his own magical mystery tour of Sydney! At some point on his extended journey he realized that something was up and had got off the bus and started the long walk back to the hotel. He had gone into another hotel to ask directions to where we were staying and started the journey back. Martyn and Marion had got into taxi and were driving around the central city streets of Sydney in search of Bert and finally found him making his way home with his determined stride. We all had a worrying hour wondering where he had got to but Bert took it all in his stride and we added that escapade to the "stories of Bert!"

I was able to see Bert one more time before he passed away. I was at the Gold Coast with Marion and Martyn and Bert was also there. He was quite ill then but he carried it with great dignity and presence. There was a tiredness about him and to me a feeling of having slightly stepped away from everything. He was on his final road and was simply living it. He had a few more years before he went home but when I said good-bye I told him how much I loved him.

My dear friend Bert, you're home now after such a long life and I know you would have liked to have reached one hundred but you obviously had other plans. You were such a bundle of joy and I know that you have visited me now and then, so thank you. Thanks also, Bert, for producing the wonderful son you have that is Martyn.

He's gentle like you, Bert, and just as determined if not more! And like you he likes to go on his wanders. I think of you a lot as you made such an impact on my life and I will never forget that. I wish I could have had more moments with you but whenever I'm with Martyn and Marion I know that you are not too far behind. I love you, Bert.

Chapter Ten
Blue Boardies

I'm haunted by the memory of a pair of shorts I should have bought. They were in a shop called Esprit and they were white boardies with large pale blue hibiscus all over them. When I saw them they spoke of sunshine and white sand beaches, a forever tan and a life that was filled with ease and fun. I don't know why I didn't buy them, but ever since I have been on the hunt for them and I have never found them again or anything close to resembling them. I'm wondering in fact if they really ever existed and that perhaps on the day I went into Esprit, I had walked into some sort of boardie dimension that only exists when we have a dream of something but can't quite get to the core of it. Every summer I live in the hope that I will find those boardies again. When I was in Coolangatta, Australia, recently I had to buy some boardies as I had left what I had back in New Zealand. Perhaps I subconsciously did it on purpose in the hope that I would find them in Australia. In fact I was sure I would, seeing that there's so much more sunshine there and white sand beaches, a great place for a pair of white, hibiscus-clad boardies to hang out. But no, anything I found was very subdued and boring, background boardies as I called them, ones that never want to shine in the sun.

The thing is, those boardies made me feel happy. When I looked at the pale blue hibiscus on the background of pristine white I felt lighter, I felt like light! I wanted to feel like that all the time. Who wants to feel subdued and background?

I've come to realize over the years of working as a channel and being involved in my own self-development that life, and everything in life, is rather like a whole mass of vibrational markers. The more I have paid attention to that idea, the more

I started to see and feel those vibrational markers and what they were saying or leading me to. More often than not, the most obvious markers are the people that we bring into our lives. Regardless of what the relationship may be that person represents a frequency in your life that is offering up something to you. It may be to simply direct you or inform you. It could be to advise or to love you. Places, sounds, smells, people, nature, well basically EVERYTHING is telling us about EVERYTHING.

We have all heard or read at one time or another that there is no such thing as a coincidence. There simply can't be if we identify with the idea that we really are creating our reality and there is never a time be it awake, asleep, conscious, unconscious, human, spirit whatever that we are not involved in laying before ourselves the framework of our existence for that moment.

Consider for a moment the theory that we exist everywhere and that we are intrinsically everything. All of that is a "*state of being*" that has a "*mind*" of its own.

That state of being is in a constant state of "*feeling, observation, preparation, creation, and participation.*" Its individual experience allows it to structure source energy to suit its purpose. As this happens it draws information from the collective source that is made up of all "*states of being.*"

It consequently permits itself to be influenced by the vibrations of those other states, therefore recognizing which of those vibrations is needed to put together the modus operandi. From that point, it will have established itself in the best frequency that will support the chosen outcome. So from the moment we awaken to start our day we are emitting signals that consciously align with everything. When we are asleep we are doing the same but subconsciously. Now this brings to mind an observation. When we are asleep we must be gathering information from sources that are unavailable to us while we are awake. In our sleep state we may be preparing for the day ahead, and when we awaken we come with the information that we need for the day. As the day progresses we begin to "recall" the information that we have gathered "out there," get attracted to the markers that are there for us, and unfold the plan for that day. I don't know about you but that makes an awful lot of sense to me and makes me feel very encouraged and secure that this is happening. As we go through the process of the day there must be a gargantuan of information that we take back with us into source to "sort out" when we go back to sleep. I imagine we must go out to some soul department where "worker souls" sift through all the information that is coming in and dispatching it to other departments that will pick it up and position the information in the appropriate ways. This makes me think how astonishing we are!

And so those blue boardies were really a marker for me to awaken something that needed to be attended to. Of course, it wasn't about the boardies themselves and me wearing them, but more about the feelings that I associated with because of them.

I recently acquired a flat mate at the advanced age of fifty-six. I've never flatted with anyone before as when I hooked up with Kay I went from home right into a relationship where we lived together. When Kay went into the care home I found myself in the position of living alone for the first time in my life. After the usual adjustments I embraced this new state of affairs. So when Kieran, known to me as Kiero, told me he was looking for a flat since the breakup of his relationship I took the news with mild interest. Kiero is my personal trainer at the gym I attend and we have known each other for about two years. Apart from the training, we seem to spend most of the training session trying to see who could come up with the most obtuse jokes. We got on well, and he is an easy person to be with. A couple of days after he told me that he was looking for a flat the idea to me started to become a feeling. When I get feelings about ideas I know that my higher nature is trying to get my attention. I couldn't ignore the feeling and so started considering having Kiero as my flat mate. It then occurred to me that Kiero was in fact a *"marker"* for me at this stage in my life and so without hesitation I put the idea to him about coming to flat with me and without getting into superfluous information Kiero moved in. Now of course the thing about life markers is that they have a *"purpose."* There is information there to gather, something to achieve, an outcome to reach thus I had to figure out what sort of *"marker"* Kiero represented and what his energy was offering me.

"All of life's markers have a purpose."

At fifty-six I feel like I am beginning my life again. Starting a relationship as I did with an older woman when I was eighteen and having that relationship last for thirty-eight years, I would have passed up on a lot of the things a normal eighteen-year-old would have experienced. I bypassed a great deal of things most eighteen-year-olds would have done as a right of passage so to speak and was plunged straight away into an adult relationship and dealing with the adult world. Most of the people I associated with were in the age bracket of thirty and up and so I found myself in the position of being in the adult world but clearly not being a mature adult male with a wealth of years of experience in the world. Looking back I think I stopped defining myself through my natural feelings and defined my world according to the world Kay lived in. I wasn't suppressing anything but rather making dormant natural aspects of myself any young man in his late teens would have been expressing. As a result I now find at fifty-six all those aspects of self that would have been expressed and experienced in my late teens are once again awakened from their dormant state. I'm sure a psychologist would have a field day with me at the moment! Now to make it clear this does not mean I have suddenly regressed into an eighteen-year-old again but rather being able to define my life now on my terms as opposed to adapting to others.

I truly feel like I am reinventing myself and facing myself in the most extraordinary of ways and I seem to be attracting people to me in my life that are a part of that journey. It makes me think of what Tabaash has taught that we all have many futures and through our life we are offering up those futures. I see now that we can never force ourselves to see a possible future but rather allow ourselves to get involved in the natural rhythm of life that takes us to that place. The markers of life are lining up and they are expressing a very potent energy to me.

This potency offers up the new potential of me as a man. I can feel latent talents and abilities emerging in ways they have never done before. I can feel a confidence and a certainty with me that is constant, allowing me to explore ideas that in the past I would have been either afraid of or simply felt unsure of my position, therefore negating the possibilities. In steps Kiero, thirty years old, sure of his position as a man, relaxed in his attitudes to life, qualified in living his life by his rules and by the experiences that he has had, therefore here is someone that at this point in my life while I am reinventing me I need. As a major marker in my life he comes qualified to assist me with the qualities that he possesses so it's no coincidence then that Kiero is a *personal trainer.*"

How I am a marker to him I haven't looked at seriously yet. I get glimpses of it now and then knowing that he is a very feeling person, but isn't spontaneous in his feelings with words or actions, whereas I'm very open in my emotional expression both verbally and physically. As a trainer he's very in his body and as a thinker very in his head. So, perhaps being exposed to all this soul energy in the house that comes with me, he is allowing the soul part of him to expand. Of course, at times it's not about the whys and the where's but about the natural state of our beings as vibrations that affects each other. The state of simply being in each other's energy is what it is all about.

As I write this a quote from a Wordsworth poem "Thoughts" comes to mind,

> Enough of sorrow
> Wreck and blight
> Think rather of the moments bright
> When the consciousness of right
> His course was true
> When wisdom prospered in his sight
> And virtue grew

Life's markers are there to make us a better man, a better woman, a better human being. They are there to make our lives better in every way we can consider so that we stay aligned to the energy of source that is there to help us. The energy will absorb our grief and show us the way out of our distress. It will show us that we grow through our adverse experiences and make us complete.

And again to quote Wordsworth:

> Our birth is but of sleep and a forgetting
> The soul that rises with us our life's star
> Hath had elsewhere its setting and cometh from afar
> Not in entire forgetfulness and not in utter nakedness
> But trailing clouds of glory do we come
> From God, who is our home.

Seeing people, experiences, places, etc., as life markers has totally changed my perspective of how life speaks to me. I realize I no longer need to look for any signs of guidance, as they are always all around me and within me.

I also appreciate that like literal markers some of them will fade away or erode so that it is impossible to see where they are leading us. And this being the natural state of our personal evolution we will seek new direction. Think how many times we have repeated something that has an adverse effect and cried out:

"*Why does this keep happening?*"

"*I should have listened to my instincts.*"

"*If only I had read the signs.*"

That last one really says it all. The signs are there and we have to basically recognize them as that and act accordingly. Amazing what a pair of blue boardies that I am still looking for have had to say. And considering the fact that I've yet to find them, means I obviously still have something to do. The markers are all around me urging me to notice them and listen and act. I'll let you know if I ever find them.

Chapter Eleven
People

Let's face the fact, we can't avoid that people will always be in our life. Even if we try our best to isolate ourselves, we are forever and a day going to be affected by people, what they do, what they think, or even if they are simply standing still supposedly inanimate, these "people" have a say in our lives. And of course you are a person, meaning you participate in being people yourself on Earth, though there are those who would dispute this and claim that they originate from somewhere else. Ekatahuna perhaps, or Saskatoon where different life forms are said to be found. In fact there are those that do seem to come from some other far-reaching universe; Donald Trump and those that participate on the *Jeremy Kyle Show* are examples. And yet aren't we fascinated by each other? We simply can't create enough opportunities to beguile ourselves. If we can't put the effort into attaining more knowledge and experience that inspires us away from our mediocrity, we turn mediocre people into A list human beings whose main purpose to me is to distract people from that fact that they *ARE* leading mediocre lives.

We are not mediocre human beings.

Our greatness is rising to the surface; this is what we are all currently swimming in. We are mastering the human stroke, creating our own soul Olympics where everyone can win a gold medal if they choose. I'm really excited about the energy that 2017 has brought to us as I *FEEL* it as an energy of living the life you want, fulfilling your desires, rising completely to the surface and feeling the light. If we don't rise to the surface then we get a very distorted sense of what our greatness can be as the light never shines in or on us completely and we end up with indistinct images of ourselves.

The deeper you go under, the less light there is and you will experience more pressure.

I think over the last few years we have been sorting out the distorted views of ourselves and have now come up clean with our reorganized selves. Who wants to spend more of life working it out while we can have the adventure of living our greatness? In my conversations with clients and friends over these first few months of this year many people have expressed their recognition of the power of 2017. There's been an immense amount of self-realization over the last few years as we were assailed with the energy tsunami of change that has made us revolutionize our thoughts, feelings, and ways that we have to participate in life. It's all different and the constant now seems to be our developing relationship with this difference that we have invited in.

As humans, not only do we come in a variation of heights, shapes, sizes, and genders, we also come with a distinction that is based on our personal vibration that we emit as individuals and the collective vibration we emit as a mass energy. As we consolidate our individual energies we are in fact creating a new personal energy where we simply become one and all.

Becoming one and all gives us access so source.

One of my personal observations about 2017 is to align yourself with as many like-minded individuals and make them a part of your life. The more that I project the intention of who I am and what I want from the highest energy I've noticed I am attracting those like-minded individuals in my life. When I speak of like-minded individuals I don't just mean those who believe in what I do spiritually, but those who align with all aspects of my personality. I find people coming into my life that intellectually are in harmony with me, stimulating me with great conversations and opening myself to new ideas. Physically bringing those into my life that inspire me to look after my body more and to create the best physical reality I want for my soul to be in. Emotionally being drawn to people who are able to express honestly and openly their feelings and for me to reciprocate. You find that you are totally open to the experience of like mind, like body, like spirit, like emotion, and so the list goes on. It becomes a plethora of like-mindedness on every level imaginable.

Always there will be certain people in your life that are going to get your attention more than others. These are the people that you have made specific agreements with to consent to experiences that will advance your understanding and position of your life. These people may be the bane of your life, a proverbial pain in the butt, but they have still got your attention so that you evolve. That's why it's so important to not make the "issues" with them all consuming as that hinders your ability to be objective, and the more you involve yourself in your reaction to this person and the issue, the more you get involved in the energy, therefore extending the problems that may arise. I like to refer to them as *minor vendettas*, though the more common turn of phrase is *bearing a grudge.*

Simon Blackwell (not his real name) lived most of his adult life with the support of social welfare. He was intelligent, articulate, and a man with the potential to do well in life and on the surface capable of developing good friendships and relationships. He came from a good family and was well brought up with excellent values and chances to be able to find great success in his life. On meeting him, he was kind and well mannered and the sort of person that you would be more than happy to get to know. You felt that you would like to help Simon and assist him in his life. However, Simon always seemed to be against everything and everyone at some point. And so because of this Simon Blackwell was a bit of a bastard. He was always involved in some minor vendetta, usually imagined, against someone or something and consequently ran his life with deep suspicion of mostly everything and anyone. Invariably people would be wary of him, reject him, and by doing so feed his vendetta. As the years went by that were historically filled with failed relationships, failed career, failed friendships and his family completely ostracizing him, he lived on welfare in council estates and lived his life as a victim, just surviving. His health began to fail in his fifties but he embraced that as part of his now vendetta against life. Fear and paranoia began to take hold of him more and more till invariably his anger started to portray itself through loud and raucous spontaneous rants and raves. He gave up his council flat and threw away most of his possessions and now lives in his car. He drives from pillar to post pretty well waiting to die. He has been tested for mental illness but it was concluded that he was as sane as can be.

Simon Blackwell turned his vendettas into something viral and created a path of destruction. His case is extreme but it brings one to the point that we are *all* in some way like Simon Blackwell. Okay, he's an extreme example but the point I'm making is that when we *do* bear those grudges and carry out those vendettas we are doing damage to our *whole* constitution and not only that we are *adding* to the collective melting pot that carries all this stuff and quite frankly I don't think that's very good for any of us or good for this world we are living in, I'm sure you agree.

I'm a Libran and Librans like to have the last word, even when they *KNOW* the futility of it they will hold onto anything they should have let go of trillions of years ago, just to make sure that they have the last word. This of course can be exhausting to the senses and the body as it takes quite a lot of concentrated effort to carry around trillions of years of energy that everyone else lost interest in some history ago. And so after many years of self-development I realize the importance of what Tabaash advises, "*PUT IT DOWN,*" because if we don't it becomes rather like a lead weight that we drag around with us rendering us into an anxious, obsessive, and exhausting state!

From a global perspective vendettas are pretty destructive. What have we created, what have we become that we have had to create weapons of mass destruction? What point as a collective energy are we making that we feel we have to make the choice to obliterate each other? A scary thought is that we inherit these vendettas as individuals, families, countries passing on through history grudges that only lead to more dissension. We are affecting the reality of our very existence through these inherited grudges. The intention to change this is always there but as we quickly write the intention we as quickly erase it so the intention has minimal affect. On occasions I wonder if we really do want to create the reality that it can all be put down and something new created. Is it that we just don't really believe that we can or is it that we are so caught up into this pattern of dissension that's been going on for so long that it's just what we have become accustomed to and for that reason see it as the norm and so just carry on doing what we have always done because *that's what we've always done.*

As people we seem to be pursuing life from the point of survival as opposed from a point of living. By doing this we become aligned to our own personal and collective survival tactics that bring about experiences that interfere with our desire to *live in a state of accord.* At times we can create these experiences from a deep-seated place of self-sabotage, therefore repeating events or circumstances that will stay with us until we stop feeding that part of us. This reflects in our personal life as much as the way the world is. If we build up enough of this energy then we externalize this by being challenged by an event. This will keep presenting itself to us until we distinguish what we are doing or thinking and make the relevant alterations to perfect a remedy.

Feel what you feel then put that down and as an observer see what your new course of action is so that you stop repeating the situation.

People challenge us all the time consciously and subconsciously about the patterns of our lives and we want this to happen so that we can bear witness to the need to evolve from patterns that do not serve us or anyone else. This isn't necessarily a pleasant experience at times as we invariably face aspects of ourselves that we may not like. We can be awash with a myriad of emotions that make us feel defensive, upset, confronted and also bring up worry, fear, self-doubt, and depression. Part of our nature seems to possess an aspect that is all about self-preservation and justification that usually creates a bigger hole for us to fall into or a greater entanglement of the issues. This can be very difficult to face as we can also create the need to hide, such is our shame or discomfort, not wanting to leave oneself open to being questioned for fear of greater exposure.

We can run from nothing as we are running from ourselves and when we stop in the belief we have created some distance we discover that we are still there.

All of us people, populating each other's conscious and subconscious realities with what at times must seem like a population explosion demanding of ourselves to accommodate it all. And like cities that can't cope with overpopulation the infrastructures of life seem to totter on the brink of insanity and yet we all seem to adapt and find coping mechanisms that make sure we don't get in each other's way too much. That makes me think how wonderful we all are and that we *DO* all have this innate ability to keep reestablishing our living mechanisms as we are beset with each other *All The Time!!*

I had such a good day yesterday. It felt like a day of rewards as good things came my way and happened to me. There were some pleasant surprises and some validations, there was love and laughter and joy. I acknowledged the energy of what that day gave to me and felt peaceful and content as I went to my bed. When I awoke this morning there was tiredness and rawness to me, and I went through the morning with a feeling of something nagging at me. I thought about it, I sat down and felt it. It soon dawned on me that something good that had occurred the previous day had shone the light on an aspect of myself that needed to be addressed. By this occurring I established a process of *balancing out* something that was out of balance. Now this made me think that good things can lead to challenges as the good things illuminate everything, offering up the prospect of growth and advancement. Certain states of emotion are often attached to this process and can't be ignored. Appropriate expression has to be found to expunge the emotion. Over the course of my work with Tabaash several people have mentioned that as they attain a greater state of awareness it often makes them more aware of the issues that they are to address in this life. As one person succinctly put it,

"I thought all this soul stuff was supposed to make me feel better."

I laughed and replied that inevitably this is the case as we persevere but we often have to wade through the heaviness of life's unresolved issues to get to that lighter place. Facing all of what we are IS a challenge but therein lays the adventure and when we do persist we advance our position in life to our advantage. It's tough, though, and the more you do persist, the more honest you find that you have to be with yourself as you know that there is nowhere to hide. The selves that need to be acknowledged will keep on rearing their heads until you pay them the attention that they demand. The more we ignore or try to brush aside, the more we increase the power that particular self will have on us and so accordingly the issues will expand and weigh us down until we can no longer bear the weight of them. That's when we force self through pain that can lead to some form of self-destruction. Self-destruction comes about because you want to destroy the part of you that is causing the issues. Destruction of course is not the cure but more so finding ways of supporting the crucial changes that will allow you to proceed in such a manner where you create positive outcomes.

Reconstruct, don't self-destruct.

All people equal human life and as all people pay more attention to creating life in a more conscious manner, we then have this effect that not only are we creating our own reality but we are also the reality of someone else's creation. If something changes then we are automatically thrown into a place where we observe, is that real? If that doesn't resonate with you as the reality that you want to embrace then you keep creating until you hit upon the reality that *does* resonate with your whole being and that's when you feel *this is right for me.*

We are in a constant state of pursuing knowledge through experience.

If as people we are not in a better place, then it is because we haven't created the reality to be in a better place. It's as if through history human beings are toying with the idea of making life better, getting along better *In the Future* instead of creating the reality of it in the now. Why should peace be something we strive to attain in the future? Why can't we promote the energy of it in the present and live in that state now?

We keep hitting out as people, blow by blow, at ourselves and at each other creating such mistrust and putting our poor souls through such trauma. We are exhausting this planet and ourselves by this reality and I can see that there is a strain in the world as we try to make some sort of sense of what is happening and to find some solution that takes us away from this tragedy that has been created. Our souls are crying out for some common sense to prevail and that's why we so need to feed that soul, to comfort it and to give it words and actions of encouragement and hope. It's obvious that it is through our connection as souls that we will be able to move through the terror that is all too prevalent in our world and alters our destiny away from all this destruction that is around us.

It's no mistake that at this time in our history where conflict is the constant in our lives, as people we are finding our souls. We are to establish a new collective belief that will be the salvation of humankind. I'm not meaning from the religious perspective as that is where much of the trouble seems to stem from but from the deep and sacred understanding that comes from being purely spiritual.

Living as the Gods we truly are is the only way to access the source energy that will balance out everything. I recall reading some years ago this quote:

> *Living life with God is constructive;*
> *living life without God is destructive.*

How many more blows can we all take? How many times do we have to keep repeating the same negatives, the same stupid actions, repeating the same cycles of destructive life before we comprehend the futility of negative actions? How awful to think that we are adapting to terror and fear and seeing it as a part of life. That is more terrifying than any terrorist action, that we are allowing ourselves to be conditioned to that and create a life around that rather than find a solution. This attitude deforms us and disables our soul and causes us to be dysfunctional, denying us of the life we can live.

We are living in a time of great spirituality but we are overwhelmed by a reality that we have all had a part to play in creating. We did that by the way we thought and the way we have participated in life. We did that by the choices that we have made that were built on negativity, prejudice, and fear. By the petty vendettas that we were caught up in and the ways that we have made enemies of our self and others. As people our greatness comes from our divinity that allows us the ultimate expression of creating life. This divinity does not come from the dogmas and creeds that have been created as ways of seeing God as a ruling entity but more it is simply what we are, it's simply the way of life.

Chapter Twelve
NZ AS

I was one month short of my eleventh birthday when we arrived in New Zealand from Canada. It was September 1971 and we were leaving the Canadian summer behind and going to another summer on the other side of the world. I recall thinking that if you kept moving around all the time then you would always have a summer and never a winter, and though that was the imaginings of a young naive boy I know now that the seasons in your life are as important as the seasons in nature. When my parents made the sudden decision to move away from Canada and everything and everyone that I had known I felt like a young tree that had just started to grow and was reaching out my roots of life to begin to grow more. And then I was ripped out of the ground and replanted in foreign soil that I was expected to adapt to. I found that some trees find it more difficult to adapt and may take many seasons before they grow. It's easy as a child to become caught up in the dreams of your parents and think that they are your dreams as well and I suppose they are from the point of what your soul has created to experience. There's always the bigger picture, but of course I didn't know that then and the repercussions of the move we made were a revelation to me as much as a rude awakening into a new reality.

I do find it intriguing that once upon a time while I was up there being a spirit and minding my own business being nonphysical, I was abruptly compelled to reincarnate into yet another human being. I suppose once you've done it a few thousand times you rather get used to it so why not give it another go? And so I wonder, at what point during my celestial ponderings did I decide that I would be born in Canada, spend the first eleven years of my life there, and then want to move to the other side of the world and be totally reformed? I think most people can look back at their lives and isolate certain events that propelled them into another form of life's reality that redefined who they were and who they were to be in the future. I always think of myself as "Born in Canada, made in New Zealand." In all the years since I've been here in New Zealand I never once considered how my life would have been had we stayed in Canada, no point in getting serendipitous over what could have been. And yet I can't help think how much parents assume that their children will easily adapt to such a major change. When we are younger our lives are easily formed by the thoughts and actions of the adults around us. As we develop our own abilities to think for ourselves and have opinions I think we rely on the security of being a part of a familiar arena that we can comfortably rely on. As much as children are adaptable they also find security and certainty of being a part of a group that reflects back the same energy. When I came to New Zealand I might have been thrown onto another planet so great were the differences. It was those differences, though, that established in me a sense of freedom that I can now as an adult know I would never have experienced had we stayed in Canada. The Canadian was gradually squeezed out of me year by year, experience by experience to make me NZ AS!

Now as an adult with far too many decades behind me I can see how traumatic being uprooted was to me. I know that children have the ability to adapt to change but children also thrive on the security of the familiar and to being taken from that and to assume that you would easily adapt was a big ask of my parents. They were also steeped in their own uncertainty about such a move as well as holding together a marriage which was no longer suitable to them, and so the intuition of a child would be sensitive to all of this. And yet there I was exposed to a whole new country and everything it represented and I had to formulate quickly a survival plan! Interesting that I thought of it in survival terms but that's how it was for me then.

My first NZ day of school was revelatory to me in ways that I never expected. First, I noticed that quite a few of my fellow classmates were going to school in bare feet. My assumption was that their parents could not afford to buy them shoes and I carried that assumption for the first few weeks until I realized that in 1971 Auckland, New Zealand, it seemed to be the norm for kids to walk to school without shoes and socks! Needless to say it was not a practice that I took up! My Canadian sensitivities preferred to be encased in leather. The second thing I was introduced to was the morning assembly. Basically, the whole school would assemble outside on a concrete courtyard in classes. The principal would make some announcements that to me seemed fairly inconsequential but then what did I know about stuff like that, I was simply the new kid on the block. Then we would all move to our classes and begin the day. Recess was called "playtime" and there was a thing called a "tuck-shop" which I assumed was a derivative of "tucker." There you could buy a meat pie, a long doughy thing filled with cream with a dap of jam on the top, which was the ubiquitous New Zealand doughnut and other "lollies" which turned out to be candies or "sweets." And there was this thoroughly disgusting confection called a "custard square," which was two fairly thick pieces of inedible pastry filled with gluttonous custard—nauseating.

The school that was called Anchorage Park Primary was built on a big field next to an estuary that seemed to be a nursery for mangroves. They grew in this thick gray gooey mixture of sand and mud that was most pleasant to walk in and even more pleasant when having done so the sun would bake the mud into a nice light gray encasement onto my legs much to the consternation of my mother! I still remember to this day the mud smelling of rotting vegetation and the sea. This area was out of bounds to us at school and was saved for after school and weekend exploration but it was a great novelty for me being at a school next to an estuary where through the classroom windows you could keep track of the tides, far more interesting than schoolwork! The sports fields seemed to surround the school and seemed to take precedence over the school itself as "playing sports" was compulsory. The boys had to play rugby or soccer and the girls played netball, which was like basketball except you passed the ball instead of bouncing it. All of this was alien to me and also I didn't have the slightest interest in running around a field kicking a ball or from what I saw of rugby getting smashed around and squashed by a whole lot of other guys in the pursuit of a leather ball the shape of a pig's bladder. This was the national sport, though, and it was sacrilege to not be involved. So I did my best, but it was pretty obvious to the others at some point that my best was my worst and thankfully I was always in the reserves! Rugby and soccer were played in the winter and played outside when the elements were usually of the "sodden nature." In the summer it was cricket, surely the most boring game ever created to send anyone into a somnambulistic state! I soon learned that if I stayed way out field there was little chance of the ball heading my way as the batters were too young to have any real strength to hit the ball that far therefore leaving me peacefully to my own devices. One day the ball did actually head my way and without thinking I actually caught the bloody thing to my immense surprise and no doubt everyone else's. Apparently by doing so the game had been won and for awhile I enjoyed the adulation of my peers who thought me "a great mate" and not weird at all because I came from some other country and for other reasons that was only obvious to them, perhaps my very existence?

I gradually settled into some sort of normalcy and started to adapt to this new country and everything it had to offer. I rolled with the punches that life threw at me and gained a thicker skin; character developing, I think they call it! I was still on the outer as far as some were concerned but I began to gain a new "inner" that was food for my soul. Even then I was searching for what God meant to me, though I would not have used those words. There was something that was awakening in me and without knowing why I knew that all the things I was going through, positive and negative, were establishing in me an expansion of myself as source and my future abilities to align with it. It was transformation through living life and the feeling of the changes and the possibilities never left me despite my fears and my aloneness. I suppose these feelings carried me through the isolation I felt brought on by the way I was rejected by my peers. Now I know that I was in training to "Be God" on a conscious level.

There was then and still is, a great spirituality to New Zealand. One can truly feel the soul of this country and the power that it exudes. I see it as a sacred place on Earth where one can truly have the opportunity to advance your soul self without the disruption that other countries have. It is an honest place and though sacred as it may be, it seems to also expose you to yourself in ways that can be advancing to one as much as painful. If we are beyond doubt on this planet to progress with our understanding of soul, then it makes sense that there will be certain countries on Earth where we can accelerate our transformation on a deeper soul level. I believe New Zealand is one of those places and I also believe that my soul organized myself to be able to come here and allow myself to unfold what occurred in my life. When one considers life from this perspective, it's interesting to look back on one's life and note the experiences that manifested challenge, transformation, acceleration, knowing that all these were manifested to advance yourself. I think now, if I had conscious awareness of this from an early age would I have made the same decisions, and I think, yes, there will always be situations where we "don't know" because it's important for us to be exposed to circumstances. "Knowing" allows us to eventually organize those situations to our advantage. So, it seems from that, we are as children doing a great deal to establish platforms that eventually when we're older lead to experience that at some point we learn to control to our advantage.

Me creating to be in New Zealand gave me a look at myself that I would never have seen had we stayed in Canada. I'm not saying that I would not have delved into my spiritual self, but I know that it would have been different, as what I needed as a soul was obviously to be found in moving to the other side of the world.

On a hill overlooking the Panmure Basin in Auckland is a little church built in the 1800s. When you walk into the church you are instantly transported into a sacred peaceful energy. There is a silence in this that demands of you for that moment to put down your human nature and allow your soul to be embraced. This church is called St. Mathias and it is where we went to church, where I was confirmed, and also where I was an altar boy. I could feel the presence of God in this church and I could feel life in this church. It was like a vortex that emitted its energy through the whole complex, the very wood in the church soaked up the energy and held it in its aged beams. When I arrived there early on a Sunday morning before the service started I loved the fact that I had the whole church to myself. I felt that I was having a personal audience with God and it brought about a peace and connection that filled me with a great sense of completeness. In that space the world outside with all its challenges did not exist and all made sense to me during that great silence. I felt that I was able to make a claim on something that was unique to me and it inspired me and made me feel like everything is possible. It also triggered feelings that this was all so familiar to me, that somewhere and another time I had walked this path and my body knew the rituals of the church. In my book *Don't Change the Channel* I wrote about the fact that I knew that I had been a nun in a previous life, and perhaps it was this memory and other memories from other religious lives I have had once again found its voice in my soul, awakened hundreds of years later in a small church on the top of a hill. I believe that when we have these memories we are also able to access the energy of that time and this energy can help us and comfort us. I believe that the vibration of everything we have ever experienced is constantly accessible to us, and as we become more involved in ourselves as source energy we can call upon this energy at will. I also believe that as we advance ourselves spiritually our soul spontaneously presents to us the energy of a memory that it knows will be useful to us. We may receive this as a sudden surge of energy that lifts us or perhaps a deep sense of peace when we are in despair. It can be where courage comes from and will power. It may make us feel inspired and powerful as a communicator when we are to be authoritative when we are not normally so.

Our memories, and our experiences, are vibration libraries that we have full membership to all our lives, and I really do mean *ALL* the lives that we have led! Theoretically this can bring greater meaning to the notion that we all carry the answers within, and not just answers but indeed to access the abilities that we have possessed in other lives that can be fruitful to us in this lifetime. Why is it that we should simply cast off our ability to succeed to be happy to be confident simply because we have moved into another life? Of course I understand about the new deals we make with each life that we live but why give up the right to access the old files?

And so our soul seems to have come up with a clever way of reminding us that undeniably we have not given up the right, but more since we are in new life the old password so to speak to access those files has expired and so we gain access by putting ourselves into familiar territory that speaks to our soul of the past.

Looking back now on those early years in New Zealand I can see that because New Zealand was more isolated in the

1970s than it is now it didn't conform to what was going on in the rest of the civilized world. It was way down here at the bottom of the world and so simply got on with being what it was. In a way it was left alone as I think some bigger countries assumed it was this little backwater country in the South Pacific that had no real relevance. I think that was a good thing as being left alone allowed Kiwis to simply get on with life, make the most of what they had without being dictated to by bigger countries. That produced in the people an attitude where you "just got on with it" and made the most of what was available. As New Zealand opened up to the world and its global influences change was imminent but Kiwis have still that "She'll be right, mate" approach which is unlike anything you will find in other countries.

As those first years in New Zealand rolled by I created a niche for myself despite the difficulties I had fitting in with my peers. Beaches and extinct volcanoes that were an amazing playground for any child surrounded us and we made many a trip to one particular volcano called Mount Wellington. It was pretty well in our backyard and it was a perfect cone standing sedately among the hustle and bustle of the townscape that surrounded it. Always clad in lush green grass it made an interesting landmark for the area and a great place for sheep to graze.

Dad would drive up the long winding narrow road and as we got higher the views of Auckland area were spectacular. Once in the car park we would all leap out of the car and run up to the edge of the crater and slide down its grassy slopes only to climb back up the steep sloop and repeat the process and I thought it was the greatest slide that ever existed. Occasionally you would slide across a nice marbled pile of sheep poo and hope that it wasn't a fresh deposit! Though I visit Auckland and have passed by Mount Wellington it's been years since I was actually up there but the memories I have of our times there are stored happily in the mind of that young boy I was.

Place-names flood back to me now as I write, Buckland's Beach, and Eastern Beach. I could never figure out why Eastern Beach had white sand and palm trees where Buckland's had gray sand and *no* palm trees. Cockle Bay, Howick and Pakuranga, Panmure Township where we would go on Friday night as the shops were open late. Crossing the Panmure bridge looking down at the small sailing ships always docked and wondering if anyone ever took them out. Going for Sunday drives to places like Titirangi and Helensville which then were way out in the country and it was a real excursion. These days with the urban sprawl they seem to be just a part of extended Auckland. That is a pity as we lose so much of the feeling of a country as more and more buildings encroach on nature devouring the very essence of what a country used to be. To me it appeared as raw and real and untouched and there was an energy of simplicity that made me yearn for something that was not quite forgotten but was slipping more and more into the shadows.

At times we would drive across the Auckland Harbor Bridge to the East Coast bays with its pristine white beaches and expansive views of Rangitoto Island a vast volcano that last erupted about 900 years ago. Rangitoto sits smack in the middle of the Waitamata Harbor and was like a sentinel guarding the city. We never went there as a child and I allowed my imagination to run riot wondering what and whom may have been on the island. From a distance it seemed to me to be guarding its secrets protectively. A couple of years ago I went there with some of my siblings and sister-in-law and as we were traveling back to Auckland on the ferry I felt that I wished I had never set foot on the island as it was no longer a secret to me! Perhaps some things are simply best left observed and not experienced!

I loved walking through the New Zealand bush, there is definitely something Jurassic about it. Sacred hills and mountains that when surrounded by the mists would transport you interdimensionally and align you with the spirit of nature embracing long winding ancient rivers. The air you breathed seemed to be air that was just made, it appeared so fresh and brand new. The soul of one's surroundings observed you, welcomed you but asked of you to respect the environment that you were a part of. And you *DID* feel you were a part of it, as there seemed to be no division to anything, all was simply life, living. Respecting this energy was respecting yourself and so your experience became all the better for doing so.

I recall one summer where a friend and myself were staying the weekend with my friend's grandmother. She lived in a big wooden house on the banks of a river. The house itself seemed to be rooted into the very ground as if it too had grown there of its own free will. The sloping banks were covered in native bush and the chorus of the native birds was a choir of birdsong. A long dirt path descended from the house to an unstable wooden jetty stretching out over the muddy river.

The river was shallow so you could easily stand feeling the muddy bottom squelching through your toes. In an old wooden canoe my friend and I would explore the area floating nonchalantly at our pleasure and leisure with a child's privilege of having no responsibilities. We would ride the gentle current of the river allowing it to take us where it chose knowing that we were secure and certain of our position. We were lulled into a silence that became meditative as our thoughts were rocked quietly into stillness permitting our souls to feed our young minds and bodies. It was unadulterated bliss and we could be like this for hours simply existing. A summer rain shower would come and go and we would lay back and let the warm rivulets of water bathe and drench us, having no concern as in half an hour the sun would dry us. The scents were the pungent sweetness of the river mud and the caress of the wild honeysuckle that grew along the bank of the river. At some point we would pull the canoe up to the bank and unwrap the tea towel that my friend's grandmother had wrapped our lunch in. Fresh-baked cheese scones that were smothered in thick yellow butter, pikelets with homemade raspberry jam, buttery and crunchy shortbread. Homemade ginger beer completed this epicurean feast and we had dangled the bottles in the river in a net sack to keep it cool. We would lay back and pleasantly doze off before we started our paddle back up river.

At night curled up on the big lumpy but comfortable sofa made into a bed for the night we would talk and laugh and see who could make the loudest and longest farts (my friend always won). Then silence, as we were lulled to sleep by the crackling of the fire and the night chorus of crickets chirping their nightfall lullaby.

This all seemed very Godlike to me though then I would not have understood it to be so. It was that "*Something More*" that always seemed to be in the background intermittently announcing itself, reminding me about what I really was and what life was really about. And always attached to that something more was that yearning of reaching out for it but never quite being able to grasp and hold onto it. If I awoke in the middle of the night and became conscious of this I would concentrate with all my will to draw the energy closer but it seemed concentrated effort pushed it away rather than attracted it. I now know it's in the *BEING* not in the *TRYING!* I realized that even when I was young so of course I then tried to *BE* but then realized I was still *TRYING* therefore *BEING* was eluding me much to my frustration and consternation as I recall thinking how can I *BE* without *TRYING!* Well, it made sense to me!

Two years after coming to New Zealand my parents decided to end their marriage and so new hurdles to leap were suddenly thrown up. Marriage separation may have been more common in Canada at the time but in New Zealand though not unheard of it wasn't common, and so I could add another title to my list of abnormalities that of a child whose parents have "split up." I could consciously feel the breakup of the energy of the family unit. It was like an instant gear change and from that moment things were never the same, as parents and children alike be it consciously or subconsciously adapted into new roles and new agreements. Our realities all changed and with them the rules of living. I'm glad that they decided to do what they did in New Zealand rather than Canada.

Yes, there would have been more family support over there but since we were on the other side of the world that was out of the picture and so as kids we were simply thrown into the deep end and had to swim, fast, and New Zealand was a better place to do that. The cost of living was still reasonable and my mother found work easily but also received the Domestic Purpose Benefit knows as the DPB that supplemented her income. I think there was a certain amount allotted for each child. I really can't imagine how things would have panned out had they split in Canada, but then perhaps their souls simply positioned themselves here in New Zealand knowing on some level that was going to happen?

It was during this time that I noticed the absence of that *"Something More"* as the reality and repercussions of human nature presented themselves. Being plunged into human experience with all its emotions and challenges overnight altered my life and it is obvious to me now decades later that human experience was licking its lips and had complete autonomy over my life.

"Yum, Yum," it was saying. "Time for some revelations."

All of us are laid raw before ourselves at times in our life, and for some this occurs frequently, too frequently perhaps. I see now that when it does it is without a doubt a process that we all have to encounter and to quote Tabaash:

As we evolve internally from all our experiences,
thoughts and actions we have to ensure that we change our lives,
our attitudes, our futures to align with the new ways we have become.

Growth was imminent and for me to grow, those old vibrations and ways simply had to depart. By departing I was open to the elements of change and acceleration that were to become the foundation stones for my future. A new arena and game had been formed and new rules had to be established thus enabling the new formula to be put into practice. If we lock these new formulas within, never giving them life, the force that is suppressed transfigures into emotions that are detrimental to a positive outcome. We may have strong glimpses of what can be possible but we are disabled by our internal incarceration.

Everything must change, nothing remains the same.

And change it did, making me feel like I had been thrust upon a tightrope between two cliffs and told to walk across it thinking that was the only way to the other side. I felt unsupported, alone, and in despair. The *Something More* wasn't there and so I realized that I had to create survival mechanisms that would get me across that tightrope. I think my pride helped me quite a great deal, as I never liked to feel that I have exposed my weaknesses. Doing so made me feel a lesser person and from past experiences when I have done so opened me up to ridicule and judgment. It created in me an indifference to the situations that arose and in that the indifference became a way of dealing with what I was feeling. During the next few years we made several moves that were really unsettling and yet as a younger person I had no choice but to navigate carefully through my mother's decisions. I was in my mid-teens by this stage and more of a Kiwi than a Canadian. I'd completely lost my Canadian accent but didn't really sound totally like a Kiwi so people were often asking me where I was from. New Zealand at that stage was taking a big step into the world and the influence of that could be seen particularly materially as the open market of the world brought its goods to New Zealand, whereas up to that point most things in the country were New Zealand made.

Living in New Zealand for forty-six years now—a fact that on writing this staggers me—has made me realize what a unique and spiritual country this is. I've been fortunate to see a great deal of this country and others and one thing that springs to mind is the order. Take LAX for instance, if ever there is an airport that can be deemed aggressive LAX is a good contender. I'm always astounded at the seeming lack of order, the indifference, and the fact that it actually works! Out of all that disorder miracles do actually happen, planes take off, okay not exactly on time, as had been my experience several times, but it works.

One of the things that you notice in any airport in New Zealand is that it is relatively quiet, and that there seems to be an order about everything, even the people. In major airports worldwide it seems like once you are off the plane it's every man and woman and child for themselves and GOOD LUCK! I'm not being judgmental here but simply stating the facts as I have experienced. So many countries seem to have lost their soul or lost sight of it and so how can you have peace, balance, and equality among the people when there is no soul or indeed how can you have life? It makes everything so tired when it's like that and I am so fortunate that I don't live in a tired place where it is hard to really live. I suppose that's why we have to wake up to this God part of us so we can stay awake to create.

To create, we have to be awake.

I can fully understand the implications now of what creating your reality really does for one's life. It sets you on a course that aligns you with a way of living that will offer up the best result. That absolutely struck a note in my soul as I wrote those words. We are always looking for the best result and we are forever and a day creating the ways to permit that to happen. Our soul really does know what is essential for us and it will go to astonishing lengths to ensure we are following a path for the best result. Then I think, is the soul's perception of the best result the same as human nature's perspective? Obviously not when you look at the quantity of resistance that human nature has to following the soul at times! To me this changes the dynamics of what my life has been all about. It means that all the challenging experiences I have were a crucial part of my journey to the best result. I'm getting an image now of myself in a Formula One racing car on the track. I am weaving and winding my way through the course, changing speed, changing gears, having to pull in at the pit stop to get "topped up." It's not a race I am involved in, though, but purely the course of life that I have set up for myself and I am deciding the best way I want to drive it. Interesting that I did not create the image of a gentle peaceful ride through the countryside with no sense of urgency!

We are living to create the best result.

When we create the opportunity to work or live in other countries our soul must know the significance of how the vibration of those places will augment our position to get a good result. And of course it's not just about the countries themselves, it is the energy of the people we align with and the experiences we have that make this occur. This is not saying that those who don't have the prospect of being in other places are missing out; they have simply established themselves in a place where all is to be had!

I'm glad my parents made the decision to move to New Zealand in 1971. I was able to experience a world that will never again exist where it was all so simple and there seemed to be such a respect for each other. Everything is so convoluted now and there doesn't seem to be such a thing as innocence anymore. The thing I think of now the most as I write this is that living seems to be such a struggle now. This morning while I was making my breakfast I heard in the radio of a terrorist attack in a train station in St. Petersburg, Russia. I felt a rage come up inside of me for these ignorant people who are stooping to such a low degree of existence that they have to do this to others. Tears of anger came to my eyes and I walked around the kitchen feeling frustrated and angry. I so wanted God to step in and intervene, and even said so. That's not what it's about, though, is it? Wherever we position ourselves that's where we want to be too, so we can advance our position as souls. I get that, I really do, but how do you tell that to a mother whose five-year-old had their legs blown off in a bomb put on a train? How do you tell that mother that the soul of their child wanted to experience that so that they could advance their soul?

Of course, you can't tell her that. Instead we all find ways of being more powerful against the tyranny that is engulfing the world. We find ways of changing ourselves so we can change each other and the world. Sometimes it's best to keep our beliefs to ourselves and do the best we can for ourselves and others in the hope that we will make the world a better place while we are here.

I think living in New Zealand made me a better person. Yeah, life pushed me around a bit here but then it probably would have been worse if we had stayed in Canada. I learned to push back here in New Zealand and embraced the qualities of being a Kiwi. Some of it's called the number-eight-wire attitude. That's a sturdy wire that farmers use for fencing, and it's useful for all sorts of things so meaning that a Kiwi can just plunge in there and get the job done, and do it well. They are not going to invest in a whole lot of discussion and worry about stuff when something needs to be done.

Will you stop mucking around, mate, and just get on with it?

I'm certainly proud to be NZ AS. This country has given me so much life, and I am very grateful for the opportunity of living in such a place. I think it's a place that "youths" you up, for want of a better word. People here really do still pay attention to each other; it's hard to be lost in the populace, as everyone's individuality seems to stand out. It's the country that launched my spiritual journey and gave me an early platform for my abilities. It's been a tough place sometimes but never brutal. There was always someone around who cared and that has been one thing that New Zealanders are good at doing, caring.

Chapter Thirteen
Something More

All day I had felt this oppressive heaviness upon me. I felt like I was dragging life around with me through the day and it was depressing and very lonely. It had been six months since my wife, Kay, had gone into a permanent care dementia unit because of her advancing Alzheimer's, and though after five years of being her primary caregiver the burden of her care had been lifted I still felt the repercussions of her leaving home. I would visit her daily, sometimes it was a good day for her and she was very lovely and gentle and funny. Other days she would look right through me or just walk away. When that happened, I would simply leave. I knew there was no point in being there, as that would agitate her. It had been one of those days when I came home and felt so sad and so suspended wondering how much longer this journey would carry on. Surely we had completed what we needed to, surely we had both let go of what was necessary so that Kay could go home to spirit and give up this life that was locking her up in her tangled brain? Obviously not, as the months unfolded and Kay's state continued to deteriorate, leaving her to live her half existence. I could feel the old anxiety and stress I had experienced in the last year of her being at home move down through me, draining me and exhausting my soul.

When I got home I felt I could hardly function. I sat down on the sofa in my office and stared into nothing, feeling completely emptied of myself. I heard the key in the door as my flat mate Kiero came home and so I pulled myself together and made the effort to show that all was well, but inside I knew that was far from the truth. We spent a quiet evening and then at 9:30 I announced that I really had to go to bed, as I was exhausted. We said our good nights and off I went to bed where I instantly went into a very deep sleep. An hour later I was aware that I had been dreaming odd scattered dreams that made no sense and I was suddenly wide awake as I felt energy in the room. When I opened my eyes I looked up to see energy in human form, all white, hovering about a meter above me. There were tendrils of white light emanating all around it and for a brief second I lay there in amazement before the fear kicked in and I gave an almighty yell and flung myself out of bed, grabbed my dressing gown, and fled into the living room.

My heart was pounding so hard I could hear it in my head. I sat down on a chair, my hands to my head, as I tried to make sense of what had just happened. Kiero had been in the bathroom cleaning his teeth and as he came out he saw me sitting there in some sort of obvious state of distress, and came over to me.

"Are you alright, buddy?" he asked in a very gentle voice.

He put his arm around me, and the instant he did that I simply burst into tears.

He held me for a moment as I calmed down and then relayed to him what had just happened.

I then began to feel like a fool. I knew that I had just been visited by spirit and that it was positive and there I had sat up and yelled with fright! Feeling more composed I went back into my room with Kiero following me. I could still feel a presence in the room and wondered if Kiero was thinking about this crazy house he had moved into with his crazy flat mate! I could still feel the concern in his voice as he talked to me and I assured him that I was okay now and that I was going back to bed. He gave me a comforting hug and went into his room across from mine, saying,

"I'm glad I can't do what you do."

I chuckled and then turned out the light with a fleeting thought about checking under the bed but dismissed that as ludicrous. Lying there, feeling the obvious energy of spirit about me, I started to think about what had just occurred.

Had Kay passed and was this her spirit coming to say good-bye? I put that question out to source but got an instant negative. Then I thought about other people who may have passed, my parents, and other people whom I was close to but again got a negative. So I lay there for a minute or two and felt that some sort of apology was needed from me.

"Look," I said aloud. "I'm really sorry that I yelled at you but you gave me one hell of a fright not expecting to see what I saw. I'm afraid I let my human nature get the better of me. I feel very stupid and if you want you can come back."

I listened hard in the darkness and then in my head the word "Angel" presented itself. The moment that occurred I felt—something? someone?—stroke the back of my neck very tenderly and I felt myself drift into sleep. For the rest of the night I dreamt that I was visiting all my friends to give them the news that Kay had passed away. Awakening the next morning I felt rested but still intrigued about the occurrence the night before. I thought about the emotions that had burst out of me when Kiero had comforted me and realized that because of the pent-up energy over the last days a bubble had to burst and that the "Angel" had obviously been doing its work. Of course, me being who I am I had to look at the bigger picture and the part Kiero played and realized he had to be put in a situation where he was the comforter in a way that he had never experienced before with any friends of his age. So there he was comforting some spiritual channel that was telling him about floating entities above the bed; what a conversation for the breakfast table. I laughed out loud at the amusing absurdity of the whole situation and how it was to him. When I sheepishly greeted him when I got out of bed I apologized but he took it all in his stride as part of living in the house of a channel.

After breakfast I went into my soul room, a closet that once had contained some of Kay's clothes that I had turned into a small meditation area. I've created a little shrine with statues of master teachers and other spiritual bits and bobs that have meaning to me. I lit a scented candle that I have in there and turned out the light and tuned in. Once again I felt the need to apologize for my reaction and told spirit so. I got the word "preparation" in my thoughts and instantly realized that I was, am, being prepared for Kay's passing. The dream that I had the night before then made sense to me and I felt what I would call the energy of a "logical peace" flow through me. I say logical because it all made complete sense to the thinker that I am and I accepted that "all is what it will be" and that everything will be okay. It sometimes surprises me my lack of emotion around Kay's circumstances. And I have asked myself, am I repressing some emotions here? Am I not facing up to what has happened? Or perhaps I am just allowing that "something else" that is within me to guide me through what has been an arduous occurrence in my life.

When I look at the sometimes laborious task we are all going through as we live on Earth at this time, are we not tapping into that greater part of us that actually knows exactly how to cope with the conflict we are constantly being bombarded with daily? It makes me think that we really are a resilient lot as humans or is it our souls that are resilient and our souls send that energy to our human nature as coping mechanisms? Looking through the history of human nature and the enormous amount of relentless adversity we have all experienced one can't help but admire the fortitude we seem to have. Has this been because the soul with all its access to source continually guides us toward allowing a more conscious awareness knowing that inevitably we will all get it right? The "something more" that I was so aware of when I was a child is with all of us and the unfavorable experiences we go through in life are taking us to the realization that we are so much more and can make things so much better. I see this now more and more as the energy of my years of looking after Kay become part of my past and I emerge as a better man. I see now that allowing this knowledge to be a conscious part of one's life is crucial to the evolution of one's self as much as the collective self we all create by the fact we are all in this life together. We simply can't be separate anymore from what gives us life.

That makes me come to the conclusion that all of us are in "preparation" for the immanent passing of how we have functioned as a collective over the last hundred years or so. We can no longer abide by the principles of "what was"; we have as a human race evolved from those. That has come about because as individuals we have changed our own personal mind, body, spirit principles consequently altering the vibrations of everything and inviting in that "something more." This has given us a new portfolio of life's doctrine that we are more consciously accessing and sharing. It seems important that we share with each other through our honesty, love, and clear communication the information we are as individuals receiving from our personal experiences in our self-development. To me it seems as if we have all been hiding from each other this great something that makes us. By being more open with each other from a platform of respect and love we can help to evolve each other. We hide our feelings from each other, we hide our deep love for each other, and we hide our talents and our abilities for fear of failure and ridicule. We hide because we fear each other, and when the fear becomes too much, we hurt each other in the myriad of ways that occur on this planet. And by doing this we are hurting ourselves by pushing away the "something else."

As a child growing up in Canada even though we had a large backyard I preferred to play in nature's back yard that was the big forest area behind our house. To me it was full of mystery and adventure that spoke to my spirit and appealed to the young boy's sense of adventure. My preference was to go alone as if others joined me I felt that the sacredness of my place was violated. The forest was saturated with the energy of the "something more." I entered this sacred place from a small path from the road and was instantly transported into the realms of spirit. All outside noises seemed to cease and even though I *was outside* I knew by a child's innate instinct that I had really *gone inside*. Before me was a wide clearing, the earth hardened and scattered with pine needles and cones. It was like a small circle and I would look up and see the towering trees above me like sentinels on sentry duty. To me it felt like they were looking down at me and telling me that it was okay if I were there and that they would watch out for me. I never for a moment felt afraid of being alone in this sacred place. To me the whole place was like an altar that I had come to worship before and I felt my wishes were respected and understood by all that was natural.

There were many paths that snaked out from the main central area and even though I had walked those paths many times they presented themselves to me as if I had just found them and was to discover what was to unfold. There was a sense that I was never alone on my wanders as if guardians of nature had been assigned to care for me, making sure I would come to no harm. Regal and rather splendid mature trees stood solid and qualified, protecting the young saplings that were growing around them. The scent of old and new wood blended luxuriously with the damp rawness of the ground cover. I found a place once just off one of the small pathways. A large tree, one of the elders of the tree tribes, had completed its life cycle numerous decades ago and had simply fallen where it stood and established itself as part of the ground. Over the passing years other forms of life had been born upon it and around it, establishing a village of flora and fauna resplendent in its variety of green hues. Here was a soft carpet of light green moss that had laid itself before the fallen elder, blanketing it with its seductive velvety mass. I laid down and felt the caress of life coming from the ground beneath. Light seemed to sparkle all around me as the sun reflected itself on the diamond drops of water on plants and each drop was its own rainbow. And it was there that I felt God spoke to me through my feelings and presented into my soul an understanding that one day I would find and create more life from that discovery. Looking back now at that moment I realized that what had occurred is that I had in fact accepted a mission to do God's work and by complying I not only changed my future but I set up for myself a long road of discovery that would be forged through difficulties. Had I known that then I probably would not have understood and simply would have brushed it aside as some childish notion. I can see now after all these years how very real it was and that God was touching me and guiding me. I was there for hours simply existing in the energy of source and melded into the physical and energy atmosphere around me until I felt like what I was as body had simply disintegrated and became one with the very ground. The sun shone down on my young face and it was warmth I felt not from the sun but from something greater and I felt it was the "something more" bathing my soul.

Reflecting on this decades later, I see it as a spiritual right of passage that I had set up for myself and accepted. I also see how by doing so I separated myself to a degree from life in the way that most people saw and felt it. A vocation must feel like that to those that took religious vows, and I understand that what I accepted was indeed my vocation, something my soul had planned and needed to fulfill. For most, bringing God into one's life is more an idea where around that idea a ritual of some sort is created and practiced. To those who have a vocation they are creating a relationship with God in such a way where they are prepared to step away from living life the way most people do. And that does mean for some relinquishing certain experiences that most people will have. I see now that to have the "something more" for some means having something less of human experience. This is not a bad thing; it's just that you choose not to have the influence of certain things in your life that may distract the outcomes you want to create.

We can become so drawn in to our human experience,
we forget the vital component that allows us to have that experience.

Interesting to note that most of the conflicts that have occurred on Earth are often based on "beliefs." We seem to be lost as a people to the common element of what God is and have so many scattered and varied perspectives of "God" that this creates a conflict of interest as the varied factors vie for supremacy. To me this is simply tearing to shreds the "God" energy, scattering the energy of it to such a degree where it almost becomes suspended while human nature sorts out its ideology. It amazes me how as people we can turn such a basic and simple truth in to something that brings out the conflict in people instead of the love. Separation from source creates a separation from our higher self. If we do that then we are moving away from the source of our knowledge and the answers that so many are desperately seeking. At the end of the day when we do connect with that, we find the truth out about ourselves and perhaps some people just don't want to know that. It's not that they don't want to know about all the goodness and love and greatness that comes from aligning to God but more the truth that they indeed are responsible for their lives and ALL of life. I can see that is too much for some and so they stay detached from what really makes life happen and prefer to believe that it's just happening randomly.

Life is not a random act, it is a choice.

The *Something More* that I speak of is always following me around as it is I. It's the me that is the *everything* that we all know is us. Paying attention to it makes us see the importance of reorganizing our life around this belief, consequently inviting in the energy that allows us harmony. Its voice is subtle and factual as I often find out. One day driving after getting a coffee and sitting near the beach I thought I would go home and meditate before my first client of the day.

The moment I had that thought the "voice" said in my head, "write." So rather than have a dialogue with it about why, and shouldn't I have a meditation instead, I simply accepted and therefore complied with the instructions that I had allowed to come to me. I say allow because it was coming from my higher self, therefore I was directing myself from my higher self for my higher good.

Over the years people have asked Tabaash and myself, what's the best way to align to your guides, to source? From my own personal understanding based on my own experiences I know that the answer to that question is to align to your own sense of God; it really is as simple as that. For in that alignment you automatically connect with the *something more*. It is the knowledge of self that expands our ideas of our self *beyond* the human nature and in that place is where you will find your connection with whatever form of guidance you require. When I first was made aware of Tabaash and my abilities it was not because he came and presented himself to me. It was that I extended my vibrations through my evolution; therefore it was possible to go to the level of consciousness where he resides. I expanded my awareness and by doing so opened up infinite possibilities.

And to me *THAT* is what enlightenment is. As we recognize the futility of some of our human nature thoughts, actions, etc., we begin to question and by doing so put light onto the areas that need to be changed. Making the relevant changes takes us to a *Higher Level* of understanding that *Expands* our perspective of ourselves, consequently giving us access to that *Something More.*

All of us are in the process of being involved in that now. Some are more conscious than others and action the changes. Those who are not are finding out through the disruption of what was their life's structures and are trying to find the solution through their human nature, not the *GOD* nature.

What are we all holding onto that we no longer need? All of us are carrying ideas around that have come from all the experiences that we have had in life and other lifetimes and some of those ideas are destroying our aptitude for love, for success, for having the lives that we all want. It's like this big battle of ideas that is going on in all of our heads. Some of us are winning the battle, others are heading toward losing. What choice do you want to make? I can see now more clearly what spirit means when they say, *"PUT IT DOWN!"*

We are allowing to be influenced by thoughts that demoralize our light nature and we descend into a place of such heaviness feeling the full weight of ideas that empty us rather than fill us. The *"Something More"* is accessible to us all and in the simplest ways that we can find. Every day we all owe it to ourselves and to each other to feel this, to see it, to put it into practice so that we can continually raise the energy of this planet, to continue the survival of life on Earth and ourselves. Many teachers are speaking of the new Earth and that we are moving toward it. It already exists, it's in the *"Something More."* We are by developing our *God Nature* creating this new Earth and its new ways. We are all of us quite purely the *"Something More."*

Chapter Fourteen
Lifetimes of Travel

Do you believe that places call to you? I do, and when you think of the many lives that we have all had it makes sense that we leave some imprint of our past in those places and we are in the future called back to those places. Let's face it, when it comes to reincarnation we are all seasoned travelers. For those who have traveled, most have had feelings that they felt familiar in a certain place, that somehow they "knew" that they had walked certain streets and knew a certain town or city. We all relate to certain cultures more than others and perhaps that's because we were a part of those cultures in other times.

Some years ago one of my neighbors who lived in the house behind me invited me to his and his wife's place for dinner. He was a building contractor and basically a real Kiwi bloke. He loved his cars, and his rugby and loved to hunt and fish and basically all the bloke stuff. I had the idea in my mind that his house would be filled with giant plasma screen televisions to watch sky sport, a beer fridge, and a big comfy sofa, and there would be gumboots and work hats in the hallway. What I saw instead was pretty much a miniature of what you would find in the Palace of Versailles. Big gold gilt French mirrors were on either side of the walls as you walked into the entrance. There was a long thin delicate French side table under one of the mirrors with a marble vase full of exquisite flowers. Marbled floors were covered in superb rugs and some of the walls were iced in colorful tapestries. I felt like I should be wearing a powdered wig and an embroidered jacket. My mate bounded down the stairway in his t-shirt and shorts and work socks, a complete anomaly to his surroundings. Beer can in hand he proceeded to show me around this beautiful home and with real knowledge explained the furnishings and pieces of object d'art he had collected over the years. To me it was obvious he was surrounding himself with some past life that he was comfortable with and still related to through his taste in décor.

It's an interesting way to get a sense of what sort of past lives your friends and family have had by paying attention to the way they portray themselves through their interests!

When I was about twelve, I came across a book called *Flambards*. It was about this teenage orphan and heiress who went to live at an impoverished estate in Essex in England. It was set before, during, and after World War I. There was something about that book that triggered a memory in me that I couldn't fathom. It all felt so recognizable and I knew that I related to the characters in the book through some sense of familiarity that gave me great comfort. Interesting that I mostly related to the description of the countryside as if I knew Essex County. I have always been drawn to Edwardian England; I seem to know the social energy of that time, the rules, and the structures. Having had some regression done I found out my last incarnation was as an Edwardian woman who had high social status.

The influence of that lifetime is evident to me in the way I have decorated my home and the way socially I am able to relate to people easily. All of us have this inner library that is filled with what must be trillions of experiences, thoughts, feelings, and events that we can access. Most of us access this by the way we present ourselves in our lives, the way we dress, walk, feel, etc., and all of this has a bearing on how we present ourselves now. When I look at people who have been put into positions of power, particularly world leadership, I like to remind myself that those "*souls*" made the agreement to be in such a position. Their motives for their position of course defines if they are good leaders or not. If they fail in the ability to lead positively and abuse the position they are in then of course that soul will create other life deals that they will have to resolve. The leaders we create as a collective are an indication of the collective vibration of how we believe we need to evolve. A bad leader can simply be an indicator that on a collective level people are not really paying attention to the role that they have in creating reality. But then given the bigger picture haven't we all been in other lives a leader just like that ourselves? Are we not simply giving ourselves an opportunity to look at how we can lead *ourselves* differently and by doing so improve the vibration of collective energy, the outcome being that we create leaders who are positive?

Our lives that we live are giving us the opportunity to lead ourselves away from past misdemeanors and to quote an appliance commercial that was aired in New Zealand:

"It's the putting right that counts."

The lives we live are also reminding us how many times we *have* got it right and that we can still access the information and energy of those moments. I get quite nervous when I am about to do a public presentation and feel rather shy when I am in crowds of people whom I don't know and yet there is a need for social interaction. I find myself naturally wanting to pull away and can feel my natural barriers come up. Recently I attended a function where I sat at a table where everyone was a couple, in fact to me the whole room seemed to be filled with couples who all knew each other and I could feel myself being overwhelmed by that. As I observed I noticed that being a part of a couple was a way of carrying each other in social circumstances, as they were a supporting act for the other. This created an energy that became attractive to others so others joined in. I sat there a man on his own feeling slightly ill at ease and no doubt that didn't help my cause at all. I looked around and reminded myself that this was my reality and that everyone in this room had created the need to be at the function. We were all participating in this energy exchange that was evolving us.

No doubt some of us had been involved in previous lives together and once again were drawn to this common energy so we could reconnect, consciously or not.

The man next to me turned and asked how I came to be there. It was through my work as a channel and I wasn't about to divulge that until I was asked. Silence, then of course the inevitable question.

"And what do you do for a job?"

I looked at him and he seemed to project the energy of someone who wasn't going to understand about someone channeling disembodied spiritual energies but I told him anyway. Silence again, he stared blankly at me and made a few polite sounds as if he knew exactly what I was on about and then turned to his wife and conversed with her. I'm such a conversation stopper, I thought to myself, feeling in fact quite amused. Then the lady on my left engaged me in conversation.

"Are you with someone?" she asked.

"I'm actually married," I replied, "but my wife couldn't be here."

"Oh, did she have to work?"

"No, she has Alzheimer's and lives in a secure dementia unit."

Another blank stare, but this time with a hint of embarrassment. Well, I certainly was becoming the life of the party, I thought as she turned away not knowing what to say or do. Blair, you really have to make the effort, you really have to dig deep into some part of yourself that can just get on with this, I conjectured. Just call on some past life you've had where it's all flowing and this is all easy. The trouble with doing what I do as a job is that people either don't want to or can't engage with you or they want to hear all about it and how it works and how you got into it. I feel like carrying my first book around with me, *Don't Change the Channel*, and telling them to read it and they will find out all they need to know!

Sometimes I get tired of the *"I'm a channel conversation and tell me all the details."* It's like talking shop all the time, and when people hear about my wife and her illness they assume that she is young and so I have to go into the explanation of the fact she is twenty-four years older than I am. That's another conversation stopper; my list of oddities gets longer all the time. I must admit that in this lifetime I seem to have chosen a life as unconventional as possible.

Whatever we have chosen in our life we have to remember that it is a life that is giving us chances to express, learn, resolve, create, and advance. I've read that each life is an opportunity to return to your original source. I think that we live each life to remember that we are all source and we don't have to *return* but more stand still and *remember* what we are. So whatever body we happen to find ourselves in, whatever country we are living in, and whatever personality we have fashioned for ourselves this time round, it's all part of the arena that allows us to put into practice what we know and to expand upon that knowledge so we can remember more. I think it's important to know that whatever life that we are living we can still access the energy of ANY lifetime and still be influenced by this. That doesn't mean that it's going to creep up on us and smack us around, though!

I believe as we advance our position as *GODS* consciously it increases our abilities to tap in to these vibrations. We can then call in the vibrations that are positive and that will enhance our ability to progress in this life. As we resonate more to the *GOD* frequency we are stimulating the part of us that *knows* what will best serve us. What I have noticed in my own development is that past-life memories seem to follow me around. I've come to the conclusion that this is not some random experience but more we *want* those memories there because they carry important information that we need to use.

And when I say information, I mean personality traits from other lives that may be important to use in this lifetime.

Where does leadership come from, our creativity and great compassion? Where does our natural athleticism stem from and our alignment with nature and animals? What indeed are our personalities but just energy made up from innumerable experiences that we now carry as a vibration.

When I visited the country of Oman some years ago I was taken by friends for a drive up into a mountainous region. From the moment we ascended up the long steep road I felt a great sense of familiarity and peace descend upon me. I felt a great kinship to the mountains and all the ruggedness of the life around me. It felt like home and made me feel secure. I saw a vision of myself, a man in dark robes sitting on an outcrop of rock overlooking an immense valley. A horse was quietly grazing by his side. The man was deep in thought and observation, and the thought that came to me when I saw this vision was how *complete* he was. There was an absolute acceptance of who he was, what his life was like, where he lived. He never questioned what his life was but at the same time knew that life could change and evolve if he so allowed it. He was totally a part of the environment that he lived in and he saw the beauty and felt its power. He was also aware that he could never take for granted what he was a part of and so he was living in a conscious way, ensuring that he participated with all around him and within him in a companionable way. He did not see himself as separated from anything but that he was everything.

He was certain of his position.

So, why do I choose to allow him to present himself as he was, as I was, to who I am now? I've struggled with the idea of myself in this lifetime not knowing where I fit in and how I identify with myself. I've not felt *complete* and at times have not had an *acceptance* of who I am. He never struggled; I have and at times still create the need to do so despite what I understand. I've questioned too much at times and forgot that I had choice and that it was my choice how much and in what ways I would evolve. And so, I have called him in as reference energy to remind me of *what I am*, not *what I have been or wish to be*.

Have you ever felt like you could be really great at doing something and yet when you make the effort to do so it doesn't quite work to plan? I think we gather the inspiration for such a feeling from past lives and if we want to pick up the thread again in another one we still have to learn new techniques for this lifetime to be able to succeed. The feeling we get that *WE CAN* is inspiration and motivation to evolve something we may have started centuries ago. Maybe we got distracted by the events of that lifetime and didn't get round to picking it up again until now?

When I contemplate the life I had as that man in ancient Oman I feel like I could do anything, and that I totally understand the order of everything. Aligning to the idea of what he is allows me access to the vibration that he still is and so when it is needed I suppose I simply become him. Does that mean that when we need to we become the very aspects of ourselves that we have portrayed in other times? Are we actually still living the vibrations of everything we have always been and when we become more conscious of this we can use it? If that is the case, what really is identity? When we drop the need to be something, we become everything, as being something seems to bring about emotional structures that limit what we are. We are trying to *fit* into a recognized formula that also fits in with convention. When we focus on *this is who we are now* we are not focusing on who we are physically or even our personality, we are focusing on this is the experience *my soul is having through this body at this time*. The meaning of *Being Yourself* changes then, as it becomes *Be Your Soul Self*.

The intricacies of having lived before perhaps are simpler than we believe. We are living libraries of experience that we always have access to. Our souls seem to know exactly what we need and it knows that because it *chooses* all of the vital information that it will need for the new life it will embark on. Life therefore is never a random act of existence, but more a considered decision based on specific experiences we want to have. As we inevitably come to this conclusion this changes the futures that we are always creating. Knowing that we *can* access information from selected lifetimes means we can accelerate our progress without the trials and tribulations we have had and can still go through, to get the results we want. Our day is determined by what has gone before, and what was gone before was determined by what went before that. I can see now our whole existence reaching right back to the beginning of our history on Earth and before that, each existence adding another layer of information that we can have admission to. It is a *selective* process, though, as we don't want to open the energy door of the past and admit memory that would be traumatic to us. So how can we make more use of the lives that we have had? I know the importance of being in the present and not getting caught up into the curiosity of living before. That can be very distracting and detaches us from the importance of what we are all about in this life. And so, getting back to my thought that we have chosen certain lifetimes that are useful to us makes sense. I think I will call them *INPUT LIVES* that are actually vital to the ways we wish to advance ourselves this time round. They offer up a specific contribution to our life if we utilize them. Everyone who is presently alive now *MUST* all have *INPUT LIVES* that they are accessing and most probably have no idea that they are doing so. How do we then make ourselves conscious of these lives that we have chosen to employ? I can only but offer up my own experiences to answer this.

Let's go back to the Omanian man I was whom I shall call Amir, simply because when I asked for a name that's the first name that came into my thoughts. I know that the idea of Amir is not just some fanciful notion dredged up from fantasy as the feeling and visions I had in Oman were far too real to discount them. This is what I did to align to him.

I held strong onto the vision that I had and I really took notice of what he was wearing. I noticed his stature was not of a tall man, but I could see that he was strong in body. I noticed his hands were powerful and hardened by life. As I noticed these things I began to *feel* more like him. Then I started to ask questions about what he was like. I asked about his personality and received the relevant information in my thoughts. The more questions I asked, the more I felt that I was identifying with his energy and felt like it was blending into me. I felt his silence, his ability to think deeply, I felt his strong male energy and particularly his ability to observe quietly and unobtrusively. Images of the life he lived, where he slept, people who were in his life flashed through my thoughts too quickly to hold onto but long enough to create a picture and a feeling of his life. As I did this I began to understand him and consequently recognized what use he is to me in this life. The more questions I asked, the more information presented itself to me helping me to develop a connection with who I was and what that life was for me. I was once again *developing* a relationship with this aspect of myself that I deemed important for me in this. Before I was born I had *arranged* the connection with this aspect knowing it would be of use to me. I knew I had really made the connection when I was attuning to him one day. I usually get the same vision of him sitting on the outcrop of rock overlooking the Oman landscape. One morning as I was aligning to him he suddenly turned to me and looked straight at me giving me this enormous smile of recognition. It's a strange feeling having yourself as a past life look at you so directly and connect in such a way! It reminds me that our soul is always connected with everything and regardless of what life we live we are always related to what we were. And then that made me think, was Amir so aware in that life of what his futures were that he was able to recognize himself in me as what he was to become? Was he attuning into me as Blair the same way that I was attuning into him as Amir? I wondered if he was receiving the *visions* of the future through thought or was he simply getting a feeling. Was I influential to him as I am now?

This is the real fine-tuning of past existences and how, if we are open to it, we can utilize what has been. This is very exciting as it exposes to us what alignment of source can mean. Can you imagine world leaders putting this into practice to balance out the struggle for supremacy? What would become of all the conflicts based on religious differences if the religious zealots were to align with an aspect of themselves that could show them the futility of God through conflict? Imagine if we were all to use these *Input Lives* we have brought with us, how this would dramatically alter our way of thinking and acting out our lives. The more I feel this, the more I realize that we are indeed made up of a selection of experiences that have been put together to create what we are now and that this process even as we live never stops. It's like a cell that continues to divide itself creating another form of life.

We are not living out our past lives in our present life,
we are utilizing aspects of the past that will help us this time around.

On Saturday I went to a Sangeet, as part of an Indian wedding and the guests were encouraged to dress in Indian clothes. I went up to a shop in Newtown that sold such things and explained to the owner what I was doing and he showed me upstairs where there was a vast array of outfits. He brought out several things for my inspection but they all seemed a bit boring to me until I caught a glimpse of an outfit that was hanging up encased in a protective covering. It was a long gold tunic that went just below the calves. The collar was all embroidered and encrusted with little diamantes. There was a sleeveless overcoat that was the same length and it was all gold and red. There was a cream-colored pair of cotton dhoti pants as well.

"That's the one," I announced with a high level of certainty.

When I tried it on I felt like I had worn something similar before and couldn't help smiling in recognition. Diamante-encrusted satin slippers finished the ensemble and I was ready to party! Many people said that night how much I suited the outfit. I felt like saying that's because I wore clothes like this in some of my past lives.

Lifetimes are like clothes really, we put them on, we take them off, we store them in the wardrobe and we forget about them. They go out of fashion and are replaced with the new trends. At times we have to clear out the wardrobe as there is not enough room in there for some of life's issues. At times we must look at them and conclude *"Whatever was I thinking?"* We never get rid of them, we simply return them back to source and they are recycled for another time. We certainly are seasoned performers; it's like a giant catwalk and we are ourselves the designers. Another point to consider is that while we *are* living our present lives we are also creating our future lives by how we live now. It's that old biblical adage again *"What you sow, you shall reap."* Looking at the state of world affairs it's easy to see that we really haven't learned much from past reaping, though. Back then, though, people were not aware of the idea of collective consciousness and how it affected everything. Now we are aware and yet still get caught up into *"All for one and one for all"* mentality. Since we do all create our reality, it's obvious we all *want to* on some level experience what is going on in the world at this point. The extremities we are all faced with on every level is making us *think* differently about the roles we are all playing in life and what effect we are having not just on our own lives but the lives of others. So who can say who is right and who is wrong? That way of thinking may have worked in the past but we can't be so simplistic in our belief systems now. We beyond doubt have an effect on everybody around us and as we align more with the knowledge of that we have to be more attentive to our responses to each other. What we may have been able to brush off in the past comes back pretty quickly to us now as we face the fact that we are all manipulating life to evolve individually and collectively. It's a responsibility we've all come with at this time and the more we acknowledge that not only are we the players but we are the creators as well, the more we pay attention to the story!

We know everyone on this planet, and we are being influenced by everything that everybody does, thinks, and acts out. The way we respond to this is telling us something about ourselves. We can be in total control of this and therefore gauge more carefully the way we respond. We can get so caught up in our indignation about stuff that we often react in such a way where we are creating a vibration of negativity and this has an effect on our whole being by moving us *away* from our well-being. Yeah, some people do stupid things but do we really have to respond in the way that we do at times?

We have a choice.

The other night I went out for a quick meal with my best mate David. As we neared my home I noticed that some dickhead (I'm writing this as I felt it at the time so forgive the language) had parked their car halfway across one of my garages. It's a garage that I use for storage and so I wasn't putting my car in it and yet despite that I saw red. I could have had it towed away; I could have rung up and had them ticketed. I could have written a nasty note about them being such a dickhead to not see that they were halfway across my garage door. For about two minutes David and I stood there and thought of all the things we could do to *prove a point.* In the end I did nothing, I decided that I *had a choice.* I chose not to indulge in pettiness and let it be. Then I felt a bit righteous thinking how noble I was to let them get away with parking that way, as if I was doing them this big favor. Then I thought, *what the bleep am I doing?* I was allowing myself to be influenced by something that really was no big deal. I was upsetting my own personal equilibrium because I was deciding to be pissed off about something that didn't really matter to me. *I was proving a point that I was right and they were wrong.* It occurred to me then that it was *I who was being a dickhead.* Then I laughed and let it go. Maybe I had left my camels in front of their house in a past life and they had shit all over the road.

I suppose life is at times piles of shit on the road, and when we look at it we realize that most of the shit is our own. We seem to have an aversion to cleaning our act up when we feel that there is an injustice being done to us. And how very petty those injustices can be. You only have to read some of the social media comments people make when they get a bee in their bonnet. I guess everyone will be a dickhead at times. It's the response without having any sense of responsibility that gets me. It's not very dignified, but then dickheads usually don't have much dignity when they are like that. I find that because of the increase of the vibration that we are all facing, we seem to be confronting very rapidly the issues that we need to put to rest. My God, that's not as easy as it sounds, though, is it? I watch myself at times going round and round in circles knowing I am doing it, knowing what to do about it. I keep watching my own circus unfold before me as if I don't have any influence over it. See, even when you do know, you don't necessarily live it all the time! Having great intentions is all very well but when it comes to facing self and changing self, the information we need seems to come out of a manual from some dimension we don't have access to. Well, it seems like that anyway.

All of us are interconnected through all the lives that we live, and some of us keep following each other around life and after life. I imagine it like multicolored lines of light all floating around in consciousness, some intertwining, others separate.

Some of those lifelines are all tangled up as if they are strangling the very existence they are living, depleting themselves of the vital life force that allows us to create life without complication. We've all been there through our history, untying the knots of energy that we established endeavoring to allow once again the power of source to flow through us.

Looking at my own connection with my wife, Kay, it's easy to see that we must have had many shared lifetimes when I look at the awareness we have with each other and the intricacies of the deals we have made with each other this time around. We seem to be using Kay's health issues as great catalysts for advancement and this is enlightening as much as it has been challenging. When she had cancer she really took charge of the situation and carried on pretty much as usual, doing the best to look after the situation herself even though I was there to support her. It was as if there was a part of her that was saying she did not want to be supported. Very typical of Kay's personality, to feel that she is the only person that can support her and give her the answers. At times I felt like I was a bit player in her life's movie feeling and wanting to do more but having to stay in the sidelines. With the Alzheimer's it was completely different. I was plunged into a main role and it was impossible not to play the role. For the first time in her adult life she found herself in a position where she was not in control and never would be again. I had to step out from the sideline and read from a different script. As the years of caring for her unfolded I realized the script was not written at all but one that I had to write as her illness progressed. I do know of a life we had lived where she had cared for me and by doing so had neglected her own life. I know of another life where I had actually taken her life, and so in a way I was giving her life this time around by caring for her. This makes me think, what are we creating NOW for our future lives because of what we are experiencing together now? As her illness worsens I can see different levels of connection we are making on a human level but I can feel very powerfully our *SOUL* connection making itself felt in the silences we have when I am just sitting with her when she is not very cognitive. We all have so many ways of loving each other and speaking to each other.

We are involved in this journey because of the arrangements we have made to evolve. It is because of our soul travels through many lives that we have come to the place we have and have had to play it out in the way it has. Her illness and the roles I have had to play in her care is not some random act of life but an important deal that was made and is still being made as we keep writing the story. And that is what we all do, write the story of who we are. I'll finish this chapter with this quote from Tabaash.

You have only ever had one life;
you have just lived it in many bodies.

Chapter Fifteen

Down to the Very Bones

Our physical bodies are great receptacles. Our bodies hold onto all our emotions and they store away information, holding it quietly or at times not so quietly. When we don't pay attention to our lives our bodies have a way of unleashing a storm that can be mildly disruptive or extremely destructive. The sort of storm we create is entirely up to us.

I recently created a destructive storm and ended up spending two weeks in hospital and have a long clean up in front of me. The thing about storms is that regardless of their destructiveness they do clean things up and they change the landscape. As humans we need to clean things up too and sometimes need to wipe the landscape clean and start again.

I became conscious of the pain after a rather intense workout at the gym. It wasn't anything major, just a niggle in my upper left arm and a little at the back of my shoulder, I paid attention to it but thought little of it and relaxed my workouts in the hope things would ease up. At night the pain was worse and at times excruciating. Painkillers helped but there obviously was something wrong. I saw the physiotherapist at the gym and they worked away at the knotted muscle in the back of my shoulder and told me the pain I was still feeling in my arm was referred pain. I was given a piece of rubber to stretch out and told to press a hard ball into the knotted muscle. I did my best to convince myself that it was making a difference but I might as well have been scuba diving in the Sahara Desert for all the difference it made. I went to the doctor and he seemed to also think it was muscle related and so I didn't have any concern. At night the pain was worse and I would writhe in agony rubbing my arm in desperation. I don't know why I never insisted on getting an X-ray done. I was about to take a trip offshore to visit a mate of mine in San Diego and perhaps didn't want to do anything that might jeopardize my trip. Looking back now it's like I was setting myself up for some inevitable crash that seemed necessary to occur. And so I went on my trip to the US, and the pain got worse and I was popping painkillers to the point where the effects of them were useless. On the day before I was to come home I got my mate to take me to A&E in San Diego. The moment they heard pain in the arm they sent me for an ECG, and when that proved inconclusive to have an X-ray of my arm.

I sat there in the small cubicle hospital gown around me listening to the sounds of some woman screaming at the top of her lungs. I felt completely detached from my circumstances and surroundings and just quietly sat there waiting for the doctor to come with the results of the X-ray. Eventually it was a female registrar who came in and showed me the X-ray. She said that there was a seven-centimeter lesion of some sort on my upper arm bone and she announced in a very matter-of-fact way,

"It's probably cancer."

As she spoke those words I calmly stared back at her and this immense sense of peace flowed through my body and I knew it was spirit's way of telling me that it was not cancer.

We stared at each other like this for a moment and then she peered closely at me as if expecting me to break down into hysterical sobbing or something of the sort.

"Would you like to be left alone for a moment?" she asked me.

I replied that I was fine but if she wanted to go and attend to other things that was fine with me. She gave me an odd look and then started talking about MRI scans and the like.

"Look, I'm heading home tomorrow and I really prefer to deal with this back home so if I'm free to go now I'd like to," I said.

So with discharge pages in hand I made my way out the entrance to where my friend was waiting in his car and one of the first things I did was to ring my doctor in New Zealand and explain what was happening. It was pouring with rain and I was full of mixed emotions and pissed off that this was the way I had to spend my last full day away. I had been given some stronger painkillers so that at least was relieving some of the discomfort I was feeling. At that time I felt about as far away from my God nature that you could be, as I felt thrown into my human nature in a major way. I wasn't feeling numb or depressed or anything like that; in fact, I realized I wasn't actually feeling anything at all. What was happening was happening and I was doing what I had to do. I felt no attachment to what was going on in my arm, and maybe that was a good thing. If I had been perhaps I would have been more involved in the issue of it and therefore would have worried more. I didn't, though, but I also knew that I wasn't in some sort of denial either. Here was a situation, these were the facts to date, and this was the best way for the moment to deal with it. No point in getting hysterical about it.

Thinking about it now of course the part of me that was able to be objective had stepped in and was guiding my emotional response and physical reactions. It was a greater part of me that was aiding me in my time of need. This enforces my belief that we are all created with everything we need in life. It wasn't that I was consciously allowing this to happen but more that the greater part of me knew what to do and the weaker part of me simply stepped aside so that the greater could get on with the job. Perhaps as humans we get rather too involved in our situations to the point where it doesn't help the cause. Obviously it's important to pay attention in the way that is necessary but getting overtly emotional or overthinking is not going to keep things in perspective. My mate Leonard, whom I had gone over to see in the US, had a good outlook; he just stayed calm and said you have to do whatever is needed. I love you and I am here for you, he told me. He saw the bigger picture as well and told me that there were things that I had to sort out and that this was the time to do so. I laughed a bit, cried a bit, and hugged him a lot.

I had an email from Air New Zealand informing me that I had been upgraded to first class. It was rather bittersweet but at least I could fly home miserable in luxury! Actually, I wasn't miserable at all. I just felt very tired and wanted to get on with getting things sorted.

My darling friend Hetty Rodenburg picked me up at Wellington airport and whisked me home and then accompanied me to my doctor's office. An MRI scan was organized and I duly presented myself at the appointed time and for an hour lay in the confinement of the machine trying to meditate while it whirred and clunked and generally made a lot of noise. I was told to stay very still, which was hard as I had been positioned to lean slightly to my right, so though I wasn't in any great discomfort I did not feel like I was laying on some nice fluffy bouncy cloud. It was another process that I had to go through and I still maintained the detachment to the situation. At 2:30 the next day, that was a Wednesday, I had a call from my doctor telling me to get right down to his surgery, he didn't tell me anything, just told me to get right down. Driving down I didn't have any impending feelings of doom and gloom. I just wanted to know what was what and so at last I was going to have an answer. He had finished seeing patients for the day and so I was shown into his office the moment I arrived. Sitting in front of his computer he was looking at the scan of my arm. There was a dark mass in the middle of the bone and on the side what looked like a small bit of bone sticking up a bit.

It was then explained to me that what I had was something called osteomyelitis.

There was a chronic infection of the bone marrow and bone. The little bit of bone I saw was in fact just that, a small break in the bone that had been weakened by the infection. Within half an hour I was driving up to Wellington Hospital referral letter in hand and presented myself to A&E. Despite the fact that I had the letter I still had to wait an hour and a half before I was seen. The pain had kicked in big time and I was doubling over in agony. The room was packed with people who seemed to be mostly friends and family waiting. Some drunk hooker who had fallen and skinned her knee provided us all with a bit of light entertainment as she sauntered in and announced her predicament in florid vocal terms. And still I waited, wondering if I collapsed would I still be waiting? Finally I was called and a male nurse who was a Godsend escorted me to a room where I was made comfortable. In that first half hour I was basically stamped and labeled and x-rayed. I couldn't sit still as the pain was unbearable. I had texted my best mate David and within ten minutes he was up there by my side. I was given two shots of morphine but still the pain hadn't depleted. David told me afterward he didn't realize how much pain I actually was in until he saw how much morphine was needed to settle things down. He took a lovely pic of me in agony; my arm has a blue arrow drawn onto it by the staff pointing to the area that was damaged or in my way of thinking pointing to where the pain was! I'm pointing to my arm, the expression on my face said it all. After a while I settled into a weird sort of stupor where time ceased to exist. I gauged everything by what they were doing to me. Needle in arm moment, having to pee moment, David helping me into a hospital gown moment, and so it went on. Then suddenly I wasn't in A&E anymore but in a bed in a ward, I don't even recall getting there. People were fussing around me and I could hear some guy in the next room and another patient talking loudly a whole lot of shit. Then David wasn't there like he had disappeared or something and I suddenly became more settled and I saw I was attached to a machine that when I pressed a button it would feed morphine into my system every five minutes, which probably accounts for David vanishing as I went into a sort of no-time zone. He no doubt had made his farewells but I have no recollection of that at all. Body didn't like the morphine, though, and it was making me feel sick and wanting to retch so they changed the meds and things became easier. I slept a surface sleep as too much was going on in me and around me to go deep, and besides the nurses kept waking me up often to take my blood pressure. I was nil by mouth as I was to go into surgery in the morning. Food was a foreign object to me at that point; just give me the drugs to keep the pain at bay. Spirit was with me though; I could feel them just there on the surface of the whole experience somehow monitoring everything and me. It made me feel like I knew I was in good hands, the greatest hands that could carry you in fact.

The night blended into the early day and daylight brought me being wheeled into surgery. Porters, hospital corridors all blank and gray walls, no glimpse of a world outside. You felt like you were being swallowed up in the blankness of it all. Suddenly a small room like an antichamber and a nurse in gown and surgical headgear asking me what my name was and what my birthday was. Others like her, surgical clones buzzing around like medical insects. Then being wheeled into theater, seeing the narrow surgical table and pushing myself across. Green surgical sheets being positioned, the medical insects hovering around positioning themselves. I felt like I was their prey as they waited to pounce once I was unconscious. The anesthetist talking somewhere above my head telling me to count, me knowing I would not get to one before I was temporarily shut off from life like a switch being flicked off.

I awoke who knows when, thinking I had been dreaming something silly or stupid but didn't know what. Looking down on my arm I wasn't distressed to see that it was almost bright red knowing that it was simply a disinfectant that they had painted on me. My arm was tight and swollen and there was a new pain, a better pain than before. To me it was the pain of getting better and healing up fast. I wasn't hooked up to the automatic drug feed anymore as any pain relief was given me orally from there on. Once I got back to the ward I wanted to be mobile and so got up and wandered around my surroundings. I met a young guy who was also wandering around and he had a bandage around his leg.

"What are you in for?" he asked like it was a familiar statement for him to make.

I explained about my arm and then to be polite asked about his leg.

"I got shot," he replied proudly like it was the crown achievement of his life so far.

He wore a stupid grin on his face and wandered around talking at the top of his voice never for a moment considering other people's predicaments or the fact he was actually in a hospital. He seemed to be treating his experience like he was in some hotel and could do what he wanted. He even had his girlfriend sleep on a mattress on the floor beside his bed. All through the night they would be talking and at about 2 in the morning I had enough and called the nurse. She said that the other nurses were too frightened to speak to him and if they called security he might cause trouble. So what they did was basically nothing. The lady who was behind the curtain in the bed next to me was moaning and talking in her sleep. She kept repeating in a resigned but frustrated voice, "Oh come on ..."

I later found out that she had been there for four months. She had gone in for a hip replacement and it had become infected. I'd be saying more than "Oh come on" if I had been there for that long. That afternoon the nurses came in and told her that they were moving her into her own room but she declined. My ears pricked up and I cheekily said that I wouldn't mind moving into my own room. I didn't think for a moment that they had paid me any attention and so to my immense surprise and relief, about ten minutes later a nurse came back telling me that they were moving me. So within minutes I was ensconced in my own room with a view over the city and surrounding hills. It was bliss; I could even close the door and shut out all the other hospital noises around me. As they settled me in I asked the nurse to open the secure drawer so I could get something out of my wallet. When the drawer was opened, there was no wallet and I realized I had in my pain/morphine state when I first arrived omitted to lock it away and it had been stolen. I had a pretty good idea of whom or whose opportunist's mates had done the deed but I could pretty well say good-bye to it and its contents. I rang up the bank straight away to cancel cards and was relieved to find that nothing was used. So they got the cash that was in there and I had a little meditation on it later and gifted it to whoever took it. I'd rather be living the life I have with all its opportunities than the life they were living in all its survival. My choices were unlimited and theirs were not.

About a day later when David and I were taking a stroll down the long wide corridor we found ourselves walking at a distance from Mr. Shot In The Leg. I stared intensely at his back and projected forgiveness of him and whoever of his mates had taken the wallet. He never turned fully around but I could feel his discomfort and he kept looking side to side nervously, and then I let it go.

On the first day of being in my own room a nurse of Irish descent came in and there seemed to be an automatic rapport between the two of us. I could feel she was more than just a person; she had soul.

"What's your name?" she asked when we first met.

I don't know why but she brought out the mischief in me.

"Cyril Bottomley-Slythe," I announced.

She stared at me not cracking a smile and then asked where I lived.

"The ninth planet of the sixth universe of the fourth dimension," I announced with a straight face.

She rolled her eyes heavenward, knowing we were going to get on just fine.

The next day after she had administered to my needs she asked me what I did for a job and so I told her and asked her if she knew what that was. She replied that, yes, she did and that in fact she herself read auras. Then she proceeded to ask me if I was left-handed, to which I replied in the affirmative. She told me that my left hand was holding onto all this gray matter and that I had to let it go and hold onto the light instead. We had a conversation for about fifteen minutes and I recall giving her some information she needed to hear but can't recall what it was. I thanked her and told her that what she had said to me made a great deal of sense and would help me. I never saw her again. It's like she had to be there for a couple of days as some sort of messenger for me, and perhaps me for her. Again, here were two souls thrown together in those circumstances serving each other. And we both recognized that's what we were doing and because of that we were able to make good use of the information we both received.

I decided to use the time in hospital as my own spiritual retreat. Apart from the time I had my visitors and when the nurses were giving me my meds I was alone and I savored the opportunity to make good use of what I had created here. So to begin with, what in fact had I created here? I had an infection so something was *festering* inside me. This had created *pain* so apart from the physical pain there was other pain I was not facing. I had to be *quiet and still and rest* so there was disquiet in my life and I was not standing still or at peace. I therefore created a situation and an environment that would enable me to face what I needed to face. I had to step away from my human world for a moment and let my soul do the driving. It was like the last six years of my life had now emotionally erupted in my arm, as evidently I could no longer carry what I had been carrying. I looked back at the last seven months and was appalled that I was actually a mess.

The day I drove home after leaving Kay at the care home I felt relieved and almost elated. The last two years had been particularly arduous and though I settled into the routines of caring for someone with Alzheimer's it was taking its toll on me. I wasn't allowed to go and see her for the first two weeks of her moving there, a positive thing for both of us. Her to get used to her new environments and routines, me to accustom myself to the fact that after almost forty years of being together it was over. I thought it would be harder for me than for her as I knew that when I wasn't there she really had no sense of my existence.

It didn't seem hard for me though. As I walked into the house for the first time knowing she would never live there again I felt no overwhelming emotions of any sort. No sadness, no tears, just a sort of blank. I sat for a moment wondering if I was suppressing my emotions but as hard as I tried I could not find them. I made dinner and sat at the table staring at the space in front of me where she would normally sit. The only thing I noticed was that the placemat that we usually kept on the table, well, she had actually put hers away as if she knew she wasn't going to use it again. Even then I didn't feel any particular strong emotions. I went to bed and stared at the empty space beside me. I didn't feel good or bad that she wasn't there anymore. It was like she had always been there but had never been there, like she was in a way still there. I went to sleep and slept really well.

I kicked into practical mode and I didn't change anything. The routines around Kay's care were no longer my responsibility in an emotional and physical way therefore relieving me of that. I found that I was creating situations that would keep me away from the house and in the back of my mind I knew I was doing it but didn't want to see that. Being at home wasn't about the fact that Kay wasn't there, it was about the fact that I was there and I didn't want to face that. I did everything I normally did, I didn't shift my routines in any way. I wasn't exactly avoiding myself but more I was avoiding what life was now like without Kay. I felt so odd like a switch that had abruptly been switched off after all those years. She was there, and I was looking after her and adapting my life to doing that and in within a moment she wasn't there and I had to look after myself.

The two weeks passed and I was allowed to go and see her. And so what did I do?

I went to see her every day. I created another routine that made me reliant on looking after her in some way. She had settled well into her new environment and was making it more her life and here I was carrying on with the old life by being there too much. She still knew me and her smile would light up when she saw me. After a while I realized I wanted that smile, I wanted her to look at me with love, but I wanted it for myself. I knew that when I finished my visit with her she had no sense at all of my existence. I would leave and be full of her existence still and also with the knowledge that it would never be the same again and of course gradually get worse as her condition deteriorated. I was seeing her more for me than I was for her. It was hard to let go of the old routines but it was also harder to come to terms with the fact that we were no longer a day-by-day part of each other's lives. When you are with someone for so many decades you establish what I will call the "code" of the relationship and I believe that all couples create their own personal code that is as unique to them as the relationship is.

The last six years with Kay were pretty intense as I settled into the routines that best served her and the care that she needed. I pretty well shut down my own life in order to look after her and that's something I would do again in a flash. And so after so many years doing that there I was overnight in a position where I didn't need to do it anymore. I was losing sight of myself and routinely carried on with work and the gym but I had no sense of myself and no sense of what was in front of me. I could feel the stress and strain of looking after Kay still with me. A while back I had started to smoke again. It was one or two now and then, or when I felt the need to "relax," so to speak. I hated doing it, I knew my body didn't want it but I still kept at it. One or two started to become five or six until it was getting up to ten a day. I never smoked at home or even around outside. I would get in the car rain or shine and drive up the hill to this little park and smoke there. Even when it was pouring with rain I would drive up there and try to keep dry by standing under the cover of a tree and that was usually useless as I would be dodging raindrops between branches. I would never smoke in my car ever. I started to create places where I would go and smoke at certain parts of the day. The little park in the morning, a car park near a beach that was on the way to see Kay, I would stop on the way for a smoke and then on the way back. It was crazy and I knew it but I was so caught up into it that it was hard to stop.

The routines of life continued and I thought I was coping and moving on with life. A heaviness had descended upon me, though, and I could not shake it. I did not feel depressed but the heaviness prevailed and inevitably I just put it down to adjusting to my new circumstances. I obviously wasn't listening to the "whispers of life," as Tabaash so succinctly puts it. I made the decision to pack up all of Kay's things and so went into the practical efforts of doing that. I put in a box all the things that I wanted to keep; the jewelry went into a safe and her earrings I still kept in an oak box on the dresser, partly because I wanted them there, partly because I didn't know what to do with about fifty pairs of clip-on earrings! While I was doing this, I felt nothing as I folded up jumpers and dresses and coats that were so familiar to me. Box after box of her life was being packed away, and with the knowledge that she had been so fastidious about the care of her clothes I took extra care to fold things properly and even put tissue paper between delicate things even in the knowledge that most were going to a charity shop.

As I completed the packing of the clothes I turned to the shoes. Boots, court shoes, casual and everyday ones she used to wear in the garden, they were all there hanging on the shoe racks that she had installed. Into the boxes they all went and again I felt detached from the whole process until I came across one pair of beautiful black velvet dress shoes that she really had so loved and had looked so elegant in when she wore them. I held them to my heart and sat on the floor and wept over those shoes, such a simple thing.

I thought that by doing all these things I was dealing with my loss, but I kept getting a message in my head that I needed to see someone and talk. My dear friend Hetty Rodenburg is the first person who came into my head. She practiced medicine in several areas over the years but invariably turned to counseling and supporting people. She was a good friend of Elisabeth Kubler-Ross, the pioneer of modern-day hospice care, and facilitated her workshops. She understood the processes of grief, and here I was obviously grieving but internalizing and I needed help. So I went and saw Hetty a couple of times and talked with her and it helped enormously! After my first session with her I felt very light and of course drove down to the beach and had a celebratory smoke! When she listened to me talking, there was a lot that was brought up from my youth and the situations I had gone through. I covered all of this in my book *Don't Change the Channel* so won't repeat myself here. Anyway, after hearing this and the stuff that I had been going through with Kay, Hetty said:

"Blair, I'm surprised that you haven't had cancer after all you have been through!"

I was surprised as much as she was but brushed that aside. Of course when she recently visited me in hospital recently I brought up what she had said and suggested that perhaps she was being a bit prophetic! The energy was obviously there and it was creeping out little by little. It was all festering inside of me, though, and I wasn't dealing with what I should be dealing with. I plummeted into not feeling again, I went through the motions of my everyday life, I worked, I went to the gym, I saw Kay, I lived but I wasn't living. I had no sense of a future for myself and that didn't seem to bother me at all as I just thought I was being in the present. And then, bang, it all came out in one big mother of an infection and I brought myself down.

When it happened I remember thinking something Tabaash has spoken of many times over the years:

"In order to be something, you have to know what it is to be nothing."

So, this was obviously one of those nothing times for me and from that vantage point I had to make some fundamental changes in my life to relieve me of what was festering inside of me and to establish a new contract with myself from that point onward. David would come every day bearing love, friendship, fruit, prunes, and his magnetic mattress. He would wrap the pillow bit around my arm and set it for the ultimate setting and I would lie there feeling the magnetic waves of energy pulsing through my body. One night while he was doing this the nurse came in to give me the antibiotics through the IV. It was a process of about half an hour as the machine pumped the drug into me. She looked at the silver mat wrapped around my arm but said nothing. And so I lay there, holistic healing doing what it needed to on my left and the IV antibiotic orthodox doing what it needed to do on the right. And I felt my beliefs were somewhere in the middle directing the whole show. Hariata, a beloved friend who so cared for Kay in those last months at home, came and brought me coffee and a cheese scone and books and her joy; she was sunlight in the room.

I Googled meditations for bone infections and was presented with a plethora of choices. I lay back and listened to guided meditations and sounds and music all feeding new energy to my arm and no doubt the rest of me that couldn't help but be a part of it as well. At night I listened to the sounds of rain and thunderstorms on my IPad and once a nurse popped her head in the door thinking there was a storm outside; after that I made sure I used my earphones! My brain was so full of "I AM GOD" that there was hardly any room for other thoughts. I became aware of myself doing a big unwind and realized as it was happening how much I must have been wound up. My vanity took a hit as I gazed in the mirror and saw how much the workouts at the gym were fast fading. I had lost about three kilos in muscle and though my body looked healthy I mourned the loss of my biceps and shoulders!

You're going back to basics, my lad, I thought to myself looking at my left arm and shoulder, the skin looking like some shriveled old balloon. I began to feel like I was participating in my life once again and could engage once more in feeling. I had no idea what was going on in the world as I read no newspapers or watched any television. It didn't matter as this experience was my world and there was enough news in that to satisfy anyone! I was allowed out on leave from the hospital as long as I was back for my meds so I took full advantage of that. First thing I did was get a haircut, and then I had to catch up on mail and business stuff. I chose not to go and see Kay while I was on leave; it didn't seem to be the thing to do. I went home and made sure everything was tickety-boo there and then made my way back to the hospital. It felt rather odd being a part of the world again and then having to go back to the hospital environment. There was really no need for me to get back into "hospital scrubs" and get into bed but it seemed the appropriate thing to. This routine carried into the second week there and I was starting to get the feeling of energy changes and the eagerness to get back home and get back into this new life that I was creating. The surgeon came and chatted with me and said they were still considering putting a titanium rod in my arm, but they had to wait until the infection had gone down more. Actually, I suspected it was because one of their colleagues who was on my case was away in Australia on holiday and they were waiting for him to get back before they made their decision.

I could feel the tide of change, though, knowing I was moving into the next level of this experience. On the late afternoon of the Saturday of the second week I was in there, this officious nurse came in and announced that they were moving me out of my room and into a mixed ward across the hallway.

"Oh what!" I announced rather ungraciously.

I could suddenly feel myself getting enormously pissed off at this news and watched as other staff came and organized my departure. I knew I was being an ass about it but I couldn't help feel put out that they were putting me out! One of the younger nurses who could sense what I was feeling tried to jolly me along by announcing that at least I had a corner next to the window with a view. I looked out the window and saw that the view was looking across at another part of the hospital where all the elevators were. There were big windows looking down to my side giving everyone a great view of anyone who wanted to be viewed. I sat down on the bed feeling like a grumpy child. My ward inmates were three elderly men whom by the looks of them were in various stages of demise. Of course I created that the one next to my part of the room was the one who moaned and sighed and was unsettled all night. It was not lost on me that "I" was the one who was moaning and sighing and feeling unsettled due to the change of room circumstances. I couldn't imagine how I was going to get on in this environment if I was here longer. I seemed to have thrown the God in me out with the bedpans and so my human nature was having one big sulk and the implications of this were interesting. I went and bought a television card so I could watch TV. Visually it all worked but I couldn't hear a thing. When the technician finally did come, the program I had wanted to watch was finished. I couldn't turn the main light off in the ward as it would plunge everybody into darkness and so had to wait until the nurses thought it was "bedtime" and time to turn out the light. The guy next to me seemed to need constant attention by the staff through the night and of course they would all talk at the tops of their voices. What ever happened to hushed voices in the hospital so you don't disturb the patients?

It seemed to me that they were doing all they could to disturb the patients, or in my case TRY my patience!

Once I decided to accept my fate and stop my sulk things improved. The lights went out. The man next door went to sleep, the staff stopped talking, and I felt peaceful. I was still pissed off, though, that I had forked out sixteen bucks to use the television that I didn't want to watch now. They had given me some credit to compensate but given the chance that I might go home the next day I wasn't going to benefit from that! I plugged myself into my rain and thunder music and allowed it to calm my inner storm and drifted off into a light sleep feeling like I was in a suspended place and ready to take the next step.

Well, that happened pretty quickly the next morning as the consultants arrived fairly early informing me that I was able to go home and as long as all the paperwork was done discharging me I could go. Well, I wasn't going to hang around anymore; the moment they left I bounced (carefully) out of bed and had a shave and shower and got dressed. I had texted David and he was there helping me pack up and by 10 a.m. I was out of that place and ready to be back in the world. I wasn't really sure what I was feeling at that time, perhaps just relief to get out of the hospital and back into life. I knew, though, that I had evolved in many ways and that I now had to change my life to fit in with how I had evolved. David drove me back to my place and then we went out to lunch.

Doing that was a complete assault to my senses, and I probably shouldn't have done it but rather stayed at home and rested. I argued to myself that's what I had been doing for the last two weeks and I wanted to get out and about again.

As we walked into the crowded café people gave me a wide berth and I didn't wonder why, considering my appearance. My left damaged arm was incased in this plastic armor to protect the bone, as it was very fragile. I had an IV drip in me feeding me 24/7 antibiotics that, of course, I had to carry around with me. It was no easy task trying to camouflage the plastic bottle that I named Baxter because that was the name on the bottle so it seemed obvious! There was no hiding a small portion of the thin plastic tubing that was going from Baxter into me and I could see the curious glances of people as they observed my situation. I must have been a dreadful sight as I had lost about four kilos and was also quite pale. I wasn't on death's door, though I was giving a good imitation.

I found trying to make conversation hard and the noise around me was exhausting me and I made the effort and ate my food and drank my coffee but I really wanted to go home and lay down.

My flat mate Kieran had decided to move out and be with his new girlfriend, a move I welcomed as I just wanted to be on my own, in my own space and have peace. Having someone around me at that time seemed too demanding on my senses as they were in a state of flux as I obviously was settling into a new pattern and a new energy. I really only wanted to see and spend time with David as he was the shoulder for me to lean on and he instinctively knew how to be there for me but also when not to be there.

And so I settled into my post-hospital routine. Sleeping became a chore as I could really only lay on my back since my left arm was still incapacitated and my right one had the IV in it. I'm a side sleeper and I summoned every meditation, thought, etc., I could muster to assist me. I discovered on YouTube meditations for bone infections and of course instantly used those. Many were annoying "guided ones."

I say annoying for the reasons that the voice of the person was not conducive for a meditation and made me far from relaxed and the other because some decided to embrace a whispery ethereal spiritual voice which made me want to laugh out loud or feel I wanted to punch them!

Finally I hit upon one which was all based on binaural beats, which are specific sounds that stimulated something in my brain waves to promote the healing of my bones. The ancient Taoists saw the human skeleton as an antenna channeling the source energy to sustain life and also serving as a communicative medium for sending energy frequencies through the body's meridians and vital organs. So basically they developed sounds that activated the "Chi" in the body to promote well-being through the whole being. I would lie there on my back feeling the vibrations of the sounds penetrating my brain and envision the energy healing my arm and any other bone that may have needed it! I would eventually fall asleep while the vibrations were still "sounding" and awaken a couple of hours later wondering where the bleep was that sound coming from. I also used my rain and storm sounds but after a while that started to irritate me and so I gave up the subliminal irrigation. I was having night sweats due to the infection and would wake up saturated and sulfuric smelling. This must have been something to do with the antibiotics I was on and it was not very pleasant. As the infection decreased so did the sweats. I have great sympathy for menopausal persons!

If anything I have a very determined nature and it's this determination that saw me through that first week and allowed me to create some excellent routines. I couldn't work and the antibiotics I was on were making my head fuzzy and my body tired. David lent me the energy pads and I used them three times a day combining its use with meditation. I invested in an excellent juicer and drank three large glasses of vegetable juice a day. I had Googled what vitamins were important for infections and high antibiotic use and vitamin K was suggested to help. There was some irony in that as emotionally the issue with my arm was chiefly to do with my wife, Kay, and the anxiety created due to her care and yet here I was being told take more vitamin K! Life's a funny old chestnut sometimes!

Every morning a district nurse would come in and change Baxter and weekly take my bloods and check my dressing. The first nurse who came was supposed to be the regular but on the first day she came to me she had slipped on her back after seeing her first client and hit her head. When she got to me I could see she was a bit wobbly but she rallied through. She ended up having to take time off due to concussion, the poor love! Can't say enough about the dedication and expertise of these nurses, they are gems. Once they had finished administering to me I would wrap the energy mat around my arm and have a meditation while communing with my higher self. I would always ask if it would heal my arm and it set to the task immediately. It told me when I asked that it was raising the vibrations of the cells that made up my bone and raising them to meet the equivalent energy from source. You could say that they are meeting halfway, he told me. As he explained I could see it in my mind as energy swirled to meet and as they did I was aware of the light energy turning into molecules and then settling into the shape of my new bone! Then in a very matter-of-fact way and I could not help notice with a grin on his face, higher self picked up the new bone and placed it into my left upper arm with a satisfying click!

I can't tell you enough how different I felt. Whatever I had been carrying around with me, I truly felt like it was put down and I was so filled with determination to ensure that not only would I never do that again to myself but as I moved forward I was going to progress in my life to the greatest of all my Mind, Body, and Spirit abilities. I thought about the teachings of Tabaash and the teachings of others I had gathered over the years. As always the one I kept resonating with was that we are GOD. If we are GOD, then we have the power to create and to change, and subsequently to move away from the adverse situations that we create.

Regardless of the negativity we are experiencing
we are still progressing.

It is the idea of this progression that I hold onto and I become very aware of my thinking so as not to engage in thoughts that would bring me down. Being more conscious of my thoughts as a vibration makes me attentive to my ideas and how I am attending to myself as the *creator of my life.* If I find myself slipping into some thought that would not serve me I would automatically think that *I KNOW THAT I AM GOD.* The moment I do that I feel a peace and an alignment back to source and back to conscious thought. Doing this also makes me aware of how easy it is for our thinking to stray into territory that will upset our energy. As an observer of this it was easier to feel detached from this straying and the emotions you would feel as a participant. I simply choose *NOT* to participate; hence, I have no emotional involvement and that keeps me free of undesired results.

As the days progressed I set up an excellent routine that satisfied every aspect of myself. One thing I've learned about myself in the almost fifty-seven years of life is that once I get into something that I have to change, I hurl myself onto it with everything I have and there is no looking back.

People who live in the past have no sense of a future.

I wanted to get back into work but I found I didn't have the mental energy to do so. The antibiotics were making me so tired by the middle of the day that I found myself having little Nana naps in the middle of the day. Still in recovery mode I had to be careful not to carry on as if nothing had happened. I went back to the gym looking all wired up with plastic tubing and plastic armor to protect my arm. I had lost quite a bit of weight and looked a bit pale. People either looked at me with great concern or gave me a wide berth, probably because they didn't want to be in proximity to me when I would obviously from their observations drop dead at their feet! Within a week of gentle exercise, I could feel my body getting back to strength and once I had the IV out, I got into training the right side of my body; the left would simply have to catch up! I was surprised how much there was of the pik line in me when they finally did take it out. I sat there expecting to feel strange movements through my veins and was surprised when the nurse held up this LONG tube of plastic that had been a house guest so to speak inside of me for the last month. Needless to say, I had no sense of attachment to it and bid a happy farewell to that and of course Baxter with no sense of sentimentality whatsoever!

When I first received the letter from the hospital about out-patient follow-up appointments I was irked somewhat to read that I had to present myself to the Infectious Diseases Clinic at Wellington Hospital. I pictured myself at the appointed date making a furtive appearance in the hope that no one would recognize me. I imagined a giant sign in enormous bright letters with giant spotlights glaring down at the people who had to make their way to the clinic. In fact, when I arrived there wasn't really such a clinic at all but it was a general clinic for all sorts of things.

I presented myself at reception and dutifully handed over my appointment letter and hoped that the receptionist would not announce at the top of his voice: "The Infectious Diseases Clinic is to the right," given the place was full of people.

Instead I was told to take a seat in the area on the right where the red chairs were. I looked around and noted that all the other chairs in the other areas were a sort of pale gray. Was this a subtle way of letting people know that the red chair people were contagious? I was also told not to take a number and that made no sense to me so I just sat down and behaved myself. As others came and sat down I glanced furtively at them wondering how infectious they were as I moved myself across to the other side of the room. I also noticed that they all went over to a little machine and took a number. What was that all about? Did it mean that I was more infectious than them or perhaps they were far more infected than myself? I moved a little further away. We all sat there in silence, no doubt wondering what sort of ailment we all had. I felt like going up to them and saying,

"Hello, what sort of infectious disease brought you here today? Isn't this fun!"

It transpired that the seating area was also where people who were to have blood tests had to go, hence take a number. In fact, one by one they all were called, leaving me sitting there feeling very conspicuous as if I must have been the only one with a chronic bone infection. There was one man, though, an older man, and at his feet was a Styrofoam container of not unreasonable size. I couldn't fathom for the life of me what it could have contained. Perhaps some diseased part of him had fallen off and he had been given the container in the event if this was to happen. He was called before me and he picked up the container and was gone simply ages. When he returned he was without the container but he looked quite cheerful so it must have been good news.

The weeks went by and I felt healthier and more focused than I had for such a long time. Facing up to making changes is one thing and making the changes is another but I made sure I embraced the new ways with a very focused and disciplined manner. It wasn't a hardship as I simply followed the rules of feeding one's mind, body, spirit. I listened to what the higher part of me was saying and I followed my thoughts around so as not to engage in ones that took me off course.

I made sure that I fed my body the appropriate nutrition for my situation. I used the energy mat three times a day and during the time I used it I also meditated.

I listened, and I observed, I followed through with the ideas that came to me and I sat in deep silence that gave me the state of being that GOD exists in. I realized that even after Kay had gone into the home I still had held onto my own reliance on her in my life and I knew that our life together was over now and I let that reliance go. The love I felt for her was so deep and when I felt it I could feel how it had been forged through the many lives that we must have had together. It is as profound as it is simple.

When we embark on a road of self-development through our spirituality we can often be under the misconception that by doing so everything will be all right and negative experience will never again touch our lives. Being spiritual doesn't stop the pain or the problems. It doesn't mean we will never suffer loss or grief or have issues that we have to deal with. As we do pay more attention to who we are in the "God Way" we begin to see how we can navigate through life with a more defined way of thinking and participating. This engages us with more productive ways of responding to adverse situations. Being GOD never takes our issues away; it shows us how to manage them better. In fact, it brings out the strength of our human nature so that we can practice these strengths. After all, we are Gods in bodies and we are on a planet that gives us the opportunity to live the human nature we all encompass.

I knew I was in pain, I didn't know how bad the pain was. Never prone to hysterics and catharsis of any sort I simply got on with what I felt I should do, thinking I was coping well with all that had gone down. And the thing was, I was coping well but didn't realize that there was also a need for me to ensure that I wasn't burying the hurt inside. In retrospect here are some points I have considered that I would have done differently. I've written them as a list; if you need to use them, they may be of use to you.

1. Don't do it all alone.

No one ever needs to bear the burden in a manner where it weighs heavily upon them. There is *ALWAYS* someone or something that can help you. You don't need to be a hero.

2. Cry when you need to.

It helps, it's nature's way of releasing stress. Crying is strength and a way of healing your hurt as well.

3. Don't think your issues are things you have to see through.

See them all as a part of your life and you are simply involved in them in this way.

4. Hang out with the people you love.

You love them because they are there for you and you are not a burden to them. Have fun with them as well as share with them how it is for you.

5. Take a break.

Get away from it all in the way you can. It makes you feel real. And don't think there's no point because you have to go back to your issues again. There is always a point to stepping away for a moment and catching your breath.

6. Get outside.

There is so much beauty around us all the time. It's often our own front door. Breathe the air, walk the paths in the park, and sit by the ocean. Feel the sun on your face and let the wind toss you around for a moment. Lean against a tree and marvel at the way life is speaking to us by everything that is natural. It also reminds us that we are bigger than our problems and it's that bigger part that can carry us through.

I know there is more I can add on the list but that will do for now. We give ourselves chances all the time to advance our position in life. At times those chances *are* our adverse circumstances. It's our responses to those circumstances that will define what the outcome will be. Two things that I carry with me are that I could have lost my arm had I not had gone to hospital when I did. And the other is that when I felt the pain get worse, I didn't do anything about it straight away.

My authentic self was warning me and I didn't listen.

I am listening now and for the rest of this life that is what I will do.

Chapter Sixteen
Inner Worlds

Just because it's your imagination doesn't make it any less real.
—*Dumbledore*

Embracing your journey into the world of soul is embracing the most enriching of experiences. It is quite simply if you excuse the pun, *"Out of This World."* Out of this world and into other worlds that we have access to. Worlds that agitate our minds to think beyond the human nature, worlds that fill our bodies with delicious sensations that expand the perception of what we can feel. Worlds that show us that beyond the ideas and rituals of life that most of us are accustomed there are places within our own being that not only are real but we can use the energy of this reality to enhance the world we now live in. As we unfold more of our authentic self it is these very worlds I speak of that we begin to access. One thing I am very clear about is that if you are completely involved in life without any sense of spirit then the vibrations of your mind and body will regulate your life. Your mind and body will establish its own creed that you will live by and as a result of that belief you create a reality that you deem to be the essential way of living therefore you will limit the worlds that are put there.

You live by the rules dictated by your beliefs.

Most people live a limited human existence; I've done it myself. Living in that existence is not wrong, but it has its restrictions and I think because of that we are often left feeling that we have so much more to gain and access and yet the world we live in simply doesn't seem to offer up the ability to "*fulfill our wildest dreams.*"

Our human nature will only take us so far.

By delving into our spiritual nature we are exposing our human nature to our soul. That in turn enhances our human nature by introducing the worlds that the soul has access to. Those worlds are full of infinite possibilities that can only but augment the human world for the better should we consciously choose to access these energies. One only has to experience the visual symphony of art through the ages to see that many of those artists were indeed tapping into a level of conscious thinking that went beyond the human nature. Many have spoken of inspiration through dreams and there are those who literally spoke of visions they received which invariably became great works of art or literature. Child art prodigy Akiane Kramarik, who is now seventeen, spoke of dreams and visions of heaven. At four years old she experienced visions of different dimensions and she expressed these through art. Her parents realized that she was having supernatural encounters with God. Colton Burpo, whose spiritual experiences as a child inspired the book and film *Heaven Is Real*, recognized Akiane's portrait of Jesus as the closest representation of the Savior that he had witnessed in his visions.

When I made the decision to write my first book, *Don't Change the Channel*, I was in Christchurch, New Zealand, taking a walk through beautiful Hagley Park. I told spirit that I was going to write the book and asked for a good title. Without any delay I received the answer in my head and promptly burst out laughing. I found it hard thinking of a title for this book, playing around with all sorts of rather trivial concepts, and then asked spirit again and they did not disappoint me and also showed me the benefits of having a catchy title.

I find it not only thrilling but rather comforting to know that we have all these other layers of consciousness that are available to us. The more that we as individuals become alive to our great source potential, the more that these layers of consciousness open up to us and *they* become alive.

I have had some pretty astonishing meditations over the years that have exposed me to the unlimitedness of life beyond our human ideas. Some have filled me with such joy and peace while others took me so far away beyond my human self that it took a while to come back to earth, so to speak. When I got out of the hospital after my surgery I was determined to use my recovery time at home to do as much spiritually to assist my healing. As I mentioned earlier I would use the energy pad three times a day and would use this time to meditate. While I was having my morning meditation I found myself transported into a place that was one of those other worlds. It was as real to me as if I was actually physically in the state of consciousness I found myself in. I could smell, feel, observe, and participate as if I was actually using my physical senses.

I was sitting quietly in an open veranda that was all stone. Before me was a small square of lawn with a fountain in the middle. After observing for a moment I noticed in the distance in front of me an entrance and I knew I wanted to make my way to it. I stood up and walked to the left following the veranda. Even though I knew that I was sitting in my chair at home having a meditation I had the sensation that I was moving. I came to the entrance and saw that there was an iron gate and it was open. I walked out and there were many steps that went down to a path that went to the left and right. I stood for a moment and could see huge snowcapped mountains towering before me. There were trees and bushes but I was not aware of any flowers or wildlife of any sort and I could not hear any birdsong. I put out a thought about what I should do and the answer "stand still and observe" came to me. And so that's exactly what I did, soaking up the beauty that was all around me. I was then aware of the presence of energy to my left and I could see a human form that was enclosed in light; in fact, it was totally emanating light. I had no sense of this being as male or female. The being gestured for me to follow them and we walked a short distance to the left to a small gazebo. I walked into the gazebo and sat down on a cushioned bench on the right. As I sat the being placed its hands on either side of my head and a surge of energy went through my body. I felt my damaged arm receiving this energy and it felt like the energy was literally rippling under my skin such was the sensation. I then felt myself expand and I could see my body sitting but also the whole area outside of where I was sitting. The mountains were massive around me and a large complex made up of many buildings that were all joined to give the impression of one huge edifice was built out of the mountain itself. It felt Chinese then Indian then Japanese.

As I saw all of this the thought "*This is your place of learning*" came to me and with that thought the meditation ended. For the rest of that day I walked around feeling connected to the energy of the place that I had gone to. Each time I was aware of the energy I could feel myself smiling in the joy of the connection. I even carried the very scent of the clear mountain air and the huge pine trees that seemed to be a prominent feature. Every day after that I tried to go back there but I could not make the connection so perhaps it was not needed. And then two days later within two minutes of starting my meditation I was there. This time I was standing in what I will call a lookout or observation platform. The floor and walls were stone and the roof was of wood. I was standing there taking in the view when a man appeared behind me. He was short and had long white hair tied back into a ponytail. He wore pants that were quite wide and a top that was like a short jacket but it was tied with a sash. His clothes were yellow and orange, and he and his clothes seemed to shimmer with the radiance of source. The wisdom he exuded was evident and his face was smooth and ageless though I knew he was not young. He told me to call him Master Jay Sai.

He started to walk and made for me to follow him. I looked down and realized I was clad in plain white pants and jacket that were very soft to the touch. I followed him down a path and past the gazebo where I had my energy experience previously. We walked on a little till we came to an enormous door that seemed to be a part of the mountain itself. In fact, it seemed that whatever was behind those doors was actually carved into the very mountain itself. It felt austere and not a little foreboding. We did not go through those doors, however, but turned to the left and directly up three shallow steps that led into a room. The room appeared to me like a small events room and the floor was covered in woven reeds. There was very little wall space, as the entire room seemed to be made of long wide windows. We sat on the floor and Master Jay Sai spoke these words to me.

"You have been through a great ordeal but this is all over and now you begin this new journey of creation."

He then took me through some directed breathing and chanting for about a minute. I then had to think a certain word that came to me and hold onto that word to sow the seed of energy of that word in my energy field. This all took about half an hour and we sat quietly for a moment and then he led me back to where he had met me. As we passed by the giant doors I asked him where they led to and he replied that they were doors to the inner sanctum and that I was as yet unqualified to pass through those doors.

The days passed and I was religious in my endeavors to make the connection with this Master who had presented himself to me. Every day I would put a thought out to him but to no avail but one morning I did and I got the reply that he was busy and to go and do something else! Even though I didn't connect with him daily I would always in these meditations find myself in this alternative reality. I could feel that my physical body was adapting to the energy of this place and the result of this was I could feel my brain adopting this new energy that mentally I experienced as an energy alignment. This had the effect of making me feel even more focused in everyday life. My ability to recognize what life was saying to me increased. I became more aware than ever of my thoughts and how the vibrations of them were influencing my life. I started to get very specific in my intentions and this made me more aware of the thoughts I used that were counterproductive to me. All of this was experienced in a state of peaceful logic that made it easier to recognize where change was needed and what thoughts were power thoughts that would work to my advantage. I could feel more clearly and see more markedly how we work as vibration. The lines of life that make up everything were no longer lifelines that I was attached to but that I and all were actually these very lifelines. The idea that there are no degrees of separation became more apparent to me. The concept *of paying attention* made better sense to me now as I realized paying attention was not just about being *the observer*, it was about continuously being the participant. By participating in the new ways I had embraced I had united with source, had become source myself, thus had access to all life information that I so wished. Getting to a place like that in one's life is not just liberating but also daunting as it brings the realization that you really *are* making life happen.

During World War Two there were underground rooms where a great board game was being played out. On massive tables the continents of the world where the conflicts were taking place were depicted. Battleships, planes, armies were all depicted in miniature. As the battles ensued these "toys" were moved as information of successes and defeats came to the attention of those in authority so they were able to "see" what was happening. It all seems rather archaic now considering the advent of technology but that's how it was done in those days. I can imagine our higher nature doing the same, maneuvering around all these aspects of ourselves as we progress in our life, positioning us at certain points always ever present and vigilant in its guidance.

On the morning of my meditation where I did meet up with Master Jay Sai he led me down some very steep steps. I watched as he almost flew down the narrow stairs that were carved out of the rock whereas I took my time not wanting to slip and fall. I remember thinking at the time, how funny that even though here I am in a place of higher learning I still embraced my human fears. We came to a pool that I took to be a hot mineral pool as it was steaming. After undressing we got into the pool and even though I had the sensation I was stepping into some substance I saw it was not water. I was told it was an energy pool and that the energy of this pool would heal all the discrepancies I had created since the beginning of this incarnation. I asked how the energy came to be a pool and was told that as everything is God then all of source is consistently flowing through all things. The energy can center itself in certain places, things, people, and so source energy becomes more concentrated. He told me that this is what happens when we have complete mastery over our lives. We allow the concentrated energy of source to center itself on us because we make a concentrated effort to accept that we are this energy, therefore we become the very source itself.

I looked around me as he spoke and the majestic mountains seemed closer and more alive than ever. As I sat there I suddenly felt very overwhelmed and almost sad. I could feel tears welling up and spilling down my cheeks. I sat there for a while and was conscious of the deep silence that pervaded. There was no sound from anything or anywhere; even the energy that I could see coursing into the energy pool did so silently. Master Jay Sai and myself sat for a little while longer and then moved out of the energy pool and up the steep steps. I was aware of the solidity of the mountain rock on my right and the precipitous way the mountain rolled down to my left. I was feeling thoughtful and serious but the energy lightened as we reached the top of the stairs. I thought Master Jay Sai had gone but saw him sitting on a stone bench that looked out over the mountains. He gestured for me to join him and we sat for a while in the silence and then he spoke:

"Everything that you behold possesses everything you will ever need to know."

I looked at the mountains before me and all the surrounding area. I looked at Master Jay Sai. I said nothing to him.

"You possess within you everything you will ever need, you just have to listen," he continued.

"Listening is the key, not seeking any great knowledge or finding anything but daily listening to what you are saying to yourself. The more that you listen, the more that you will hear."

I looked at him and tried to "listen" to what I was feeling to what my life was saying to me as I sat before him.

"Let me take your hands," he said.

He took my hands in his and then moved his hands up to my wrists where he held firm and then asked me what I was hearing.

"I hear your strength and your love and I hear your dedication to me and I hear your wisdom," was my reply.

Then he said something to me that struck such a powerful note in the very core of my being and I felt the tears well up.

"Let me hold onto you, but never hold onto me."

He was there to hold me, to guide me, and to propel me to myself but it is never intended that I hold onto him. Becoming dependent on someone or something will never allow us to accurately listen to ourselves. It is about holding strong onto our ideas of ourselves that move us forward in life with ease. If we hold strong onto the ideas other people have about us we still move forward but it becomes a challenge to maintain sovereignty over our life. And then I thought of all I had been through over the last years looking after Kay and how I had held onto her and by doing so had become infected with an energy that no longer served my purpose. It made me think of people that I had known and know now that I can see hold onto experiences that have demanded of them but no longer do and how this is weighing them down. Kay was responsible for me in the early years of our relationship. I was young and though not exactly naive was inexperienced and still needed the guidance. And then life's circle turned and I became responsible for her and guided her. She had to let go of me so I could look after her and now I have to let go of her, as she no longer needs me in the same way. And so when Master Jay Sai spoke those words to me I could see that Kay and I no longer needed to hold onto each other as our life together had finished.

I continued with my meditations over the days and each time explored various parts of this spiritual world that I had access to. After a very deep relaxing moment I found myself flying down a great valley and was conscious of the steepness of the mountains on either side of me. I knew I was in the valley where the Master Jay Sai resided and soon I could see below me the vast edifice of the spiritual complex below me. I floated down and came to the inner courtyard I had been in when I had first visited this place. I was standing at the entrance and went to the left where there were two doors at right angles to each other, one being blue, the other green. I felt to go through the blue door that was farthest from me and stood before the door wondering if I should walk right in or wait for some guidance. The moment I had that thought I heard a voice say knock and upon doing so the door opened and I entered. Directly in front of me was a set of narrow stone steps that went into a short spiral. I walked up the steps and found myself in a room atop a small tower. The room was round and the floor a very highly polished wood. There were desks built around the room all facing outward toward the windows. I was told to sit at one of the desks and on doing so noticed what I thought was a giant gong not quite in the middle of the room. On closer inspection, I saw that though the frame and shape were of a gong, the gong part was actually a mass of energy waves. It was as I was informed an energy gong. I was told I would hear certain sounds and I was to record what first came to me as I heard the sound. I looked down at the desk expecting to see paper and pen but there was a mass of energy in front of me that recorded my thoughts as I heard the sounds. I heard four sounds and was told that whatever I recorded would be useful to me.

Now this made me think of all the times I have had strange noises in my ears or heard deep humming sounds the energy of which seemed to reverberate through my whole body and so this is what I think. As we become more aligned to source and understand that all is vibration we attune our being to the sounds that we need most. These sounds stimulate aspects of our consciousness that go on to promote ideas, feelings that invariably become the events of our life. We turn these sounds into people as well who are attracted to our energy as much as we are to them. It is the music of consciousness playing out around us and within us all the time and we are in fact orchestrating this life symphony. So when we are taught to listen to what life is daily saying to us we are in fact listening with our souls for the vibrations that we attract to us. Daily we put out a vibration call that is relevant to our thoughts, words, and actions. So we will only receive the vibration that matches with what we have emitted. I would think that most people are simply randomly putting out a myriad of mixed vibrations not being aware of what they are most of the time, and of course not realizing that they are receiving messages back from source. This formula that we work with is one that is prevalent through all of life, be it physical and nonphysical, and as we come to this awareness we change the very frequency we as human beings resonate to and adapt our whole being of mind, body, spirit to expand. We are always reaching out for more, as we know in our deepest place that we are more and we must be fulfilled in this knowledge. If we have a healthy body that is totally functional in every way we don't just use one arm or hop around on one leg. If we can, we see with a pair of eyes or hear with a pair of ears; we do not close one eye or one ear. We use *all of our body* to function properly and so that's what our soul wants. It wishes to use *all of itself* as well so it can function in the way it was created to. Intrinsically what we all want is full function of all that we are made up of to give us complete access to everything that we want. Sometimes to get that we have to go to worlds that are a different *REAL* than what we are presently engaged with. And the only way to have right of entry is to engage with our soul that has other world rights.

The world we live in is a world where change is the constant. It is a world where the natural harmony of life is disturbed. When we access other worlds, we go to places where the natural state of all life is harmony. That *is* our natural way of being and so putting ourselves into a state where we can access more of that harmony enhances our prospects.

I found myself in my meditation near the stairway I had descended to go to the energy pool, but I did not have the feeling to go down to it. I stood and contemplated my options and the view around me. I could see that I was at the back of the edifice that was carved into the mountain. A road lay before me that meandered through the surrounding country. I decided to go sight-seeing and started to wander down the road. A forest of delicate cheery blossoms whispered intoxicating fragrance around me. Long lush green grass grew at the base of each tree like a velvety protector. To the left was the solid citadel of mountain that kept a constant vigilance of the surrounding area. The road sloped gently for about fifty meters and then turned to the left. At the turn, a meadow of wildflowers cascaded before me, their presentation of color a botanical performance at its best. In the distance was a large tree, an atmosphere on its own with its generous branches triumphant in their long reach. I made for that tree through the meadow of flowers that united me with a carpet of green lawn that encircled the whole of the tree. I sat with respect against the trunk of the tree and I say respect, for truly everything around me was alive and expressing in what it was. I was simply another part of life that had found expression in quietly being myself, and the life around me made me a part of the all and that gave me great peace. From my vantage point I could see that the mountain itself was made like a great peninsula where immense cavernous valleys fell on either side. This peninsula was massive though it shrank in comparison to the mountains that were its embrace. As I sat drinking in the beauty that was all around me I couldn't help but remember that this was all my reality. I had created it specifically for the purpose of my growth.

When definite changes have to be made in our lives the whole of our being expunges unessential vibrations from our personal fields. So, what are we then left with? We are left with an array of vibrations that are all powerful but we still have to organize their potential. We do this by getting the "feeling" of them first and when we get those feelings this is the vibrations way of "speaking to us." There would have been times in anyone's life when they had thought or said:

"That really speaks to me."

I thought this as I sat drinking in the landscape before me. I was creating a relationship with this place and its vibration was having a conversation with my vibration. I had created a place of harmony where my powerful vibrations could be organized to their definitive potential. In this place I was actually living as source energy. This was the place of harmony that I had created so that I could exercise the part of me that is in harmony. And then that made me think how difficult it is to be in harmony let alone practice it when we live in a world where so much is not in harmony. And so no wonder we have to create other worlds that give us access to harmony. Perhaps as human beings we are actually trying too hard to find harmony in the places where it can never be found. Are we needlessly pressuring ourselves by trying to find the answer we need only in this world where many of them in fact will be found in other worlds of consciousness we have available to us? Is this why those worlds exist, because in the grand scheme of things this is actually how it was established to begin with? The more I consider this, the more that makes sense. In the Bible it cites that *"In God's house there are many mansions."* Perhaps the true meaning of this is that as Gods we have available many worlds within that we can access to guide us through life. If we can't find what we are looking for in one world we simply can go to another to find what we need.

When we meditate we are relaxing our human nature so that we can access our God nature. The deeper we go, the further we move our self from the idea of our human nature and we involve ourselves more in our God nature, which opens up these other worlds that are there. We then use our God senses as opposed to our human senses. Our God senses are finely tuned to experience vibrations that our human sense can't, consequently in our altered state we become conscious of other levels of life. Those other levels carry information that can only be accessed by moving away from our human senses. It's like levels of a library where you may need to gain special access to certain places of knowledge. It's not that the "*Soul Section*" is restricted but more like you have to be qualified in some way to gain access. And the qualification in this case would simply be that you consciously recognize your *God Nature* as an essential commodity to life.

We are already an established source of energy that only has one direction and that is to expand. There is no purpose to this expansion, by simply in its state of being it expands. And along the road of that expansion the opportunity to create and participate in creation occurs. So that becomes thought manifested in forms that are tangible to our soul and human senses. And this is done because we can. These other worlds that we can access are created so that we can find the right vibration for the thoughts and actions that we depict in life. And through life we are involuntarily calling on these other worlds as our soul knows that it has access to them. Thus how much more are we able to advance our position by voluntary accessing these worlds?

How I'm feeling it and thinking it is that "*ALL*" is a replica of God. And this all has all, is all that God is. We are cloned from this source but given freedom to express this all in the uniqueness of our human nature while we are here on Earth. God self-positioned in the human self, experiencing the ability to express. If we have mastery over the human self we therefore also recognize that it too is source energy capable of receiving source power through it. As we guide this power intentionally through thoughts, words, and deeds we are training our human nature to recognize the God nature. Inexorably this training aligns us completely and we recognize the state of *being* that opens up all the worlds that are within. And when we do that the whole of everything makes sense for the reason that we simply exist as *The True Source* and what we created and how it all works because *we know*.

How would it be living in a world where we are all like this? We would all become self-governing and have total autonomy over the life that we lead. The nature of karma would change, as there would no longer be the need to resolve issues and that would change the dynamics of why people are involved in relationships and the very reasons why they have incarnated on Earth. As a result conflicts between people, countries, and beliefs would probably cease. Would there then be a need for the religions that have been established that are so much the cause of the conflicts of this time? No one would be going around needing to prove that *their God* is the ultimate God. It would change the way we coexist with animals and nature and the Earth itself as we would move away from any need to exploit, and live in the state of harmony that deep down in us all we know exists. And of course we would have access to all those other worlds that I have been speaking of. And those worlds would have altered to align with our higher vibrations.

I find it perplexing and sad when I see that so many can be so very challenged by what I am saying, preferring instead to stay locked into domineering autocratic beliefs that give them but one world and one way of seeing and living in it. I feel that from our creation we were given everything that God is, and it was meant to be that way. I hardly think that the God force would create anything less than itself. As we open ourselves up to these other worlds that are within us we are also opening up each other to be a part of each other's worlds in better ways.

Yesterday when I was having my morning meditation I found myself back in my world of harmony sitting in the same place when I first encountered this world.

Directly in front of me stood the Master known as Yeshua (Jesus). He held out his hand and told me to come with him. I was overcome with his deep love he had for me and this love coursed through my body. I followed him and he took me to those big doors that Master Jay Sai had said were doors to the inner sanctum. Yeshua placed his hand on the doors and they opened before us. We stood in an atrium, the floor of which was covered in colored mosaic tiles; I thought of Morocco when I saw them. There was a central garden where there were others gathered around in conversation. I asked Yeshua if they were like me where they were in a meditative state in body and had come here. He replied that some were but that others were actually souls who were going to reincarnate into important lifetimes and that in this place they were in preparation for those lives. He said that if you choose a specific lifetime where you would make some massive impact then this is where you would come to prepare. I thought of people like Nelson Mandela, Diana Princess of Wales, Earnest Rutherford and wondered if they had come here first before they were born. I guess if you are going to have some major impact on the world, you want to be well prepared!

He led me away to a small balcony that overlooked massive cloud formations and we stood there for a while and then turned to the left and walked down three marble steps that were under a wide arch. We walked into a space that was a very cloudy red and though not concerned I could feel myself hesitate. Yeshua gently took my hand and told me to stay by him and all is well. The idea came into my head that this place had something to do with the base chakra, and the moment I had that thought Yeshua told me he was going to replant my soul in the new energy. I was informed that we do many replants through our lifetime though mainly we are unaware of them. When we become aware it is because we know that we have reached some major zenith of development in our life and that it was like beginning again an incarnation while we are still alive. A great energy pod appeared and Yeshua placed me in it. I felt myself drift off into a peaceful state and then the meditation finished. Later on in the day I received information as a thought that while I was in that other world being re-sown, the benefits of my development out there would be filtered through to me in my present day-to-day living here in this world. Another reminder to me of how we are advancing by the influences of higher nature experience. Also I knew then that I would not have to "wait" for some process to occur and complete but that I would benefit straight away by anything my higher nature was doing.

This was yet another clue to me of the complex nature of source and what we are able to experience once we open up to the realms of possibility. If we look at one life that we live and we consider all the events, ideas, feelings, people, and movements of that life it's quite astounding that we are able to function! How do we really hold it all together? We have to have help from some other sources apart from the ones we have in our human nature.

*Human nature simply isn't qualified to give us
everything we need in life.*

I imagine all these other worlds are like specialized shops that offer up specific goods that you won't find in the mainstream shops.

You want lumber, you go to the lumber store.

You want ice cream, you go to the ice cream parlor.

You want source energy, you go beyond your human nature.

I'm having a lot of fun participating in these other worlds that I have created and every time I visit one of them it is yet another validation of my true nature and the developing relationship I have with it. Of course this changes completely the way I see and run my human nature and accordingly the way that I view the human nature of others. When we can see and feel beyond that nature and go to the higher nature we also are able to sense the energy of the other worlds that other people have created and this aligns us with the energy that promotes the well-being among all beings. Months later I was having a meditation and found myself in this special place with Yeshua standing beside me. I was no longer in the energy pod and I was standing on the edge of a great precipice. I looked at my body and it was a pale shimmering blue light body. Behind me stood other beings who were also light bodies. Yeshua came up and whispered to me,

"You have been reborn, now fly."

I spread my arms out like they were wings and tipped myself off the edge of the precipice and like a bullet fell rapidly down and down. I could feel the air rushing around me as I continued my fall and then I soared up and with a great feeling of joy and freedom flew through the great canyons. I could hear the others applauding me as they rushed to the edge to watch me fly, it was truly exhilarating and felt this was the most natural thing to do! I landed back next to Yeshua and he took me into a massive hug and held me.

"You have returned to source!" he exclaimed. "This is your new beginning."

I would like to end this chapter with a quote from Buddha.

Face your past without regret
Handle your present with confidence
Prepare the future without fear

Chapter Seventeen
You Never Know

Have you ever had the thought of just how much we are all carrying around with us all the time? It's quite mind blowing when you think about that right now as you read this that not only are you possessed of all this life's experiences but also all the experiences of all the other lives you have ever had. That's an awful lot of ideas, feelings, reactions, responses, etc. We are also being exposed all the time to the energies of everyone and everything else that in actual fact is information we are downloading as vibration. The fact that we are able to function while all of this is happening is a good indication of not only how powerful and complex we are as beings but also of how resilient we are to be able to allow all this to happen and still function in a sane way! We were obviously created with theses coping mechanisms, otherwise we could never function.

I was at the supermarket early in the week doing the weekly shop. Kay used to come with me even up to the point when she needed to go into care. She loved to push the shopping trolley though I suspect it was more that it was something to grip onto and make her feel secure while she walked around with me. It was sort of a "she pushing a little" and "me pulling a lot" arrangement but I could see she felt happy doing it as it made her feel she was still participating in the world. When we reached the checkout she would grip onto the side of the counter while I placed the shopping on it. I was thinking about this while I was at the checkout this week and the operator, a lovely gentle Indian woman in her early sixties, smiled at me with recognition. We started to chat and she asked me where the lovely lady was that used to come with me. I explained the situation and how Kay was now in care. Tears came into her eyes as she continued to push my shopping through.

"You just never know," she said. "You see all these people all through the day and yet you never know what they are going through in their lives."

I then asked her about her family assuming she had some as I wanted to direct the conversation away from my situation with Kay; as of late I was finding it more difficult to talk about it without getting emotional. She spoke to me of her children and how they were not living in the country at present and I could feel her own pain at the separation from them. For a moment, we stood on common ground and I then thought, "You never know," as I looked at her and smiled. Here she was doing her job and most people probably never gave her the time of day or even saw her as a person with a life. I often notice people blankly looking at checkout operators as if they are some kind of mechanical apparatus attached to the checkout. No conversation is passed in the time of the shopping transaction.

And I have seen checkout operators give the customers the same look, not engaging with them at all, everything becoming a mechanical transaction with no emotion or connection. When I had paid for my shopping and was leaving I put out my hand to my checkout friend and she took it warmly in both of her hands. We looked at each other and smiled; we had an understanding and for a moment we had turned on a light for each other.

This little exchange made me think as I was driving home just how easy it is to ignore what is going on around us. Here we all are, billions of us sharing a planet, and country, a city, a street and despite that we seem to do our best to not bump into each other. And yet we are all desperate for each other because our souls yearn for the connection. We seem to be creating more ways to ignore each other, be suspicious of each other, or be afraid of each other. Of course, what this does is to build up an intense mistrust of human nature, creating thicker walls of energy that take us further away from the opportunity to love and respect.

You never know when you might be giving someone life. A simple act of kindness, a smile, or small way of paying attention can be a lifeline for someone.

It's meant that we pay attention to each other; I believe that we daily look for the opportunities to do so since it's natural to serve each other. We are all a big energy family together; we seek each other out through the day and we create lots of varied opportunities to do so. We meet each other in supermarkets or at a petrol station. We stand next to each other at the pedestrian crossings or in elevators and waiting rooms. We are all involved in this energy intimacy but most are totally ignorant of this fact and stand alone in the need to protect the space we live in even though we live obviously among so much and so many.

And sometimes we are specifically guided toward a certain situation where we are going to be of some use as I found out recently. A friend was visiting from the US and I enjoyed playing tour guide around the Wellington region. I live at the base of Mount Victoria and there is a lookout at the top that offers 360-degree views. It's a prerequisite for any visitor and the views are quite spectacular. It's a short drive up winding and narrow roads and you have to be careful, as some drivers are not as courteous as others when it comes to speed and giving way when you want to. I turned a corner and gave way to a guy on a scooter coming down; we traveled about fifty meters when there was that awful sound of vehicle hitting vehicle. I looked in the rear-vision mirror to see the guy who had been on the scooter laying on the road. A motorist turning right into a street had failed to give way to the guy on the scooter and the scooter had plowed into the side of the vehicle.

In an instant, my friend and I kicked into rescue mood. I felt myself getting all practical and authoritative as I rang emergency services and asked the injured man his name, and if and where he was feeling pain. My friend took the man's hand

and she went into healing mode. She grabbed my hand and our energies connected, sending to the man healing energy as he lay there on the road. The man who had hit the guy leaned down toward him and started asking him his cell phone number and email address. I looked at the face of the injured man who looked as if he couldn't believe what he was hearing and he even said to the guy,

"Why are you asking me all this right now?"

A pedestrian who had witnessed the accident was hovering around not quite sure what to do and she kept looking at a blue car parked on the side of the road and asking who it belonged to. I found myself wondering why she felt it so important in her reality to know. My friend and I felt calm and peaceful, obviously an energy that we had been called upon to bring to the situation. Once the emergency services arrived we stepped back and let them do their job and luckily the guy was able to stand and walk to the ambulance. We didn't need to give any statements and so we left after another ten minutes. I thought about all the people who in that short time had all been gathered together to be a part of that experience and the diverse rolls we played. I also remembered how important it was to put that situation down and not carry it. Another frame of life was being played out and then you move on to the next one. What was it about the law of attraction that we all pulled together that experience so that we could all serve each other in the ways we did? And the answer is, so we could all put into practice who we are and what we know and what we can do.

We can always be more than what we are, know more than what we believe we know, and do more than what we are doing. We have given ourselves this great chance called our life to portray ourselves beyond what we believe and it is a belief within us all that urges us toward our achievements. The test is not so much can we, as we would never have created a chance if we believed we could not. The test is more in the way we resist by portraying ourselves as weak or afraid or any of the other ideas we have about life that are counterproductive. We can spend a lifetime tossing around our potential and never actually do anything with it. It's like constantly having meetings about what you want to do but never actually doing anything. The thing I have come to realize is that you really do have to *feel* the potential before you are truly able to engage with the power of an outcome. In the feeling we know the prospects of our ideas and this encourages us to pursue the most appropriate course of action.

Our investigations into self-realization allow us to know that there are realities that we can only make possible through our deep investigation into ourselves as source energy. I believe that one of the keys to each individual is actually through the living of the qualities that we have brought with us into our lives. The talents that we all have are in fact platforms for awakening on all levels. So, early recognition of your qualities gives you the food to nourish all your potentials. You never know that right now you are harboring great advances to yourself because you have a particular ability that you may have thought of as something you can "just do." This is because your qualities carry specific vibrations that are aligned to source energy in such a way that they assist in stimulating the collective energy. As this happens it raises the frequency of collective energy to enhance its potential. Can you imagine what collectively we would all achieve if we all realized this about the talents we have all brought into our lives?

There are powerful messages in our personal qualities.

I found recently a powerful message in the qualities of someone who was suffering a great loss. A client who had come to see Tabaash had lost a child and after the session with Tabaash I felt the desire to sit and talk more with her and shared with her some of my situation with Kay. Later in the day I received a text message from her speaking of her desire to meet Kay and come and sit with me when I visited Kay. Naturally I am protective of Kay particularly in her declining situation but my instincts were to agree to the visit and so we arranged a time to meet up at the care home one Sunday. She arrived with her partner and while he waited in the reception area we went in to visit Kay. She was sitting next to a caregiver who was assisting her in drinking juice from a plastic cup. Kay smiled up at me when she saw me and I sat next to her and she reached out to me. I introduced Kay to the visitor I had brought and she looked at her and smiled. Kay let her take her hand and I could feel the acceptance Kay had of her. I could also sense that somehow Kay knew of the pain this woman was suffering and Kay reached out and smiled at her and then touched her nose in some sort of salutation to the situation.

We sat awhile and this lovely lady brought a simple gift for Kay of lavender cream and oil. She put a little on Kay's hand and helped her raise her hand so she could smell the fragrance and in that gesture there was such caring and love from someone who was traumatized by the passing of her child. I was very moved and reminded that through our personal pain we can still have the ability to touch others with grace and love and also be helped ourselves in our own need to be healed. As source energy we emit signals of need like a call of vibration that reaches out as tendrils of energy to connect with some source that helps us. And so at times we will feel drawn to a shared experience where we give life as much as receive life for ourselves. That's how I saw the visit that Sunday and we all received that day the gift of love and healing.

Visiting a dementia care unit is a very raw experience, and there are those who would find it exigent to do so. A lot of exposed emotion is always evident whenever I go up there and you never know what you will be faced with in the complex dynamics of people's befuddled energies. I've had some fascinating discourse with some of the residents in the unit that Kay is in. A recent arrival came up to me last week and what transpired was a lesson in how important it was to simply "go with it." She came up to me and asked if there was enough transport for everybody. I assured her there was but she got quite agitated and starting going on about how she had worked for days to ensure that was the case. I told her that I had just been in touch with head office and that they had assured me that there was sufficient transport for everyone and that head office was very pleased with her. Her face, which had developed signs of tears, suddenly broke into a great smile at this news. Then she asked me if my limousine had arrived and I assured her that it had and I thanked her for doing such a great job in looking after my needs. She sat down and her expression was of one who looked relieved! I see all of this as simply visiting the worlds that these people find themselves in. Rather than trying to explain otherwise it was best to be a part of their world as it stood at that time. And who's saying that it wasn't real as it certainly is to them. Even when our brains get all muddled we are still functioning beings of consciousness playing out the parts that we have created. If we are disabled in our minds or bodies we are still *GOD* and our souls are always a part of source and are whole and able.

Living with a disability is teaching ourselves
and others how truly able we are.

We have all of us, at some point, chosen a life where we have had a permanent physical or mental disability. This may come about from the very beginning of our life or occur at some point through our life. That is a *conscious* choice that as a soul we have made and from that choice we will make valuable progress. If we are living a life where we are totally *able* in all respects and we *disable* our life because we don't pay attention to our abilities we are disrespecting the qualities that we all possess. Making a conscious choice to be born with a disability is in fact a *respectful* choice as you are respecting your soul's desire to evolve from whatever the chosen disability offers you. Being disabled when you don't need to evolve in that way creates unnecessary challenges and is an indicator that you are not aligned with your authenticity. Here are some ways that I can disable myself and I'm sure that you can relate to some of these.

I disable myself on the road by making
disparaging comments about drivers.

God, this one really pisses me off, as I have zero tolerance for those morons who for some act of miracle (or someone's inability to see that they were morons) managed to get a driving license. I see it all the time, people going through red lights creating a moment of excitement for some unaware pedestrian, others not indicating and then making some thrilling maneuver causing several other drivers to express certain expletives and wear down their brake pads by sudden and violent braking. And my all-time major disabling act of moronic ineptitude is when you are behind someone waiting for the lights to go from red to green. The individual in front of you is picking their nose or on the phone texting or simply staring into space. Then suddenly they see the light has changed and realize that they have some responsibility to move forward, but only giving *THEM* enough time to go through the light. Leaving you smoldering behind at the now red light, imagining innumerable ways of carnage upon their person!

And so this argues the point, what would my *ABLE* self have done in such circumstances? It would have sedately sat in a very aligned place emotionally knowing that I would get to my destination and that two more minutes of delay were hardly going to make a difference. It would journey through its life while in a vehicle with great reference to others on the road and acknowledge the value of its experience.

(I can feel myself disabling myself as I write this so I need to practice the able part a bit more.)

I disable myself at the supermarket when at the express checkout
I am behind someone who is not express.

Now this seems to be a repetitive pattern for me when I visit the supermarket. Without fail I find myself at the express checkout only to be confronted by it being the least express of all the checkouts in the whole of the supermarket. The sign after all is clear enough *"Fifteen Items Or Less."* I stare pointedly at the person in front of me with the trolley full that is almost exploding with groceries and make a point that in my stare I am counting, yes, counting the amount they have. I then stare pointedly at the sign but they seem to have lost the mathematical ability to count and become temporarily blind, as they seem unable to see me and continue in their non-express ways. The able part of me would offer to help unload the gargantuan amount of groceries they have loaded up and I would make appreciative murmuring noises that all of this is no trouble at all and being held up like this was no issue to myself. I would even be more amiable and offer to wheel the trolley to the car and even unload the bags. With the advent of self-checkouts this had made the situation somewhat easier apart from the odd occasion where a customer completely loses their head in regard to having to check themselves out.

I disable myself by swearing at recorded help lines.

As a baby boomer I am one of those who are on the cusp of the machinations of the digital age. I have managed to adopt a certain amount of cyber facts that have allowed me to write this book on my computer, access emails, and use Skype. I occasionally astound myself when I try to move a file from documents to a memory stick and it actually works. However,

I am on occasions confounded by a request from my computer that obviously assumes I have a PhD in computer science. In the old days, there was a manual that you could look up the correct page and follow the instructions. Manuals are archaic now; instead you get a disc that will inform you how to go about setting up and dealing with problems. The problem is that when you put the disc in it makes the assumption that you have already done the prerequisite applications that permit you access to the disc. And of course the reason that you are trying to follow the disc is because you can't figure out how to access the prerequisite information in order to follow the information in the disc! I look up on the computer screen and push the "help" icon that proves to be only of help to those who do have a PhD in computer science and also have been speaking computer for decades. I feel like a tourist in a foreign country with my little pocket translator trying to be understood but to no avail.

And so, onto the next step, the telephone help line. God help us all as we spend the next three minutes listening to all the options that will connect us with a number to push in the hope of the light at the end of this rather long tunnel. You have to really listen, though, because if you don't listen you'll miss it and then you have to hang up and start the whole ruddy process all over again. Your anxiety levels are rising; you are plotting revengeful unfortunate events that will occur to the person or persons who have instigated the procedure.

Your brain is perusing its memory banks finding certain expletives that will verbally occur given the chance that this event is more prolonged. Then a recorded voice comes on and tells me to explain in a few words what the problem is. I pause too long as I try to think of how to put my issue in a few words and by that time the recorded message is telling me that it does not understand.

"OF COURSE YOU DON'T UNDERSTAND, SEEING AS I HAVEN'T ACTUALLY SAID ANYTHING," I reply rather ungraciously.

"I'm sorry, can you explain in a few words what your issue is?"

"I WILL IF YOU GIVE ME A BLOODY CHANCE TO TALK!"

"I'll see if there is someone else who is able to help you."

And usually at that point I either hang up or actually get disconnected. And then I sit in frustration and annoyance at the fact I've been verbally abusing a nonhuman apparatus that after all is simply programmed to serve me and ignore any form of abuse hurled at them from customers at their wit's end. And the other bone of contention is when they tell you that there is a waiting time of fifteen minutes or years or something undesirable but that your call is important to them so please don't hang up! My reactions obviously state how much more I have to go on the road to being an enlightened being of energy.

And so, you never know what life is going to offer us up in the way of opportunities that allow us to regard how we respond to life and its circumstances. Here we all are billions of souls, in billions of bodies on a planet that was created to sustain us in our natural state. And what has happened, we have evolved into an unnatural state of being going completely against the laws that govern the state of harmony. A turn of phrase that is too often said and heard is, "I don't know." This constant affirming of our ignorance of who we are, what are choices are, where we are going, is disrespectful to our intelligence.

I think too often, too many are disrespecting each other because we are not seeing each other in our true light and that's really what we want. If that wasn't the case then why are we bothering to find better ways to be in harmony? To find harmony in each other as human beings we first have to be in harmony with each other as spiritual beings. By doing that we truly can bring out the very best in one another. I don't want to sound all self-righteous and preachy here as that is the last thing that any of us need. We are seeing now that the issues of conflict that are created and lived out are because of our lack of conscious connection with source. How can we fix the issues of humanity when we cannot respect that we are as souls, the same?

By seeing that we are souls we *will know* that we all carry the potential of making it all work. We *will know* that we have this common thread that holds us all together and feeds us the power of life, advancing our own life because of this. We *will know* that in fact we are carrying each other through our pain and our joy. You never know, by doing this we will all know.

Chapter Eighteen

True Friends Know How to Be Weird with You

I recently celebrated my fifty-seventh birthday and for the first time in many years I actually felt like it was a birthday and an actual celebration. Last year my birthday came up a few weeks after Kay had gone to live in care, a few friends gathered at the care home, we had cake and a chat but Kay wasn't really in the loop at all and it all felt a bit flat. During the years of looking after Kay I sort of forgot about birthdays. I've read lots of stuff about how you should not recognize your birthday as it means your recognizing that you're aging and all that stuff, but I sort of see it like, hell, if I'm God then I should believe anything I want to and not have it affect me one quivering vibration portal!

My best mate is David; he's the realist person I know, and I can always rely on him to tell me how it is. As our ages—and I like to think our wisdom—have progressed we have started the ritual of taking each other out for dinner on our birthdays. This has mostly been a highly satisfying experience except for last year where I was a bit flat and down. I choose this restaurant that was basically shit and I ordered as an entrée fried sardines, which when they came to me crumbled into nothingness, eating air would have been more satisfying. Those sardines rather summed up my life as it was then. We would have been better off getting fish 'n chips and drinking a nice bottle of champagne at my place. However, a ritual is a ritual and these traditions between mates need to be respected. David and I respect these traditions often, even when it's not our birthday. We like to get together and hang out over a meal and beer or wine or both, and talk. Our conversations are not "what do blokes talk about when they get together." It's the coming together of two souls who have obviously had a lot of history between them and so the dialogue is all soul related. We automatically disperse with all the human stuff and go direct to the soul, straight to the substance of everything. Even when we hang out for a cuppa the conversation always turns to the soul stuff. We are going to an A&P show in a couple of weeks, which for those readers who don't know is an Agricultural and Produce show where a local farming community gets together, sort of like a farmer's fair. It will be fun, but we will probably end up discussing why someone would want to reincarnate as a cow.

David came from a farming background up north. We were both born in the same year though he in July and me in October, the same day. Interestingly, our parents share the same birthday month and day though different years. From all accounts, his was a normal farming upbringing in rural New Zealand.

He was a "bit of a lad" growing up fast, and I mean fast cars, fast girls, fast life.

He became a vegetarian in his twenties and seemed to do a hell of a lot of growing through his experiences in a short time. He had his share of traumas but that hard shell (he's Cancerian) protected his gentle heart and he moved forward and was able to advance his soul. When I met him his soul was strong but his human nature was still vulnerable, and we recognized a kindredness in each other and became friends.

Kay, always possessive of me and wary of anyone who might take me away from her or lead me astray, was instantly wary of him. It took her a few years to trust him and accept him and yet when she did she learned to love and trust him unequivocally. Now in Kay's advanced state of Alzheimer's her face will light up in a smile of recognition and love when she sees David. It's wonderful.

I can't help but think about the many experiences we all must have shared in other lives to meet up again in this lifetime. I think of the qualities that David has brought to Kay and myself that have supported our journey in life through all the years we have known each other. David tells me a story of Kay when she was a few years into her Alzheimer's. Kay was always full of projects that needed to be done around the house and never made time to "smell the roses," so to speak. It was summer and the garden was full of exquisite color. I had made a special effort with the garden, as I wanted it to be a paradise for Kay. I wanted her to be surrounded by beauty and the good energy that the garden emitted. It was a very warm summer and the sky was always a backdrop of cornflower blue. The birdsong was a symphony and the air filled with the contented vigor of long summer days. David had come over and while I was making a cuppa Kay had gone out into the garden with him and in wonder pointed out the butterflies and the song of all the birds. He had never had a conversation with Kay like this; it was not about what she was doing but about what was, and life as a state of being. He told me it was beautiful to have that conversation with her and to see a part of her that she would never show.

And so once again we realize that the vibrations of our soul make a difference to one another.

A few years back Dave's mum, Doreen, started on her final road in this life. Doreen was a straight shooter, you always knew where you stood with her. She had a heart of gold and a tongue sharp as a razor. I loved her. She had been ill for a while and being massively independent didn't want anyone to fuss over her. David respected that for a while and then realized he had to disrespect that and made the move up the line to look after his mother. I would drive up there some weekends and spend time with Doreen and David and would always have Kay with me. Kay's response to Doreen was remarkable; here was one woman suffering from Alzheimer's wanting to look after another woman who had a terminal illness. Kay would fuss over her, I'm sure much to Doreen's annoyance; it was like

Kay wanted to protect her. I often wondered what karma they must have had together in this life.

One day we drove up to spend the weekend but on arrival I could see that Doreen was not up to having visitors despite who it was. We stayed one night and then drove back the next day. I knew that I would never see Doreen again. A few weeks later I got the text from Dave saying that she had passed. I cried for Doreen and I cried for my mate David and then said a blessing for Doreen, helping her soul along the road back home. And so once again, the completion of a life and yet the beginning of another adventure for the soul that was known as Doreen in this lifetime.

When the funeral was held, it wasn't feasible to take Kay with me so I organized care for her and made my way up to New Plymouth. It's a lovely drive through small towns and green hills and I could feel Doreen's presence with me as I made my way up. I thought about the people that come into our life, I thought about all the planning that we must make out there in spirit before we are born connecting with all the souls that have been a part of our life. And I thought about the fact that every single one of those beings has helped us to evolve in some way. If only we could see that more often, and if only those people on this planet that bring pain and suffering to the world could see that, how much we would all be in a better position.

The day of the funeral was a blue sky day, warm and inviting. Rather a sort of heaven day, I remember thinking. I was driving David to the funeral and was meeting him at Doreen's home where other family members had gathered as well. David and I were standing in the living room near a cabinet that held ornaments that Doreen had collected from her travels. We talked about her and could feel her presence. As we did this we looked over to see one of the ornaments—I can't recall what it was but it was something that had a small pendulum on it—and it began to move. David and I stared at the ornament as it swayed back and forth and then we looked at each other in amazement. David had asked me to speak at the funeral and so when the time came I stood up but before I read the poem I had chosen, I spoke to the congregation of the love and dedication that David had shown to Doreen and told him how proud I was of him. I knew this would embarrass him but, what the hell, he had to be acknowledged. We all gave him a great applause as he cringed into his seat, his head down. At the graveside we lowered Doreen into her grave and sprinkled rose petals on top. After the funeral I went to my hotel room to change and when I opened the door I looked down as something caught my eye. There on the floor was one rose petal.

I would like to think that there are more people on the planet who care for each other than don't, though it's hard to see that happening at times. We will let our human nature so get in the way when it comes to stepping forward when we should. The social rules that have been created make it so difficult for us to serve each other. We seem to be tangling ourselves in more rules to stop being there for each other and I think that's really sad. When people are too scared to speak up or get involved we have to ask ourselves what have we done to create this fear and more importantly what can we do to reverse this? I look at the way David stepped in unequivocally and cared for his mother. It never occurred to me to not look after Kay as long as I could. In my wanderings through town and about I see how people do their best not to engage with each other, so caught up are they in the survival of life and missing the love and service, missing the living.

Is it so hard to see how vital we are to each other?

Think of the people that are in your life right now, the people that you are really glad are in your life. Those people are there for your joy, your happiness, your fun and pleasure.

They are there to help you advance your position in life. They give you the chance to show and receive love, to adventure with and share stories. They are in your life so you can create memories. They will hold you and comfort you, be honest and real. You want them there; they want you there. We are vital to each other's well-being. We are all in each other's lives because we want to be, there is no chance thing about it, we are each and every one of us each other's creations.

For most of us it is our families that first shape our lives; these are our first relationships. We define our early life through the thoughts and experiences of those people and the protective energy of that collective. We grow and observe life; we step into the world and through our new experiences we begin to add new dimensions to our life. As these dimensions present themselves they match up with the dimensions that we are all made up of. The more we advance our life through experience, the more we become aware; this awareness gives us a knowledge that we are so much more. Once we tread this road we seek for being more in every way possible. This is the way of life, to be consciously multidimensional. Our first friendships allow us to develop our social and communication skills. They make us aware of ourselves outside of the family reality and help us to understand that there are many other realities beyond that which we have grown up with. Our friendships also show us our individuality, as we are alert to the fact that we are separate from them and part of a different collective energy.

As I have become older and more aware of myself in my God nature I have seen that the friendships that I develop are all source based. Meaning that as a spiritual being I now seek for people who are aligned to their own God nature. When this occurs, there is an instant recognition and familiarity and openness to share and express love instantaneously. There doesn't seem to be the "getting to know you" period as you feel that the knowing is already there and so you simply pick up that thread of life and get on with it. Allowing this to occur in your life gives you the chance to be your authentic self while you bypass all this etiquette that comes about as you develop a relationship. This etiquette creates a need to wear a mask and little by little show yourself as time goes on.

In source-based relationships, masks are never worn.

Relationships on Earth are all karmic based, filled with the intricacies of human emotions and needs. In approaching each other purely from our human nature we engage in a human experience with all that it has to offer. This can be extremely satisfying or destructive. The nature of human relationships points us toward our relationship with our self and how we manage it. Each relationship we develop is in fact a chance to face our self in some way. We face this by the responses we have to the people we bring into our life. Developing close friendships brings constancy to our lives presenting us with a platform where we can practice knowing our self without the stop-start energy that can come about when we don't have the steadiness of solid relationships. In the vast picture of life, we are all soul companions sharing a planet, creating life, fitting into the complex and astounding experience that is life. That we do it and most of the time it flows is a validation of our ability to corroborate with each other despite the supposed massive discrepancies that seem so prevalent. Perhaps the discrepancies are not as substantial as we believe?

Our relationships with each other are forged through history.

One of the questions that people often ask Tabaash in their sessions with him is,

*"Have I had connections with the people
who are close to me in other lifetimes?"*

The answer of course is yes. We seek for those souls whom we have had many experiences with. Through these experiences we have occupied each other's energy fields, committing ourselves to sharing life in many ways. Doing this builds up emotional bonds that need to be expressed, shared, and sometimes resolved. When we leave things unresolved, we find each other again to resolve the situation. When we find great alignment with each other we often wish to seek that alignment again and advance it. Sometimes we just like being with each other and the joy of being able to find each other again through history is an exciting and fulfilling adventure. We also come together for a specific purpose that may have an impact on humanity. The combined energy of specific qualities from souls uniting has brought about great advancements on Earth in every conceivable way.

As we advance ourselves I believe we seek out those souls whose vibrations complement ourselves and also enhance the qualities we possess. We are more motivated by some people than others; some people bring out the best of us while others the worst. Whatever the case is, we are all triggers for each other's growth.

I recall many years ago a good friend who was inspired by my own spiritual development in such a way where he initiated his own awakening much to the annoyance of his girlfriend who felt threatened by the positive changes he was making because it was upsetting her plan! She told him that she didn't want him to hang out with me anymore because she thought I was having a negative influence on his life! In other words, she didn't like the idea that he was moving forward in his life and it didn't fit in with her plan. How many times have people adapted themselves to suit other people because they didn't want to upset the apple cart? What is this doing to you but suppressing your qualities that are there to advance you? As children we have a natural instinct in whom we want to hang out with and parents can often throw a spanner in the works by placing embargos on our friendships with some people because the parents don't like them. I recall my own mother saying,

"Why do you have to hang out with those guys? Why don't you hang out with that nice boy who lives down the street?"

I'm sure there are many of us who have heard that before!

All my friendships are now source based. I suppose you can't help but see people as Gods the more you become one yourself!

A few years back I met a client online who was having a session with Tabaash via Skype. To make a very long journey short we became great friends, soul brothers in fact. It was like we were one being, at times the parallels in our lives being so similar. It's become more so over the years to the point where he jokes that to find out how he's doing he contacts me. One night I awoke with the sudden realization that his whole last name was almost an anagram of Blair Styra. And to top that, his first name is Anthony (Tony), which is my middle name. Tony organized a seminar for me in Sedona, Arizona, and when we met at the airport in Phoenix there was none of the awkwardness of first meetings, it was the reunion of soul brothers who knew each other very well. As we developed our connection we also developed an energy connection where we could feel what the other was feeling or know what the other was going through. Sometimes we were feeling the same emotion or going through the same thing at the same time. It was and is very powerful when you connect with someone on that level. It totally goes beyond human nature and can only be found in the nature of God.

Tony introduced me to Leonard, a native of New York City. Leonard is street savvy and a gentleman. When we first set eyes on each other I felt like I was looking at a younger version of myself. We look like we are brothers; we dress alike and have many similar tastes. I know that if I walked into his wardrobe I would find something to wear, we call it the

BLENORD effect! When I shop for clothes I always think, "Leonard would like this." The three of us recently got together in Sedona to have some bro time. I had spent time with each of them individually and they with each other but this was the first time that the "brothers" had been together in this life and it was a very sacred reunion of three souls who obviously have had a great deal of history together. For me personally it was an important experience. When I established a relationship with Kay when I was eighteen I bypassed a lot of the things that I would normally have done at that age, hanging out with my mates being one of them.

So spending time with Tony and Leonard offered up to me a kinship in friendship that was liberating and revealing. The three of us together were like components that were created to work together. Each component enhancing the others and because of that life seemed to work better. They were lights shining on me that revealed me to myself in ways I had not seen and giving me opportunities to express myself in ways I had not done. Our combined spiritual energy was a pool of our God natures swirling with infinite opportunities to advance each other.

Our joy in each other's company was intoxicating and contagious, as often I would see people smiling at us in our obvious satisfaction of being together.

There's nothing quite like being your total authentic self with others who are doing the same thing. I felt the fact that we were all three meeting for the first time in Sedona meaningful to our personal and collective development. The energy of Sedona was exposing us to new aspects of ourselves that would shape our collective energy. We were reuniting as souls to establish a powerful energy that we intended to develop to serve humanity.

On my first visit to Sedona while I was touring with Dolores Cannon and her daughter Julia we visited the Grand Canyon. My first visit was a revelation to my soul and so I suggested to the bros that we visit it. To my surprise neither of them had been before and so after an organic breakfast in a café just outside Sedona we drove the two hours to the Canyon. It was autumn and the trees were displaying a horticultural fashion parade of color. The skies were an intense blue and the red of the mountains against the blue of the sky and the colors of the autumn leaves made it all quite spectacular and it was one of those times where you truly marveled at nature. The conversations with my like-minded God brothers on the journey were always easy but so were the silences as none of us felt an obligation to fill up the empty space. As we drove through the terrain that extended in front of us I imagined what it must have been like when there were no roads and convenience stores. This vast expanse of land having never been violated by human nature, the land reaching out to the edge of the Grand Canyon must have been a great marvel to those who came across it. No sealed car parks and out-buildings, no signs pointing you in any direction. A place devoid of public toilets, coffee shops, and deals that offered you the Grand Canyon experience. You didn't need to find a deal, you were experiencing it. How the ancients of the place must have revered this and simply embraced its sacredness and adapted to the power of nature rather than exploit its potential.

When we arrived I could see that since my last visit there had been some retail development around the area. So now not only can some people be exposed to one of the wonders of the world that would speak many things to their soul, they could do it while drinking a coke, filling their face full of potato chips and pizza and then have the privilege of desecrating the landscape by dropping their litter on the ground even though there was a litter bin two feet away, which their big fat feet had an aversion to walking toward. You just felt like lifting these people up and dropping them over the edge. And then there were those who were wandering around plugged into music and doing stuff on their mobiles the whole time they were there, which made me wonder why they bothered in the first place as they could do that anytime anywhere. It amazes me that some people cannot turn off for a moment and pay attention and homage to real life and what it can do for them. What do they say when people ask, "How was the Grand Canyon?"

"I don't know," they would reply. "I was too busy filling my already empty head with noise that would make sure that I didn't have to engage with anyone or the world. And to ensure that I would totally miss out on everything I had to keep texting my friends who are just as brain dead as me so we could all ensure that we really never participated in life at all."

Right, having got that out of my system I return back to my bros and me. I was keen to see what their reaction would be when they first set eyes on the Canyon and it was the same I had when I first saw it, it stunned them into silence. There is a respect in that silence as not only are you being shown how beautiful our world is and it did it completely without any human interference for billions of years. That's one of the frightening things about human nature, they can obliterate in a few thousand years what took billions of years to craft and not feel bad about it.

A few years back my folks decided to sell the family home and they moved into an apartment in a retirement complex near the beach. When we were children we used to visit this beach area and though close to the city it was still untouched countryside. When the folks moved into their apartment the view across the road was one of rolling green hills and vast landscapes. Four years on its rolling gray roof-scapes and the lush tall trees were replaced with streetlights. A once quiet road is now a constant hum of traffic. All the surrounding hills that stood the nature of time quite well were in a month or two leveled flat so human nature can expand. A flock of geese that used to nest in the bushes near a stream now wander through the streets shitting all over the place. I admire their fortitude; in the face of adversity they have the right attitude. I suppose in a way that's what human nature is doing to Earth, it's shitting on nature, and shitting on life as it was created to be. Maybe that's why the Earth is shitting back; makes you think, doesn't it?

In the meantime, I've left Leonard and Tony and myself hovering somewhere in the Grand Canyon. We had such fun being together. Hanging out with people that you are in harmony with is a blast. When you love them and know how to be God as well with them the blast ignites a power and an energy that is quite combustible! We wandered around for hours mostly together but occasionally having a quiet reflective moment to ourselves. We took a lot of photos of each other and when I look at the pictures there are a lot of light beams surrounding us obviously enjoying hanging out with us as well. Some people would say it was the trick of the light, I say it was God. The energy being what it was, Tabaash couldn't help but urge me to allow him in so he could talk with the boys and generally participate. So, I stepped aside and he walked with the guys and chatted and told them stories of the energy of the place, walking between the two of them his arms around their shoulders. Leonard said afterward that a couple walking toward them and Tabaash gave them a gracious bow and wished them a good day. The look on the woman's face apparently was one of amazement but also one of recognition that Tabaash was not quite of this planet.

He spoke to some crows and they spoke back, one particular one hanging around as long as Tabaash was hanging out with the boys. When I came back in I felt the openness of my body to great energy and was filled with happiness.

The three of us moved away from the crowds, wanting to feel the sacred tranquility of the area. We found a flat stone where we were able to sit and meditate and so we joined hands and I could feel the electrical charge of life flow from one to the other, a lifeline of source energy stimulating our higher thoughts and taking us into deep places within our soul. I had a vision of us in a past life where we lived as indigenous people, our village about a hundred miles north of where we sat. Tony was the father to Leonard and me, his two sons, and we had a great harmony with the environment that allowed us to benefit from the land because our people worked together with the forces of life and revered the Earth and all it was offering us. I felt a great respect and love for these two men who had come into my life once again knowing that our combined energy was going to give something to humanity.

When we finished our meditation we sat for a while longer looking at the greatness before us, talking and watching people. I observed that some people were basically bobbing from one photo opportunity to another not even seeing what was around them. They would stop for a second and then move on as if this experience was something they had to get over so they could get onto the next one. Then there were those who were caught up in the sacredness of the place and as I watched them I could see the gift they were receiving by being there. I know that every experience we have in life changes us regardless of us being conscious of it or not. How more fulfilling, though, if we are conscious of this and just think what we must be participating in when we do engage on a conscious level. The way some people live their lives is like bobbing from one experience to another, never fully understanding what they are doing and why they are doing it, they get so caught up into getting to the next destination.

We are denying ourselves life by living too much, too fast.

After our meditation the boys and myself wandered around for an hour more and then headed back to the car. I knew that this was not the last time I would visit this place and so I thanked source for the opportunity I had with my brothers, knowing that we had sowed some very imperative seeds for the work that the three of us will do in the future. It felt like it was a starting point for us in regard to being positioned in a place where there was a particular energy that was essential to our personal development and the common ground that we had created. From this ground would be built the foundation of our further service to God and humanity. Tony and Leonard and myself have evidently come together to serve humanity by uniting our individual qualities. Meeting together in Sedona was like we were welcoming each other back into our lives and establishing the source link that would create a formula for future work. As I said to Leonard this morning on video call:

"Each of us has things that we need to do and change that is vital to our individual development and as we make these changes it becomes much more evident how we will come together to serve, we are in preparation for something big."

Before we do any of that, though, we really need to eat something. Being only thirty Leonard still needs to go to the feeding trough several times a day whereas Tony and I being of a more mature age often forget to eat! With Leonard I've never seen anyone order so much food and not eat it. He must have had a diet that never varied in a past life as whenever I've been out to eat with him he will order a variety of dishes that he will surround himself with. The day we left Sedona we had breakfast at a local popular café that was humming with the contentment of well-fed human beings. Leonard obviously wanted to be one of them.

On that last breakfast he ordered an omelet with hash browns, dill pickles, and potato chips. He also ordered a side of corn chips, pancakes, and a bowl of fruit. Oh, but wait, I forgot the side of guacamole and salsa just for good measure. I've got a picture of it. I did have a pick at the corn chips; they were delicious.

I get ahead of myself, though, as we had a few days to go before this final epicurean breakfast feast. After our day at the Grand Canyon we went to a place called Bell Rock that's not too far out of Sedona township. Bell Rock is named for its characteristic bell shape and is an easy climb with a little effort. It's also a powerful vortex and sightings of UFOs are quite common in this area. I had been there once before with Tony a few years back, but it was in the middle of summer and the temps were in the high 90s (40s C) so we abandoned the idea of a climb. This trip, though, it was autumn and a tolerable 70s (20s C) degrees made a climb highly acceptable! We got there in the morning and the place was packed with sightseers and possibly people looking for quivering portals vibrating with a powerful spiritual energy; well, you never know? The climb was far from arduous at the beginning and soon we were standing on a veranda of red rock taking in the grandiose view of the surrounding area. Tony and Leonard did some Chi Gong for a few minutes and then we sat down and meditated together for about ten minutes. There was not even the gentlest of breezes and not only could you feel the stillness, you could also hear it. There is so much that is being told to us in those silent moments. That's when it's good to attune to what life is saying to us.

As I sat there with my brothers I felt like I was downloading information that was going to be useful and I had the sense that it was data that was already in my soul memory but it was awakening. Have you ever felt like that when you know you are being given information or something in you is stimulated to recall something deep or vital to your life? If that happens to me I always put out the thought of recognition and that I am open to receiving the information.

After our meditation, we wandered around and climbed a bit higher but not too high as climbing up is easy; it's the climbing down where the challenge is as the process of descending seems harder than ascending! I could see people who had climbed right to the top looking down considering their options for descending. Apparently quite a few people get stuck up top as they panic trying to get down and have to be rescued. Not that we were stuck but as we made our way down though not precarious, we had to be careful not to do a header down the side of Bell Rock! Leonard and I being who we are of course had to take a difficult route to no doubt prove our masculinity or something of the sort. It was quite steep and we had to slide down on our backsides and make funny concentration faces as we did so, which completely took the cool out of us. Only briefly though as when we hit the bottom we stood tall, adjusted the sunnies, smoothed back the hair, and strutted back to where Tony was. I could wax lyrical about Bell Rock but there's a danger of sounding like a travel brochure so I shall simply leave you with the image of the trio reunited, sauntering off into the early afternoon back to the car, ready for our next adventure.

About a month ago Tabaash mentioned to Leonard in a session about a Lemurian crystal that Leonard was going to buy and he described it in some detail so Leonard was keen to find it. We actually did find it on our first day in Sedona but it was on our last morning that Leonard went to buy it. We couldn't recall which shop it was but Leonard was certain that it was on the right down the road and so like a man on an important mission he took off, leaving me and Tony to follow in his wake. We did eventually find the shop after popping into every shop on that side of the street that looked like it sold crystals to find that it was pretty well right in front of where we had parked the car. Men and directions, eh?

Being from New York, Italian, and basically being Leonard, he managed to get the price down and so the owner of the shop did a cleansing and a blessing of the crystal and also on the three of us as we stood there. It was quite extraordinary and very special and significant and not one customer came into the shop as he was doing it. The minute he finished, though, several people instantly came into the shop. I hoped that they would spend lots of money in this shop owned by this very generous spirit. As we drove out of Sedona and started our two-hour journey to Phoenix I knew I would return to this unique town and once again it would embrace me with its sacred energy. We were all heading home and would be picking up our day-to-day lives once again. I was the first to be dropped off and as I said good-bye to my brothers I felt like I should say something profound but all I wanted to do was cry. And then suddenly they were gone and I was checking in my bags and heading to Los Angeles to get my flight to New Zealand. I felt quite disoriented and rather blank; the time the three of us had together had shifted something in me and I knew it was the same for them. We can all trace back through our life the significant people and see how they have shaped us. Looking back now at my life I can see how certain people appeared in my life for a myriad of reasons. We have made an agreement with these people to present themselves to us and we to them so that we can all encourage each to evolve in life. Some stay with us right through our lives while others come only for a short sojourn and then blend into the past. The friendships we develop are like keys to doors that open to our relationship with ourselves. We seek, though, for so much more and at times it's nice to travel solo but nevertheless we must embrace the opportunities that we find in each other. As human beings we are essential to the survival of one and all, and so I encourage you all to hold strong onto the wonderful friendships that you have and encourage yourself to develop others.

In doing this we are giving each other life and life to a new idea of how we can all be as people sharing this Earth. Being too separate is making enemies of each other and losing the common ground of respect that allows us to build the energy that manifests as the New Earth Energy. We all carry the sacred energy of source and we all have the great aptitude to love.

There is never a greater moment than now.

Chapter Nineteen
The Life of a Coin

A few weeks back my friend Marion gave me an old Roman coin that was struck when Valentinian 1st was emperor of Rome from 364–375. I had never heard of him and it seems to me that Rome had an awful lot of emperors in its time. Every Tomious, Dicksus, and Harryium seemed to want to wear the purple robes of Rome, not something to be taken lightly considering the fact that there would always be someone around who wanted to rip those robes off you and a fair amount of your skin and limbs in the process. From what I have read of Valentinian he seemed to be quite the socialist, establishing schools and setting up medical care for the poor of Rome. He was intolerant, though, of magical practices, witchcraft, and some healing practices so that makes me glad that I was not alive at that time doing what I do now! Apparently, he had a brute of a temper and at times wasn't a very nice person to the people around him but then it must have been difficult being the ruler of what was known as the Great Roman Empire. I mean, no pressure, right?

I am quite in awe of this coin. It's a historical storybook and when I look at it I am thunderstruck by the fact it started its life when most of the people of the time had no idea of the existence of much of the world. I wish that I could hold the coin and have it talk to me of all the experiences it has had. It would tell me the story of its conception and of the person who had worked the metal to give it the shape it has and of the person who would have stamped Valentinian's face on the coin. Who were these people and what sort of lives did they have? As the coin went into circulation I think of all the men and women, soldiers, slaves, children, shopkeepers whose hands would have held this coin and used it for whatever purpose. Did it reside in a silk purse or a leather pouch? Was it passed over to buy a beer or a loaf of bread? Was it ever used in a gambling game by a group of soldiers passing the time while they waited for orders from the commanding officer? Whatever the value of this coin was I have no idea but the value it has to me now as an object that was used every day passed from person to person place to place makes this coin a valuable traveler through history. I wonder if I was alive in that time in history living out yet another life perhaps possessing this very coin. And if I was alive at that time what was it that my soul wanted from that lifetime and since that time have I progressed in the ways that I wanted to?

Like the coin we have all existed through history. We are no different from the coin in the sense that we ourselves are living history. Our soul is a great storyteller full of the adventures and experiences of life from the very conception of each life we have lived. We have value in each lifetime as the coin did while it was in circulation. The coin of course is no longer valid as a form of currency but we never lose value as souls; in fact, we gain value with every experience with every life that we live. If we invest well in life, the value increases securing a positive future. The value we place on our life stems from the original plans that we come into life with. One could say that you come with specific intentions that are your investments; rather like an investment portfolio, the content being thoughts, feelings, personality traits and more, I'm sure you get my point. You are your investment and the market is the world that you create. Based on events that you establish and participate in, you may create fluctuations in the market and the "value" of your life is defined by these fluctuations. When you get good returns, you celebrate and hopefully invest more from that point. You have to be careful that you don't invest too much in certain thoughts, actions, and experiences, as you may not reap the best returns. GOD is your broker and will give you advice now and then but life is speculative and to make it work you have to learn how to read yourself, to best read the market! At times we create investments that are a great challenge for us that take us to the outer reaches of our abilities to cope. I'm a firm believer that we don't create something we can't cope with. To find how we cope we have to invest in the market of our live's emotions and responses. This can mean extra vigilance on our part to ensure the greatest returns.

I mentioned in an earlier chapter about the woman who had lost a child and wanted to visit Kay at the care home. She had been in contact with me about visiting Kay again but for some reason I felt I did not want to encourage another visit. I made some excuse or another but when she came to see Tabaash for a session I asked afterward why she felt so compelled to visit Kay. She told me that since Kay was close to death she felt more connected to her daughter in spirit. This confirmed my need to discourage her visits to Kay and as the weeks went by I heard various reports of her odd behavior and her desire to kill herself so that she could be with her child in spirit. She was investing so much in her idea that once she died she would be with her and it would be as it was when they were mother and daughter. I knew that we could do nothing more for her and even though she wanted more sessions with Tabaash I knew it was fruitless.

I heard a couple of weeks back through a text that she had indeed taken her life.

I looked up to the heavens and said out loud, "Oh you stupid woman, you had so many other choices!" With all due respect to her trauma and loss, I felt angry that she was making all this effort to understand her loss but obviously she had invested so heavily in her pain she was unable to feel connected to ways of being that would help her move on with living. Her investment in grief overpowered any other investments she was making in life to the point where the grief became the main investment in her life's portfolio. In her way of thinking there was no more value left in her life, it was like she had cashed in all her investments and closed the portfolio. The heaviness she felt must have been so unbearable for her to take her life, I wonder now how she sees what she experienced here on Earth while she lived and hope that she allows the souls that are there to help relieve her pain.

In my years as a channel I have dealt with people who are terminally ill and others who are suicidal and always I have been able to feel compassion and sadness for the journey they have been on and their passing. I have always been able to go to the God in me and understand that there is a bigger picture but for some reason with this woman I just felt anger and it made me examine why I was feeling it with this particular situation. I believe it's because I knew that she could have found a way of being able to bear her loss and move forward in her life. I am sorry that she was not able to find her way through her trauma and I couldn't help but think of Kay and her situation, wishing we had more years together of life without the Alzheimer's and here was someone who had so much life to have if only she was able to feel that through her pain. Usually when I hear of the passing of someone I send a prayer and thoughts to help that soul transition. I found with this woman I could not do that right away. Days and days later when I was meditating, her name came into my thoughts. I know that when this happens it is the soul of the person coming onto my radar. I spoke to her in my thoughts of how sorry I was that she had taken her life and that I had been pissed off with her. I told her that I understood that her trauma was too great to bear and that I hoped she had found the peace she had been seeking. I sent her love and strength to support her and when I did I felt this great sense of peace come upon me and I knew it was her telling me that she was peaceful. I was able to share this with some of the people who had also tried to help her as they had been quite shocked when they heard she had taken her life. They felt very comforted after I had shared with them what I had experienced and were able to be at peace with it.

As I wait for Kay's passing that is imminent I wonder about the emotional pain that I will feel and how it will affect me. In many ways, I have spent the last few years going through grief as Kay's grip on reality shifted to where it is today. With the woman who lost her daughter it was so sudden and she was not prepared for the impact of what occurred. I've had years of getting used to it but even so the loss will be great. Of course my connection with source has shown me that our souls never die and so I am able to invest well in the idea of what we have access to when we pass and what Kay will access once she passes.

Every person we make connections with has had an impact on our life, some more than others. This impact I believe is important to pay attention to as it offers up a chance to think, feel, and respond in a particular way that seems important to our development.

Our responses to life and its situations tell us about ourselves.

There is guidance offered up to us in our responses that assists us in healing our own issues from the past. This shows us where we stand in our present and presents to us the infinite possibilities of our futures, and all of this because of the way we choose to respond and invest in those responses. I see this more clearly as I accept the fact that the day-to-day stories of our life are ways of directing us through life. The challenges that we face as a human race are epic stories that speak to us of the possible outcomes that we all create for ourselves and the Earth. I think of the coin and consider the way the world was then and of all the conflicts that were happening. You would think that we would have as a human race evolved from the need to grow through conflict. Over a thousand years later we haven't changed much in that sense, have we? What is it that we have invested in that still makes some of us believe that it's fundamentally acceptable to inflict upon people belief systems that proliferate acts of violence against each other? People speak of dark forces and negative energy that keep us aligned with destructive ways of living life; that's a thought I suppose, but is it also a fact that for millenniums we have invested in ways of thinking that have created belief systems that place us against each other and ourselves? Are we ourselves creating the very dark forces that have been spoken of simply because a belief system held by many creates a collective energy that if focused on long enough can disrupt that balance of life? Emperor Valentinian had a social conscious that made him establish systems that helped the community but despite that he still went to battle. Does that need to be the way of the world today? Since the time of Valentinian as a human race we have advanced mind, body, and spirit. Advancing is one thing but to live those advancements to the positive benefit of all seems to be something that still eludes us. We have advanced our technological aptitude to a high degree and have made great inroads with science and medicine and yet we use science to create more weapons of mass destruction and the medicines that are being created don't seem to have an impact on the new viral strains that are prevalent. We talk a lot about climate change but while we talk we make few changes that have a major impact. We are aware of the changes that are considered necessary but no leader seems to want to take the absolute lead in what needs to be done to bring all countries together in agreement and so we seem to be content to be observers rather than participants. Meanwhile, the world Earth reasserts itself and we believe that we have nothing to do with what is happening or we are of the belief that we can't do anything as it's too late and the balance has been tipped.

Are we really wanting to be tipped out?

Today as I write it is New Year's Day and through the morning I have been receiving New Year's wishes. One message that was sent really struck a note in me.

You have 12 new chapters.
You have 365 new chances
Waiting for you.

I like the look of the numbers 2018; there seems to be a harmony in the numbers. They are pleasing to the eyes and to me seem powerful and sacred. We have twelve months in front of us to invest in life more consciously. Twelve months to be creators of something wonderful that can bring about positive change to the world and ourselves. Twelve months to see what it means to be true believers of ourselves as source energy and healers to each other and the Earth.

Are we true believers who can live what we believe?

When I spoke at the New Earth Conference and retreat in Sedona in November last year I thought about what the New Earth Energy means to me and how I interpret this in life. This is obviously a significant time in Earth's history as it sheds some old layers and empties itself of energy that is no longer considered necessary. We are used to the belief that when we look at something we believe that what we see is true and absolute and constant in its finite existence. Of course, all life is infinite in its evolution and we must create a new platform for the new energy to thrive. If we as people understand this then we can be in harmony with these changes and subsequently make our own personal changes to align with the new energy; in fact, we MUST make the changes if we are to continue our time here on Earth. And this is when as true believers of the New Earth Energy we look toward advancing ourselves in the ways we can make possible. This is very exciting, we have 365 days to prepare, create, and participate in a whole new way of being that engages us in positive evolution.

So, where do you start? I've compiled a list of what I believe are changes we can make that aligns with the New Earth Energy.

BE GOD CONSCIOUSLY.

From the moment you awaken affirm in your own way and words that you indeed are *GOD*. And what greater starting point can you have to begin a day considering this is the point of creation, the point where all the power is? Whatever you need for the day it's going to start from this place.

CREATE THE DAY AND ALL IT ENTAILS FOR YOU.

The day is before you and you have all the infinite possibilities of what it could be. Whatever the structure of your day, inform your life from your *GOD NATURE* the rules of the day and the outcomes that you choose to create. Information we pass on to our human nature daily is essential to a greater outcome.

NURTURE.

It's your day, your creation, relax and start this new day with peace and ease, knowing that all the systems that make you are going to work better when you have a relaxed beginning. Don't rush your breakfast; use it as a time to awaken yourself to the day, it's a good preparation time.

MEDITATE.

Create some time to go within and visit your higher nature and the places that exist deep within you. Allow yourself to know that through this you are *SOURCE ENERGY* and connecting in this way will enhance the day that you have before you.

BE CONSCIOUS OF THE DAY.

Have a day where you are *AWARE* of how you are creating the day, how you are listening to the day, what it's telling you, and how you are responding to what you hear.

STAY CONNECTED TO SOURCE.

As often as you can through the day reinforce your connection with source that indeed *YOU ARE GOD!* It's keeping you logged in for the day and doing this aligns you with the guidance that we all have through our lives from source and the energies that work with us. It's also a simple way of evolving our body's relationship with the higher part of us.

PRACTICE SOME OR ALL OF THE QUALITIES YOU POSSESS.

What a great way to affirm who we are and to create more!

SHOW AN ACT OF KINDNESS TO SOMEONE.

We are here to look out for each other so by expressing some act of kindness or finding some way of serving another human being is a way of loving which is vital for all of us to feel and express.

EVEN IF YOU DON'T AGREE WITH SOMEONE'S PERSPECTIVE, SHOW RESPECT.

This doesn't mean you can't have an opinion but respect that others have one as well. It's very easy to become indignant about someone else's perspective if you are not respecting their right to have one. Your response or reaction tells you about yourself, not the person. Know when to walk away or say nothing; it's useful to keep your opinions to yourself at times!

THIS IS A LIFE YOU HAVE CHOSEN, IT IS YOUR DEAL.

As odd as it may seem to some people, no one else had a hand in making your life deals. You have always had complete sovereignty over everything. One can struggle with this notion, as most believe the deals you make in life are influenced by others and outside circumstances, but circumstances and people only occur because of you. The New Earth Energy carries a frequency that amplifies the ways you can make the best deals in life. If you are willing to be a participant in this energy then *What Was* does not come into the picture. The New Earth Energy has nothing to do with what has passed. Using the new energy takes you away from the old ways and what you were. It encourages you to live in a fulfilling way, it shows you productive choices and makes it uncomplicated when it comes to making the deals in your life.

LOVE, BE LOVED, AND BE DIVINE.

Love is the word that is used to describe the ultimate vibration of life.

When we are loved we are given life, when we love back we are giving life.

When we love ourself, we are standing on the point of creation energy, and we align with our divinity when we give this love to ourselves. This love gives you the feeling of how you are connected to everything and it shows you how you and all are carried by this energy through life and directed in wondrous ways.

Love empowers and heals, it calms us down and lights us up. Love encourages us to advance all our potentials and it is the vibration that makes the most sense.

Why does it make the most sense, I hear you thinking?

Love is what God feels.

GOD knows no other feeling but love and so it is the ULTIMATE FEELING. When we engage with love it will organize all our other human emotions in such a way where we will only but benefit. Creating from the ultimate feeling gives you a more definitive platform on which to create your life. This makes me think of when I go to see Kay and when I walk into the room her face lights up with love. Because of the Alzheimer's the walls are down and when she is aligned the love flows out of her in such a gracious and divine way it astounds me. In her eyes I can see that ultimate feeling. So I suppose that what we want to experience in each life we have is this ultimate feeling. No wonder when you ask people what they most want in life the answer usually is *Love*. The soul knows where the power comes from and without the energy of love the soul feels detached from life and struggles through the body. And so, is this really all we have to do in each life? Are we simply to strip back the layers of our human nature to expose love? What of all the experiences and events of our life, what are they all about? Perhaps it is just how it is on Earth and regardless of life being positive or negative by approaching everything with love you gain a greater understanding. Therein lays the challenge then, to find love through adversity as much as through the productive events of life. That's a massive thing to face when humanity is used to being angry at adversity. Most people would find it very difficult to find love in brutality, abuse, negativity. I don't believe for a moment that approaching adverse situations with love is showing an insensitivity or indifference to suffering but it must empower some part of our soul that shows us a way to cope better and direct us toward positive outcomes. We have made conflict a constant in our lives, be it through association or our own self-inflicted conflicts.

Conflict seems to be something that we accept whereas love is something to attain like a reward that we have to earn because of the conflicts we have been through.

Why earn the right to the ultimate feeling when it is freely given?

Inflicting upon ourselves ideas that harbor feelings of guilt and unworthiness seems to be a major conflict for a lot of people. I don't believe the world needs to be like this anymore. Perhaps in the past it was like that because that's where we are at as a collective, but I really believe that we have moved away from the idea of that energy as a constant in our lives. That way of thinking and believing has nothing to do with the New Earth Energy and that's why we question and react against it, as intrinsically our souls know we have advanced and find no need to think in such a manner. In the time of our old friend Emperor Valentinian, conflict was an unvarying part of life and accepted. That was our history as it was then, people still feeling the need to conquer the Earth and each other. And yet where have all the conflicts through our history actually taken us? Empires come and go, beliefs do the same, and so do our lifetimes. Some things, however, remain consistent like the energy of love and the coin that I possess even though the emperor is long gone and so is the world that he lived in.

Chapter Twenty
A Long Walk

I have a good friend Hirini who has just walked the entire length of the country in one hundred days. This was no stroll through the countryside but a walk for the rivers of Aoteoroa (New Zealand), a walk with the spirits of the men who made up the Maori Battalion that fought in WWII. He carried them with him in his pack, their faces lined up in several rows on a piece of paper. They were his guardians, his warriors urging him forward on his mission to bring attention to the people the desecration of the liquid arteries of life that flowed through the country. These rivers are becoming congested and poisoned by the ignorance and exploitation of people who believe that these arteries are to be treated like sewers where the waste of human life and its toxins can be poured. For centuries these rivers have been the lifelines for all that exists close and beyond these rivers, capillaries reaching to give life further out. The God force created everything to be in harmony. All the formulas that make life occur are all made to be in harmony. They all work together and when the formula is followed, harmony exists. Human nature has evolved as a very disruptive part of this formula and by doing so has taken the harmony away. In our need to be human in our nature we are taking nature itself to the brink of disaster, consequently disrupting human nature as well. I have great admiration for a person such as Hirini, who, literally in this case, "walks his talk." Through our history there have been many human beings who have walked long and hard to bring attention to what we are doing to this world and each other. There are always going to be those who will make a great stand when they see the injustices that are all too prevalent on this planet. They have been pioneers in every walk of life, reminding us by their actions that we disrupt life when stop our walk and get off the road.

I have this picture forming in my mind of the very first time that we came into life on Earth. There we stand at a starting point with all of life before us considering the directions that we would like to take. It's all new as we have never been here before and the vastness of what is before us is exhilarating and we are trembling perhaps with a little trepidation of the roads that we will travel. The Earth is still brand new itself and is still developing physically and emotionally as we are. There are no disruptive influences that will distract us from our ultimate life experience and we have our connection with source energy still intact giving us the power to create the adventure of that lifetime.

The beauty of the Earth is quite exquisite, the energy intact and untouched by disturbing influences that are not in harmony with Earth. Life is sacred and all life forms on Earth work in concurrence so conflict has never been experienced. Everything naturally adapts as life evolves and the rhythm of life is such where all things pulse with this one rhythm connecting all life forms to create one big collective vibration. This vibration becomes the sound of life on Earth and it is a sound that gives life. And as we take our first steps on this new plane of experience we too are in harmony with this rhythm. It speaks to us through our thoughts and feelings, opening itself up to our investigation. This was our inauguration into life as a human being on Earth, we commenced our own long walk from that point and we have been walking ever since. I see this image of our soul within a body, a light being with no features, walking and guiding the body through the many lifetimes it will have. The walk continues but the bodies and the scenery changes with each life. As the soul continues its long walk, it dispenses of energy that are not fruitful to its journey. Imagine what it must have been like knowing that everything existed to support everything else, there being no degree of separation at all. The vibration of life must have been quite astonishing. Fear, anxiety, tension, conflicts would never have been experienced and so to roam through life in such a place was indeed paradisical.

To think that we have lived all this, seen all this, felt the world in this state and within us all the time is a deep-seated memory that we have accessed through our many lifetimes opening us to this state, reminding us of what we can attain.

I feel like all that time ago we all started a long walk together on a journey of exploration, adventure, and creation. Not only have we shared history together but we have been creators together in the human experience so that's an awful lot of sharing we have done! No wonder we keep seeking out each other again and again to further extend our relationship with each other and to swap creation stories! This particular long walk, though, seems to be coming to an end and as it does, we can no longer walk at the old pace or be involved with the old intentions we had when we began this journey. Our intentions are different now, though, different in the sense that we seem no longer to be so lost in our human nature and this discovery has led us to our spirit and the energy of source itself. We have made once again the natural link with GOD and its power.

We can once again claim our right to be engaged wholly and holy with source.

2017 seemed to be a brutal year for so many. Since the advent of 2018 I have had many conversations with people who were glad to see the back of 2017 and all it represented and I'm no exception. I understand that if we are completing the old model of life reality there is bound to be acceleration in our circumstances directing us to *completions* that are essential to the advancement of our being. These completions have had many faces and from my observation many were faced with huge fundamental choices in their lives, altering the very basis of their life's constitution. Each of us seemed at times to be walking very separately perhaps at times feeling unsupported but knowing also that it was a walk that we had to do alone at times. Occasionally we would run into each other and the look of recognition that we were all going through the same thing could be seen in our appearance. Emerging from our experiences we seemed to come out exposed and raw but lighter and wiser. To me I could feel the dispensing of the old energy as if it was slowly being drawn away. I was walking along a very long stretch of beach in Auckland recently and it was an extremely warm and windy day so much that standing on the beach in my shorts and no shirt I felt like I was having a total body dermabrasion session! The drier sand seemed to be sucked away and it skirted along the beach, tendrils of grit skimmed away by the action of the wind seemingly vacuumed up into oblivion. I took a movie of it on my Iphone and set the app to slow motion. When I replayed it, it made me think of the old energy and how it was just like this sand. It also made me think that around us are fields of energy skimming through us impacting our lives. I believe our soul knows this and I also believe that our soul knows what to do with these energy fields. The soul with its awareness would be monitoring these fields and would pull in what it felt necessary to our understanding. I also believe that over the last few decades it seems like we have all been prepared for the shift of energy and the impact this has on our lives. Of course not only does this shift affect us physiologically but mentally and emotionally as well. My belief is that this new vibration is able to resonate with us because of the way we have been evolving over the last decades. These changes have given us awareness on all the levels that I have spoken of and have heralded important changes that expose us to even more of the new vibration. We are, "simply put," being meddled with in a positive way!

We have been repositioned to align with the new vibration.

It's rather like we have been looking out a window and seeing the same view for a very long time. We have got used to that view and have adapted ourselves to the view. Our opinions, actions, ways of participating in life are all based on the view out of that window. We then look out another window and the view is different. We are so used to looking out the previous window that we keep going back to it because that's the view we have become accustomed to. Having looked out the other window we are curious about what we see and so we keep going back there to have another look. Every time we have "another look," we are creating new images of life for ourselves until eventually we stop making visits to the old view. We do this through our whole life. At times the window is open exposing us not to just the view but the energy of what we see. With the window, we have invited in the experience of what we see. When we have the window closed, we can just observe, gather more insight, and make the choice to open that window or not. If we see a view we really like and want to open that window but it's jammed, we evidently need to put more effort into opening the window!

When I was a child and we still lived in Canada we used to visit my maternal grandmother (Nana) at her place in the seaside town called White Rock. Usually we would drive down but during the summer holidays my father drove us to the railway station where he dropped us off while he went to work. We boarded the train to White Rock and the memory of this trip I still carry with me, not just the trip, indeed the whole feeling of it. It was about an hour's journey and it was a coastal journey full of appealing and mysterious sights and sounds that were woven into me like a magic spell. The seats were deep green leather with a table between the seats. An expanse of glass gave you full views of whatever was going on outside and the air seemed to me to crackle with the energy of our adventure. It was that real holiday feeling when all the usual routines and rules and old energy were put away and you felt like you were permitted to be someone else that somehow seemed better than everyday life. It was infectious and my sister and brothers all seemed to support each other in this journey and were in total harmony with each other, no doubt much to the relief of my mother! Sitting by the window as we pulled out of the station I was transfixed by the changing scenes as we moved from city to suburban areas and then out into open country and finally along the coastal track by the sea. I remember that the tide was out and the gray wet sand was a table of glistening wetness reaching out far away where I could just make out the silver line where the ocean was. Such scenes always made me conscious that there was something rather great going on around me and within me that had nothing to do with what I was actually seeing in regard to human nature. I suppose looking out the window as the train progressed in its journey lulled me into some contemplative meditative state allowing me to feel beyond my human nature. And do we not do that now as adults, finding a view that encourages us to be meditative? Some windows in life are just for that and I believe as we participate in those views we are reaching into those other worlds that are available to us and bringing back some information that can inspire us.

The journey to White Rock on the train though not a long walk was a journey that encouraged me to be braver and more authentic. I understand now that it was a state of being I was in that had nothing to do with the survival energy that was the prevalent energy through my childhood. The gentle rocking of the carriage and click clack click clack of the wheels on the track and the metal-on-metal heat smell that came through the open windows is with me to this very day, allowing me to be lulled into that part of my past. I loved looking out the wide windows that offered up such a generous array of changing scenery.

In life our perspective defines how big or small the windows of life can be. Sometimes there are no windows, leaving us with no view and making it more problematical when it comes to making decisions, or does it? Being able to look out a window of life and "see" what the possibilities are adds greatly to our choices but does it actually stop us from really using our feelings more concisely?

Seeing too much can confuse our issues if we are given too much information and this can actually cloud our natural judgment. Having no view allows our soul self to step in, giving us a clearer outlook and perhaps a more honest one at that. It gets us out of our brain and allows us to make choices through our feelings. If we are given a little bit of a view we have to build from what we see and if the view is expansive we seem to be embraced by it and become a part of it.

Next to my house on the right is a small block of apartments. They are three levels and the upper levels can see into my back garden. I love to fill the garden with color and so those upper apartments next door get a visual feast through the year. One day I was out front pottering around when one of the occupants of the apartments came over and told me how much pleasure it gave them when they looked out the window and saw my garden. Now that gave me pleasure knowing that I was able to share in such a simple way. And so now when I'm planning what to do in the garden I always think about what the neighbors will see when they look out the window! So to quote what I had written in a previous chapter:

You never know when you are giving people joy.

We have been walking through life from the moment we were created by source. As we have done this we have accumulated essential ingredients that advance our experience as source energy. We have taken forms and shapes that at times are not human and we have qualified as creators. I believe we stand in a position now where collectively we feel this more than ever before. And so what are we being faced with daily? Life, to put it in one word, we are facing *life* and in a way where never before have we been more practiced. And yet as we emerge into this light age we seem to be bombarded by rules that are stifling honest assessments in our lives. There are numerous self-appointed saviors that seem hell bent on making up rules that range from stupid to disturbing. People seem to have become so oversensitive to any form of reality that they hide behind the political correctness so they don't have to grow some balls. (And, yes, no doubt that there are those who might be offended by that term but that just proves my point.) I can't believe that we keep finding new ways to be offended by life! I heard on the radio this morning that the singer Lourde is being sued by some Israeli group who are seeking compensation for the young people who may have been traumatized by the fact she canceled her concert over there. Do we really want to continue walking this path? It's making people not only pissed off with each other but also afraid of being themselves for fear of reprisals.

I have compiled a small list of political correctness gone mad:

1. The word "man" as a prefix or suffix has been ruled as politically incorrect. A "manhole" is now referred to as a "utility" or maintenance" hole.
2. The English pudding (dessert) Spotted Dick has now been changed to "Spotted Richard" to avoid offense.

And this one really had me rolling my eyes and making expletives.

3. A UK recruiter was stunned and I quote: When her job advert for "reliable" and "hardworking" applicants was rejected by a job center as it could be "offensive to unreliable and lazy people."

But wait there's more!

4. A school in Seattle renamed Easter eggs "spring spheres" to avoid causing offense to people who did not celebrate Easter.

And so I shall endeavor to use all of this in one sentence.

On the way to the recruitment agency I had to apologize to the unreliable and lazy for my aptitude and avoid the utility hole, for fear that I would drop my Spotted Richard all over my spring spheres.

The walk seems so much longer.

Chapter Twenty-One
Sedona

Places speak to you, they put out a call to you inviting you to participate in their energy. For this to happen you yourself have put out a call asking in your vibration to align you with a place that would be fulfilling to your soul and healing and empowering to your body. For me one of these places in my life has been Sedona, Arizona.

We have to go back a few million years ago now when the area known as Sedona was covered by sea. The sea diminished over a slow period of time and the land transformed through seismic activity became the template for what we see as Sedona today. Wind and erosion created the majesty of the mountains that make the landscape of Sedona so seductive and mesmerizing to the eye. History speculates that the first inhabitants of Sedona known as "Paleo Indians" go back to 8000 BC. It was thought that they had migrated across land connecting Asia and North America. Other nomads followed during the period of AD 500 to AD 700; they were referred to as the Anasazi Indians. The Navajos called them "The ancient ones who weren't us." For reasons unknown the Anasazi departed the area and other tribes established themselves. There is a theory that a giant volcanic eruption around AD 1060 erupted, forcing the nomadic people to flee the area. Gradually other tribes established themselves but then in the 1300s the area was once again abandoned, possibly because of tribal conflicts. Spanish explorers made their mark around 1583 in their search for gold and silver but this proved to be fruitless in the Sedona area.

By the early 1900s there were a few squatters in the area, T. C. Schnebly and his wife being two of them. Schnebly had petitioned the US Postal Service to establish a postal stop in this area and was successful. The names he suggested for the area were not so successful until Schnebly's brother suggested the name of his sister-in-law, whose name was Sedona, so that is how Sedona got its name and I must say it's so much nicer saying that I have visited Sedona, Arizona, than Schnebly, Arizona, with all due respect to old T C!

From there on Sedona's history varied from fruit orchards to being utilized by Hollywood as the setting for over seventy films. Today it is a tourist destination with close proximity to the Grand Canyon and attracting millions of visitors a year because of its unique landscape. Of course, it has also gained quite a reputation over the last few decades as a bit of a spiritual and UFO mecca, drawing thousands to visit the sacred sights and camp under the stars in the hope of extraterrestrial connections. The Native Americans acknowledged Sedona as a sacred place and though they chose not to live in this powerful energy field, they often traveled to this place for healing and to perform other sacred rituals. There are a lot of powerful spiritual vortexes, the energy of which seems to amplify our own personal vibrations. I have personally felt the power of these vortexes and have experienced quite obvious transformation and healing. I have also noticed that once you have had this experience the energy that you have drawn in will never leave you. In fact, it seems to lodge itself into a part of your being allowing consistent transformation, perhaps for the rest of your life? I felt like I had plugged into source energy and wherever I am in the world I know that I am able to utilize the connection I have made.

I first visited Sedona many years ago when my friend Dolores Cannon and I did a speaking tour in several American states. We were accompanied by Dolores's daughter Julia, a gifted writer, speaker, and teacher in her own right, and the three of us hit the road "touring." In Sedona we were to present at the Sedona Creative Life Centre that was founded in 2000 by Shirley Caris, whose vision was to create a place dedicated to the creative and spiritual energy of humanity. Through the year it provides the most extraordinary environment and energy for presenters who offer up their particular brand of magic in spiritual and creative programs. It's a place where you feel the embrace of source energy.

The drive to Sedona from Phoenix is about two hours and once you get out of the airport area and onto the freeway it's pretty much a journey through the arid desert landscape of Arizona. I can tell you nothing about Phoenix as I've only got as far as its airport! There is something about the aridness of this sort of desert that speaks to my soul and as we drove to Sedona I felt the vibration of the area reaching out to me in a great massive energy hug. I think I smiled the whole way to Sedona. I felt Sedona before I saw it; as we were driving I noted a very distinctive shift in the vibrations, we had without doubt moved into a dimension that instantly spoke volumes to me and it wasn't subtle. Julia felt the same and as we drove into Sedona proper we felt like we were in some sort of energy bubble.

My first visual opinion of it was that it was very much part of the landscape. There were no tall buildings to interfere with the landscape and the colors of all the buildings were in harmony with the natural hues of the surrounding hills and rock formations. A progressive town council made sure there were no garish neon signs and even the streetlights at night were not allowed to be too bright lest they should interfere with the night sky! Now I like that idea very much and wish that other civic leaders would be as sensitive to the natural environments of towns and cities. Sedona presented itself to me as very ordered and peaceful and gave no impression of the hippy, new-age community that I had been led to believe. In fact, it seemed about as far away from that as you could imagine but it had presence and you could feel that everywhere. It is a place that touched you wherever you were and whatever you were doing. I felt like there was always this guardian energy in a constant vigil.

Once we had checked into our hotel Julia and I went out to explore, leaving Dolores to rest and work on her latest book. As we wandered around the area every corner we took exposed to us a view that could have been hung in any national gallery except this was natural and the gallery was the world! It was stunning and I must have looked a sight as we walked, my head swiveling all over the place for fear of missing something spectacular. I felt like I was being very warmly welcomed by the spirits of this land and that they were glad that I was there; it was an exceptional feeling and one I had never experienced before. There was no sense that I had been there before but more that I recognized the sacredness of the place and the sacredness was recognizing my soul.

Dolores and I presented at the Creative Life Centre and this magnificent venue seemed itself an energy vortex in its own right. What a perfect place to speak at in a perfect town of such consecrated magnitude! I was in an altered state the whole time we were there, seeing and feeling from many new levels of myself that had opened up. During the breaks I would wander off by myself walking through the gardens that had been established, discovering more energy and more magic and felt very much that I was being spoken to from sources that had nothing to do with human nature. It was not the spoken word but words that came to me through feelings and I knew that information was being downloaded into my soul for future reference.

After the day's work Julia and I would go off exploring, not wanting to miss a single moment of this opportunity we were being given. One day we drove out of town and basically did a loop, albeit a big one! The thing about a place like Sedona is that you want to stop every second to look at the view or take a picture or simply marvel at the sacredness and energy of the place. You can't do a place like that in a few hours or even days; it certainly deserves your undivided attention. We drove up through Flagstaff and then got onto the freeway and I saw a sign that said Sedona so I directed Julia, who was driving that day, down that road. We drove for a while and then the road stopped being a road and pretty well became a large wide track. We were in a four-wheel drive and so decided to risk whatever was before us. OMG!! does not do it justice! In fact, words completely failed me, it was so majestic and spiritual and so off-the-planet stupendous. The massive red rock formations hugged the road like a wave that was about to break on the shore but for some reason had stopped in mid-motion. It was an ocean of terrestrial brilliance manifested as these rock formations. We would drive (carefully) and every five minutes or so I would yell out for Julia to stop as I saw another sight we just HAD TO LOOK AT! There was no one else around and as we gazed at the terrain before us the silence was full of ancient magic and memory. We had for a moment stepped away from the world and felt we were in an altered state and were being gifted the energy of something very primordial. It was like the ancients of the land were looking down on us and giving us their blessing.

The road was, for want of a better word, shit, and Julia was very impressive as she managed the potholes and uneven surface. Occasionally another vehicle would struggle past us and once to our amazement a Porsche was doing its best to look cool but was fast losing it as the struggle with the road was fast defeating it. God knows what damage driving in such a road was doing to such a car; what were they thinking? We traveled on like this for about half an hour before we saw in the distance Sedona township and eventually ended up much to our surprise, or perhaps not, on the road where the Life Centre was. The car and us were pretty well covered in red dust but hell it was well worth it and I advise anyone who is visiting Sedona to immediately book a four-wheel drive vehicle and make the effort to drive up Old Schnebly's Road! Keep your windows up, though, or you will end up looking like you have been rolling in the terrain of Mars. Oh yeah, if you come across a Porsche or any other dick in an unsuitable car, point at your four-wheel super-charged all-terrain vehicle and then at theirs and go HAHAHAHAHAHAHA!

I mean, really?

The rest of the week I seemed to float around in a sacred bubble of energy, my whole being pulled into pieces and put back together. Not only was I experiencing some inner transformation but mentally and physically I could feel myself shift onto a new platform that was giving me a new outlook on myself and the world that I was creating. Every time I stepped outside of my hotel room and looked at the surrounding majesty that embraced Sedona I felt a gentle electric surge pulse through my body that was exhilarating and empowering to all aspects of my soul.

The day of our departure had arrived and we had to get up in the early hours for the two-hour drive back to Phoenix and the airport. While the ladies were still getting themselves organized I stood in the small garden that was on the side of the hotel complex. It was about 2 a.m. and it was cool and still and the awning of the night sky was still in place, allowing the shimmering stars to perform. I walked around the garden and spoke to God and spirit, thanking them for one of the most life-changing and amazing weeks of my life. I pledged my life to continue the work I was doing and created the intention to return to Sedona in the future. I looked at the stars and saw there were three above me that seemed to be in a row. One of the stars unexpectedly flashed and then took off rapidly to the west. I stood there transfixed while another did the same and went east and then the last star took off straight up and vanished. I'm not going to say I couldn't believe what I was seeing as I DID believe what I had just seen. My whole being felt full of charged energy and a door seemed to open within me allowing knowledge and certainty that was previously unknown in my life. I didn't have a feeling of amazement or anything like that, but it just all seemed to make sense. That was my first experience of the extraterrestrial kind and it was not to be my last.

My next trip to Sedona was in late June 2014 where I met up with my great soul brother Tony and his partner Michelle. I had just been a key speaker at the 2014 Transformation Conference in Arkansas run by Ozark Mountain Publishers and Tony had organized for me to run a weekend seminar at the Creative Life Centre.

So much had happened in the years since my first trip to Sedona and I was thrilled that I was able to once again visit. This was also the first time that Tony and I were to actually meet in person as our connection up to that point was via Skype. My connection to Phoenix was delayed by several hours due to delays in Arkansas so by the time I reached Phoenix I was feeling pretty exhausted and more than a little pissed off about all the waiting around. Our meeting of two souls that had such a sense of familiarity about them that we simply picked up the thread of life and carried on. I just love it when you meet up with people where you have such a connection. There is no "getting to know you" as that's already been established and so you simply get on with creating more adventures! That's how it is with Tony and me; it's a bit like,

"Oh, it's you again. What have you been up to the last few lifetimes?"

The airport delays were unfortunate as it meant getting into Sedona about 11 p.m. and since I was staying at the house of my friend Linda this time around I was concerned about our very late arrival. She took it in her stride, though, and as Tony and Michelle went to their hotel Linda and I had a quick chat before retiring for the night.

I was so excited to be in Sedona again and once I sensed the first light of the new day I was wide awake and even though it was some ridiculous hour like 5 a.m. I had to get up and go for an early morning exploration. I quietly left the house and walked onto the road. Of course there was no one around at that time of the morning but there was plenty of wildlife around making the most of the coolness of the morning. Being the height of summer the temperatures later on would get into the 90s (40s C), not that I minded as I think I must have been a lizard in a previous incarnation as I love the heat of the sun on me. The morning birdsong was in full chorus as I started my walk and desert lizards made a gallop across the road as they saw me walking. It was not uncommon to see snakes and coyote and deer at this time of the day, but my morning companions were mainly the birds and the occasional jogger looking terribly serious in their athletic pursuit! The surrounding streets had names like Pony Soldier Road and Mount Shadows Drive in reference to the surrounding landscape and the fact that western movies had been filmed in Sedona. The houses were still deep in slumber as were their occupants and due to the arid conditions not a lawn was to be seen but there were plenty of trees and cacti and other desert-type plants that made a pleasant garden among the red earth. There were lots of bugs buzzing away so it wasn't exactly quiet as I walked up the road toward the imposing rock formations before me. One was called Coffee Pot Rock for obvious reasons while another had been christened Sugar Loaf. It was thrilling walking toward these and I had to stop every few seconds to marvel at the awesome sights all around me. I don't think I have ever been to a place where not only were you able to feast visually in such a satisfying way but feel the atmosphere as an actual sensation upon and through your whole being. I had yet to have breakfast but I felt that I was already full.

The sun had risen by now exposing the colors of the rock formations, and against the background of the most striking blue sky the show had begun and it was an extravagant performance. I stood under the bastion that was Coffee Pot Rock and looked at it with my soul. I wondered at its age and the history it had experienced. I thought of the ancients who had maybe stood where I was and what they had thought of this place and how they had utilized the energy of Sedona. I closed my eyes and imagined that I was absorbing the power of this history and wondered also if I had ever been there in another life. I opened my eyes and turned to the view in the distance and felt the now hot sun on my body.

I made my trek back to the house feeling very aligned with my surroundings and very happy to be here again. I knew that this visit to Sedona was going to be very different from my first one.

The next day found me once again at the Sedona Life Centre. Tony had organized for me to run a seminar and people came from all over the US to attend. While the others were setting things up for the day I made a private pilgrimage around the center remembering the last time I had been there. I was particularly eager to go and see a bronze bust of a First Nation man who was centered in a small courtyard between rooms. The last time I had been there was just before Dolores and I had presented there and I had been mesmerized by this splendid artwork and had felt the sacredness of its energy. Dolores and I were to speak in the main conference room that was adjacent to the courtyard where the bust was. I stood in the main room projecting my intention for the day to come and something caught my eye and I swear that the bust had turned and looked straight at me and then retained its normal position. To say I was stunned is an understatement, and I walked over to the bust and looked at it. I looked at it hard and I felt like there was life coming from it and that it knew that I was staring at it. The feeling that I had was that it had recognized me and was acknowledging me and was giving me the OK. I could feel spirit all around me and I told them how grateful I was for their energy and to be back in Sedona and here at the Life Centre. Through the whole time Dolores and I were there I felt that they were walking with me. And so of course it made sense that on this second trip I would go and pay my respects to the First Nation gentleman.

It was a hot late July day but the courtyard was shaded and didn't seem to draw the heat into it all, leaving a seductive coolness in the area. I stood by the bust and greeted it and watched for any signs of it moving. It was not like last time but I vow that there was a little grin on its face and the words came into my mind as if it were talking to me.

"Well, it's you again, is it? Come back for some more?"

Again the feeling of being surrounded by the spirits of the place was there and I knew through the whole weekend they were there watching, supporting, and teaching with us. The center hosts so many wonderful spiritual and creative Gods through the year and one could truly feel the way the energy of it all had blended and created a supportive energy that was always there and I liked to think that we were also doing the same. There is a unique energy that is created when a group of like-minded spiritual beings get together to share and learn. I find the energy to be full of each other's wisdom but also each other's vulnerability as we perhaps go to expose some aspects of our self that need to be faced. We are teachers and healers for each other and we are supporting acts for each other. The common ground that we create by participating in these events is something that we will always carry with us as we have made a commitment to imparting that energy in our soul; the energy becomes literally a part of us. It is such an intimate experience to share with like-minded beings on this level and I feel so blessed in my life to be able to do that. Before I start presenting and bring Tabaash through I always like to remind myself that all these people before me are aspects of myself that are helping me to evolve. They are souls that I already have common ground with and that we have been in communication on some other level for some time, and that's why we are all together because we put out the call to each other. It's never about what is it that I am doing for them but what are we all doing for each other? Yes, there are always roles that one portrays but that's simply the script and we must play our roles to the maximum but there would be no role to play if there were not others in the play! When I speak at events and look at the mass of people before me I think how fortunate I am to be able to have all the energy of these people as we share in the event and carry each other at that time in our lives. We bless each other and we love each other simply by participating and it's even grander when we know that we are doing it consciously!

On a day before we started the seminar Tony wanted to take the group to a sacred place not too far from Sedona township. It was in the Coconino National Forest, which spreads out to an impressive 751,000 hectares (1.856 million acres) in northern Arizona. It literally was in the backyard of Sedona but once we got out of the car park area we were instantly transported into a time and energy and place where human beings were utterly out of place. There were quite a few people around and I wanted to go off and be by myself and enjoy the deep silence of this place. Massive slabs of red rock towered around and above us and there was a great hole in the Earth where slices of rock as large as a house had tumbled and lay intact on top of each other like slabs of cold butter that had been cut and positioned. The relentless summer sun beat down, baking the rocks into a permanent primitive sculpture. Even though there were many people around silence prevailed as we all paid our silent homage to the Earth. There is no way that you can't be moved and touched by such an atmosphere and it made me think how the power of life must have been before human nature had a hand in changing it. I envied the original ancients of the Earth who would have been in complete harmony with this energy, they themselves recognizing that they were like everything else, just a part of the landscape.

The creeks and riverbeds were dry and signs of flash floods were evident among the terrain. Vegetation had been bleached to silver green by the sun but you could smell the subtle fragrance of them, an aromatic blend of many plant energies. We found a place to sit and for a while we accustomed our human nature and our souls to where we were and then Tony took the group through a guided meditation. His words trailed off after a while and we were left to our own feelings and thoughts. I love being with a group of people who with you are sharing and developing the Gods that they are. It's a very unique energy that is created, a very intimate energy of the advancement of people's lives. We all bring a specific vibration to the group that actually activates an amplified energy. It's the old "United We Stand" concept.

After the weekend seminar, I had the joy of leisure time with my friends and I looked forward to creating some adventures. Always an early riser I would take my morning constitution by walking up to Coffee Pot Rock and logging in to whatever energy I felt. Linda and I would then go down to a local shop where they made really good coffee and then off somewhere to breakfast.

Just outside of Sedona as you head south there is a café/shop that makes excellent organic breakfasts. I think it's called Oak Creek but it might not be. It's built under the canopy of the red rocks and surrounded by trees. You can sit in or outside and we opted for out and all the food is organic and delicious. We sat under a canopy of delicate trees and enjoyed the warmth of the morning sun as we breakfasted and talked. Linda had made some suggestion that we go walking in another part of Coconino National Park but this time to a part of the park that had a major energy vortex. I was keen to visit this vortex and I knew that Michelle and Tony would be as well. I contacted them and we made plans to meet at Linda's within the hour.

When they arrived they presented me with a straw hat (that I promptly left behind by mistake when I left) to ward off the fierce Arizona sun. When we went for our walk I decorated the front of it with bits and bobs I found, a feather, a flat piece of interesting stone, a weird-looking twisted twig, you know, it's the sort of thing you do when you are on holiday and have been presented with a hat!

We made another coffee stop along the way as Michelle and Tony needed their fix and Linda and I needed another one, too. And so after satiating ourselves with caffeine and taking pictures of each other and ourselves in front of a statue we went off to the vortex. We drove out of Sedona heading east and then made a turn to the west. The area unfolded into what looked to be ranches and there were signs pointing toward a resort (expensive) where later in the evening we had a drink. Linda had mentioned that the area was popular and that we would probably encounter quite a few hikers and people on bikes. As we pulled into the car park there was a definite lack of other vehicles and there didn't seem to be any other people around. We walked over to the start of the path and as we entered two hikers passed by. They were the only other people we saw the whole time we were there. I definitely sensed a change in the vibration as we walked on; I felt like I was pushing very gently through a force field and the whole area had been laid out for our investigation. The whole time we were in the area I had the feeling of being observed by the ancestors of the land and it felt like we were accepted. I believe it's important to respect the ancestors of such places and I put out a silent acknowledgment and thank you. They could probably tell that our intentions were sacred and so gave us the thumbs up!

There were signs warning us about bears and snakes, etc., that I pretty well ignored knowing that we were well protected and I wondered if there were signs for bears and snakes warning them about people!

The path was narrow and dusty and very uneven and definitely not the sort of place you would want to go in heels. We all settled into our own rhythms and after a while our conversation stopped as we each felt embraced by the force of our surroundings. The conversation of the land was subtle and you wanted to hear what it was saying. You could hear it in the gentle rustle of the bushes as a slight breeze invited a tête-à-tête with the land. You heard the laughter of the heat-baked rocks as the sun made a joke, and the dry riverbeds and streams were wide open to any discussion that would ensue. We would stop often and plant ourselves albeit temporarily into the land so that we too could be a part of the ongoing natural dialogue. I looked up at the sky and the surrounding ranges extending themselves upward. The sky was a white blue and the heat haze melted upon the ranges adding to their ethereal presence. Heat and calmness danced together in the air making you feel like you were reaching out of your body to join in. Wherever I looked, whatever I felt, the smells, the sounds, all sensations spoke deeply to my soul and carried me into the layered worlds that made up this revered place. As we neared the position of the vortex I felt a slight dizziness in my head and a sense that I was walking in my body but had no feeling of actually being a part of it. I was observing my surroundings—in fact, experiencing my surroundings—from a very disembodied position. It's amusing to note that everything seemed to make much more sense from that position!

It was obvious that we were in the vortex area as the trunks of the few trees that were around had grown twisted and seemed to be leaning inward toward some centrifugal source. The path had inclined gradually and we reached the top of a small hill and stopped. Separating and saying nothing to each other we took ourselves off to where we felt drawn and sat and meditated or just walked around or sat and observed our position. I was drawn to what looked like a wide stream that denuded of water exposed a smoothness of red rock and I went and stood in the area that if there had been water in it would have been a deep pool under the base of a small waterfall. I lifted my arms into the air and closed my eyes and felt my body pulling up energy from the ground. My heart chakra that for so long had been constricted opened up, and I could feel an emotional anxiety and physical tension depart my body and to this day it has never returned. I was still caring for my wife, Kay, at this stage and knew that all the stress was taking its toll on me and the release of this was liberating.

An interesting follow-up to this was the next day when Michelle and I had a wander around the township of Sedona. I felt drawn to go into a small shop where a woman practiced aura readings after having your aura photographed by a special camera. I decided to have it done and when the results came through she was looking at my heart chakra and I kid you not literally told me that yesterday I had done something that had cleared my heart chakra and balanced it all out. She then basically pointed out what was happening in my life through what she saw in my aura and it was exactly what was happening. Michelle was with me and she knew my story and looked at me in amazement at what was transpiring. After I finished she quickly had her aura photo done as well. So you see we are carrying our life around with us all the time!

I get ahead of myself, though, so let's get back to Coconino. We were all in a no-time place; we could have been there a few hours, a few days, who knows, we were just there. In great synchronicity, we all seemed to come out of our reverie.

At the same time, we all gathered together and spoke a little of what we had personally experienced. I could feel the "Ancients" around and Tabaash was making his presence felt and I knew he would like to channel through me at that time and talk to the others. And so, I departed from that part of my human nature for the moment and let him in. Usually when I channel I have no memory of what is said but on some occasions I am watching everything transpire from a high vantage point where I am able to see all and this was one of those occasion. I could see my body being directed by Tabaash and he was standing very still and powerfully with his hands in the air and he was calling out in some other language. It sounded like it was some sort of incantation and I looked at the surrounding rock formations and they seemed to suddenly shimmer with an energy that felt like a presence of spirit. I knew then that he was calling to the spirits of the land and the mountains and was invoking a sacred energy. The others were standing there watching him in amazement and I could see their own energy fields expanding with the energy that was being called in. Tabaash then spoke some words to the others present and then departed and I came back, my whole being feeling very expanded and empowered. We didn't really say much as we walked back toward the car; what could possibly have been said!

We were nearing the sign that had warned us about snakes and bears and as we passed it I felt the change of energy again and in a moment some hikers and a family appeared and so obviously our sacred time in the area had passed and it was others' turns. I wonder about the experiences other people have in these places. I suppose it depends on the person or group and what collective energy they carry. Some may have the most remarkable experiences while others may have none at all. For some they walk a sacred path filled with the enchantment that sacred energy harbors. Others simply walk a path that is made up of dirt and stones and things to be wary of and look up and see a rock formation and never hear the voices of the ancients. I often wonder what people feel and see when they visit other towns, cities, countries; are they simply seeing the bricks and mortar, the "things to do?" When the boys and I were at the Grand Canyon in November with a mass of other tourists wandering around, were they capturing the spirituality of the place or was it simply something that had to be done on their list of things to do? I always want to have a great taste of wherever I visit, to be a total glutton indulging in what is on offer. We live on this extraordinary planet which offers up so much naturally, and of course there is what we have as humans created as well to indulge in. We have senses and feelings and desires and tastes, so why would we want to deny ourselves of such a repast?

Why dip into life when we can dive deeply?

I liked the fact that the energy of the afternoon stayed with me well into the evening and we decided at once to go and freshen up and have a drink at the resort that was near where we had been in the afternoon. We sat outside with our drinks watching the landscape change as the sun set and changed the colors of life into more subdued hues. The rock formations around us seemed to take on faces that were looking curiously at the antics of these human beings. We decided not to eat at the resort as the prices were rather "extraterrestrial" and so we drove into town to find somewhere. Well, I don't know what people did at night in Sedona socially but it certainly didn't seem to be eating out as wherever we went the restaurants had closed about 8 p.m. Reluctantly we ended up in a place that was built like a UFO. It was like walking into a tin can but a tin can would have been better. The menu was full of things that had titles relating to UFOs and space stuff like Nova Nachos, Andromeda apple pie, that sort of thing. I opted for something that was like a grilled cheese sandwich and it probably did come from some far-reaching galaxy but one where they obviously didn't eat food; it was disgusting.

The next day we decided to visit the old mining town of Jerome that is in the Black Hills of Yavapai Valley. It's more than 1,500 meters above sea level and was founded in the late nineteenth century. Mining was the reason for this town as the copper deposits found were rich in abundance and in its heyday the population was around 10,000. Eventually the mines ran out and the population dwindled to around one hundred people by the mid-1950s. In efforts to preserve its history it was granted a reprieve by becoming a National Historic Landmark in the late 1960s and today it has art galleries, restaurants, bars, and a myriad of interesting shops selling things from jewelry, fashion, and the most marvelous shop that sells kaleidoscopes that was truly magical. I urge you all to visit this place, but just to warn you the streets are winding and steep and parking is a pain but it's well worth it. On top of the hill known as Cleopatra's Hill is the Jerome Grand Hotel that was opened in 1927 as the United Verde Hospital. It's a fairly imposing structure seemingly keeping a vigil over the town and the place gave me the creeps. A supposed 9,000 people died there during its hospital history and it has quite the reputation for being haunted. Linda and Michelle didn't want to climb the steep street up to the hotel so Tony and I made the trek and the views were spectacular. The minute I walked into the reception area my whole being wanted to turn around and walk out again. It was as if life had deserted the place, leaving it hollow and sad. I only stayed a few minutes and had to go out again as it was making me feel dizzy. There was another entrance to the side which led into the dining room and that felt slightly better so I went in and had a wander. I have never been in a place where I felt such despair. How people could possibly stay there was beyond me. I didn't feel any particular spirit presence but more the whole place was saturated with despair. I took a few pics thinking that I might pick up a few spirits or energy but there was nothing to be seen.

When I was in Sedona in November 2017 I suggested to Tony and Leonard that we visit Jerome. My impression after four years was that it was struggling and I think that's a great pity, as places like that really should be preserved. The same businesses were there and there didn't seem to be any new ones. And of course the Grand Hotel was still atop the hill looking down in a menacing sort of way, or perhaps that's just the way I chose to perceive it and I had no inclination to go and have another look. We had a quick lunch and then got back to the car. Being November the sun had gone off the hill and so there was quite a chill up there. It was nice to get back down into the valley where it was warmer and the energy was happier. I don't think Jerome was a particularly happy place in its day; it seemed to be a rowdy town and full of rather erratic energy which still seems to linger after all this time. Obviously one can change the energy of a place over time but history always lingers one way or another and that is true in any place in the world.

After our "UFO" dinner we went back to Linda's place and lay out by the pool in the dark looking up at the starry sky and hoping we might see some of our extraterrestrial family. They must have been having a night in as the sky sparkled with stars and the occasional satellite but no more; however, we enjoyed talking under the stars and hanging out. Our time together was at a close as Michelle and Tony and I were departing the next day. I thought about how certain visits we make in life and people we connect with are closer steps to something in ourselves that we wish to relate to and this is how I felt about this trip to Sedona. When we get a chance to revisit a place or develop a relationship with people we are positioning ourselves in order to advance our lives in some ways or perhaps all ways. I feel that Sedona is in me now speaking to me daily. Whenever I look at the pictures I took I feel a sense of home and when we get that feeling it's good to engage with that. Every time I have been there I have thanked source for the opportunity and have always had the feeling that I would return, and that I believe is a very good thing.

Chapter Twenty-Two
The Rainbow Bridge

My friend Jesse sent me a message the other day saying that spirit wanted to tell me about the Rainbow Bridge and that it's something he has been on most of his life. It's the weaving as he said of *"Heaven into Earth"* and part of the reason why in this life he does not want to be tied down by the densities of others. But then to quote him:

"Yet in such a strong position one's own densities become acutely present."

The Rainbow Bridge has been around for a long time and it's becoming more evident to those who have been on their personal soul journey. As I have written previously all things are there for those who choose to see and so access to this bridge is not open to a selective few but to anybody who has opened their soul so they can see what's always there. It is a strong position to be in and an acknowledgment that you are your own creation. In each life we live, we create many bridges to cross the many divides that as human beings we establish. The Rainbow Bridge is becoming more obvious to so many as they endeavor to establish more consciously their relationship with GOD and how they translate the energy of GOD into human nature. The weaving of this energy onto Earth and into human nature is equivalent to the turning on of all the lights in life's room revealing the essence of everything. I see the crossing of this bridge as a metaphor for *adding another dimension to your life* and once you have done this there is no turning back. Crossing this line is a massive challenge to so many as once you do this you become acutely aware of yourself, *ALL* yourselves in fact. We are exposed to the productive and counterproductive aspects of our personality but we also have the comprehension of the ways to accept what needs to change and accept what can remain the same. Crossing the bridge exposes us to the *awareness that we are souls* and in doing so we expose more light into our human nature. This doesn't necessarily come about through having a spiritual experience or expanding our spirituality as the Rainbow Bridge can give us access to the greater qualities of our human nature and the settling of human emotions or facts that have been unsettling. I recently read a book, a novel that had a profound effect on me in such a way that as I was reading it I could feel that I was changing. As I read the last paragraph of the book a great tingling went through my body and I felt that I had released something that I had been carrying with me all my life. In a moment, I knew I was different and could feel my whole being becoming more powerful and more open and more alive. I had crossed the bridge and by doing so had moved away from something limited that had been affecting me, and a thought came to me that *I am more conscious now of what I have always known.* I could also feel my whole being literally adapting its energy to this knowledge; it was very profound and very empowering. It must have been a great relief to my body to no longer be affected by whatever it was that I was carrying. I wasn't even aware of what it was and had no desire to go digging. After finishing the book I knew that I had crossed a bridge and would never again forget what I had once forgotten. As we walk away from what was, we leave behind the energy of who we were for those times and we walk toward a different self that we choose that has diverse energy. It is a self that will take us toward the something more that we all so crave. That's why we never really forget that the Rainbow Bridge is always there for us to cross. We have a constant craving all of our lives to walk toward that bridge and cross it. At times we get as far as walking by the bridge and yet we don't cross it because we are so embroiled in our human nature that we forget that the blending of the Heaven/Earth energy is the way of all things. And it is this way that is ever prevalent now as bridges are popping up all over the place. Eventually there will be so many bridges that even the most stalwart skeptics will be unable to ignore that there is indeed a bridge to higher consciousness. We are plainly being bombarded by higher consciousness now and there is no turning back from it. There will be those who stand on their human ground regardless of the evidence that is before them and all they are doing is staving off the moment and putting themselves through excessive and avoidable challenges.

We will all cross the Rainbow Bridge.

I've got into the habit daily of watching out for when a bridge might appear, and in the evening thinking about how many bridges I may have crossed or could have crossed! Every time we do cross a bridge it's another layer of source energy that we now are conscious of and another layer of source that we can access to create a greater life. This afternoon I was visiting Kay at the care home. Of late there seems to be less of Kay in her body and what is in there wants to sleep a great deal. Regardless of that I will still spend time with her and wheel her out into the gardens where we sit for about half an hour. It was quite gusty today and I thought it was going to be sheltered but after a few major gusts that gave us a fair whack a lot more of Kay was in her body and she gave me the "Kay look" that pretty well said what she thought about being assaulted by the elements. Anyway, I wheeled her back inside and we sat in one of the lounge areas where she promptly went to sleep again, occasionally waking up and giving me a smile and then off she went out again. One of the residents of the retirement part of the complex whom I had become acquainted with walked by and stopped for a chat. She asked a little about our background and how Kay was doing. Then she asked me how I was doing and bent down and gave me a big hug. Her love and compassion were so fulfilling and sincere and it really touched me, so much so that I felt she was a Rainbow Bridge that was empowering me. I watched her as she walked away and felt so grateful for that brief connection. I could easily, as many would, not have seen her as anything more than a kindly person being empathic but I instead saw it in the light it was meant to be. I was soul who needed the light and her soul in her way saw that and gave it.

Some years ago I heard of a client of mine that I had not seen for a while who was in a very troubled way. I made contact and wanted them to know that we were there to support them and to not hesitate to contact me whenever they felt the need to.

I knew they were hesitant and so I made contact every few days just to make sure they were doing all right and to remind them that they didn't have to stand alone. They appreciated the contact but then surprised me by asking, "Why are you doing this, why are you making the effort?" I simply replied, "Because I care." The reply I got rather surprised me as they said, "But people just don't do that."

It made me think what belief did they have in themselves that made them feel that. And it made me think that the Rainbow Bridges are there for them but something in themselves won't allow them to cross it or when they do get to a place where that's possible they get suspicious. Over the thirty or so years I have been working with spirit I have seen people invest much effort, time, and money into their self-development only to stop and doubt once they get to the place where it is all amounting to something, and this confounds me. There always seems to be that doubt among human nature. Is this really happening? Now that I'm here, do I actually believe and believe in myself? What's the catch? Do I deserve this?

Why do we invest in so much when we still have doubts?

The answer to that is that our higher nature is always in the background urging us on to take those steps, make those changes, create the new realities as it knows that the Rainbow Bridges are there just waiting to be crossed. And, of course, it comes down to what you believe.

This morning when I was out in the back watering the garden I found a monarch butterfly on the path. It was dead and by the look of it had come out of its cocoon to be battered about by the wind before it had a chance of life. I picked it up and held it in the palm of my hand and then the thought came to me that perhaps I could resurrect it. I sat down and had a meditation on this for about five minutes but to no avail. Placing the butterfly on the desk in the kitchen I went about the morning and this afternoon when I was having my lunch something caught my eye and I looked up and saw the butterfly moving. I did the shake of the head, not believing what I saw, and then it did it again. My whole being went blank, and then I realized that with the back door open a gentle breeze was moving the butterfly. I laughed aloud, but thought for the briefest of moments I truly believed that the butterfly had come alive again and that made me happy! And when I saw it was the wind I stayed happy because for that moment *I HAD BELIEVED.* So, I may not be the Lazarus of butterflies yet but the more I keep believing, the more I can, be it butterflies or life, I know I can create life. I think that's one of the ultimate realities we have to recognize in this time and when we get that, cross that Rainbow Bridge that blends the energies of life, we stand autonomously with the power of source. So you would think the realization of that would make it all simple to us human beings. No, we have to complicate things by doubting that we can create, be skeptical of the whole process, become suspicious or competitive. We will punch at life and try to find a sure-fired quick way to get what we want rather than go with the natural process and in doing this we are totally missing the point which is to *enjoy the creation process.*

I see all around me the way that life is like making a cup of instant coffee; we put a teaspoon of life in the cup, add some life ingredients and stir, add a few things to our taste and then drink. There's not even the moment of savoring the aroma of experience before we drink and then life goes back on the shelf until we need another cup. We all seem to want instant happiness, instant financial gain, instant well-being, instant enlightenment and because of this we tend to get drawn into situations which may gratify us for the short term but then we have to start again. Are we creating a world where we are simply hanging out for the next experience but are never really living? Are we looking for the quickest way to "get life" in the hope the fast route will give you the best results? Well, according to several websites that I checked up on we seem to be able to do all this in just a few steps! One sight was offering great wealth in seven easy steps, while others added a step or two and one brought it down to five steps. Some were easy, but others were simple. Enlightenment and Happiness were the same, just a few easy steps or perhaps more and you could be happily enlightened with great wealth and all you had to do was walk a step or two!

Through my own experiences in life I know that you can't cut corners in anything. If you do, you just end up having to make it up somewhere along life's road. Funny how we seem to want to short change ourselves in life because of our fears and doubts and beliefs that we can't cope with what life gives us. And that's not just the bad stuff but the good stuff as well. So many have denied themselves success, happy moments, great relationships, more chances in life and so, so much more because they cut the corners thinking that's the way to drive life. And it makes me think how can people possibly bear to be alive and not be living? So another message that these Rainbow Bridges bring to us is the magic of what life can be when we are aligned to the source of life. I can respect the choices we make that define the experiences of our lives and that sometimes those experiences may be painful, but no one comes into life with only limited choices despite how arduous the journey may be. I don't believe it's about seeing the good in everything for let's face it, sometimes it's just plain simple crap and impossible to feel good about some stuff. It's about allowing ourselves to realize that means that we don't have to suffer long term by what happens when life hurts us. It's telling us that we don't have to keep hurting, that we can put that down and pick up something that makes us feel better. And we don't have to wait till we feel we have got over something or deserve it. We have the choice all the time to move forward and keep moving forward until we have moved so far away from what was that it becomes a distant view that we only have an idea of and no longer an attachment to the experience. God, I look at what we all put up with when we all should be daily looking at what way we can live our lives. I'm not talking about the basic structures of our lives necessarily or our jobs or our relationships but more our beliefs around all these things and what those beliefs do to the way we live.

What are your beliefs doing to your life?

Being bullied through my school years made me defiant and defensive but also afraid of just being authentic. I built up beliefs that I thought were protecting me, I think they call it *growing a thicker skin,* but all that seemed to do was to create a wall that was easy to hide behind and the whole time the real self was looking for ways to scale the wall. And that real self eventually will do that, it has to, it's the way we are wired, to succeed to move beyond what was and hopefully in a way where you're not dragging everything you don't want along for a permanent ride. I can feel clearly now that this time in life is the time where we no longer need to be brutalized by life's past offerings and to see that it all made us wiser (even if we don't feel that it has, and that's just the way of life). So having now got that, it's time to get on with it. When I read stuff about embracing your pain, make friends with your anger, and all that sort of stuff that really pisses me off as sometimes I actually want to *feel* angry, I don't want to go out and have lunch with it! And pain sucks, why should I embrace it? I'd rather feel all those things, have my moment, and hopefully be grown up enough to be able to put it down and no longer invest in it. And you know I think that's okay, I think that when we cross those Rainbow Bridges that whatever we find when we do it's going to tell us that it's okay as well and I think there's a sort of passion involved in feeling those things that makes us more qualified in truth to get a life! I think we have to be careful that we don't mollycoddle ourselves through fatuous beliefs and experiences that render us incapable of facing the truth of our life and its situations. Human nature seems to be very good at creating methods that give us the impression we are dealing with things whereas in fact we are simply creating diversions from the truth.

- Life hurts sometimes and when it does we have to feel the hurt and then move on.
- We don't need to understand everything; understanding often comes about through what we are feeling and what we are going through. Isn't that enough without having to have understanding?
- Some people will never get you or what you represent and you don't need to spend your life trying to get people on your side or get them to understand you.
- You will get pissed off with life, people, the weather, price hikes on everything, politicians, long lines in the supermarket, TV ads, yourself, red light runners, and a myriad of other things that no doubt add up to the thousands but hey sometimes life sucks but we will and can get over all those things but one thing is for sure, we can't ignore them!

- We will be depressed or if not, feel flat some days. We will want to cry and we don't know why, we will feel unhappy and oversensitive, and we will have days when we don't want to get out of bed and be involved in life. We will push away the people that we love the most and sometimes we will hurt them and they will hurt us. We will be let down by people and life and sometimes we feel we are let down by God and we will question if we really believe all this stuff. We will want to whack the ass of the guy on the bike as we drive by because for the last five kilometers he's been holding up the traffic as he peddles at his leisure not giving a rat's ass about who's behind him because he's a biker and that's more important. And all of that is simply part of the journey and we can't repress what we feel but we do have to organize what we feel so that it doesn't hurt us or anyone else. And feeling all that and thinking all that doesn't mean that you are any less God than God itself!

- It also doesn't mean that you have to have lots of therapy or go and find yourself and get rid of the selves that you found and didn't want when you found them. And all those Rainbow Bridges that are appearing are always going to be there for you and there is no toll to cross them. You will always be your own creator and you will always have choices. Each day you stand in a place that is infinite with possibilities and it is only you that can direct the course of your life with all this wonderful source energy that is constantly at your disposal.

I made my usual afternoon visit to Kay today and found her in her room. She had a small tummy bug over the last day and they were keeping her in her room just in case it might spread to the other residents. They had positioned her in front of the television that was up on the wall but as the dulcet tones of Ellen filled the room she was simply staring into space and with the saddest expression I have seen on her face since she went into care. I sat next to her but she didn't even register that she knew I was there or if she did she didn't care. She looked so fed up and so empty. I just sat by her side and watched her as she fell in and out of sleep and on waking making her take sips of water. *What does it take for a person to recognize when it is time to go home to source?* I thought as I watched her. I stayed for about half an hour but later on in the early evening I had the feeling to go up again and just sit with her. She was in bed and asleep, curled up on her left side, clutching at the side of the mattress. I've noticed that she holds tightly onto things these days, my hand, the side of the chair, the bed, making me wonder what is she feeling that makes her hold on so much? I can't imagine what the machinations of her damaged brain were making her see and feel.

My poor love, she looked so fragile in her sleep and she kept moving her legs as if she were running. Perhaps she was in a dream and she was feeling free and mobile again. I cried a bit and sat in silence and just watched her and thought about our long life together and how everything is now. Of course, there was no answer to anything that I was feeling or observing, it simply was. And now as I sit here and write this I see that the two of us are simply involved in a process that has no answer and we will live through this situation until it is no more. I've tried at times when I have sat with her in the past to imagine that I am taking her to the Rainbow Bridge and handing her over to the spirits who will take her back to source but I know that she has to get to that bridge on her own. I guess I'm saying that we have to get to the place where we simply leave things alone and let them take their own course. As humans that's hard as we want to make things better or help or simply be a guiding hand. We can feel so inadequate because we really do want to serve the cause and when we can't it doesn't feel right.

The best thing I did tonight then was that I was there and I cried and I loved and I wept for what was, when things were full and whole and happy. And I sat and thought that one day soon she will be gone and all this will be what was.

Our Rainbow Bridges take us back to our absolute self, the self that is God. We come into our lives so full and laden with the ideas of what we want this life to be. As we begin to step forward in life it seems that we create the separation of the selves that are all so imperative to our successes. Without all our selves how can we truly be the one source, how can we recognize the Rainbow Bridge when it is there? I have compiled a list of ways that I believe we cross those Rainbow Bridges each day and through the life we are living.

- By acknowledging our God nature when we awaken each morning.
- By preparing our day of Mind, Body, and Spirit.
- By nurturing and loving our bodies from the moment we awaken with food it loves that will sustain us through the day.
- By paying attention to what life is telling us through the day and following its guidance.
- By through the day, reminding ourselves of our God nature through a thought or action.
- By showing an act of kindness to someone.
- By giving love and receiving love.
- By being authentic to ourselves through the day and not allowing our self to be distracted from what is authentic to us.
- By accepting that what we are involved in is a reality we have created and that we have the choice to change that reality should we wish.
- By recognizing what is important to put down that is no longer productive.

- To pay attention to the qualities that we possess and to express those qualities.

- To be leaders when we need to lead, listeners when we need to listen, teachers when we need to teach, and healers when we need to heal but to also know when to step back and respect that though you may have an answer it is not your place to give it.

- To know that through the day you have paid attention to life and that you have lived that life Mind, Body, and Spirit to the best of your ability.

- To love yourself and respect yourself even when you think that you cannot find it in you to do so.

- To know that you create the creed of your life every moment and to know when to make the changes that one must make to evolve.

- And finally to complete each day by emptying yourself of the day's energy, thanking source for the opportunity that you had to be a creator once again and put that day to bed with great peace and love.

Chapter Twenty-Three

Feeling Grief Doesn't Always Mean Being Sad

I was thinking this morning about my time with Kay last night and the way I was feeling and realized that though I was grieving I was not sad. Without the sadness I was able to use the grief to understand something profound that I was not quite able to put my finger on. The feeling of grief spoke volumes to me that didn't need to be transcribed or translated in any other way, what I felt was simply enough. I see now that the energy of grief is an emotional vantage point that allows one to observe from a place of surrender. You have surrendered up the need to understand, be adversely affected, be damaged in any way, and when we don't surrender to this emotion then we will dilute it with things like sadness and anger and counterproductive thoughts and actions. There's honesty in allowing self to feel raw grief without diluting the experience. I remember many years ago there had been a massive midair explosion in a Pan Am flight that was making its approach to Heathrow in London. It broke up and landed in country outside of London. On board were a large group of US teens heading for a trip and there were no survivors. As usual the media dived on all this like vultures and on the news that night there was a clip of a woman at the airport in the US who had just received the news that there were no survivors and that her daughter who was on board was not coming home. The poor woman was so assaulted by her grief that she had collapsed onto the floor and was laying on her back screaming like a baby, her arms flailing around her and her legs and feet beating on the floor. It was human nature in its rawest form possible, and I was mesmerized not by her pain but the power that I felt was coming out of her needing to get out. Sadness would obviously present itself to her at some point but in that airport on that floor she was expressing the power of grief. Years later, I think it was a documentary on grief, I saw this same woman being interviewed and she spoke of how mortified she was that such a private moment of her torment was made public. If I had known her or known where she was I would have told her that she should never feel that as she was showing the world what it was to be real and that one can never sanitize or moderate an emotion such as grief.

In our human nature we are used to believing in the finality of death; in our spirit nature we believe in the ongoing of our true nature, our soul, and embrace the infinite possibilities of what we are. I think that if people who have passed away could send a letter to those still here on Earth then human nature's perspective of grief and loss would alter dramatically! I like to imagine it would be something like this:

Dear Friends and Family,

Well, I arrived here safely and I must say it was a very pleasant journey and much better than first class! On arrival there was such a welcome committee of those I had not seen for such a long time, it was the best of reunions. I was taken to reception where I checked in and then was taken to a lovely place where I was given a wonderful soul cleanse that got rid of any human residue I may have brought with me. Very strict rules up here about what you can bring and not bring with you.

Now I can imagine some of you thinking it sounds a bit like going through customs and being asked if you have anything to declare! Well, there were no spirit sniffer dogs wandering around checking my bags but just lovely souls helping to make the transition from human to spirit in a loving and magnificent way. I was taken to this room that was round and had a massive domed ceiling that seemed to be a part of the sky though it was made of great panels of sapphire and diamond, ruby and emerald; in fact, I realized they were all the colors of the chakras. I was positioned in the center of the room under this dome and the moment I did this I heard a sound like a hum but it was the most beautiful sound I have ever heard, like the sound of pure love. Then all the colors of the gems touched my soul and I felt this great relief as all the human nature issues that had been a part of my life were cleansed from me and from that moment I felt like I knew exactly who I was and what was possible. The joy I felt was exquisite and I was told that I had now been returned to my original state, the state we all are when we were first created as souls by source.

I noticed that there was a line of other souls waiting their turn and afterward when we all talked we were like one big positive hum! I noticed that some souls were enclosed in a cocoon of light that looked rather like a pod and I asked one of the guiding souls what was happening to them. I was told that those souls had experienced some extreme trauma in life and though they were cleansed they had to go into a meditative sleep to ensure that they don't lock back into the energy of what they had gone through.

Afterward I was asked if I would like to rest or if I was happy to go on to the review.

I opted for the review as I was eager to see what that life had been all about for me and I knew I would have to do it eventually even though here I have all eternity to decide. I was quite pleased with the result and feel more qualified when I make the decision about future incarnations. There are some souls here who seem to struggle with looking at the life they lived and some are quite insistent that they lived a good and honest life but the thing about these reviews is that you can't hide a thing. Of course you're not being judged in any way but simply shown what was what. Well, there was one soul who had been quite a successful man in life but perhaps had been rather arrogant and pushy who said that whoever they were (the spirit helpers) they were setting him up to look bad and he wanted to speak to their superior! I'm not sure what happened but considering WHO the superior is, I thought, well, if anyone can sort it out God will! Don't know what happened to him as he went off in a huff. All the helpers here just respect your responses and know that at some point they all come round. The accommodation here is out of the world, if you will excuse the pun! You can create, literally create what you want, you think it and there it is! I've got a nice cozy bungalow by the sea, that's something I always wanted when I was in body but I never made it happen. I said to the spirit who was helping me that I wish I had been able to manifest like this on Earth.

They told me that we can but people seem to take their belief systems only so far and then in creeps the doubt. It all makes so much sense here and I can see how I could have done so much better while I was in the body. So I'm urging you all to give yourself that chance and don't wait till you're here with me! I didn't really know what to expect before I came up here. I know I had my belief systems and knew that God was real but what I have discovered is how real I AM in every way possible! And the thing is that it makes so much sense, now why didn't I see that while in body? Time has no meaning here and so I have been able to allow myself a good honest look at my whole being and what it has been all about for me. I'm able to access all the information from all the lifetimes I have had and I can see certain patterns that have emerged that have been important for me to resolve. I'm able to look at all these without any emotional distractions as I simply experience them as the facts of life that they were. And I see my connection with all of you from this perspective and it's been interesting to see what lives we have shared and why we had chosen to be together. Everything inexorably blends together into collective wisdom. Initially I was still involved in human nature patterns of thinking and living but you soon learn to let that go and enjoy the liberation of being pure source energy. I'm beginning to really understand the machine of life and how unlimited it is. Where I am right now is just one level of consciousness that is available and I am eager to move onto other levels to learn and experience more. Without the confinement of limited thoughts all the doors of life are wide open for any soul who makes that choice.

There are a great deal of events that you can participate in as well. (I must admit that rather surprised me, the last thing I thought that would be here would be concerts and lectures and all sorts of entertainment!) I attended a lecture where a soul was talking about God and never to ask God for an answer! Instead the soul explained that we should ask GOD for the POWER so you could create the answer yourself. The soul went on to say that GOD does not give answers, GOD gives you the POWER to create them yourself. I must say I felt very empowered by this concept and realized once again that we are all the masters of our reality and that we all have the ability to create the answers in our lives. It made me think about all those people back on Earth who are so caught up in the struggle of life and they have no idea how simple it all is! Mind you, when I was in body I made it pretty complicated for myself at times so I was no exception. After that lecture it made me believe more that everything is possible and I've been having fun manifesting realities just to see what I can do. I manifested an eighty-foot hot dog just for the sake of doing it! I made a lake freeze, though it seems to always be summer here, just so I could go ice skating. Of course, after a while you get a bit bored with doing stuff like that but everyone does it! Since time has no meaning here you are always experiencing what you want to when you want to at any moment. There are no "systems" in place, simply choices, and this makes you really aware that what you believe is essential to your development.

I can't find enough words to explain the beauty and serenity here. Probably the best word I can use is COMPLETE. There's a place that is like an enormous Italianate garden that is quite spectacular and when you go there you can talk to master teachers, I tell you, it's all here for you. I have visited an area that was called the Temple of the Rose and it's where you go when you really want to advance your spiritual understanding. Apparently when you are going to incarnate again and want to be a light worker or someone who wants to bring spirit to Earth this is the place to go as you are working with very advanced souls and teachings. The longer I am here, the more I am aware of my unlimited self and all that is possible with it.

I realize that the time that we have spent on Earth is but one of the innumerable places of consciousness that we can access. There doesn't seem to be any form of hierarchy or stages as some people put it but simply life, presented to you for you to organize at your will. There are always souls here who will assist you in all ways to ensure you create the best opportunities for self. After a while you simply forget about times and structures, routines, etc., and get on with the process of just living.

I have become so aware of my whole self that at times I forgot that I was actually that person on Earth in the life when you knew me, here I am EVERYTHING! It all blends together and you realize the concept of collective consciousness. I am aware of how things are on Earth and how everybody is doing but the souls here say that you don't want to get too distracted by what was and to remember that we no longer have emotional *attachments to that life. That's not saying we don't care and we do send love and guidance when it's needed but it's no longer our journey and it would be far too distracting for all of you if we were appearing all the time!*

I can't tell you enough how wonderful it was to be able to share life with you all while I was there. Each of you was a valuable part of my life and the way I developed and I would like to think that I was the same for you all. There is never an end to life and I look forward to the time we will unite again in spirit. Even though you might mourn my physical loss, please don't do it for too long because as this letter tells you I'm fine and thriving! I will always keep in touch when it is needed but it does not pay to dwell too much on what was as there is always so much to create that can be. You have a life there to complete and make sure you do it in the ultimate way you can! I have a life here that is ongoing and I know that wherever we are, we are always in touch through our souls and the love that is everywhere. I hear your words and I feel your love and give you reassurance that all is quite well with me! So thank you for being in my life and I look forward to all the times we will have together in the many futures we all have.

With deep love for you all,
Good-bye for now.

Wouldn't that be wonderful if we were able to receive such a letter from those who have passed? Not only would it comfort us to know all is fine on the other side, but it would also be a reassurance to those who fear death that there is the other side and that we simply carry on life even when we may not have a body. Of course we do correspond with spirit through our dreams and thoughts and feelings, and at times through gifted light workers who are able to bring us messages and guidance from source. The easiest and most evident way, though, is through our own God nature as when we can truly accept this and live this then our ability to access spirit is simply there naturally.

Our grief can be an energy that can so weigh us down that it disables us to the point where we find it renders us almost immobile. That sort of grief seems to permeate the very core of everything and all reasoning seems to be thrown out the window. I've seen people in this grief who are so involved in it that even though they may seek out assistance and gather useful tools to help them they choose to wallow in the energy of grief and end up asking the same questions over and over again. Even when they may have answers they seem to either reject them or not use the tools that they have picked up. They seem to isolate themselves in a cocoon of energy that makes them separate from life even though they may give the impression that they are involved. I think in situations like that there are no answers that can be given to the person that will satisfy them as the journey they are on is about being able to create their own answers. I can't imagine how hard it must be for them to find ways of creating answers since they are so burdened by what they are feeling and one can only turn the light on for them a little more in the hope it will make a difference. We have to become night-lights for them like a child who takes comfort from that light when they are afraid of the dark. If we grieve beyond our need there is a danger of turning the grief into depression. One thing I certainly learned from having had the bone infection last year was to let my grief out.

I went to a party last Saturday afternoon, an annual event hosted by two wonderful friends. Yearly they call together friends and family and have a catered gathering, and it's awesome. As I was driving back home I felt the stirrings in my stomach that spoke to me of impending acquaintance with the toilet bowl. A friend was with me and I was dropping them off at a place they were house sitting and I was doing my best to ignore the cacophony that was going on in my stomach that was aiming upward looking for an exit. Me, I took another exit to the closest public convenience, and with apologies to my friend informed them I needed to chuck my guts up! And so I did, with hardly any time to lock the door I took aim and spewed! It wasn't very graceful either but one of those gut-wrenching, rib-clenching loud spews that left nothing to the imagination. I felt immensely better afterward and when I got back into the car Christina informed me that she could hear me. There really was nothing to say in reply to that, but that wasn't the end of it and after dropping her off I had to get back home with some sense of urgency because I could feel that perhaps I was in for a night of this. Actually, it ended up being an hour and half of intense intestinal and bowel cleansing as it was going out both ends, fast. Why do I tell you this? you might well ask. Well, it made me think that this is what grief is like, no holds barred, emptying of your whole being that weakens you and grabs at you when you least expect it. It's awful when you are feeling it but the relief when it's out is considerable. And it makes you vulnerable and tired and your strength is gone. Once you complete the cycle, though, you get back into the saddle and on with things as I did the next morning when feeling much better. I hooked up with friends for brunch and indulged in THE WORKS veggie breakfast and my stomach didn't complain once!

I don't think one can ever presume we know what someone is going through even though you may have had similar experiences. The way that we respond to life and other people's situations is unique to each person. We can only but give the perspective and wisdom we have gained, hoping it will assist someone in creating their own. I think people can load themselves too much with the sense of being responsible for finding a solution for others and I also believe there are many who want someone else to find the solution to their issues. We must find ways to support each other and serve each other in honesty, love, and strength and to accept that there is only so much we can offer.

Chapter Twenty-Four
Dolores

This book would not be complete without a chapter on my sacred friend Dolores Cannon. In fact, I probably would not be writing this book if I had not met Dolores. Since her passing there has not been a day when I have not been aware of her presence in my life. We must have had a great deal of past lives together as when we met we simply seemed to just settle into knowing each other again and getting on with the things we were to do. It's like that with some people when you first meet them.

"Oh, it's you again, is it?" I feel like saying sometimes.

Dolores was smart and shrewd and determined as well as kind and motherly and vulnerable. She carried a lot in her life and sometimes when she should have put some things down, she didn't. Well, we might be Gods in human bodies but sometimes the human nature gets the better of us, even when you are Dolores Cannon! She created a big mission in this lifetime to be able to pass onto us through her work, information that has been valuable to our evolution. She had filled in a lot of gaps and was greatly respected. Meeting her for the first time in Christchurch, New Zealand, was auspicious and I was greatly aware of the impact of the meeting even then. I recall thinking that here was someone who was going to make a difference in my life and set some important foundations for me.

The longer I work in this field, the more I am so grateful for the opportunities I have had to connect and in some cases work with amazing light workers. Dolores was an investigator, a gatherer of information that was to be transcribed into books. What she created with her quantum healing technique opened us up to more of the infinite possibilities that are around us. What I liked about her work is that she dealt with facts and not a whole lot of ambiguous new-age concepts. She laid it out straight and I admire her courage in doing so. I believe the information that she was able to access has been imperative to the way we are developing our human and Earthien natures. Nothing is ever random, things occur when we are ready for them, when we need to know. And of course one of the most important things about the information Dolores collated was that

It made us think way beyond the square!

That's what we have been doing for the last few decades now and because of that it has evolved the way we think and changed what we believe and consequently set us up on a rather astonishing inner adventure. Dolores was real, she wasn't airbrushed in any way. I admired her guts and her rawness and her determined nature to get the information out there. When I look at the journey of someone like Dolores Cannon I think of what they as a soul had experienced to come into life with such agreements. When you look at a life that you live where you have been there to raise awareness that's a big ask of yourself. Dolores was a pioneer of her time, as self-awareness, UFOs, past lives, all that stuff when she first started were put in the drawer of either unbelievable or just plain crazy. Here was this woman who had a husband, children, who was living in a small town in Arkansas stepping forward and pretty well announcing through her work that we were not just human in our nature but that we have lived many lives through history, ETs do exist, oh, and by the way, I'm really good mates with Nostradamus and I am helping to transcribe his quatrains so that people can understand them.

Her work took her all over the world and she has touched, and still does, millions of people who are looking to advance their understanding of life. I recall her saying once that people in her town thought she was odd because she traveled so much, not because of her work! Her daughter Julia was her right-hand person and traveled with her making sure that everything was ship-shape and, man, she did an awesome job! She wasn't just supporting her mother but supporting the whole Dolores Cannon Enterprise, a huge responsibility in my way of seeing it. The thing I love about connecting with a soul that you know and that you have a mission with is that it's very easy to simply step into what you need to do. There doesn't seem to be that getting-to-know-you period, all that has already been established previously and so you can simply get on with what you have come to do.

When I'm working with other light workers I always when I can sit in the audience. I think it's respectful to do so when it's possible; however, I make sure I sit in the back so no one can see me as I have found in the past that people keep looking over at me and I think that distracts them from the person on the platform and is disrespectful to that person who is speaking. And so I find a corner in the back where I can participate, listen and watch. I loved watching people's responses to Dolores and what she was saying. The first thing I noticed was you could feel how much the audience respected this woman on the stage. I could also feel the love for her coming from people and I do hope she felt that when she was talking. At the beginning of her talks I could see that some were frantically scribbling down notes but that after a while they stopped doing that and simply listened. The information that Dolores gave was thrilling and mind blowing and thought provoking and she always had her audience in a firm grasp. Her delivery was matter-of-fact and more powerful because of that.

She was not telling us a story, she was giving to us facts and facts that were imperative for us all to hear at this time in our history. If you were there you wanted to be there because your soul was telling you that this was really important for you at this time in your life. You might be there because it was curiosity that took you there or simply because you were interested and wanted to know more but whatever the reasons, and this is for everything you attend, you are there because your soul wanted to hear. And this hearing created in you an awakening that will never shut down and it also established the law of attraction in you so you could gather more and develop more.

Dolores helped us all to wake up!

I liked that fact that she seemed totally unaware of her impact on the audience and was simply getting on with the job she came to do. She had nothing to prove but a great deal to impart and I know that's how she saw it. I could also see that the work she was doing was highly stimulating to her and that she enjoyed the diversity and the travel. Apart from Julia she traveled alone; there was no need for her to have a huge entourage with her that would have annoyed her. As long as she had a good bed to sleep in and a hairdresser who knew how to do her hair the way she wanted she was content! The information that she gathered over the years is timeless, and for decades to come I know that it will still be of interest to human nature seeking for a bigger truth. More often than not I get clients who have found Dolores on YouTube and can't get enough of her information and I recommend to others to read her books to give them a wider perspective about life.

A Missouri girl, Dolores was born in St. Louis in 1931 and she lived there with her family until she met and married Johnny Cannon, who was a career naval man. That was the start of her transient life as navy wife, and once the kids came along, a navy mother. Dolores and Johnny became interested in hypnosis and became efficient in the skill, helping others to stop smoking, lose weight, etc. Then in 1968 a medical doctor referred one of his patents to them who had major health issues and was suffering from a nervous eating disorder. He thought that perhaps hypnosis would be a useful tool. What transpired was the opening of a major door in the career of Dolores Cannon. The woman halfway through her session went into spontaneous regression and started to describe a past life she had in Chicago as a woman in the 1920s. She presented different mannerism to what she normally had and even spoke differently. Intrigued, Dolores and Johnny regressed this same woman over a period of months, and five different past incarnations were brought through, even one when she described when she was created by God! These sessions culminated in Dolores's very first book, *Five Lives Remembered*, written in 2009. This must have been astounding to Dolores and Johnny, as we are talking about the late 1960s when, despite the age of free love, drugs, flower power, etc., there was no such thing as "Consciousness" and "Past Life Regression," "Source Energy," "Quantum Healing," and all the metaphysical concepts we are so familiar with today. They must have felt like they were pioneers in their covered wagon heading for the new land! I suppose the good thing about that was that there was nothing to compare their experience with and therefore there were no rules so they were able to create their own.

In this day and age it's hard to find something that hasn't already been discovered or experienced. Dolores and Johnny were living in a time before Google and Siri and all the other sources of information we have available today to find out about things. To me they were true pioneers in their field, and I am in awe of what they did and take my hat off to them. I'm laughing a bit to myself now as here I am writing all about Dolores but to get this information, did I get in contact with Julia and other family members and do consistent research? No. I simply typed into Google Dolores Cannon Bio and there was all the info I needed!

In fact, that's exactly what people are doing to find out more about Dolores and her work. They put in the groundwork, though, and it must have been very exciting to know that very few had traveled that road before them. These days everything is yet another version of something that had come before but what Dolores and Johnny Cannon did was tantamount to walking on the moon. The theories they were investigating of course were not new but it was obviously time for this information to become more mainstream and from a karmic perspective that was one of the missions for the Cannons! Knowing that we all create the lives we live and what we do fascinated me, that particularly Dolores came here to give us access to history and of course to ourselves who created history.

In late 1968 Johnny on his way to the naval base was seriously injured in a car accident caused by a drunk driver. He spent the rest of his life in a wheelchair, and this situation changed the life of the Cannons. They moved to the hills of Arkansas where Dolores dedicated her life to her husband and the raising of their four children. Her interest in regression therapy never waned but it took a back seat for the moment. I think now that those years of caring for Johnny and being a mother were part of the way she had to develop so she could do the work she was to do in the future. Life's experiences throw us into ways of preparing ourselves for great things to come. I think of what Tabaash has taught that we are always in a constant state of *Preparation, Creation, and Participation.*

I have visited the house that Johnny built and the surrounding land is very sacred and exceptionally beautiful. One can feel the history of the land and I'm sure it has many stories to tell. I call the area Cannon Mountain, and I think that is highly appropriate! So up on Cannon Mountain, Dolores, while attending to her family's needs, was preparing for her life's great work. As the kids grew and moved into their own stories Dolores once again picked up the thread of hypnotherapy and started to advance where she had left off. This time was rather like her apprenticeship that lay down the foundations for the complexity of her future work. She had to take these steps carefully to adapt herself not only to the information that was coming through, but also to the energy that she was receiving while she was working. When you are working as a light worker you are dealing with the energy of source in a very amplified way. One can't just be "blasted" with this energy without "easing into it." It was the same for me when I first started to work with spirit. My body and all its levels on consciousness had to be primed for a bigger energy.

Dolores was very thorough in her investigations and she would go to great lengths to research the validity of the information she was gathering from her regression clients. There never was anything "New Age" about Dolores and she often affirmed:

"I am an investigator."

And investigate she did, working with thousands of clients in those early days, collating information that invariably became her books and opened up to us all a wealth of life information that took us way outside of the paddock gates! With all her investigations Dolores realized that she was tapping into the subconscious mind of her clients and from this realization she perfected her own brand of hypnotic technique called the Quantum Healing Hypnosis Technique. This enabled her to have direct connection with the subconscious mind that provided answers to questions and was the basis for instant physical and emotional healing.

Dolores had a wealth of material that she wanted to publish but the book publishers of the day didn't believe there was a general interest in the subject and so the door remained closed to her. Unflinchingly she established her own publishing company, Ozark Mountain Publishing, in 1992, which now publishes fifty writers worldwide and Dolores's books have been translated into more than twenty languages, so you sort of want to raise a finger to those unwilling publishers, you know what I mean?!

One must remember that whatever life you are living you are advancing your own self and Dolores Cannon was no exception. As her work progressed she seemed to reach certain milestone experiences that would take her to another level of belief. She was presented with concepts that were alien to her and she found that she was expanding her own beliefs as time progressed. In her series The Convoluted Universe, she goes into depth with some of the information she was faced with. These books are a golden library of our history from the level of meta and quantum physics and I highly recommend them. They really stretch your imagination and your ability to think way beyond the square. When I read them (and I'm still reading them, such is the wealth of information) it makes me realize how much as human beings we accept what we are told to believe without questioning that there might be more. Perhaps there had been a part of human nature that did not want to know the truth of unlimited consciousness, perhaps at times in our history that was too much for us to comprehend? Whatever the case, I believe that now we are more than ready to accept the new theories that are presented to us and to accept that they have validity. We were educated to think within the box and now we have evolved to think outside of the box. I can never understand why some people would find that so threatening, particularly when it has no bearing on their own lives. Mind you, humanity has got an excellent reputation for persecution, prejudice, and bigotry.

As Dolores continued in her work she was exposed to advanced ways of thinking and being that opened her up to the world of multidimensional reality. She was taught that time as we know it here on Earth did not exist in a linear way. All events exist in the now. So simply put, we right now exist in our own creations of Past, Present, and Future. There are no degrees of separation. We are all standing at one point, and our beliefs will define which aspect of ourselves goes where from that point. If we walk down the street and we turn left, another aspect goes right, and another doesn't walk down the street at all. That's why it's so important to consider our options from that point of consciousness we find ourselves in. As we weigh the options and do so from a point of ourselves as the God nature then we are able to see the most productive road we can take. And so we get right back to the old maxim:

Whatever you pay attention to becomes your life.

The thought just occurred to me that the reason people feel so challenged by such a concept is simply because we have been trained to think and believe and respond in certain ways and that becomes our security. When the old ways are challenged then we resist and become suspicious of the new ways of thinking. Well, that's been going on all through the history of this planet! And so Dolores's work was asking us to pay attention to the new energy. Through her work we have been fed new information about how to live with the New Earth Energy.

Of the books that Dolores has written, truly some of the most fascinating are in the Nostradamus series. Through hypnosis Nostradamus was able to speak *directly* from the sixteenth century to Dolores in the twenty-first century. He explained he wanted her to write a book to clarify the meanings of his prophecies as because of the inquisition he had disguised his messages so they were not destroyed. So in the sessions that Dolores sat with him he explained what the meanings of them were. He was quick to point out a message that has come time and time again to us through source, the message being *that we are the ones creating our realities and by recognizing this we can avert negative occurrences and produce positive results.*

In a conversation I had with Dolores once about her relationship with Nostradamus she told me that it hit home one day to her that he was actually really talking to her from the past as midway through a conversation she was having with him he said he had to stop for the moment as his wife was telling him that dinner was ready, which rather put it in perspective! I wonder, though, if Dolores was talking to him through the hypnosis subject, was Nostradamus in a state of meditation talking to her or was he simply sitting there in his room being able to see her and just directly talk? The other message that Nostradamus stressed was that we absolutely do have the ability to change the outcomes of our lives, be it individually or collectively, such is the power of the mind. Again, this is something that is being stressed to us at this time.

In the 1980s Dolores work expanded as she moved into the subject material of extraterrestrials, UFOs, life beyond Earth. Once again we are reminded through this work of the multilayers of life that exist and also the opportunities we all have through our personal incarnations that we have many lives on many planets, in many dimensions, and in many forms. I have also come to realize that people who believe in ETs and life on other planets don't necessarily embrace spiritual truths as I found out at one of the Transformation Conferences I was speaking at. Ozark Mountain Publishers regularly presents a UFO conference and Transformation Conferences but at separate times of the year. One year, however, it was decided to combine the two over a period of a week, the Transformation Conference being held mid- to late week and the UFO over the weekend. There was a dinner where the two factions were to blend, a sort of "getting-to-know-you" dinner. Well, the UFO people at my table made it pretty obvious that they wanted nothing to do with spiritual channels, past-life regressions, and the like as when I was asked by some man who I was and what I did when I started to talk to him he simply turned his back on me and talked to another UFO person next to him. I was literally in midstream and he simply turned away. Nice, eh? I think he needs to incarnate on some planet where they can teach him some manners. Interesting how some people's belief systems can reach beyond the stars but can't reach deep within themselves. A lot of the UFO groups are very "in their heads" but not in their hearts; they simply wanted to deal with the facts as they saw them so feelings had nothing to do with it.

The Transformation Conferences are fantastic and I have had the pleasure of speaking at them many times. To get together with a group of like-minded speakers and participants is truly magic and I always come away with a feeling of deep satisfaction having learned so much and made new friends. After Dolores transitioned into spirit it was a bit odd attending the first conference after she passed but I could feel her presence the whole time and I know she was there to make sure that the work that she started continued!

Just because you don't have a body anymore, doesn't mean you don't have an opinion—or influence, for that matter!

I am so happy to have met Dolores and her family; she opened up a door for me for which I am truly grateful. I know that she is around me at times, and I felt her presence very strongly particularly in the months prior to Kay going into care. It was not a good time in my life and I felt the situation weighing heavily upon me day after day. One afternoon I drove up to the top of Mount Victoria near where I live to have some time out among the trees and the surrounding area. The ever-present mobile phone was on the passenger seat but I had turned it off as I was feeling like shit and didn't feel up to calls, etc. As I sat there in the car simply feeling miserable, my phone literally turned itself on. It was face down on the seat and when I turned it up, there was a picture of Dolores looking up at me. I laughed and thanked her for her love and support and it really did help.

I loved hanging out with her and working with her and knowing her. She visited New Zealand a few times and I organized a couple of evenings that we presented together; the place was always packed, Dolores Cannon was in town! I've been fortunate in my career to work alongside some extraordinary people and when you come upon a person that truly complements you as much as you do them then you know that is something you have planned to do. And when you do that it seems it's always easy to just get on with the project in hand. You already know each other and so you can dispense with the getting-to-know-you bit and move on to the soul deal you have made.

Dolores can be proud of the life that she lived and the difference that she made to our world, and she *did* make a big difference. The information that she gathered will be as informative in decades to come as it is now. She was a woman, a mother, and grandmother, a teacher, and a reporter. She was a presenter and a creator. She was "GOD" doing it her way and she did it well. Dolores wanted to be an opera singer and though she may not have sung at Carnegie Hall or Covent Garden as an opera singer she learned how to sing to a very different tune, and boy could she carry that!

Thank you, Dolores. I love you.

Chapter Twenty-Five
"God Watching"

Driving through town today I was passing a pizza shop and I noticed sitting on the steps outside was a young Chinese woman with her face buried in her hands. She was sitting like a person who was feeling some sort of emotional pain, all hunched up, and she reminded me of a puppet whose strings had been cut and she had simply fallen, her limbs lifeless. As I drove past I could see her face was contorted in anguish and I wondered what event or events had led her to such an emotional place. It was just after 3 p.m. and the schools had just finished for the day and students from Wellington Boys College were congregating in masses at the bus stop. You could sense the puberty oozing out of them as they postured in groups, eyeing up the girls from Wellington Girls College (or perhaps each other) who either took no notice of them at all or pretended that they were not noticing.

They were exquisitely playing the boy/girl game. I smiled at myself as I recalled the time when I was one of those guys playing the same game. Let's face it, we all do it; we *still* do it sometimes! The traffic lights had turned red so I was able to spend a few moments observing all the GODS around me playing out their own personal stories; it was a great day to *God Watch.*

How astonishing to think that right now there are 7,530,103,737 (I asked Siri) people on this planet and all are mostly unaware that they are presently involved in their own creation called their life. They know that they are alive on Earth in their human bodies but the majority would find it hard to fathom that the reason they are is because this is the way they have made it happen.

> *We want to be who we are.*
> *We are always watching ourselves all the time.*
> *And we are all one way or another watching each other.*

As a species we seem to be rather a voyeuristic lot on the whole when you look at the technological advances (I seriously question the word "advance" here) that permit us to snoop on each other. We even *ALLOW* ourselves to be snooped upon legitimately by posting videos or pictures of ourselves cutting our toenails, waxing parts of our bodies that in some people's cases the hair was in fact *shielding* the world from such atrocities, or being on the *Jeremy Kyle Show*. And yet I suppose in its own grotesque way all those things are *God Watching* since we are all God and you have to admire the species called *people* who have found ways of making the world sit up and pay attention to them where in the past they would have simply faded into the murkiness of anonymity. The message of today seems to be,

LOOK AT ME!!

And so we do, look, I mean, and by creating all these ways of looking at each other is it simply because we actually want and need to see what we're doing because if we don't then how can we really move on from the place where we are? By paying attention to each other, we pay attention to what we are doing, not just as individuals and all our quirky and endearing little ways, but as a populace that is forever creating this world we live on. It's an odd thought that we have created a need to pay attention to the most facile aspects of life, perhaps this is a ploy to avoid the way we should be looking at each other. Or we go to the complete extremes to be noticed. One evening I was flicking through all the TV channels in hope I might actually come across a program that had nothing to do with cooking or house renovation or going feral with a group of people on an island and hit on a British program called *Naked Attraction*.

The gist of this program is to meet someone totally naked first and then having got that out of the way go on a date fully clothed. There were six contestants weekly, sometimes male, sometimes female, who stood behind a screen; some weeks there were straight couples, others gay couples. Then there was the person who had to choose from the contestants whose bits and bobs were gradually (and clearly) exposed as the screen was raised. I was so disgusted with this program that of course I had to watch it right through. People were eliminated through the show, leaving two contestants. Before the winner was announced the person who was doing the choosing also had to come on naked. Well, it really was quite a beguiling exercise in *God Watching* taken to the extreme of voyeurism. Now, this program wasn't on at 11 p.m. or a time when the children would be safely tucked up but actual prime time! How do parents explain this to children if they come upon it and how would you feel as a parent or friend or work colleague if you saw someone you knew on the program swinging their bits around on national television? I know of another program that is American that is *Naked Dating* or something like that where having been introduced the couple pretty well get there kit off as quickly as possible and prance and frolic together in the hope that at the conclusion of the program he or she will be the one! Whatever happened to the Saturday-night thriller? And how do you even decide that you want to be on one of those programs? Are you sitting at home one day or at the office and suddenly this compulsion to be naked on television overtakes you? Do you have to audition for these shows or is it "we will take you as you come?"

It bemuses me as much as it amuses me, but then I can say the same about human nature in total! And who comes up with the idea? Only a few short years ago it was considered risqué to show a breast or buttock on the television and any programs that might have were relegated to the depths of the night and came with a severe warning should one be mortally offended. Now it seems that people can't wait to be mortally offended and keep creating more ways to look at bodies rather than find ways to look at souls.

Can you imagine a reality TV program called *Soul Attraction* where people stand behind the screen and little by little their souls are exposed? Well, we don't have to look far because we all happen to be staring in that program and it's called our life. Each life we live we are showing a little more soul than we did before and I think people sense that's happening even though they may not be sure what's going on. And I think that's frightening to people for the reason that they are seeing themselves and rather than do that, they have to find ways of distracting them from the truth of their authenticity with all its power and the responsibility that comes with that power, that being they are responsible for creating their life.

God watching is not just watching people.

We are quite simply surrounded by source energy, breathing in source energy, watching source energy, and always *BEING* source energy so how could we possibly miss it! On some mornings I drive to a local beach with a nice coffee in hand and love to spend some time with the beach energy. We are in the middle of autumn now but the last two days felt and appeared more like the midst of winter. So all rugged up in a winter coat that would have rivaled anything worn in the Arctic I stood outside my car doing my best to convince myself that being buffeted by the southerly icy winds was an excellent idea. Within a few seconds I realized it was a completely stupid idea and so took refuge in the warmth of the car. Leonard from the US started to message me while he was waiting to fly to California and when his message came through a splendid rainbow manifested in the distance against the backdrop of dark rain clouds. The colors were deep and rich and as I gazed at its beauty I realized that I was *God Watching*. I also had the thought that as much as I was watching life it was watching me back. Most people would carry the concept that much around us is inanimate and therefore has no interaction with us. What we are seeing, hearing, experiencing at any moment is not only changing our moods but is actually having an effect on how our nervous, endocrine, and immune systems function. So if we are a vibration before we are anything else then our environments also being vibration will sense our frequency. The combined energy will have an impact on both ourselves and the environment that we are in, which brings up this point, that when we respond negatively to a positive environment it's not the environment that's the problem, it's us!

Our bodies are an environment.
Our minds are an environment.
Our spirits are an environment.

When there is stress or tension placed in any environment, there is going to be a negative impact on all the components of life creating a negative environment to our well-being. So, it makes sense what Tabaash and other teachers have said about the importance of listening to what life is saying to you. So when I was looking at the rainbow it made me feel good and made me smile, which had a positive outcome on my well-being. And that positive energy touched all the environments that I was involved in and had a positive impact on them. And by doing that life smiled at me and I smiled back and for that moment not only was I in a better place, so was the world. Well, that's what I believe! I could have easily ignored the rainbow or just given it a cursory glance, but it got my attention and by me acknowledging that meant that I knew that it was speaking to me. I think that we give life just a cursory glance at times and by doing so miss out on what it is saying to us. We do this for lots of reasons emotionally, but I think all in all we are also rather a lazy bunch of beings when it comes to paying attention to our true nature, preferring to attend instead to our human nature.

Are we involved in a major mind, body, spirit environmental crisis?

Perhaps crisis is too strong a word, but fundamentally the way we are looking at life, looking at ourselves, is changing, has to change if we are to involve ourselves in evolving positively.

Yesterday I received a package in the mail that was from a client. It was a piece of lapis lazuli that had the word *joy* etched into it in gold. They said they had a dream that they were to send it to me and were told to write,

It is from the Great Spirit that enfolds us all to bring comfort and joy.

I was touched by this gift and it made me think that there seems to be a bit of *God Watching* happening out there in spirit! I also seem to be attracting stones and crystals to me at present. At a friend's summer party my great friend Mary-Helen said that she wanted to give me one of her crystals that was outside in her backyard. I am not wrong in saying that Mary-Helen literally has thousands of crystals and me having one of them was not going to make a big dent in the collection. She was going away for a few days and told me to drive around to her place and have a look over the back fence and that it was near the washing line.

So one fine day I went over and saw this lovely crystal geode that was about a foot high and wide, easy to lift and transport. I rang her up when she came back from her trip and thanked her and said it was lovely and made all the right appreciative sounds but in the midst she interrupted me and said,

"NO! Not that one, it's the bigger one further around the corner."

I must admit I hadn't looked further around the corner and so went back and was blown away by this 200 kilogram quartz crystal that was about the width and height of a coffee table. I imagined that spirit was out there looking down and sardonically saying,

"Not so easy to lift that one up, Blair, is it?"

And so what does one do when one wishes to take ownership of such a sacred and powerful crystal that weighs a ton? One calls one's mate, David, who has a truck and muscles. I thought between the two of us and our combined strength, it would be a breeze, but the breeze was not blowing the day we went to get it. For a start, it was in an awkward position slightly embedded in a slope of the lawn. The multisided shape made it hard to grasp and we had to be careful not to chip the terminals. So we huffed and puffed and grunted and generally made men noises but to no avail. And then we did what men do when they have to contemplate their next move: we stood with our hands on our hips and looked at it. You could almost hear the cogs of our brains turning as we considered our options.

"I've got that small trolley I threw in the back of your truck," I announced. "If we can lift it onto that then we can just wheel it through this narrow path and then down to the truck." We looked at each other the way men do when they know that they have hit upon a brilliant idea and are in total agreement. We placed our hands on our hips again and stood and stared at the crystal as if aligning ourselves with our brilliance before we got on with the task.

David having agreed that my idea would work nodded, and so with some more huffing and puffing and men sounds we managed to get the crystal onto the trolley where it very properly buckled the wheels, rendering the trolley a now useless commodity. So, more hands on hips and more staring at the crystal as our next strategy carefully formed under our sweating brow. There was a tarpaulin in the truck and so we decided that if we lifted the crystal onto that we could lift/ shuffle it along the path. Mary-Helen was in the background, concerned that we were going to damage the terminals, but we made reassuring sounds to her while straining and gasping and almost passing out with the effort we were putting into shifting the crystal. We got it to the end of the narrow path but still had to lift it up about half a meter and into a wheelbarrow, a job that had to be done in two stages, otherwise David and I would have been in for hernias in places where no man would want them, if yah know what I mean!

Having got the crystal into a wheelbarrow we now had to journey down a steep path and then down a short flight of very narrow and steep steps. The neighbor had rigged up some very narrow planks from the bottom step to the cab of the truck and as I neared the planks I eyed them dubiously, wondering if they would bear the weight of the crystal. I had visions of it smashed to many pieces, Mary-Helen standing there giving us that I-told-you-so look. As I descended the stair carefully the wheelbarrow took on a life of its own and started to propel me with the weight of the crystal down the stairs at a rate that I was not comfortable with, and by some sort of miracle it motored across the plank at great speed positioning itself in the cab of the truck exactly where it needed to be while I did my best to look like I wasn't being dragged behind and that this was all my idea! As much as I would love to have taken credit for such a strategic maneuver I instead gave a silent thanks to those above and patted the crystal for showing such initiative. It probably got sick of being manhandled by such novices and decided to take things in hand, so to speak! On the way back to my place we dropped in on a job David was doing and picked up some very solid metal planks that would make the end journey much faster and easier. It was slightly more uphill at my place and with more push, shove, and heave, we got it positioned. It looks superb and I visit it often through the day, giving it a hug and kiss and placing my third eye on it. When the sun shines onto its glassy surface miniature rainbows appear within its core and sparkle like internal magic. It is always cold to the touch, a sort of electric cold that makes your skin feel like it is vibrating. Placing my forehead onto its flat surface the coolness of it is an exquisite surprise that turns into the gift of energy. This draws me into a halo of light surrounded by a halo of color. I am in awe that it is a natural element from deep within the Earth and that it must be millions of years old and that makes me feel like I am participating in creation itself. It sits next to a large sitting Buddha and it is my very sacred garden spot. I suspect the crystal is doing quite a lot of its own *God Watching.*

When the weather was warmer I would sit up in that area where I had placed a small park bench and do a little bit of internal *God Watching* under the canopy of the trees, my companions being the crystal, Buddha, and a small shrine and I hoped like hell that the birds were not going to shit on me but perhaps it was their way of *God Watching?*

> *Internal God Watching is mandatory*
> *for any serious God on planet Earth.*

This is what I get when I internally *God Watch.* I always find a quiet and private place where I won't be disturbed. At times I like to be outside when I do this but I know that can be a bit distracting for some people and hard to find a place where they won't be disturbed. I close my eyes and inform my body and mind that I am going to do some *Internal God Watching.* The moment I put out that thought my mind fills up with a very light blue and I feel all floatie and peaceful. Then it usually gets a bit comical as I see small puffy white clouds appear with little signs on them and I see aspects of myself that are portraying my *God Nature.* The signs pertain to what I need to pay attention to and it is always correct and relevant. One sign may read *FITNESS*, another could read *EMOTIONS*, and one sign once read *EAT LESS*, which I was rather piqued about as I didn't think I was overeating!

The thing is you can't argue with what you are seeing as it's true and comes from your *God Nature.* Usually I see the clouds all in a row and after a while they do a little bit of a dance around and one of the clouds projects more prominently, indicating that this is important to pay attention to. I try to pay attention to the emotions and thoughts that I experience when I see what the sign says, as these are indicators of how I am responding to what I am seeing. Impatience may come up or sadness; indignation and acceptance are just a few of the emotions that present themselves. All those responses are telling you about your beliefs around those issues. At times I get quite clear ideas or information that is quite specifically telling me the course of action to take. It's all quite logical, straightforward, and clear. I am being presented facts from my own *God Nature* and it will not project anything in an ambiguous manner. One thing I have noted in this experience is that there is no interaction between the separate factions sitting on their clouds. They are single units projecting a specific intent that does not need to collaborate with other factions. They know their position, present what is necessary, and then quietly hover while I continue my *God Watching*.

I like the logical and matter-of-fact way that I am presented with this information and I have to remember that it is given to me in this manner because *that is the way that I like to receive it.* It will differ with each individual as we all have our own ways of accepting information. It's interesting to note that I have not *thought* consciously that this is the way I prefer to receive, as the minute I close my eyes and align the process begins. So I can only surmise that the higher nature in me knows exactly the way I will receive and process, but then I guess that's the job of the higher nature! When I look at the signs I will usually download information straightaway. Other times I see the sign and then ask for more information, and it is always simple. One thing I have learned over the years of asking of source is that the reply will come to you in a simple form, factual and very direct. I have never known higher nature to be anything else than this. I believe our human nature is too involved in our emotional state at times, thus making things too convoluted, whereas the higher nature not having to deal with the human emotions can basically cut to the chase! It is in our true nature to live a life that is without the complex emotional formulas that we all seem so accepting of. The more I *God Watch* myself, the more I feel and experience the magnitude of the power that is source and that this is so totally the way to always be and live. When we *God Watch* we trigger deep within our being the memory of this and so this can be defined as a form of *awakening*. *God Watching* also alerts you to what is going on with all the levels of life that we are involved in daily. There is depth to everything we do, feel, think, say through our day and I believe it's imperative to the success of the day for us to know as many levels of that day as we can. I believe this is vital because these levels harbor information that will guide us quite distinctively in our thoughts, words, and deeds. So once again we are visiting the idea that there is no such thing as a random act of life.

God watching removes the arbitrariness of life.

Human nature finds at times a great security in life being predictable, which perhaps curtails our ability to create more. Coming to Earth in each life that we live one must remember that we are not just here to engage in our human nature.

How premature to shake away other aspects of our power before we see that they are of great consequence to our human nature. It all seems too easy to cast away vital ingredients if only to scrounge around in the future looking for them again, a total ineffective exercise. I believe that each new day we bring to our human nature effective supplies specifically for that day.

It is not the nature of God to awaken unprepared.

If we have had our awakening to our *God Nature* then we are living in a state of awareness that automatically puts us in preparation mode. As we *God Watch* we see this clearly easily accessing the supplies that will take us through the day. We are consistently putting out signals that are like calls to other souls so that they too will engage in the dance that is our life. That's an interesting concept and the aim is to dance with as many partners through the day. The connections we make are varied, and some are conscious, others unconscious. We may make an alignment with the soul of someone but have nothing to do with their human nature. With others, we become heavily involved in the human nature, the soul never getting a look. We may look at the physical that is nature but never see or feel the soul of it.

We may see, but we do not hear.
We may touch, but we never feel.
We may be alive, but are we living?

When we awaken we have arrived at our destination for the day and are we going to approach this with the excitement of boundless potential striving to express our soul and human qualities? There is elegance in being conscious of the power we express as we position ourselves through the day to the best of our advantage. It is like a great beauty knowing the way to position herself so one experiences the best angles of the beauty she has. The awareness she has of her assets teaches her to play them to her advantage. And so the same can be said of us all since we all have assets that we owe ourselves to exploit in a positive nature in our lifetime. Here is a little *God Watching* exercise that you might want to try.

Stand or sit before a mirror; if it is at all possible, a full-length mirror is best. Spend a few moments simply observing yourself, allowing the body to be comfortable and the thoughts to quiet. As you gaze at your body be conscious of thoughts that come to you or feelings you have about yourself. If you are feeling self-conscious and find it hard to see yourself then breathe a little faster and relax more and in your mind think,

I am not my body.

You may wish to repeat this several times in your thoughts, and you will after a while find yourself looking at your body with detachment and without bias. I've tried this and it is hard to look at yourself, as your human nature seems to jump right into seeing your imperfections and you kick into automatic self-criticism! You can't help but stretch the skin to see how much better you look without those slightly dropped upper eyelids or the puffiness of the jowls. Your hands itch to reach for that number of the plastic surgeon! So, once you've bypassed this stage it seems a little easier to just look objectively.

Now think about all your mind, body, spirit qualities.

Again, be conscious of the thoughts and feelings you have while you are doing this.

Be alert to your responses.

This is not an exercise of self-criticism so if you find your mind wandering in that direction veer away! As you become alert to your responses think,

I am God Watching.

Hold strong onto that thought and keep gently repeating it. You may want to say this out loud. Once you feel you have got to a place where you feel aligned then think or say,

I remove layers of energy that are no longer relevant to my life.

Every time you take a layer off then once again think, *I am God Watching,* and be conscious of the changes you feel are occurring through the process. Don't hold onto anything but do pay attention to anything that presents itself as relative to your advancement or anything that you know is fundamental to change. You will reach a place where you know that there are no more layers to remove and when you have reached this place think or say,

I ACCEPT THAT I AM MY GOD NATURE.
MY GOD NATURE DIRECTS MY HUMAN NATURE.
I AM GOD.

God Watching offers up many varied opportunities as I have discovered since I took up the hobby seriously. My mate David bought an old church with three Coptic crosses still intact on the roof in the suburb of Ngaio in Wellington and has turned it into an amazing home. He does this, buys places that need doing up, lives in them for a while, and then moves on. His church is on the market now and he's ready to move onto the next project. Talking to him earlier in the week he asked if I could come up and get Tabaash to empty the place of the old energy and to give a blessing to ensure a good sale and I was happy to oblige. The moment you walk into the house it's like a giant embrace engulfing you in the tantalizing energy of comfort and homeliness. I've been to the property a few times since he bought it and it's fascinating watching the transformation as he practices his magical art of creating a perfect home. The energy of it always felt fairly clear to me apart from one room at the back as it felt rather cold and forlorn and though it didn't feel like a bad or negative energy it felt sad.

Estate agents had "dressed" the house and when I entered it was inviting and enticing. David ambled down the stairs and I gave my great friend a huge hug. I'm always so happy to see him and spend time with his wonderful soul. We were going to grab a nice meal out afterward so I looked forward to his company and a great yarn. We went upstairs and I brought

Tabaash through and he started his process of which I will now explain. Houses are like sponges to energy and they will hold the residue of its history within its walls. Some homes feel like they have a real soul and you feel an instant rapport with them while others can feel totally void of anything and give the impression of simply being bricks and mortar. You can always feel a happy house and one that's not. Most of the time it's to do with the people who have lived there, other times it is because the house had been built on land that carries its own history. There are many stories about homes and buildings that have been the recipient of paranormal activity due to being on a site of an ancient burial ground or a battle. Houses that are hundreds of years old are like libraries of the past and the imprints of its previous occupants have left their mark. So what Tabaash is doing is not "ghost busting" but emptying the house of all the old energy and calling in the new. He walks around each room and blesses it and chants, calling in positive energies and chats away to whatever spirits who happen to wonder what he might be doing! So once he got going at David's he gave David a running commentary about who was around the property and told him to stand in a certain place and feel the energy of that particular vortex and the vibe of a certain room. Then Tabaash would shift the energy and tell David to come and feel how different it was. When he got to the room that I felt the negative energy he said that there was death in this area but not in the building but around the land and he cited that there had been a sickness and that there were people buried nearby. Well, whatever he did certainly cheered the room up as there was a remarkable change of energy that made the room feel positively oozing with happiness! David had put the property on the market and he told David that while he was chanting, etc., David was to hold strong in his mind the selling of the property at the price he wanted, and that the energy that Tabaash was creating should not be wasted. This all took in total about fifteen minutes and when I returned the first thing I sensed was a very deep peace, not just in the house but in David, so Tabaash had done his job well! Nothing like a soul colonic to spruce things up!

Off we went up the road to a very lovely restaurant and I must say there's nothing quite like a restaurant to do some God watching. I eat out quite a lot living in the center of town. Where I live in Wellington I'm really spoiled for choice as literally at my doorstep there are hundreds of restaurants and cafés. Café style casual dining seems to be the trend these days so it was nice to go to a place where it was quiet and cozy and there were tablecloths on the tables. The place was packed and there was a gentle hum of normal conversation as people were not having to compete with the waiting staff's choice of music. We ordered our food and I in a whim ordered a bottle of Laurent Perrier Champagne simply because I felt like it.

As per usual David and I kicked into our usually metaphysical discussions and as usual someone sitting at the table near us pricked up her ears and was straining to hear the gist of our conversation. These days whenever I am out and about particularly when I'm in a restaurant or café where you can really observe people I see it as an exceptional time to do some *God Watching AND God Listening,* for that matter. At the table next to us were two couples whom like David and I were in their late fifties but actually looked a lot older. The men were in an animated discussion about someone who was living in a tent on an island off the shore of Auckland. One of the women was staring into space, a bored expression on her face like she had heard this story one too many times and as I *God Watched* her I could sense a sadness in her as she dug her hole a little bit deeper. The other was half listening to the story and half listening to what David and I were talking about. The energy she exuded was that of someone who would love to participate in what we were discussing. She kept throwing glances our way as if waiting to be invited to join. The two men at the table were a study in themselves as pretty much through the evening they acted like the women were not there at all; the women must have felt like they were part of rent a crowd, just there to fill a space.

As we progressed with our dinner we started to talk about the way the vibrations of life were altering and moving faster. I casually mentioned that most of my life I have had the ability to spin my chakras, starting from the base and moving up. I told David that all I had to do was clinch my sphincter muscle in my bottom and everything just started to happen. We discussed this and of course had to clinch and so there we were eating, talking, and clinching. I looked around the room at all the people quietly conversing and having their dinner totally unaware that at the table in the corner were two men who were clinching their arses while spinning their chakras. I couldn't help it. I just started to laugh in a very undignified way and almost farted as I relaxed, which made me want to laugh even more. Then of course I laughed more, thinking about what would happen if I did fart and how people around would have responded. We were getting a few strange looks at this stage by some of the more salubrious patrons but, hey, we're all Gods so let's get on with our dinner and all clinch our sphincters together!

As I have practiced *God Watching* I've become more sensitive, picking up the energy around and within people. Sitting at the traffics lights at a major intersection in town I watched as a mass of people used the pedestrian crossing and a barrage of thoughts inundated my mind as I picked up on the moods and feelings of the people crossing. I watched as a big white van turned into one of the lanes in front of me and the idea that the person driving was pissed off and felt anxious came to me; I didn't even see the driver. It's like I could simply feel the energy he was filling the van with. None of this felt intrusive; I was simply listening to the life around me that is always happening anyway and there was no emotion attached to it, just the knowing.

There is a new common sense that has been established by humanity. The old common sense was based on values that were pertinent when we were all very involved only in our human nature, God being separate from us, a ruling deity who was better than us, who ruled us, told us what to do, and rewarded us. That particular design of God has been a human creation by those who wanted the power and established the idea of God as something to fear and revere. This new common sense that we have established is created by what we have become as a collective vibration. We are no longer willing to accept the word of the old systems to define how we should live our lives and we now know that we have sovereignty over ourselves. This has changed our understanding of what the force of God is and when we look deep within we have seen that there is no degree of separation between us, our souls, and the God force. This seems such a difficult concept for some to grasp particularly when one sees God as a force to be angry at when things go wrong in life.

God created the ability to be alive.
Humans created what we do with it.

I feel at times such a deep love and respect for human nature and the astonishing things we are all capable of. It seems that we really want the world to be a better place and yet there seems to be so much fear of stepping up to that place and actually living it all the time. It's as if we have come to believe that this is only something that we can have a little of rather than have the whole lot. It's the old adage where we will all be rewarded in heaven. Why can't we have our rewards now? Why wait?

My nana used to tell me to see the best in people and as a child I found that hard when I observed and experienced the nasty side of human nature. It's easy to become afraid of people and of life when you feel pushed around and unqualified to support yourself. So what I now know and understand is that actually some people really suck and I don't have to accept that. It's okay to make a stand and have an opinion when you know it's the appropriate thing to do. If I were to give advice to my nana I would say this: Some people are not very nice and not very good and they seem to find ways of hurting other people and hurting themselves. So quite frankly I can't see the best in them. What I can do, though, is see they have a soul before I see their darker human nature. When I remember to see their soul then I am able to understand that within that human nature is something better and greater and pure that is never lost. When I *God Watch* I know that even the darkest human nature will at some point turn on the light and fill life's room with its radiance so that soul can once again see how much more there is.

God Watching is the new way to observe life.

Chapter Twenty-Six
Everything Is Always There

My final X-ray for my arm and the all-clear from the hospital had come and gone a few months back and so when I felt the slight pain in my arm I didn't take much notice of it. It had been a year since I had first felt the pain not knowing what was in front of me and so when the pain occurred again and didn't go away I could feel the anxiety slowly creeping in, not wanting to believe that once again I had created the same situation. I asked my higher nature and got that I was fine. I meditated on it and asked Tabaash and he told me all was well. I felt fine and I felt strong and I felt well but my human nature kept recalling what the surgeon had said to me just before I had left the hospital after my stay there:

"If you ever feel pain get yourself straight up to hospital."

I didn't, well, not for three days anyway. It didn't feel like the pain I had before, and I took my temperature several times over those three days and it was normal. Finally something higher in me took charge. It was a Wednesday and I had a full day of clients. The morning one was a person who came to see me, and the others were offshore Skype sessions. I had in the back of my mind that maybe I will pop up to the hospital soon and get the arm looked at, but my human nature male self was stubborn and fearful. I could not bear the thought that I would have to go through once again what I had been through. I had worked so hard on healing myself and could not believe that once again I would create the same reality. My first client came and went and I was getting ready for the second client to ring on Skype; it was then the Internet connection went down. I rang up the server and they said there had been some sort of cable malfunction and it would not be fixed till later in the afternoon. I had to contact the clients via phone and reschedule. I sat back and laughed at myself, and my higher nature. We had cleared the way for me to get up to the hospital and sort this thing out.

I found a spot straight away in the hospital car park, a miracle in itself, but obviously the way was being cleared for me, and when I went up to the desk and explained the situation they sent me in straight away to have my bloods done. There was talk of X-rays but they wanted the consultant to talk to me first. I felt blank but not worried. They ushered me into a small cubicle where there was another man sitting and they sent him somewhere else; that made me worry slightly that they were treating me as urgent and bumping this guy off further down the list. I sat down and looked at the table beside me, the top of which was covered in magazines that were so obscure that it was hard to imagine they had even gone to print. They had names like "Picnic Spots in Siberia" and "Train Spotting in East Afghanistan." I didn't pick them up as I thought they were probably highly infested with some disease. I amused myself by looking at all the apps on my Iphone and wondered why I had half of them since I never used them or even knew what they were for. Hospital sounds drifted into my little cubicle world, and after a while I sat in a sort of slight meditative stupor not particularly feeling anything at all. I was shaken out of my reverie by the arrival of the consultant who ushered me into another cubicle. He was South African and of the age that I would call indistinctive; he could have been in his forties but more likely hitting sixty. He was quite portly and seemed frazzled, no doubt by his heavy workload.

"Look," he said. 'The results of your bloods have come back fine so I don't believe there's need for an X-ray."

He then went on to explain about something that measures the amount of infection in your blood, I can't remember exactly what he called it, but the normal for most people was between two and four and he said mine was two, but when I had the infection a year before it had been 180! There was, he continued, quite a lot of scar tissue in my arm and it doesn't stretch so the amount of gym work I'm doing was pulling the scar tissue across the muscle, hence the pain. Well, the amount of relief I felt as he talked was enormous and as he skedaddled away to administer to the sick I couldn't hide the huge grin I had on my face. The interesting thing was that straight away the pain I had been feeling simply vanished and so it made me wonder that perhaps my soul self needed to do a little bit of "*so a year later, how you doing?*"

I am more conscious now than ever that all our issues are always with us. And rather than put huge effort into "letting them go" it's best to actually understand that they always have an integral place in our life and by seeing them differently we change the impact they have on us. I have personally seen the impact of what one can do to oneself by retaining an energy that is best expunged from my system. I have also proved that you can have a huge impact on one's healing and recovery through the connection we have with our higher natures. I use my higher nature all the time now; it's a daily routine and often through the whole day. I needed also to have the medical intervention that was given to me and with the combination of what I was doing holistically I speeded up the healing of my arm. I have also realized that by practicing this process it was a way of giving new information to my human nature that it was to accept with ease that it was possible to be influenced by the higher nature and its energy. The human nature no longer needed to be involved in the energy of struggle and a healing process that was slow. Having gone through what I did with my arm gave me the chance to *arm myself differently*, if you will excuse the pun!

If everything is always there, that means the power to live a life that fulfills you in all the ways is in your life now. Let's face it, to be blunt we all go through shit in our lives at times and at the end of the day we all have to find ways of dealing with that. I think it's unrealistic and naive of us to believe we get rid of the stuff that hurts us. It's always going to be a part of our lives. This "stuff," though, is what makes us look at what we need to change, and it makes us pay more attention to the way we respond to our challenges. Seeing all this, knowing all this, and acting from our *God Nature* places us in the position where we turn our naivete into a positive experience and it makes us feel more qualified to be able to create better outcomes. We train ourselves to new ways of being, moving away from destructive outcomes. We become master manipulators of our own creations, molding life's situations until they work for us. This seems a more productive way of dealing with things we don't want as opposed to creating counterproductive experiences to resolve. We seem to be afraid of what we see and what we feel at times, and by having this fear we push what needs to be dealt with into the shadows in the hope that it will go away. While it is in the shadows it is slowly gathering more momentum until eventually it seems to *grow out of the shadows* until you have to attend to it! It's like the bag of onions I bought and put in a metal container in the pantry. I simply forgot all about them until a few weeks later when I wondered where that awful composting smell was coming from. As I followed the scent I lifted the lid of the container to behold the sprouting onions seeking for the light and a big mushy smelly mess of rotted onion. Needless to say, there was a bit of cleaning up to do! And there is life sometimes, a big smelly mess that's seeking for the light and if we ignore what's needed we have a bit of cleaning up to do.

Observe, Attend, Complete, and THEN
put the issues into the shadows.

If we have a good look at life this day, Thursday, 26 April 2018, we see that everything is simply happening. Our experiences are relative to where we currently live. We are paying attention to what we need to, attending to our jobs, the people who are in our lives today; we are participating in the experience of life as we currently know it. While we are doing this all the other residents of Earth are existing in the way they need to, thinking, feeling, doing what is relative to their lives. And we are all doing this at the same time and regardless of the fact we don't know on a conscious level what's happening,

It is all happening.

I imagine it is like I'm coming in from outer space and I see Earth as one big room. A giant door surrounds Earth and as I get closer it begins to slide open, allowing me to enter this room, and as I do I behold that *Everything Is Happening* and *Everything Is Always There.* I go to the part of the room that I want to and surround myself with what is needed by me and as I do my focus is on what is essential to my life, allowing the rest of the Earth/Room to go out of focus. I am still aware that it is there but will only bring it or part of it into focus if it needs to be an integral part of my experience. I think we push at life too much and if it doesn't like that it will push back. And remember, since everything is our creation, then this is tantamount to pushing ourselves, and if this self does not like it then it's going to give you a big shove back. If you keep pushing when you have been given the message to back off then you are going to set up some interesting dynamics that may be confrontational. It's like teasing yourself, it will put up with only so much and then when it's had enough it will fight back. That's when we get all pissed off and get a taste of our own medicine! I recall when I was a child one of my friends sitting on me and tickling me unmercifully. He pushed too far, though, as he did it for so long I threw up, right in his face, and he got angry with me! Well, honestly!

Life is going to throw up in your face if you push it too much.

It's not a pleasant analogy but we can only put up with so much, and if we push the limits then the limits are going to push back. So by learning to observe before we push we can get a sense of when to leave well enough alone or not.

I was thinking today how much I find this thing called life so challenging and so tiring at times because of the massive shift we are going through. It's not that the new energy is demanding anything of us, it's that it's just there and it's doing its thing and the best we can do at times is simply pay attention to our responses. I have to remind myself that as soul I have *chosen* to create all this so I could *participate* in all that is occurring, and it's all occurring so I can evolve. And we are all in our own boats doing exactly the same. This creating your reality stuff can get a bit confusing at times. I mean, think about it, I find life challenging at times and yet I have to remember that in the bigger picture I have actually been the one who has established the challenge. I also established the massive shifts that are occurring with everything and everybody. I am not only making all this happen but I also happen to be participating in what I have made happen. So that basically makes me totally responsible for everything that is happening, has happened, and will happen to everyone and everything. Now I can see why some people are not too happy about such a theory when you consider what's gone down through history. And to think that we have done this numerous times through history in other lives and we keep coming back to repeat it all again! I get it, I really do, but at times the human in me kicks in and stands in utter perplexity at this process. It's beyond shaking my head and trying to make sense of it, I mean really,

Hey, God, what were you thinking?

We have been traveling through the very long history of this planet and our souls' evolution on it. The moment we incarnate we come completely qualified for the task of life because we have set ourselves up for this journey and there was no way that we were going to come into life without that know-how. We have all been involved in the events of life and have now reached a place where there is

A great turn of events!

This is our more conscious venture into the world of source power and it changes everything. And like everything else this event has always been there, was always going to happen. It had to, human nature has been dissatisfied with the way it has been going, the way that certain factions seem to have all the say and control of where as a planet we are going and quite frankly human nature has had a gut full.

Before change is humanly possible, it has to be spiritually possible.
That is the new now.

Spiritually it's a time of evolution, the spirit part of us taking precedence over the human nature to establish a new form of control. With this control we can gauge quickly human nature's issues and go direct to source energy and find solutions to these issues without having to create disturbance in human nature. Looking back through the last one hundred years on Earth there have been a lot of events that have disrupted our equilibrium and this needs to be rectified and to do this it seems unlikely we will find it in our human nature. And so here we are turning inward to our soul, knowing that is the place we have now to go to in order to get back in alignment.

And aren't we all having fun, or not as the case may at times be! We have spent lifetimes building human nature layers on our souls and we seem to have forgotten to put windows in so our soul could shine through! Our poor soul, spending all that time without a decent view of anything and knowing that it has a job to do and it can't get to it as the human nature has the monopoly on everything. I think of certain phrases that have been bandied around for a while.

The challenge is in the struggle.
You can't have the good without the bad.
You only learn from your mistakes.
It's the tough times that make us stronger.
Life isn't always a bed of roses.
No pain, no gain.

How depressing to accept any of those and believe them, and yet so many really do believe them and live by those concepts. Let's do some changes then and create new ones.

The challenge is to always be source energy eliminating struggle.
Good is good and bad is ignorance.
Life's full of opportunities and experiences; we learn from them all.
We are Gods, always strong.
Life is a botanical garden of exquisite vision and senses.
No pain, only gain.

Accepting that everything is always there is going to change the way we approach life. For a start it takes away the need to get rid of anything and the efforts we put into doing so. We don't have the worry of anything coming back and the anxiety that may go with that. There's no need to go out and find something; if it's in life's room then that eliminates that need. We don't have to become something, find anything, worry that we will miss out and hope for the best. If the best is forever in the room then you access that and bring it forward into life. We go into life's room and we observe and we then recognize essentially what is needed. We accept and then establish a strategy that fits our needs. We then express what we've observed and determine the outcomes we desire. We may do some fine-tuning, but we are confident in the choices we have made because we have trusted that in life's room is everything we need and we only use what is necessary. If the lights are on then there will be no stumbling around in the dark, bumping into life, grabbing at any old thing in the hope it's going to be alright! The greatest chance that we as human beings can give ourselves is to stand in life's room as the Gods we are.

Everything is always there and that's okay.

Chapter Twenty-Seven
We All Find Out Eventually

Over the years as people have become familiar with my work with Tabaash, some who have been coming for sometime have taken to calling Tabaash "Mr. T," an endearment that I myself have adopted over time. Yesterday I spent the day up in Auckland with my friends Sandra and Keith and we were boarding our flight back to Wellington. As I stepped into the plane the attendant looked at my boarding pass and welcomed me in a hearty voice using my Christian name. She handed me back my pass and I moved on and you can imagine my surprise when she announced, "And we have Mr. T on board as well!" I looked at Sandra and Keith and burst out laughing. It was obviously the passenger who was behind me but then I always think about the importance of listening to what life is saying so it must have been Tabaash letting me know in his way that he was right behind me. That is and always has been a great comfort to me in all the years I have been doing this. Knowing that there is a being out there watching out for you is very humbling as well as greatly appreciated. Of course we all have that available to ourselves but most people would not even be aware of those "guardian angels," as people call them. How is it possible that people would believe that we have to go through any life totally void of any assistance from higher realms of consciousness? It makes me think it's like throwing a set of dice and seeing what comes up. I don't for a moment think that is what life is meant to be, some speculative exercise of chance hoping we will get a double six.

When I look at the stupid, crazy, and counterproductive things that some people can get themselves involved in (and I'm no exception), I shake my head and wonder, "What were they thinking?" That's it, of course; they weren't thinking at all or if they were then they were doing so from their human nature that directed them down the road of challenge. When it comes to making decisions, human nature tends to take its lead from *the human nature*; now with the advent of self-development we are taking the lead from the *God Nature* that has rather changed the human climate we all live in. This brings climate change to a whole new level! Emotionally, physically, mentally, spiritually we have all weathered a few storms and with the *God Vibe* stepping in to clear the storms, a few are being created in the process and the human nature *reacts* against this powerful source.

We often react against the positive powerful sources of life.

So why do we do that? I believe it's because it makes us become conscious of the fact that we need to make changes and this brings out varied forms of negative responses. Often it seems that we have to create even more disruption before we get our positive results and so I can understand why some would recoil in the wake of change. It's a process of dismantling and I think some believe that's too disturbing, so rather than dismantle they stay with what they know, which in most cases inevitably becomes an unsettling experience! When eventually you do accept the powerful sources of life it transforms everything. Recently I was speaking at a one-day seminar in the beautiful town called Havelock North in the Hawke's Bay region here in New Zealand. It's a four-hour drive north of Wellington and I was sharing the day with my friend and colleague Hetty Rodenburg. Hetty and Tabaash have collaborated before and we seem to be a very successful team.

I had a car full of ladies with me as Sonia and Raewyn from Wellington were attending and it was a car full of happy Gods as we hit the road for an adventure. One thing about God people, we are very comfortable with silences or we can't stop talking. There weren't many pauses on this trip and the four-hour trip took about seven hours as we kept stopping to peruse the shops along the way, grab a coffee, have lunch, and generally take our time! The boot of the car was crammed full with lady purchases and man purchases and though I couldn't actually see out of my rear-vision mirror it was worth it. We were to teach and stay at Taruna Centre in Havelock North that is a place of holistic and adult education. It was started by Ruth Nelson and Edna Burbury, who were lifelong friends and partners. They were dedicated to education and were early supporters of the Rudolph Steiner Education philosophy. They wanted Taruna to be a place that would encourage adult learning and encourage people to reach beyond their perimeters. The house sits atop a hill with the sweeping views of Hawke's Bay beneath them and at the base of Te Mata Peak a sumptuous array of steep rolling green carpeted hills and peaks. There was a wide and very green lawn at the front of the house that just ached for an afternoon tea party and a game of croquet or lawn bowls. The whole area had a quiet presence that felt ancient and I felt perhaps it was being swept by the constant energy of Te Mata Peak above. We settled in and then went into town where we had a rowdy dinner at a local pub and then an early night.

I was awakened early by the sound of heavy rain but when I looked out the window I could see the road was wet and yet I could see no rain falling, perhaps up here it was invisible sacred rain, most unusual. The feeling to go up to Te Mata Peak before we started the day was strong and I knew I also had to take Raewyn with me. She is a very gifted channel and healer and she could feel the essence of Taruna and the surrounding area and that there was energy there to be awakened.

It was only a five-minute drive up to the peak and the morning was fresh, glorious, and sprinkled with the day's early sunshine. There were a few stalwart joggers around but apart from that we had the place to ourselves. Raewyn went off to the right to awaken the energy and I went to the summit and gazed at the vista before me. The energy of the land and sea reaching out in front of me spoke its story and I had one of those epiphanies when you suddenly feel that in a brief second you completely understand everything and how it all works. It was encouraging and settling and I stood there for a while just being. I had the thought then that Hetty would be wondering where we were and at that moment a chattering group of four tourists ascended, breaking the spell. I turned to see Raewyn coming down from her citadel and as we got closer to each other she also said Hetty would be wondering where we were, so being of the same thought we scuttled spiritually back to the car but not before we took a selfie, which ended up with us looking something like "Howard and Hilda" on holiday. We drove the short distance back to Taruna, the trees on either side of us literally glowing with conversation, ancient lords and ladies of the forest that they were, and we felt very honored to be accepted into their kingdom.

It was a great gathering of people on that Saturday and at the end I felt saturated with love and companionship from all the exquisite souls who had partaken of the day. Here were people who had created the need to be together and serve and learn and by doing so expanded the understanding of who they were. Each would take what they had experienced and would do something unique with it that pertained to what they believed. And that is what we are all doing with the lives that we live. We all are involved in our own personal experience of life, gathering what we know is necessary to our advancement. Within us is this great desire to be something more than what we know as human nature and it's this desire that allows us to strive for more. When we understand that this more has nothing to do with our human nature then we turn a massive corner that exposes us to the "*something more*."

When I set out on my spiritual journey in this lifetime I thought it was all about being spirit and all that it entails. My enthusiasm took me deep within and as it did I found myself looking at my human nature. The God in me had led me to my human nature and showed it to me in every way possible. It is of course still doing this and will do so until I leave this life. I know more than ever now that we are not here to conquer our human frailties and foibles, we are not here to pass some big test so that we are qualified to move on to some other higher level of consciousness where we find portals of energy vibrating madly. We are here in our bodies to live as the Gods we are but having this human experience on Earth.

Our bodies are not our nemesis and neither are the lives we have created. And yet so many see it in that way and consequently participate in struggles that perpetuate uncertainty, fear, and mistrust. I see and know more than ever that we never intended to *become something* here on Earth but more *be the Gods we are.* Of course, we must bring in our own personal interpretation to being God and what that means to us. And this is something that we explore daily, and there is great adventure in doing this as we have this whole life and this whole world before us to do so. *Finding out eventually* isn't just about knowing that we are God and that there is a heaven out there, but it's also about being able to live as God in the bodies that we possess now, believing that we are able to access that unlimited power of life while we are still in our bodies. It changes the way we feel, the way we think, and the way we participate in life. It alters the ways that we treat each other, be it as individuals or as a collective. Living this way doesn't *tell us what to do and how to be,* being this way shows us that we already *know* what to do and know how to go about it. When we get this and see that others are getting this as well it pulls all the pieces together and there we have the *Oneness of All.*

As my wife's illness takes more of a hold on her and I watch her determination to live I think about what she told me a long time ago about being afraid that there is nothing there when we die. This morning when I had my morning meditation

I found myself to my great pleasure visiting the dimension I had spoken of in an earlier chapter where I had met the master teacher who helped me. I found that I was sitting in the same place where I had first begun the journey in this place and my whole being filled with great joy of being here again as it had been sometime since I had. It was during my recovery from my arm infection that took me there and I thought that perhaps I only visited that dimension for the purpose to assist my healing. Yet here I was again and I was walking through a corridor that had high arches and views to the right of the majestic mountains. I got to the end of the corridor and was wondering what this trip was all about as nothing presented itself to me. I looked over the open veranda and saw a small garden surrounded by trees. It was very isolated and lonely and I saw that sitting on a bench was Kay looking very alone and very confused. I descended some stairs that were to the left and rushed to her side and took her gently in my arms. Spirit then spoke to me and said that she was afraid and so was there in this place not knowing what to do. I spoke to her gently and told her that there was nothing to fear at all and that I was allowed to take her to the light if that was okay with her. Her eyes spoke of gratitude and such devotion and I lifted her into my arms and walked down a small pathway that led to a long and wide canoe on the riverbank. I gently placed Kay at the bow and I went to the stern and stood and raised my arms. As I did the canoe started to move gently and we made a silent journey between the great mountains on either side of us. As we moved up river I could see a great swirling circle of light ahead. It was like a whirlpool standing on its side drawing us in. I beckoned to Kay to notice and her eye's widened with awe and wonder at the sight. We penetrated the light and we were surrounded by its essence bringing great peace and happiness. I looked at Kay and saw that the light was now transforming her to full health and well-being. The canoe came to a stop and there were wide steps that seemed to be made of the light itself and we ascended the steps. I was told that I was permitted to go with Kay and so I led her up the wide steps till we came to the base of a set of steps that were narrower and shorter and led to a wooden door at the top. We stood together at the base of these steps and the door opened, revealing heaven.

I took Kay up to the door, a door I knew that I could not go through. Kay's face had taken on a radiance and she showed no fear at all. I stood before her and spoke.

"My dear love, you have to go through this door now and you will be looked after. I am not going to say good-bye to you as I know that I will see you again. I just want to say thank you for the wonderful life that we have shared and for everything that you have done for me and taught me in this life we had together. I can't go through the door with you as it's your time, not mine, but before you go through that door can you just hold me, just one more time?"

And she did, a long tender embrace that spoke of the union we have shared through this and other lifetimes. And then she went through the door and it closed behind her, leaving me alone. My spirit then took flight and I soared through the air conscious of a great peace and a sense of completion. I landed near my tree and sat and leaned against it and when I did the meditation finished and I opened the eyes of my physical body and in deep peace and silence, tears streaming down my face. A voice in my head said, *Don't move, Blair*, and so I sat in the energy of my experience for a while longer. I carried that energy all through my day and I wondered that when I went to see Kay later in the day if there would be any indication in her behavior that she knew on a deep level what had occurred, and there was.

The last few days when I have visited Kay she has been very angry and the look in her eyes can be defined as quite hostile. Spending time with her has been avoiding being hit as she flays out her fists or avoiding being spat at or just glared at like I am her worst enemy. I walked onto the lounge area of the hospital wing Kay was in and I knew straight away that she knew me as she smiled and lifted up her hand as if greeting me. Sitting next to her was an elderly man who was also a resident and he had taken quite a fancy to Kay and would sit with her through the day. When I made my daily visit he would give me reports about her condition on that day and then would trundle off while I had my time with Kay. It really is special and beautiful seeing his devotion to Kay, his own wife had passed away a year earlier, and I was happy that he had found a way of expressing his caring nature by sitting with Kay. The poor man was riddled with leukemia and cancer and though full of life he looked tired and frail. It's wonderful that even though at the final stage of your life you can still attract to you an opportunity to care and I am full of gratitude for his attention to Kay.

I like to wheel Kay out of the hospital wing and take her around the complex where we usually sit for a while in one of the many lounges. As per usual I bring some chocolate and Kay sat there eating it, staring at me the whole time regarding this prospect before her. The hostile look was still in her eyes and yet in an instant it softened and she gave me a little smile. I had been reading the paper and she made a noise of disapproval as if to say, "I thought you were here to spend time with me!" I turned to her and we stared at each other a long time and I made a face at her and she laughed. Then she winked at me and put her hand on my arm and reached for my other hand and held onto it hard. She reached up and started to touch my cheeks and my nose and then bent her face toward me as if she wanted to have a kiss. I gave her a kiss and she smiled and started to chatter away and look around her. In the last year I have never had such an animated and connected time as we did then. I could feel that she understood what I was saying to her and even though her conversation was unintelligible she was communicating to me like she knew me. At one point I bent down and enveloped her in my arms and told her how much I loved her. She went all still and when I looked at her face I could see that there were tears in her eyes. We simply looked at each other with this great understanding between us, the conversation being in our eyes.

When I left an hour later I felt like I had been presented with a tremendous gift and for the rest of the evening I felt the greatest emotion that we can feel, the only emotion that God feels, love. In love there is respect for the oneness we are and a knowing that if we approach life and live life with love then the things we want to know, mind, body, spirit, will come to us. When we stand on the platform of love before anything else we are able to recognize that we are great beings of energy creators of unbounded potential and magnificence. If we inform our human nature that this is the new way we can take that nature to glory. I have known great love in my life with Kay, a love that has taken many turns on life's road and when I think of what I "heard" when I looked into her eyes yesterday as we held each other's gaze I know that despite what human bodies may endure physically and emotionally and mentally everything is going to be all right.

About the Author

Blair Styra was born in Canada in 1960 and lived the first eleven years of his life there. He and his family immigrated to New Zealand in 1971 an event that was to pave the way for his spiritual journey. As a young child in Canada he always had the feeling that there was something more about life even though he could not define it with words. He felt very attuned to a presence of energy that as an adult he understood to be spirit. In his late teens he met up with a woman who eventually became his wife. The journey that they created together acted as a catalyst for his spiritual growth, and eventually led to him discovering his ability as a channel for spirit. From that point on he began to create new ways of being on all levels. This led to his connection with Tabaash and for the last 24 years Blair has been the channel for Tabaash. The work they have done together has since taken them throughout New Zealand and internationally. In New Zealand they presented for two years a radio program called "Talking with Tabaash" as well as presenting for 12 years monthly meditation/teaching evenings. They have also run seminars on such subjects as "Bringing God into the business world" and a seminar they have run with Dr Hetty Rodenburg on Grief and Spirituality called "Travelling Light". Blair Styra considers his work with spirit to be his authentic vibration and a life long experience. Tabaash is available for one on one personal consultation's in person and also on Skype. Blair Styra resides with his wife Kay in Wellington New Zealand.

Books by Blair Styra

Don't Change the Channel
Published by: Ozark Mountain Publishing

Who Catharted
Published by: Ozark Mountain Publishing

For more information about any of the above titles, soon to be released titles,
or other items in our catalog, write, phone or visit our website:
Ozark Mountain Publishing, Inc.
PO Box 754, Huntsville, AR 72740
479-738-2348/800-935-0045
www.ozarkmt.com

If you liked this book, you might also like:

The Curators
by Guy Needler

Living the Life Force
by Nicholas Vesey

Ghost and Me
by Kevin Killer

In Light and In Shade
by Patricia Irvine

Headless Chicken
by Manuela Stoerzer

Reconnecting to the Earth
by Aaron Hoopes

Heaven Here on Earth
by Curt Melliger

For more information about any of the above titles, soon to be released titles,
or other items in our catalog, write, phone or visit our website:
Ozark Mountain Publishing, Inc.
PO Box 754, Huntsville, AR 72740

479-738-2348

www.ozarkmt.com

Other Books by Ozark Mountain Publishing, Inc.

Dolores Cannon
A Soul Remembers Hiroshima
Between Death and Life
Conversations with Nostradamus,
    Volume I, II, III
The Convoluted Universe -Book One,
    Two, Three, Four, Five
The Custodians
Five Lives Remembered
Jesus and the Essenes
Keepers of the Garden
Legacy from the Stars
The Legend of Starcrash
The Search for Hidden Sacred Knowledge
They Walked with Jesus
The Three Waves of Volunteers and the
    New Earth
Aron Abrahamsen
Holiday in Heaven
Out of the Archives – Earth Changes
Justine Alessi & M. E. McMillan
Rebirth of the Oracle
Kathryn/Patrick Andries
Naked in Public
Kathryn Andries
The Big Desire
Dream Doctor
Soul Choices: Six Paths to Find Your Life
    Purpose
Soul Choices: Six Paths to Fulfilling
    Relationships
Patrick Andries
Owners Manual for the Mind
Dan Bird
Finding Your Way in the Spiritual Age
Waking Up in the Spiritual Age
Julia Cannon
Soul Speak – The Language of Your Body
Ronald Chapman
Seeing True
Albert Cheung
The Emperor's Stargate
Jack Churchward
Lifting the Veil on the Lost Continent of
    Mu
The Stone Tablets of Mu
Sherri Cortland
Guide Group Fridays
Raising Our Vibrations for the New Age

Spiritual Tool Box
Windows of Opportunity
Patrick De Haan
The Alien Handbook
Paulinne Delcour-Min
Spiritual Gold
Michael Dennis
Morning Coffee with God
God's Many Mansions
Carolyn Greer Daly
Opening to Fullness of Spirit
Anita Holmes
Twidders
Aaron Hoopes
Reconnecting to the Earth
Victoria Hunt
Kiss the Wind
Patricia Irvine
In Light and In Shade
Kevin Killen
Ghosts and Me
Diane Lewis
From Psychic to Soul
Donna Lynn
From Fear to Love
Maureen McGill
Baby It's You
Maureen McGill & Nola Davis
Live from the Other Side
Curt Melliger
Heaven Here on Earth
Henry Michaelson
And Jesus Said – A Conversation
Dennis Milner
Kosmos
Andy Myers
Not Your Average Angel Book
Guy Needler
Avoiding Karma
Beyond the Source – Book 1, Book 2
The Anne Dialogues
The Curators
The History of God
The Origin Speaks
James Nussbaumer
And Then I Knew My Abundance
The Master of Everything
Mastering Your Own Spiritual Freedom

For more information about any of the above titles, soon to be released titles,
or other items in our catalog, write, phone or visit our website:
PO Box 754, Huntsville, AR 72740
479-738-2348/800-935-0045
www.ozarkmt.com

Other Books by Ozark Mountain Publishing, Inc.

Sherry O'Brian
Peaks and Valleys
Riet Okken
The Liberating Power of Emotions
Gabrielle Orr
Akashic Records: One True Love
Let Miracles Happen
Victor Parachin
Sit a Bit
Nikki Pattillo
A Spiritual Evolution
Children of the Stars
Rev. Grant H. Pealer
A Funny Thing Happened on the
    Way to Heaven
Worlds Beyond Death
Victoria Pendragon
Born Healers
Feng Shui from the Inside, Out
Sleep Magic
The Sleeping Phoenix
Michael Perlin
Fantastic Adventures in Metaphysics
Walter Pullen
Evolution of the Spirit
Debra Rayburn
Let's Get Natural with Herbs
Charmian Redwood
A New Earth Rising
Coming Home to Lemuria
David Rivinus
Always Dreaming
Richard Rowe
Imagining the Unimaginable
M. Don Schorn
Elder Gods of Antiquity
Legacy of the Elder Gods
Gardens of the Elder Gods
Reincarnation...Stepping Stones of Life
Garnet Schulhauser
Dance of Eternal Rapture
Dance of Heavenly Bliss

Dancing Forever with Spirit
Dancing on a Stamp
Manuella Stoerzer
Headless Chicken
Annie Stillwater Gray
Education of a Guardian Angel
The Dawn Book
Work of a Guardian Angel
Blair Styra
Don't Change the Channel
Who Catharted
Natalie Sudman
Application of Impossible Things
L.R. Sumpter
Judy's Story
The Old is New
We Are the Creators
Jim Thomas
Tales from the Trance
Nicholas Vesey
Living the Life-Force
Janie Wells
Embracing the Human Journey
Payment for Passage
Dennis Wheatley/ Maria Wheatley
The Essential Dowsing Guide
Maria Wheatley
Druidic Soul Star Astrology
Jacquelyn Wiersma
The Zodiac Recipe
Sherry Wilde
The Forgotten Promise
Lyn Willmoth
A Small Book of Comfort
Stuart Wilson & Joanna Prentis
Atlantis and the New Consciousness
Beyond Limitations
The Essenes -Children of the Light
The Magdalene Version
Power of the Magdalene
Robert Winterhalter
The Healing Christ

For more information about any of the above titles, soon to be released titles,
or other items in our catalog, write, phone or visit our website:
PO Box 754, Huntsville, AR 72740
479-738-2348/800-935-0045
www.ozarkmt.com